Praise for John Verdon's

Think of a Number

"Verdon has written the mother of all puzzle mysteries . . . He is endlessly inventive."
—*Toronto Star*

"It's hard to remember a better debut for a crime writer . . . Good writing and good storytelling often aren't the same thing. Verdon combines them masterfully with his creation of Dave Gurney."
—*Star-Ledger*

"Simply one of the best thrillers I've read in a lifetime of thriller reading— eloquent, heart-rending, deeply suspenseful on many levels, and relentlessly intelligent . . . Absolutely not to be missed!"
—John Lescroart, *New York Times* bestselling author of *The Suspect, Betrayal,* and *A Plague of Secrets*

"Addictive and thoroughly engrossing . . . plays deliciously on our deepest, most primal fears . . . This tale will grab hold of you like a steel jaw trap."
—Joseph Finder, *New York Times* bestselling author of *Vanished*

"What makes this work is the intricate fabric that debut novelist Verdon weaves, as complications twist into what seems to be an impossible knot."
—*Chicago Sun-Times*

"A subtle and intelligent thriller of the first order . . . Don't miss it."
—Lisa Unger, *New York Times* bestselling author of *Die for You*

"Verdon is a master at controlling pace . . . and demanding that the reader use his or her brain to figure out what comes next. When you're finished, you may not trust silly parlor games ever again."
—*Salon*

"Edge-of-the-chair suspense, memorable characters that jump off the pages, and elegant and deft writing . . . a stunning debut."
—Faye Kellerman, *New York Times* bestselling author of *Stone Kiss* and *The Forgotten*

"Savor the sense of loss that haunts this strong debut."
—*Houston Chronicle*

"Will hook just about any reader ... An astoundingly addictive work filled with real life characters that jump off the page into a daring and skillful plot, this book will leave you stumped and hungry for more ... a book for all readers, not just those who revel in the thriller genre."
—*New York Journal of Books*

"*Think of a Number* is a 10, and crime fans of almost every persuasion will love it. An outstanding debut."
—*Booklist* (starred review)

"The numbers game gets a murderous spin in Verdon's deft, literate debut."
—*Publishers Weekly*

"Verdon's deftly written, erudite debut is an exquisitely plotted novel of suspense."
—*Portland Oregonian*

"One of the finest thrillers I've read in years. I devoured it. Consistently intelligent, fast-paced, and filled with clever twists ... *Think of a Number* stands out as original and exciting."
—John Katzenbach, *New York Times* bestselling author of *The Traveler, Just Cause,* and *Hart's War*

"John Verdon has ... created an incredible crime novel which could give Stieg Larsson a run for his well-earned money ... All of the characters are incredibly well developed ... The descriptions of scenes make you feel like you are there, and the plot is brilliant."
—*Herald-Dispatch* (West Virginia)

"The reader will find that it is difficult to put the book down ... hair raising."
—*Paramus Post*

"The mystery is brilliantly executed ... If you read only one thriller this year, make it *Think of a Number.*"
—*Bookloons*

Think of a Number

Also by John Verdon

Shut Your Eyes Tight
Let the Devil Sleep
Peter Pan Must Die

John Verdon

Think of a Number

A novel

B\D\W\Y

Broadway Books

NEW YORK

Copyright © 2010 by John Verdon
Excerpt from *Peter Pan Must Die* copyright © 2014 by John Verdon

All rights reserved.
Published in the United States by Broadway Books, an imprint of the Crown Publishing Group, a division of Random House LLC, a Penguin Random House Company, New York.
www.crownpublishing.com

BROADWAY BOOKS and its logo, B \ D \ W \ Y, are trademarks of Random House LLC.

Originally published in the United States by Crown Publishers, an imprint of the Crown Publishing Group, a division of Random House, Inc., New York, in 2010.

Library of Congress Cataloging-in-Publication Data
Verdon, John.
Think of a number/John Verdon.
p. cm.
1. Police—New York (State)—New York—Fiction.   2. Serial murderers—Fiction.   I. Title.
PS3622.E736S59 2010
813'.6—dc22
2009028512

ISBN 978-0-307-88545-6
eISBN 978-0-307-58894-4

Printed in the United States of America

Book design by Lynne Amft
Cover design by Mumtaz Mustafa
Cover photography by Dave Wall/arcangel-images.com

For Naomi

Think of a Number

"*Where were you?*" *said the old woman in the bed.* "*I had to pee, and no one came.*"

Unruffled by her nasty tone, the young man stood at the foot of the bed, beaming.

"*I had to pee,*" *she repeated, more vaguely, as if she were now unsure what the words meant.*

"*I have good news, Mother,*" *said the man.* "*Soon everything will be all right. Everything will be taken care of.*"

"*Where do you go when you leave me?*" *Her voice again was sharp, querulous.*

"*Not far, Mother. You know very well I never go far.*"

"*I don't like to be alone.*"

His smile broadened, was almost beatific. "*Very soon everything will be all right. Everything will be the way it was supposed to be. You can trust me, Mother. I found a way to fix everything. What he took he will give, when he gets what he gave.*"

"*You write such beautiful poetry.*"

There were no windows in the room. The sideways light from the bedside lamp—the sole source of illumination—emphasized the thick scar on the woman's throat and the shadows in her son's eyes.

"*Will we go dancing?*" *she asked, staring past him and past the dark wall behind him to a brighter vision.*

"*Of course, Mother. Everything will be perfect.*"

"Where's my little Dickie Duck?"
"Right here, Mother."
"Will Dickie Duck come to bed?"
"To beddy-bye, to beddy-bye, to beddy-bye."
"I have to pee," she said, almost coquettishly.

Part One

Fatal Memories

Chapter 1

Cop art

Jason Strunk was by all accounts an inconsequential fellow, a bland thirty-something, nearly invisible to his neighbors—and apparently inaudible as well, since none could recall a single specific thing he'd ever said. They couldn't even be certain that he'd ever spoken. Perhaps he'd nodded, perhaps said hello, perhaps muttered a word or two. It was hard to say.

All expressed a conventional initial amazement, even a temporary disbelief, at the revelation of Mr. Strunk's obsessive devotion to killing middle-aged men with mustaches and his uniquely disturbing way of disposing of the bodies: cutting them into manageable segments, wrapping them colorfully, and mailing them to local police officers as Christmas presents.

Dave Gurney gazed intently at the colorless, placid face of Jason Strunk—actually, the original Central Booking mug shot of Jason Strunk—that stared back at him from his computer screen. The mug shot had been enlarged to make the face life-size, and it was surrounded at the borders of the screen by the tool icons of a creative photo-retouching program that Gurney was just starting to get the hang of.

He moved one of the brightness-control tools on the screen to the iris of Strunk's right eye, clicked his mouse, and then examined the small highlight he'd created.

Better, but still not right.

The eyes were always the hardest—the eyes and the mouth—but they were the key. Sometimes he had to experiment with the position and intensity of one tiny highlight for hours, and even then he'd end up with something not quite what it should be, not good enough to show to Sonya, and definitely not Madeleine.

The thing about the eyes was that they, more than anything else, captured the tension, the contradiction—the uncommunicative blandness spiked with a hint of cruelty that Gurney had often discerned in the faces of murderers with whom he'd had the opportunity to spend quality time.

He'd gotten the look right with his patient manipulation of the mug shot of Jorge Kunzman (the Walmart stock clerk who always kept the head of his last date in his refrigerator until he could replace it with one more recent). He'd been pleased with the result, which conveyed with disturbing immediacy the deep black emptiness lurking in Mr. Kunzman's bored expression, and Sonya's excited reaction, her gush of praise, had solidified his opinion. It was that reception, plus the unexpected sale of the piece to one of Sonya's collector friends, that motivated him to produce the series of creatively doctored photographs now being featured in a show headlined Portraits of Murderers by the Man Who Caught Them, in Sonya's small but pricey gallery in Ithaca.

How a recently retired NYPD homicide detective with a yawning uninterest in art in general and trendy art in particular, and a deep distaste for personal notoriety, could have ended up as the focus of a chic university-town art show described by local critics as "a cutting-edge blend of brutally raw photographs, unflinching psychological insights, and masterful graphic manipulations" was a question with two very different answers: his own and his wife's.

As far as he was concerned, it all began with Madeleine's cajoling him into taking an art-appreciation course with her at the museum in Cooperstown. She was forever trying to get him out— out of his den, out of the house, out of himself, just *out*. He'd learned that the best way to stay in control of his own time was through the strategy of periodic capitulations. The art-appreciation course was one of these strategic moves, and although he dreaded the prospect of sitting through it, he expected it to immunize him against further pressures for at least a month or two. It wasn't that he was a couch potato—far from it. At the age of forty-seven, he could still do fifty push-ups, fifty chin-ups, and fifty sit-ups. He just wasn't very fond of going places.

The course, however, turned out to be a surprise—in fact, three surprises. First, despite his pre-course assumption that his greatest challenge would be staying awake, he found the instructor, Sonya Reynolds, a gallery owner and artist of regional renown, riveting. She was not conventionally beautiful, not in the archetypal Northern European Catherine Deneuve mode. Her mouth was too pouty, her cheekbones overly prominent, her nose too strong. But somehow the imperfect parts were unified into a uniquely striking whole by large eyes of a deep smoky green and by a manner that was completely relaxed and naturally sensual. There were not many men in the class, just six of the twenty-six attendees, but she had the absolute attention of all six.

The second surprise was his positive reaction to the subject matter. Because it was a special interest of hers, Sonya devoted considerable time to art derived from photography—photography that had been manipulated to create images that were more powerful or communicative than the originals.

The third surprise came three weeks into the twelve-week course, on the night that she was commenting enthusiastically on a contemporary artist's silk-screen prints derived from solarized photographic portraits. As Gurney gazed at the prints, the idea came to him that he could take advantage of an unusual resource to which he had special access and to which he could bring a special perspective. The notion was strangely exciting. The last thing he'd expected from an art-appreciation course was excitement.

Once this occurred to him—*the concept of enhancing, clarifying, intensifying criminal mug shots,* particularly the mug shots of murderers, in ways that would capture and convey the nature of the beast he had spent his career studying, pursuing, and outwitting—it took hold, and he thought about it more often than he would have been comfortable admitting. He was, after all, a cautious man who could see both sides of every question, the flaw in every conviction, the naïveté in every enthusiasm.

As Gurney worked at the desk in his den that bright October morning on the mug shot of Jason Strunk, the pleasant challenge of the process was interrupted by the sound of something being dropped on the floor behind him.

"I'm leaving these here," said Madeleine Gurney in a voice that to anyone else might have sounded casual but to her husband was fraught.

He looked over his shoulder, his eyes narrowing at the sight of the small burlap sack leaning against the door. "Leaving what?" he asked, knowing the answer.

"Tulips," said Madeleine in the same even tone.

"You mean bulbs?"

It was a silly correction, and they both knew it. It was just a way of expressing his irritation at Madeleine's wanting him to do something he didn't feel like doing.

"What do you want me to do with them in here?"

"Bring them out to the garden. Help me plant them."

He considered pointing out the illogic of her bringing into the den something for him to bring back out to the garden but thought better of it.

"As soon as I finish with this," he said a little resentfully. He realized that planting tulip bulbs on a glorious Indian-summer day in a hilltop garden overlooking a rolling panorama of crimson autumn woods and emerald pastures under a cobalt sky was not a particularly onerous assignment. He just hated being interrupted. And this reaction to interruption, he told himself, was a by-product of his greatest strength: the linear, logical mind that had made him such a successful detective—the mind that was jarred by the slightest discontinuity in a suspect's story, that could sense a fissure too tiny for most eyes to see.

Madeleine peered over his shoulder at the computer screen. "How can you work on something so ugly on a day like this?" she asked.

Chapter 2

A perfect victim

David and Madeleine Gurney lived in a sturdy nineteenth-century farmhouse, nestled in the corner of a secluded pasture at the end of a dead-end road in the Delaware County hills five miles outside the village of Walnut Crossing. The ten-acre pasture was surrounded by woods of cherry, maple, and oak.

The house retained its original architectural simplicity. During the year they'd owned it, the Gurneys had restored to a more appropriate appearance the previous owner's unfortunate updates—replacing, for example, bleak aluminum windows with wood-framed versions that possessed the divided-light style of an earlier century. They did it not out of a mania for historical authenticity but in recognition that the original aesthetics had somehow been *right*. This matter of how one's home should look and feel was one of the subjects on which Madeleine and David were in complete harmony—a list that, it seemed to him, had lately been shrinking.

This thought had been eating like acid at his mood most of the day, activated by his wife's comment about the ugliness of the portrait he was working on. It was still at the edge of his consciousness that afternoon when, dozing in his favorite Adirondack chair after the tulip-planting activity, he became aware of Madeleine's footsteps brushing toward him through the ankle-high grass. When the footsteps stopped in front of his chair, he opened one eye.

"Do you think," she said in her calm, light way, "it's too late to take the canoe out?" Her voice positioned the words deftly between a question and a challenge.

Madeleine was a slim, athletic forty-five-year-old who could easily be mistaken for thirty-five. Her eyes were frank, steady, appraising. Her long brown hair, with the exception of a few errant strands, was pulled up under her broad-brimmed straw gardening hat.

He responded with a question from his own train of thought. "Do you really think it's ugly?"

"Of course it's ugly," she said without hesitation. "Isn't it supposed to be?"

He frowned as he considered her comment. "You mean the subject matter?" he asked.

"What else would I mean?"

"I don't know." He shrugged. "You sounded a bit contemptuous of the whole thing—the execution as well as the subject matter."

"Sorry."

She didn't seem sorry. As he teetered on the edge of saying so, she changed the subject.

"Are you looking forward to seeing your old classmate?"

"Not exactly," he said, adjusting the reclining back of his chair a notch lower. "I'm not big on recollections of times past."

"Maybe he's got a murder for you to solve."

Gurney looked at his wife, studied the ambiguity of her expression. "You think that's what he wants?" he asked blandly.

"Isn't that what you're famous for?" Anger was beginning to stiffen her voice.

It was something he'd witnessed in her often enough in recent months that he thought he understood what it was about. They had different notions of what his retirement from the job was supposed to mean, what kind of changes it was supposed to make in their lives, and, more specifically, how it was supposed to change *him*. Recently, too, ill feeling had been growing around his new avocation—the portraits-of-murderers project that was absorbing his time. He suspected that Madeleine's negativity in this area might be partly related to Sonya's enthusiasm.

"Did you know he's famous, too?" she asked.

"Who?"

"Your classmate."

"Not really. He said something on the phone about writing a book, and I checked on it briefly. I wouldn't have thought he was well known."

"*Two* books," said Madeleine. "He's the director of some sort of institute in Peony, and he did a series of lectures that ran on PBS. I printed out copies of the book jackets from the Internet. You might want to take a look at them."

"I assume he'll tell me all there is to know about himself and his books. He doesn't sound shy."

"Have it your way. I left the copies on your desk, if you change your mind. By the way, Kyle phoned earlier."

He stared at her silently.

"I said you'd get back to him."

"Why didn't you call me?" he asked, more testily than he intended. His son didn't call often.

"I asked him if I should get you. He said he didn't want to disturb you, it wasn't really urgent."

"Did he say anything else?"

"No."

She turned and walked across the thick, moist grass toward the house. When she reached the side door and put her hand on the knob, she seemed to remember something else, looked back at him, and spoke with exaggerated bafflement. "According to the book jacket, your old classmate seems to be a saint, perfect in every way. A guru of good behavior. It's hard to imagine why he'd need to consult a homicide detective."

"A *retired* homicide detective," corrected Gurney.

But she'd already gone in and neglected to cushion the slam of the door.

Chapter 3

Trouble in paradise

The following day was more exquisite than the day before. It was the picture of October in a New England calendar. Gurney rose at 7:00 A.M., showered and shaved, put on jeans and a light cotton sweater, and was having his coffee in a canvas chair on the bluestone patio outside their downstairs bedroom. The patio and the French doors leading to it were additions he'd made to the house at Madeleine's urging.

She was good at that sort of thing, had a sensitive eye for what was possible, what was appropriate. It revealed a lot about her—her positive instincts, her practical imagination, her unfailing taste. But when he got tangled in their areas of contention—the mires and brambles of the expectations each privately cultivated—he found it difficult to focus on her remarkable strengths.

He must remember to return Kyle's call. He would have to wait three hours because of the time difference between Walnut Crossing and Seattle. He settled deeper into his chair, cradling his warm coffee mug in both hands.

He glanced at the slim folder he'd brought out with his coffee and tried to imagine the appearance of the college classmate he hadn't seen for twenty-five years. The photo that appeared on the book jackets that Madeleine printed out from a bookstore website refreshed his recollection not only of the face but of the personality—complete with the vocal timbre of an Irish tenor and a smile that was improbably charming.

When they were undergraduates at Fordham's Rose Hill campus in the Bronx, Mark Mellery was a wild character whose spurts of humor and truth, energy and ambition were colored by something darker. He had a tendency to walk close to the edge—a sort of careening genius, simultaneously reckless and calculating, always on the brink of a downward spiral.

According to his website bio, the direction of the spiral, which had taken him down rapidly in his twenties, had been reversed in his thirties by some sort of dramatic spiritual transformation.

Balancing his coffee mug on the narrow wooden arm of the chair, Gurney opened the folder on his lap, extracted the e-mail he'd received from Mellery a week earlier, and went over it again, line by line.

> *Hello, Dave:*
>
> *I hope you don't find it inappropriate to be contacted by an old classmate after so much time has elapsed. One can never be sure what may be brought to mind by a voice from the past. I've remained in touch with our shared academic past through our alumni association and have been fascinated by the news items published over the years concerning the members of our graduating class. I was happy to note on more than one occasion your own stellar achievements and the recognition you were receiving. (One article in our Alumni News called you THE MOST DECORATED DETECTIVE IN THE NYPD—which didn't especially surprise me, remembering the Dave Gurney I knew in college!) Then, about a year ago, I saw that you'd retired from the police department—and that you'd moved to up here to Delaware County. It got my attention because I happen to be located in the town of Peony—"just down the road apiece," as they say. I doubt that you've heard of it, but I now run a kind of retreat house here, called the Institute for Spiritual Renewal—pretty fancy-sounding, I know, but in reality quite down to earth.*

Although it has occurred to me many times over the years that I would enjoy seeing you again, a disturbing situation has finally given me the nudge I needed to stop thinking about it and get in touch with you. It's a situation in which I believe that your advice would be most helpful. What I'd love to do is pay you a brief visit. If you could find it possible to spare me half an hour, I'll come to your home in Walnut Crossing—or to any other location that might better suit your convenience.

My recollections of our conversations in the campus center and even longer conversations in the Shamrock Bar—not to mention your remarkable professional experience—tell me that you're the right person to talk to about the perplexing matter before me. It's a weird puzzle that I suspect will interest you. Your ability to put two and two together in ways that elude everyone else was always your great strength. Whenever I think of you, I always think of your perfect logic and crystal clarity—qualities that I dearly need more of right now. I'll call you within the next few days at the number that appears in the alumni directory—in the hope that it's correct and current.

> *With many good memories,*
> *Mark Mellery*

P.S. Even if you end up as mystified by my problem as I am, and have no advice to offer, it will still be a delight to see you again.

The promised call had come two days later. Gurney had immediately recognized the voice, eerily unchanged except for a distinct tremor of anxiety.

After some self-deprecating remarks about his failure to stay in touch, Mellery got to the point. Could he see Gurney within the next few days? The sooner the better, since the "situation" was urgent. Another "development" had occurred. It really was impossible to discuss over the phone, as Gurney would understand when they met. There were things Mellery had to show him. No, it wasn't a matter for the local police, for reasons he'd explain when he came. No, it wasn't a legal matter, not yet, anyway. No crime had been committed, nor was one being specifically threatened—not that he could prove. Lord, it was so difficult to talk about it this way; it would be so much easier in person. Yes, he realized that Gurney was not in the private-investigation business. But just half an hour—could he have half an hour?

With the mixed feelings he'd had from the beginning, Gurney agreed. His curiosity often got the better of his reticence; in this instance he was curious about the hint of hysteria lurking in the undertone of Mellery's mellifluous voice. And, of course, a puzzle to be deciphered attracted him more powerfully than he cared to admit.

After rereading the e-mail a third time, Gurney put it back in the folder and let his mind wander over the recollections it stirred up from the back bins of his memory: the morning classes in which Mellery had looked hungover and bored, his gradual coming to life in the afternoon, his wild Irish jabs of wit and insight in the wee hours fueled by alcohol. He was a natural actor, undisputed star of the college dramatic society—a young man who, however full of life he might be at the Shamrock Bar, was doubly alive on the stage. He was a man who depended on an audience—a man who was drawn up to his full height only in the nourishing light of admiration.

Gurney opened the folder and glanced through the e-mail yet again. He was bothered by Mellery's depiction of their relationship. The contact between them had been less frequent, less significant, less friendly than Mellery's words suggested. But he got the impression that Mellery had chosen his words carefully—that despite its simplicity, the note had been written and rewritten, pondered and edited—and that the flattery, like everything else in the letter, was purposeful. But what was the purpose? The obvious one was to ensure Gurney's agreement to a face-to-face meeting and to engage him in the solution of whatever "mystery" had arisen. Beyond that, it was hard to say. The problem was clearly important to Mellery—

which would explain the time and attention he had apparently lavished on getting the flow and feeling of his sentences just right, on conveying a certain mix of warmth and distress.

There was also the small matter of the "P.S." In addition to subtly challenging him with the suggestion that he might be defeated by the puzzle, whatever it was, it also appeared to obstruct an easy exit route, to vitiate any claim Gurney might be tempted to make that he was not in the private-investigation business or would not be likely to be helpful. The thrust of its wording was to characterize any reluctance to meet as a rude dismissal of an old friend.

Oh, yes, it was carefully crafted.

Carefulness. That was something new, wasn't it? Definitely not a cornerstone quality of the old Mark Mellery.

This apparent change interested Gurney.

On cue, Madeleine came out through the back door and walked about two-thirds of the way to where Gurney was sitting.

"Your guest has arrived," she announced flatly.

"Where is he?"

"In the house."

He looked down. An ant was zigzagging along the arm of his chair. He sent it flying with a sharp flick of his fingernail.

"Ask him to come out here," he said. "It's too nice to be indoors."

"It is, isn't it?" she said, making the comment sound both poignant and ironic. "By the way, he looks exactly like his picture on the book jacket—even more so."

"Even more so? What's that supposed to mean?"

She was already returning to the house and did not answer.

Chapter 4

I know you so well I know
what you're thinking

Mark Mellery took long strides through the soft grass. He approached Gurney as if planning to embrace him, but something made him reconsider.

"Davey!" he cried, extending his hand.

Davey? wondered Gurney.

"My God!" Mellery went on. "You look the same! God, it's good to see you! Great to see you looking the way you do! Davey Gurney! Back at Fordham they used to say you looked like Robert Redford in *All the President's Men*. Still do—haven't changed a bit! If I didn't know you were forty-seven like me, I'd say you were thirty!"

He clasped Gurney's hand with both of his as though it were a precious object. "Driving over today, from Peony to Walnut Crossing, I was remembering how calm and collected you always were. An emotional oasis—that's what you were, an emotional oasis! And you still have that look. Davey Gurney—calm, cool, and collected—plus the sharpest mind in town. How have you been?"

"I've been fortunate," said Gurney, extricating his hand and speaking in a voice as devoid of excitement as Mellery's was full of it. "I have no complaints."

"Fortunate . . ." Mellery enunciated the syllables as if trying to recall the meaning of a foreign word. "It's a nice place you have here. Very nice."

"Madeleine has a good eye for these things. Shall we have a

seat?" Gurney motioned toward a pair of weathered Adirondack chairs facing each other between the apple tree and a birdbath.

Mellery started in the direction indicated, then stopped. "I had something . . ."

"Could this be it?" Madeleine was walking toward them from the house, holding in front of her an elegant briefcase. Understated and expensive, it was like everything else in Mellery's appearance— from the handmade (but comfortably broken in and not too highly polished) English shoes to the beautifully tailored (but gently rum- pled) cashmere sport jacket—a look seemingly calculated to say that here stood a man who knew how to use money without letting money use him, a man who had achieved success without worship- ping it, a man to whom good fortune came naturally. A harried look about his eyes, however, conveyed a different message.

"Ah, yes, thank you," said Mellery, accepting the briefcase from Madeleine with obvious relief. "But where . . . ?"

"You laid it on the coffee table."

"Yes, of course. My brain is kind of scattered today. Thank you!"

"Would you like something to drink?"

"Drink?"

"We have some iced tea already made. Or, if you'd prefer some- thing else . . . ?"

"No, no, iced tea would be fine. Thank you."

As Gurney observed his old classmate, it suddenly occurred to him what Madeleine had meant when she said that Mellery looked exactly like his book jacket photograph, "only more so."

The quality most evident in the photograph was a kind of infor- mal perfection—the illusion of a casual, amateur snapshot with- out the unflattering shadows or awkward composition of an actual amateur snapshot. It was exactly that sense of carefully crafted carelessness—the ego-driven desire to appear ego-free—that Mellery exemplified in person. As usual, Madeleine's perception had been on target.

"In your e-mail you mentioned a problem," said Gurney with a get-to-the-point abruptness verging on rudeness.

"Yes," Mellery answered, but instead of addressing it, he offered a reminiscence that seemed designed to weave another little thread of obligation into the old school tie, recounting a silly debate a classmate of theirs had gotten into with a philosophy professor. During the telling of this tale, Mellery referred to himself, Gurney, and the protagonist as the "Three Musketeers" of the Rose Hill campus, striving to make something sophomoric sound heroic. Gurney found the effort embarrassing and offered his guest no response beyond an expectant stare.

"Well," said Mellery, turning uncomfortably to the matter at hand, "I'm not sure where to begin."

If you don't know where to begin your own story, thought Gurney, *why the hell are you here?*

Mellery finally opened his briefcase, withdrew two slim softcover books, and handed them, with care, as if they were fragile, to Gurney. They were the books described in the website printouts he had looked at earlier. One was called *The Only Thing That Matters* and was subtitled *The Power of Conscience to Change Lives.* The other was called *Honestly!* and was subtitled *The Only Way to Be Happy.*

"You may not have heard of these books. They were moderately successful, but not exactly blockbusters." Mellery smiled with what looked like a well-practiced imitation of humility. "I'm not suggesting you need to read them right now." He smiled again, as though this were amusing. "However, they may give you some clue to what's happening, or why it's happening, once I explain my problem . . . or perhaps I should say my *apparent* problem. The whole business has me a bit confused."

And more than a bit frightened, mused Gurney.

Mellery took a long breath, paused, then began his story like a man walking with fragile determination into a cold surf.

"I should tell you first about the notes I've received." He reached into his briefcase, withdrew two envelopes, opened one, took from it a sheet of white paper with handwriting on one side and a smaller envelope of the size that might be used for an RSVP. He handed the paper to Gurney.

"This was the first communication I received, about three weeks ago."

Gurney took the paper and settled back in his chair to examine it, noting at once the neatness of the handwriting. The words were precisely, elegantly formed—stirring a sudden recollection of Sister Mary Joseph's script moving gracefully across a grammar-school blackboard. But even stranger than the painstaking penmanship was the fact that the note had been written with a fountain pen, and in red ink. *Red ink?* Gurney's grandfather had had red ink. He had little round bottles of blue, green, and red ink. He remembered so little of his grandfather, but he remembered the ink. Could one still purchase red ink for a fountain pen?

Gurney read the note with a deepening frown, then read it again. There was neither a salutation nor a signature.

Do you believe in Fate? I do, because I thought I'd never see you again— and then one day, there you were. It all came back: how you sound, how you move—most of all, how you think. If someone told you to think of a number, I know what number you'd think of. You don't believe me? I'll prove it to you. Think of any number up to a thousand—the first number that comes to your mind. Picture it. Now see how well I know your secrets. Open the little envelope.

Gurney uttered a noncommittal grunt and looked inquiringly at Mellery, who had been staring at him intently as he read. "Do you have any idea who sent you this?"

"None whatever."

"Any suspicions?"

"None."

"Hmm. Did you play the game?"

"The game?" Clearly Mellery had not thought of it that way. "If what you mean is, did I think of a number, yes, I did. Under the circumstances it would have been difficult not to."

"So you thought of a number?"

"Yes."

"And?"

Mellery cleared his throat. "The number I thought of was six-five-eight." He repeated it, articulating the digits—*six, five, eight*—as though they might mean something to Gurney. When he saw that they didn't, he took a nervous breath and went on.

"The number six fifty-eight has no particular significance to me. It just happened to be the first number that came to mind. I've racked my brains, trying to remember anything I might associate it with, any reason I might have picked it, but I couldn't come up with a single thing. *It's just the first number that came to mind,*" he insisted with panicky earnestness.

Gurney gazed at him with growing interest. "And in the smaller envelope . . . ?"

Mellery handed him the other envelope that was enclosed with the note and watched closely as he opened it, extracted a piece of notepaper half the size of the first, and read the message written in the same delicate style, the same red ink:

> *Does it shock you that I knew you would pick 658?*
> *Who knows you that well? If you want the answer,*
> *you must first repay me the $289.87 it cost me to find you.*
> *Send that exact amount to*
> *P.O. Box 49449, Wycherly, CT 61010.*
> *Send me CASH or a PERSONAL CHECK.*
> *Make it out to X. Arybdis.*
> *(That was not always my name.)*

After reading the note again, Gurney asked Mellery whether he had responded to it.

"Yes. I sent a check for the amount mentioned."

"Why?"

"What do you mean?"

"It's a lot of money. Why did you decide to send it?"

"Because it was driving me crazy. The number—how could he know?"

"Has the check cleared?"

"No, as a matter of fact, it hasn't," said Mellery. "I've been monitoring my account daily. That's why I sent a check instead of cash. I thought it might be a good idea to know something about this Arybdis person—at least know where he deposited his checks. I mean, the whole tone of the thing was so unsettling."

"What exactly unsettled you?"

"The number, obviously!" cried Mellery. "How could he possibly know such a thing?"

"Good question," said Gurney. "Why do you say 'he'?"

"What? Oh, I see what you mean. I just thought . . . I don't know, it's just what came to mind. I suppose 'X. Arybdis' sounded masculine for some reason."

"X. Arybdis. Odd sort of name," said Gurney. "Does it mean anything to you? Ring any bell at all?"

"None."

The name meant nothing to Gurney, but it did not seem completely unfamiliar, either. Whatever it was, it was buried in a subbasement mental filing cabinet.

"After you sent the check, were you contacted again?"

"Oh, yes!" said Mellery, once more reaching into his briefcase and pulling out two other sheets of paper. "I received this one about ten days ago. And this one the day after I sent you my e-mail asking if we could get together." He thrust them toward Gurney like a little boy showing his father two new bruises.

They appeared to be written by the same meticulous hand with the same pen as the pair of notes in the earlier communication, but the tone had changed.

The first was composed of eight short lines:

> *How many bright angels*
> *can dance on a pin?*
> *How many hopes drown in*
> *a bottle of gin?*
> *Did the thought ever come*

that your glass was a gun
and one day you'd wonder,
God, what have I done?

The eight lines of the second were similarly cryptic and menacing:

What you took you will give
when you get what you gave.
I know what you think,
when you blink,
where you've been,
where you'll be.
You and I have a date,
Mr. 658.

Over the next ten minutes, during which he read each note half a dozen times, Gurney's expression grew darker and Mellery's angst more obvious.

"What do you think?" Mellery finally asked.

"You have a clever enemy."

"I mean, what do you think about the number business?"

"What about it?"

"How could he know what number would come to my mind?"

"Offhand, I would say he couldn't know."

"He couldn't know, but he did! I mean, that's the whole thing isn't? He couldn't know, but he did! No one could possibly know that the number six fifty-eight would be the number I would think of, but not only did he know it—he knew it at least two days before I did, when he put the damn letter in the mail!"

Mellery suddenly heaved himself up from his chair, pacing across the grass toward the house, then back again, running his hands through his hair.

"There's no scientific way to do that. There's no conceivable way of doing it. Don't you see how crazy this is?"

Gurney was resting his chin thoughtfully on the tips of his

fingers. "There's a simple philosophical principle that I find one hundred percent reliable. *If something happens, it must have a way of happening.* This number business must have a simple explanation."

"But . . ."

Gurney raised his hand like the serious young traffic cop he had been for his first six months in the NYPD. "Sit down. Relax. I'm sure we can figure it out."

Chapter 5

Unpleasant possibilities

Madeleine brought a pair of iced teas to the two men and returned to the house. The smell of warm grass filled the air. The temperature was close to seventy. A swarm of purple finches descended on the thistle-seed feeders. The sun, the colors, the aromas were intense, but wasted on Mellery, whose anxious thoughts seemed to occupy him completely.

As they sipped their teas, Gurney tried to assess the motives and honesty of his guest. He knew that labeling someone too early in the game could lead to mistakes, but doing so was often irresistible. The main thing was to be aware of the fallibility of the process and be willing to revise the label as new information became available.

His gut feeling was that Mellery was a classic phony, a pretender on many levels, who to some extent believed his own pretenses. His accent, for example, which had been present even in the college days, was an accent from nowhere, from some imaginary place of culture and refinement. Surely it was no longer put on—it was an integral part of him—but its roots lay in imaginary soil. The expensive haircut, the moisturized skin, the flawless teeth, the exercised physique, and the manicured fingernails suggested a top-shelf televangelist. His manner was that of a man eager to appear at ease in the world, a man in cool possession of everything that eludes ordinary humans. Gurney realized all this had been present in a nascent form twenty-six years earlier. Mark Mellery had simply become more of what he'd always been.

"Had it occurred to you to go to the police?" asked Gurney.

"I didn't think there was any point. I didn't think they'd do anything. What could they do? There was no specific threat, nothing that couldn't be explained away, no actual crime. I didn't have anything concrete to take to them. A couple of nasty little poems? A warped high-school kid could have written them, someone with a weird sense of humor. And since the police wouldn't really do anything or, worse yet, would treat it as a joke, why would I waste my time going to them?"

Gurney nodded, unconvinced.

"Besides," Mellery went on, "the idea of the local police grabbing hold of this and launching a full-scale investigation, questioning people, coming up to the institute, badgering present and former guests—some of our guests are sensitive people—stomping around and raising all sorts of hell, poking into things that are none of their business, maybe getting the press involved . . . Christ! I can just see the headlines—'Spiritual Author Gets Death Threats'—and the turmoil that would raise. . . ." Mellery's voice trailed off, and he shook his head as if mere words could not describe the damage the police might cause.

Gurney responded with a look of bafflement.

"What's wrong?" Mellery asked.

"Your two reasons for not contacting the police contradict each other."

"How?"

"You didn't contact the police because you were afraid they wouldn't do anything. And you didn't contact them because you were afraid they would do too much."

"Ah, yes . . . but both statements are true. The common element is my fear of the matter's being handled ineptly. Police ineptness might take the form of a lackadaisical approach or a bumbling bulls-in-the-china-shop approach. Inept lassitude or inept aggressiveness—you see what I mean?"

Gurney had the feeling he'd just watched someone stub his toe and turn it into a pirouette. He wasn't quite buying it. In his experience when a man gave two reasons for a decision, it was likely that a third reason—the real one—had been left unstated.

As if tuned to the wavelength of Gurney's thought, Mellery said suddenly, "I need to be more honest with you, more open about my concerns. I can't expect you to help me unless I show you the whole picture. In my forty-seven years, I've led two distinctly different lives. For the first two-thirds of my existence on this earth, I was on the wrong path, going nowhere good but getting there fast. It started in college. After college it got worse. The drinking increased, the chaos increased. I got involved in dealing drugs to an upmarket clientele and became friends with my customers. One was so impressed with my ability to spin a line of bullshit that he gave me a job on Wall Street selling bullshit stock deals over the phone to people greedy and stupid enough to believe that doubling their investment in three months was a real possibility. I was good at it, and I made a lot of money, and the money was my rocket fuel into lunacy. I did whatever I felt like doing, and most of it I can't remember, because most of the time I was blind drunk. For ten years I worked for a succession of brilliant, thieving scumbags. Then my wife died. You wouldn't have known, but I had gotten married the year after we graduated."

Mellery reached for his glass. He drank thoughtfully, as though the taste were an idea forming in his mind. When the glass was half empty, he placed it on the arm of the chair, stared at it for a moment, then resumed his story.

"Her death was a monumental event. It had a greater effect on me than all the events of our fifteen years of marriage combined. I hate to admit this, but it was only through her death that my wife's life had any real impact on me."

Gurney got the impression that this neat irony, spoken as haltingly as though it had just come to mind, was being delivered for the hundredth time. "How did she die?"

"The whole story is in my first book, but here's the short ugly version. We were on vacation on the Olympic Peninsula in Washington. One evening at sunset, we were sitting on a deserted beach. Erin decided to go for a swim. She'd usually go out about a hundred feet and swim back and forth parallel to the shore, as if she were doing laps in a pool. She was religious about exercise." He paused, letting his eyes drift shut.

"Is that what she did that night?"

"What?"

"You said that's what she *usually* did."

"Oh, I see. Yes, I *think* that's what she did that night. The truth is, I'm really not sure because I was drunk. Erin went in the water; I stayed on the beach with my thermos of martinis." A tic had appeared at the corner of his left eye.

"Erin drowned. The people who discovered her body, floating in the water fifty feet from shore, also discovered me, passed out on the beach in a drunken stupor."

After a pause he continued in a strained voice, "I imagine she had a cramp or . . . I don't know what . . . but I imagine . . . she may have called to me—" He broke off, closed his eyes again, and massaged the tic. When he opened them, he looked around as if taking in his surroundings for the first time.

"This is a lovely place you have," he said with a sad smile.

"You said her death had a powerful effect on you?"

"Oh, yes, a powerful effect."

"Right away or later?"

"Right away. It's a cliché, but I had what is called 'a moment of clarity.' It was more painful, more revelatory than anything I've experienced before or since. I saw vividly for the first time in my life the path I was on and how insanely destructive it was. I don't want to liken myself to Paul being knocked off his horse on the way to Damascus, but the fact is, from that moment on I did not want to take another step down that path." He spoke these words with resounding conviction.

He could teach a sales course called Resounding Conviction, mused Gurney.

"I signed myself in to an alcohol detox because it seemed the right thing to do. After detox I went into therapy. I wanted to be sure

I'd found the truth and not lost my mind. The therapist was encouraging. I ended up going back to school and getting two graduate degrees, one in psychology and one in counseling. One of my classmates was the pastor of a Unitarian church, and he asked me to come and talk about my 'conversion'—that was his word for it, not mine. The talk was a success. It grew into a series of lectures that I gave at a dozen other Unitarian churches, and the lectures turned into my first book. The book became the basis of a three-part series for PBS. Then that was distributed as a set of videotapes.

"A lot of stuff like that happened—a stream of coincidences that carried me from one good thing to another. I was invited to do a series of private seminars for some extraordinary people—who also happened to be extraordinarily wealthy. That led to the founding of the Mellery Institute for Spiritual Renewal. The people who come there love what I do. I know how egomaniacal that sounds, but it's true. I have people who come back year after year to hear essentially the same lectures, to go through the same spiritual exercises. I hesitate to say this, because it sounds so pretentious, but as a result of Erin's death I was reborn into an amazing new life."

His eyes moved restlessly, giving the impression of being focused on a private landscape. Madeleine came out, removed their empty glasses, and asked if they wanted refills, which they declined. Mellery mentioned again what a lovely place they had.

"You said that you wanted to be more honest with me about your concerns," prompted Gurney.

"Yes. It has to do with my drinking years. I was a blackout drinker. I had serious *memory* blackouts—some lasting an hour or two, some longer. In the final years, I had them every time I drank. That's a lot of time, a lot of things I've done, that I have no recollection of. When I was drunk, I wasn't choosy about who I was with or what I did. Frankly, the alcohol references in those nasty little notes I showed you are the reason I'm so upset. My emotions the past few days have been bouncing back and forth between upset and terrified."

Despite his skepticism, Gurney was struck by something authentic in Mellery's tone. "Tell me more," he said.

During the ensuing half hour, it became clear that there was not a lot more Mellery was willing or able to tell. He did, however, return to one point that obsessed him.

"How in the name of God could he have known what number I would think of? I have gone over in my mind people I've known, places I've been, addresses, zip codes, phone numbers, dates, birthdays, license plates, even prices of things—anything with numbers—and there's nothing I associate with six fifty-eight. It's driving me crazy!"

"It might be more useful to focus on simpler questions. For instance . . ."

But Mellery wasn't listening. "I have no sense that six fifty-eight means anything at all. But it must mean something. And whatever it means, someone else knows about it. Someone else knows that six fifty-eight is significant enough to me that it would be the first number I would think of. I can't get my mind around that. It's a nightmare!"

Gurney sat quietly and waited for Mellery's panic to exhaust itself.

"The references to drinking mean that it's someone who knew me in the bad old days. If they have some sort of grudge—which it sounds like they do—they've been nursing it for a long time. It might be someone who lost track of me, had no idea where I was, then saw one of my books, saw my picture, read something about me, and decided to . . . decided to what? I don't even know what these notes are about."

Still Gurney said nothing.

"Do you have any idea what it's like to have a hundred, maybe two hundred, nights in your life you have no recollection of?" Mellery shook his head in apparent astonishment at his own recklessness. "The only thing I know for sure about those nights is that I was drunk enough—crazy enough—to do anything. That's the thing about alcohol—when you drink as much I did, it takes away all fear of consequences. Your perceptions are warped, your inhibitions disappear, your memory shuts down, and you run on impulse—instinct without constraint." He fell silent, shaking his head.

"What do you think you might have done in one of those memory blackouts?"

Mellery stared at him. "Anything! Christ, that's the point—*anything!*"

He looked, Gurney thought, like a man who has just discovered that the tropical paradise of his dreams, in which he has invested every cent, is infested with scorpions.

"What do you want me to do for you?"

"I don't know. Maybe I was hoping for a Sherlock Holmes deduction, mystery solved, letter writer identified and rendered harmless."

"You're in a better position to guess what this is all about than I am."

Mellery shook his head. Then a fragile hopefulness widened his eyes. "Could it be a practical joke?"

"If it is, it's crueler than most," replied Gurney. "What else comes to mind?"

"Blackmail? The writer knows something awful, something I can't remember? And the $289.87 is just the first demand?"

Gurney nodded noncommittally. "Any other possibilities?"

"Revenge? For something awful I did, but they don't want money, they want . . ." His voice trailed off pathetically.

"And there's no specific thing you remember doing that would seem to justify this response?"

"No. I told you. Nothing I can *remember.*"

"Okay, I believe you. But under the circumstances, it may be worthwhile to consider a few simple questions. Just write them down as I ask them, take them home, spend twenty-four hours with them, and see what comes to mind."

Mellery opened his elegant briefcase and withdrew a small leather notebook and a Montblanc pen.

"I want you to make a few separate lists, as best you can, okay? List number one: possible business or professional enemies—people with whom you were at any time in serious conflict over money, contracts, promises, position, reputation. List number two: unresolved personal conflicts—ex-friends, ex-lovers, partners in affairs that ended badly. List three: directly menacing individuals—people who have made accusations against you or threatened you. List four: unstable individuals—people you dealt with who were unbalanced or troubled in some way. List five: anyone from your past whom you have run into recently, regardless of how innocent or accidental the encounter may have seemed. List six: any connections you have with anyone living in or around Wycherly—since that's where the X. Arybdis post-office box is, and that's where all the envelopes were postmarked."

As he dictated the questions, he observed Mellery shake his head repeatedly, as if to assert the impossibility of recalling any relevant names.

"I know how difficult this seems," said Gurney with parental firmness, "but it needs to be done. In the meantime leave the notes with me. I'll take a closer look. But remember, I'm not in the private-investigation business, and there may be very little I can do for you."

Mellery stared bleakly at his hands. "Apart from making these lists, is there something else I should be doing myself?"

"Good question. Anything come to mind?"

"Well . . . maybe with some direction from you I could track down this Mr. Arybdis of Wycherly, Connecticut, try to get some information about him."

"If by 'track down' you mean through his home address rather than his box number, the post office won't give it to you. For that you need to get the police involved, but you refuse to do that. You could check the Internet White Pages, but that gets you nowhere with a made-up name—which this probably is, since he said in the note it wasn't the name you knew him by." Gurney paused. "But it's an odd thing about the check, don't you think?"

"You mean the amount?"

"I mean the fact that it wasn't cashed. Why make such a point of it—the precise amount, who to make it out to, where to send it— and then not cash it?"

"Well, if Arybdis is a false name, and he has no ID in that name ..."

"Then why offer the option of sending a check? Why not demand cash?"

Mellery's eyes scanned the ground as if the possibilities were land mines. "Maybe all he wanted was something with my signature on it."

"That occurred to me," said Gurney, "but there are two difficulties with it. First, remember that he was also willing to take cash. Second, if the real goal was to get a signed check, why not ask for a smaller amount—say, twenty dollars or even fifty? Wouldn't that increase the likelihood of getting a response?"

"Maybe Arybdis isn't that smart."

"Somehow I don't think that's the problem."

Mellery looked like exhaustion was vying with anxiety in every cell of his body and it was a close contest. "Do you think I'm in any real danger?"

Gurney shrugged. "Most crank letters are just crank letters. The unpleasant message itself is the assault weapon, so to speak. However ..."

"These are different?"

"These may be different."

Mellery's eyes widened. "I see. You will take another look at them?"

"Yes. And you'll get started on those lists?"

"It won't do any good, but yes, I'll try."

Chapter 6

For blood that's as red as a
painted rose

In the absence of an invitation to stay for lunch, Mellery had reluctantly departed, driving a meticulously restored powder blue Austin-Healey—a classic open sports car on a perfect driving day to which the man seemed miserably oblivious.

Gurney returned to his Adirondack chair and sat there for a long while, nearly an hour, hoping that the tangle of facts would start to arrange themselves in some kind of order, some sensible concatenation. However, the only thing that became clear to him was that he was hungry. He got up, went into the house, made a sandwich of havarti and roasted peppers, and ate alone. Madeleine seemed to be missing, and he wondered if he'd forgotten some plan she might have told him about. Then, as he was rinsing his plate and gazing idly out the window, he caught sight of her meandering up the field from the orchard, her canvas tote full of apples. She had that look of bright serenity that was so often for her an automatic consequence of being in the open air.

She entered the kitchen and laid the apples down by the sink with a loud, happy sigh. "God, what a day!" she exclaimed. "On a day like this, being indoors a minute longer than you have to be is a sin!"

It wasn't that he disagreed with her, at least not aesthetically, maybe not at all, but the difficult personal fact for him was that his natural inclinations tilted him inward in a variety of ways, with the result that, left to his own devices, he spent more time in the consideration of action than in action, more time in his head than in the world. This had never been a problem in his profession; in truth, it was the very thing that seemed to make him so good at it.

In any event, he had no immediate desire to go out, nor was it something he felt like talking about, arguing about, or feeling guilty about. He raised a diversionary subject.

"What was your impression of Mark Mellery?"

She answered without looking up from the fruit she was transferring from her bag to the countertop, or even pausing to consider the question.

"Full of himself and scared to death. An egomaniac with an inferiority complex. Afraid the bogeyman is coming to get him. Wants Uncle Dave to protect him. By the way, I wasn't purposely eavesdropping. His voice carries well. I bet he's a great public speaker." She made this sound like a dubious asset.

"What did you think of the number business?"

"Ah," she said with dramatic affectation. "'The Case of the Mind-Reading Stalker.'"

He stifled his irritation. "Do you have any idea how it might have been done—how the writer knew what number Mellery would choose?"

"Nope."

"You don't seem perplexed by it."

"But you are." Again she spoke with her eyes on her apples. The tiny ironic grin, increasingly present these days, tugged at the corner of her mouth.

"You have to admit it's quite a puzzle," he insisted.

"I suppose."

He repeated the key facts with the edginess of a man who cannot understand why he is not being understood. "A person gives you a sealed envelope and tells you to picture a number in your mind. You picture six fifty-eight. He tells you to look in the envelope. You look in the envelope. The note inside says six fifty-eight."

It was clear that Madeleine was not as impressed as she ought to be. He went on, "That's a remarkable feat. It would appear to be impossible. Yet it was done. I'd like to figure out how it was done."

"And I'm sure you will," she said with a small sigh.

He gazed through the French doors, past the pepper and tomato plants wilted from the season's first frost. (When was that? He couldn't remember. Couldn't seem to focus on the time factor.) Beyond the garden, beyond the pasture, his gaze rested on the red barn. The old McIntosh apple tree was just visible behind the corner of it, its fruit dotted here and there through the mass of foliage like droplets of impressionist paint. Into this tableau there intruded a nagging sense of something he ought to be doing. *What was it?* Of course! His week-old promise that he would fetch the extension ladder from the barn and pick the high fruit Madeleine couldn't get to by herself. Such a small thing. So easy for him to do. A half-hour project at most.

As he rose from his chair, buoyed by good intentions, the phone rang. Madeleine picked it up, ostensibly because she was standing next to the table on which it rested, but that was not the real reason. Madeleine often answered the phone regardless of who was closer to it. It had less to do with logistics than with their respective desires for contact with other people. For her, people in general were a plus, a source of positive stimulation (with exceptions such as the predatory Sonya Reynolds). For Gurney, people in general were a minus, a drain on his energy (with exceptions such as the encouraging Sonya Reynolds).

"Hello?" said Madeleine in that pleasantly expectant way she greeted all callers—full of the promise of interest in whatever they might have to say. A second later her tone dropped into a less enthusiastic register.

"Yes, he is. Just a moment." She waved the handset toward Gurney, laid it on the table, and left the room.

It was Mark Mellery, and his agitation level had risen.

"Davey, thank God you're there. I just got home. I got another of those damn letters."

"In today's mail?"

The answer was yes, as Gurney assumed it would be. But the question had a purpose nonetheless. He had discovered over years of interviewing countless hysterical people—at crime scenes, in emergency rooms, in all sorts of chaotic situations—that the easiest way to calm them was to start by asking simple questions they could answer yes to.

"Does it look like the same handwriting?"

"Yes."

"And the same red ink?"

"Yes, everything's the same except the words. Shall I read it to you?"

"Go ahead," he said. "Read it to me slowly and tell me where the line breaks are."

The clear questions, clear instructions, and Gurney's tranquil voice had the predictable effect. Mellery sounded like his feet were getting back on solid ground as he read aloud the peculiar, unsettling verse—with little pauses to indicate the ends of lines:

> *"I do what I've done*
> *not for money or fun*
> *but for debts to be paid,*
> *amends to be made.*
> *For blood that's as red*
> *as a painted rose.*
> *So every man knows*
> *he reaps what he sows."*

After jotting it down on the pad by the phone, Gurney reread it carefully, trying to get a sense of the writer—the peculiar personality lurking at the intersection of a vengeful intent and the urge to express it in a poem.

Mellery broke the silence. "What are you thinking?"

"I'm thinking it may be time for you to go to the police."

"I'd rather not do that." The agitation was returning. "I explained that to you."

"I know you did. But if you want my best advice, that's it."

"I understand what you're saying. But I'm asking for an alternative."

"The best alternative, if you can afford it, would be twenty-four-hour bodyguards."

"You mean walk around my own property between a pair of gorillas? How on earth do I explain that to my guests?"

"'Gorillas' may be a bit of an exaggeration."

"Look, the point is, I don't tell lies to my guests. If one of them asked me who these new additions are, I'd have to admit that they are bodyguards, which would naturally lead to more questions. It would be unsettling—toxic to the atmosphere I try to generate here. Is there any other course of action you can suggest?"

"That depends. What would you want the action to achieve?"

Mellery answered with a sour little laugh. "Maybe you could discover who's after me and what they want to do to me, and then keep them from doing it. Do you think you could do that?"

Gurney was about to say, "I'm not sure whether I can or not," when Mellery added with sudden intensity, "Davey, for Chrissake, I'm scared shitless. I don't know what the hell is going on. You're the smartest guy I ever met. And you're the only guy I trust not to make the situation worse."

Just then Madeleine passed through the kitchen carrying her knitting bag. She picked up her straw gardening hat from the sideboard along with the current issue of *Mother Earth News* and went out through the French doors with a quick smile that seemed to be switched on by the bright sky.

"How much I can help you will depend on how much you help me," said Gurney.

"What do you want me to do?"

"I already told you."

"What? Oh . . . the lists . . ."

"When you've made progress, call me back. We'll see where we go from there."

"Dave?"

"Yes?"

"Thank you."

"I haven't done anything."

"You've given me some hope. Oh, by the way, I opened that envelope today very carefully. Like they do on TV. So if there are fingerprints, they wouldn't be destroyed. I used tweezers and latex gloves. I put the letter in a plastic bag."

Chapter 7

The black hole

Gurney wasn't really comfortable with his agreement to get involved in Mark Mellery's problem. Certainly he was attracted by its mystery, by the challenge of unraveling it. So why did he feel uneasy?

It popped into his mind that he should go to the barn to get the ladder to gather the promised apples, but that was replaced by the thought he should set up his next art project for Sonya Reynolds—at least enter the mug shot of the infamous Peter Piggert into his computer's retouching program. He'd been looking forward to the challenge of capturing the inner life of that Eagle Scout who had not only murdered his father and fifteen years later his mother but had done so for sex-related motives that seemed more horrendous than the crimes themselves.

Gurney went to the room he had set up for his Cop Art avocation. Once the farmhouse pantry, it was now furnished as a den and was suffused with a shadowless, cool light from an expanded window on its north wall. He stared out at the bucolic view. A gap in the maple copse beyond the meadow formed a frame for the bluish hills that receded into the distance. It brought his mind back to the apples, and he returned to the kitchen.

As he stood entangled in indecision, Madeleine came in from her knitting.

"So what's the next step with Mellery?" she asked.

"I haven't decided."

"Why not?"

"Well . . . it's not the kind of thing you'd want me to get wound up in, is it?"

"That's not the problem," she said with the clarity that always impressed him.

"You're right," he conceded. "I think the problem actually is that I can't put the normal labels on anything yet."

She flashed a smile of understanding.

Encouraged, he went on, "I'm not a homicide cop anymore, and he's not a homicide victim. I'm not sure what I am or what he is."

"Old college buddy?"

"But what the hell is that? He recalls a level of comradeship between us that I never felt. Besides, he doesn't need a buddy, he needs a bodyguard."

"He wants Uncle Dave."

"That's not who I am."

"You sure?"

He sighed. "Do you want me to get involved in this Mellery business or not?"

"You *are* involved. You may not have the labels sorted out yet. You're not an official cop, and he's not an official crime victim. But there's a puzzle there, and by God, sooner or later you're going to put the pieces together. That's always going to be the bottom line, isn't it?"

"Is that an accusation? You married a detective. I wasn't pretending to be something else."

"I thought there might be a difference between a detective and a retired detective."

"I've been retired for over a year. What do I do that looks like detective work?"

She shook her head as if to say that the answer was painfully obvious. "What do you invest any time in that *doesn't* look like detective work?"

"I don't know what you mean."

"Everyone does portraits of murderers?"

"It's a subject I know something about. You want me to draw pictures of daisies?"

"Daisies would be better than homicidal madmen."

"It was you who got me involved in this art thing."

"Oh, I see. It's because of me that you spend your time on beautiful fall mornings staring into the eyes of serial killers?"

The barrette that was holding most of her hair up and away from her face seemed to be losing its grip, and several dark strands descended in front of her eyes, which she seemed not to notice, giving her a rare harried look that he found touching.

He took a deep breath. "What exactly are we fighting about?"

"You figure it out. You're the detective."

As he stood looking at her, he lost interest in carrying the weight of the argument any further. "I want to show you something," he said. "I'll be right back."

He left the room and returned a minute later with his handwritten copy of the nasty little poem Mellery had read to him over the phone.

"What do you make of this?"

She read it so rapidly that someone who didn't know her might think she hadn't read it at all. "Sounds serious," she said, handing it back to him.

"I agree."

"What do you think he's *done*?"

"Ah, good question. You noticed that word?"

She recited the relevant couplet: "'I do what I've done / not for money or fun.'"

If Madeleine didn't have a photographic memory, thought Gurney, she had something close to it.

"So what exactly is it that he's *done*, and what is he planning to *do*?" she went on in a rhetorical tone that invited no reply. "I'm sure you'll find out. You might even end up with a murder to solve, from the sound of that note. Then you could collect the evidence, follow the leads, catch the murderer, paint his portrait, and give it to Sonya for her gallery. What's that saying about turning lemons into lemonade?"

Her smile looked positively dangerous.

At times like this, the question that came to his mind was the one he least wanted to consider. Had moving to Delaware County been a great mistake?

He suspected that he'd gone along with her desire to live in the country to make up to her for all the crap she'd had to endure as a cop's wife—always playing second fiddle to the job. She loved woods and mountains and meadows and open spaces, and he felt he owed her a new environment, a new life—and he made the assumption that he would be able to adjust to anything. Bit of pride there. Or maybe self-delusion. Perhaps a desire to get rid of his guilt through a grand gesture? Stupid, really. The truth was, he hadn't adjusted well to the move. He wasn't as flexible as he'd naïvely imagined. As he kept trying to find a meaningful place for himself in the middle of nowhere, he kept falling back instinctively on what he was good at—perhaps too good at, obsessively good at. Even in his struggles to appreciate nature. The damn birds, for example. Bird-watching. He'd managed to turn the process of observation and identification into a stakeout. Made notes on their comings and goings, habits, feeding patterns, flight characteristics. It might look to someone else like a newfound love of God's little creatures. But it wasn't that at all. It wasn't love, it was analysis. Probing.

Deciphering.

Good God. Was he really that limited?

Was he, in fact, too limited—too small and rigid—in his approach to life to ever be able to give back to Madeleine what his devotion to his work had deprived her of? And as long as he was considering painful possibilities, maybe there were more things to make up for than just an excessive immersion in his profession.

Or maybe just one other thing.

The thing they found so hard to talk about.

The collapsed star.

The black hole whose terrible gravity had twisted their relationship.

Chapter 8

A rock and a hard place

The sparkling autumn weather deteriorated that afternoon. The clouds, which in the morning had been joyful little cotton-ball clichés, darkened. Premonitory rumbles of thunder could be heard—so far in the distance that the direction from which they originated was unclear. They were more like an intangible presence in the atmosphere than the product of a specific storm—a perception that strengthened as they persisted over a period of hours, seeming neither to draw closer nor entirely cease.

That evening Madeleine went to a local concert with one of her new Walnut Crossing friends. It was not an event she expected Gurney to attend, so he didn't feel defensive about his decision to stay home and work on his art project.

Shortly after her departure, he found himself sitting in front of his computer screen, gazing at the mug shot of Peter Possum Piggert. All he had done so far was to import the graphics file and set it up as a new project—to which he had given a wretchedly cute name: *Oedipus Wrecks*.

In the Sophocles version of the old Greek tale, Oedipus kills a man who turns out to be his father, marries a woman who turns out to be his mother, and sires two daughters with her, creating great misery for all concerned. In Freud's psychology the Greek tale is a symbol for the developmental phase in the life of a male child during which he desires his father's absence (disappearance, death) so that he may possess exclusively the affection of his mother. In the case of Peter Possum Piggert, however, there was neither exculpatory ignorance nor any question of symbolism. Knowing exactly what he was doing and to whom, Peter at the age of fifteen murdered his father, entered into a new relationship with his mother, and sired two daughters with her. But it did not stop there. Fifteen years later he murdered his mother in a dispute over a new relationship he had entered into with their daughters, then thirteen and fourteen.

Gurney's involvement in the case had begun when half of Mrs. Iris Piggert's body was discovered tangled in the rudder mechanism of a Hudson River day liner docked at a Manhattan pier, and it ended with the arrest of Peter Piggert in a desert compound of "traditionalist" Mormons in Utah, where he had gone to live as the husband of his two daughters.

Despite the depravity of the crimes, steeped in blood and family horror, Piggert remained a controlled and taciturn figure in all interrogations and throughout the criminal proceedings against him, keeping his Mr. Hyde well concealed and looking more like a depressed auto mechanic than a parricidal, incestuous polygamist.

Gurney stared at Piggert on the screen, and Piggert stared back. Ever since he first interrogated him, and even more so now, Gurney felt that the key quality of the man was a need (taken to bizarre lengths) to control his environment. People, even family—in fact, family most of all—were part of that environment, and making them do as he wished was essential. If he had to kill someone to establish his control, so be it. The sex, as big a driving force as it appeared to be, was more about power than lust.

As he searched the stolid face for a hint of the demon, a gust of wind picked up a swirl of dry leaves. They blew with the sound of a feathery broom across the patio; a few clicked lightly against the glass panes of the French doors. The restlessness of the leaves, plus the intermittent thunder, made it hard for him to concentrate. The idea of being alone for a few hours of progress on the portrait, free of raised eyebrows and unpleasant questions, had appealed to him.

But now his mind was unsettled. He peered into Piggert's eyes, heavy and dark—with none of the wild glare that animated the eyes of Charlie Manson, the tabloid prince of sex and slaughter— but again the wind and the leaves distracted him, and then the thunder. Out beyond the line of hills, there was a faint flashing in the murky sky. A couplet from one of Mellery's threatening poems had been drifting in and out of his mind. Now it came again and stuck there.

> *What you took you will give*
> *when you get what you gave.*

It was at first an impossible riddle. The words were too general; they had too much and too little meaning; yet he could not get them out of his head.

He opened the desk drawer and removed the sequence of messages Mellery had given him. He shut down the computer and pushed the keyboard to the side of the desk so he could arrange the messages in order—beginning with the first note.

> *Do you believe in Fate? I do, because I thought I'd never see you again— and then one day, there you were. It all came back: how you sound, how you move—most of all, how you think. If someone told you to think of a number, I know what number you'd think of. You don't believe me? I'll prove it to you. Think of any number up to a thousand—the first number that comes to your mind. Picture it. Now see how well I know your secrets. Open the little envelope.*

Although he'd done so earlier, he examined the outer envelope, inside and out, as well as the notepaper on which the message was written to be sure there was no faint trace anywhere of the number 658—not even a watermark—that could have suggested the number that seemed to come spontaneously to Mellery's mind. There was no such trace. More definitive tests could be conducted later, but he was satisfied for now that whatever it was that enabled the writer to know that Mellery would choose 658, it wasn't a subtle imprint in the paper.

The content of the message comprised a number of claims that Gurney enumerated on a lined yellow notepad:

1. I knew you in the past but lost contact with you.
2. I encountered you again, recently.
3. I recall a great deal about you.
4. I can prove I know your secrets by writing down and sealing in the enclosed envelope the next number that will enter your mind.

The tone struck him as creepily playful, and the reference to knowing Mellery's "secrets" could be read as a threat—reinforced by the request for money in the smaller envelope.

> *Does it shock you that I knew you would pick 658?*
> *Who knows you that well? If you want the answer,*
> *you must first repay me the $289.87 it cost me to find you.*
> *Send that exact amount to*
> *P.O. Box 49449, Wycherly, CT 61010.*
> *Send me CASH or a PERSONAL CHECK.*
> *Make it out to X. Arybdis.*
> *(That was not always my name.)*

In addition to the inexplicable number prediction, the smaller note reiterated the claim of close personal knowledge and specified $289.87 as a cost incurred in locating Mellery (although the first half of the message made it sound like a chance encounter) and as a precondition to the writer's revealing his identity; it offered a choice of paying the amount by check or cash; it gave the name for the check as "X. Arybdis," offered an explanation of why Mellery would not recognize the name, and provided a Wycherly P.O. box address to send the money to. Gurney jotted all these facts down on his yellow pad, finding it helpful in organizing his thoughts.

Those thoughts centered on four questions: How could the number prediction be explained without hypothesizing some sort of *Manchurian Candidate* hypnosis or ESP? Did the other specific number in the note, $289.87, have any significance beyond the stated "cost to find you"? Why the cash-or-check option, which sounded like a parody of a direct-marketing ad? And what was it about that name, Arybdis, that kept tickling a dark corner of Gurney's memory? He wrote these questions down alongside his other notes.

Next he laid out the three poems in the sequence of their envelope postmarks.

> *How many bright angels*
> *can dance on a pin?*
> *How many hopes drown in*
> *a bottle of gin?*
> *Did the thought ever come*
> *that your glass was a gun*
> *and one day you'd wonder,*
> *God, what have I done?*

> *What you took you will give*
> *when you get what you gave.*
> *I know what you think,*
> *when you blink,*
> *where you've been,*
> *where you'll be.*
> *You and I have a date,*
> *Mr. 658.*

> *I do what I've done*
> *not for money or fun*
> *but for debts to be paid,*
> *amends to be made.*
> *For blood that's as red*

> *as a painted rose.*
> *So every man knows*
> *he reaps what he sows.*

The first thing that struck him was the change in attitude. The toying tone of the two prose messages had become prosecutorial in the first poem, overtly menacing in the second, and vengeful in the third. Putting aside the question of how seriously it should be taken, the message itself was clear: The writer (X. Arybdis?) was saying that he intended to get even with (kill?) Mellery for a drinking-related misdeed in his past. As Gurney wrote the word *kill* in the notes he was making, his attention jumped back to the initial couplet in the second poem:

> *What you took you will give*
> *when you get what you gave.*

Now he knew exactly what the words meant, and the meaning was chillingly simple. *For the life you took, you will give your life. What you did will be done to you.*

He wasn't sure whether the frisson he felt convinced him he was right or if knowing he was right created the frisson, but either way he had no doubt about it. This did not, however, answer his other questions. It only made them more urgent, and it gave rise to new ones.

Was the threat of murder just a threat, designed only to inflict the pain of apprehension—or was it a declaration of practical intent? To what was the writer referring when he said *"I do what I've done"* in the first line of the third poem? Had he previously done to someone else what he now proposed to do to Mellery? Might Mellery have done something in concert with someone else whom the writer had already dealt with? Gurney made a note to ask Mellery if any friend or associate of his had ever been killed, assaulted, or threatened.

Maybe it was the mood created by the flashes of light beyond the blackening foothills, or the eerie persistence of the low thunder, or his own exhaustion, but the personality behind the messages was emerging from the shadows. The detachment of the voice in those poems, bloody purpose and careful syntax, hatred and calculation— he had seen those qualities combined before to horrible effect. As he stared out the den window, surrounded by the unsettled atmosphere of the approaching storms, he could sense in those messages the iciness of a psychopath. A psychopath who called himself X. Arybdis.

Of course, it was possible that he was off base. It wouldn't be the first time that a certain mood, particularly in the evening, particularly when he was alone, had generated in him convictions unsupported by the facts.

Still . . . what was it about that name? In what dusty box of memories was it faintly stirring?

He went to bed early that night, long before Madeleine returned home from her concert, determined that tomorrow he would return the letters to Mellery and insist that he go to the police. The stakes were too high, the danger too palpable. In bed, though, he found it impossible to lay the day to rest. His mind was a racecourse with no exits and no finish line. It was an experience he was familiar with—a price he paid (he'd come to believe) for the intense attention he devoted to certain kinds of challenges. Once his obsessed mind, instead of falling asleep, fell into this circular rut, there were only two options. He could let the process run its course, which could take three or four hours, or he could force himself out of bed and into his clothes.

Minutes later, dressed in jeans and a comfortable old cotton sweater, he was standing outside on the patio. A full moon behind the overcast sky created a faint illumination, making the barn visible. It was in that direction, along the rutted road through the pasture, that he decided to walk.

Past the barn was the pond. Halfway there he stopped and listened to the sound of a car coming up the road from the direction of the village. He estimated it to be about half a mile away. In that quiet corner of the Catskills, where the sporadic howling of coyotes was the loudest nighttime sound, a vehicle could be heard at a great distance.

Soon the headlights of Madeleine's car swept over the tangle of dying goldenrod that bordered the pasture. She turned toward the barn, stopped on the crunchy gravel, and switched off the headlights. She got out and walked toward him—cautiously, her eyes adjusting to the semidarkness.

"What are you doing?" Her question sounded soft, friendly.

"Couldn't sleep. Mind racing. Thought I'd take a walk around the pond."

"Feels like rain." A rumble in the sky punctuated her observation.

He nodded.

She stood next to him on the path and inhaled deeply.

"Wonderful smell. Come on, let's walk," she said, taking his arm.

As they reached the pond, the path broadened into a mowed swath. Somewhere in the woods, an owl screeched—or, more precisely, there was a familiar screech they thought might be an owl when they first heard it that summer, and each time after that they became more certain it was an owl. It was in the nature of Gurney's intellect to realize that this process of increasing conviction made no logical sense, but he also knew that pointing it out, interesting though this trick of the mind might be to him, would bore and annoy her. So he said nothing, happy that he knew her well enough to know when to be quiet, and they ambled on to the far side of the pond in amiable silence. She was right about the smell—a wonderful sweetness in the air.

They had moments like this from time to time, moments of easy affection and quiet closeness, that reminded him of the early years of their marriage, the years before the accident. "The Accident"— that dense, generic label with which he wrapped the event in his memory to keep its razor-wire details from slicing his heart. The accident—the death—that eclipsed the sun, turning their marriage into a shifting mixture of habit, duty, edgy companionship, and rare moments of hope—rare moments when something bright and clear as a diamond would shoot back and forth between them, reminding him of what once was and might again be possible.

"You always seem to be wrestling with something," she said, curling her fingers around the inside of his arm, just above his elbow.

Right again.

"How was the concert?" he finally asked.

"First half was baroque, lovely. Second half was twentieth century, not so lovely."

He was about to chime in with his own low opinion of modern music but thought better of it.

"What kept you awake?" she asked.

"I'm not really sure."

He sensed her skepticism. She let go of his arm. Something splashed into the pond a few yards ahead of them.

"I couldn't get the Mellery business out of my mind," he said.

She didn't reply.

"Bits and pieces of it kept running around in my head—not getting anywhere—just making me uncomfortable—too tired to think straight."

Again she offered nothing but a thoughtful silence.

"I kept thinking about that name on the note."

"X. Arybdis?"

"How did you . . . ? You heard us mention it?"

"I have good hearing."

"I know, but it always surprises me."

"It might not really be X. Arybdis, you know," she said in that offhand way that he knew was anything but offhand.

"What?" he said, stopping.

"It might not be X. Arybdis."

"What do you mean?"

"I was suffering through one of the atonal atrocities in the second half of the concert, thinking that some modern composers must really hate the cello. Why would you force a beautiful instrument to make such painful noises? Horrible scraping and whining."

"And . . . ?" he said gently, trying to keep his curiosity from sounding edgy.

"And I'd have left at that point, but I couldn't because I'd given Ellie a ride there."

"Ellie?"

"Ellie from the bottom of the hill—rather than take two cars? But she seemed to be enjoying it, God knows why."

"Yes?"

"So I asked myself, what can I do to pass the time and keep from killing the musicians?"

There was another splash in the pond, and she stopped to listen. He half saw, half sensed her smile. Madeleine was fond of frogs.

"And?"

"And I thought to myself I could start figuring out my Christmas card list—it's practically November—so I took out my pen and on the back of my program, at the top of the page, I wrote 'Xmas Cards'—not the whole word *Christmas* but the abbreviation, X-M-A-S," she said, spelling it out.

In the darkness he could feel more than see her inquiring look, as if she were asking whether he was getting the point.

"Go on," he said.

"Every time I see that abbreviation, it reminds me of little Tommy Milakos."

"Who?"

"Tommy had a crush on me in the ninth grade at Our Lady of Chastity."

"I thought it was Our Lady of Sorrows," said Gurney with a twinge of irritation.

She paused a beat to let her little joke register, then went on. "Anyway, one day Sister Immaculata, a very large woman, started screaming at me because I'd abbreviated *Christmas* as *Xmas* in a little quiz about Catholic holy days. She said anyone who wrote it that way was purposely 'X-ing Christ out of Christmas.' She was furious. I thought she was going to hit me. But right then Tommy— sweet little brown-eyed Tommy—jumped up out of his seat and shouted, 'It's not an *X*.'

"Sister Immaculata was shocked. It was the first time anyone had ever dared to interrupt her. She just stared at him, but he stared right back, my little champion. 'It's not an English letter,' he said. 'It's a Greek letter. It's the same as an English *ch*. It's the first letter of *Christ* in Greek.' And, of course, Tommy Milakos was Greek, so everybody knew he must be right."

Dark as it was, he thought he could see her smiling softly at the recollection, even suspected he heard a little sigh. Maybe he was wrong about the sigh—he hoped so. And another distraction—had she betrayed a preference for brown eyes over blue? *Get ahold of yourself, Gurney, she's talking about the ninth grade.*

She went on, "So maybe 'X. Arybdis' is really 'Ch. Arybdis'? Or maybe 'Charybdis'? Isn't that something in Greek mythology?"

"Yes, it is," he said, as much to himself as to her. "*Between Scylla and Charybdis* . . ."

"Like 'between a rock and a hard place'?"

He nodded. "Something like that."

"Which is which?"

He seemed not to hear the question, his mind racing now through the Charybdis implications, juggling the possibilities.

"Hmm?" He realized she'd asked him something.

"Scylla and Charybdis," she said. "The rock and the hard place. Which is which?"

"It's not a direct translation, just an approximation of the meaning. Scylla and Charybdis were actual navigational perils in the Strait of Messina. Ships had to navigate between them and tended to be destroyed in the process. In mythology, they were personalized into demons of destruction."

"When you say navigational perils . . . like what?"

"Scylla was the name for a jagged outcropping of rocks that ships were battered against until they sank."

When he didn't immediately continue, she persisted, "And Charybdis?"

He cleared his throat. Something about the idea of Charybdis seemed especially disturbing. "Charybdis was a whirlpool. A very powerful whirlpool. Once a man was caught in it, he could never get out. It sucked him down and tore him to pieces." He recalled with unsettling clarity an illustration he'd seen ages ago in an edition of the *Odyssey*, showing a sailor trapped in the violent eddy, his face contorted in horror.

Again came the screech from the woods.

"Come on," said Madeleine. "Let's get up to the house. It's going to rain any minute."

He stood still, lost in his racing thoughts.

"Come on," she urged. "Before we get soaked."

He followed her to her car, and they drove up slowly through the pasture to the house.

Before they got out, he turned to her and asked, "You don't think of every *x* you see as a possible *ch*, do you?"

"Of course not."

"Then why . . . ?"

"Because 'Arybdis' sounded Greek."

"Right. Of course."

She looked across the front seat at him, her expression, abetted by the clouded night, unreadable.

After a while she said, with a small smile in her voice, "You never stop thinking, do you?"

Then, as she had promised, the rain began.

Chapter 9

No such person

After being stalled for several hours at the periphery of the mountains, a steep cold front swept through the area, bringing lashings of wind and rain. In the morning the ground was covered with leaves and the air was charged with the intense smells of autumn. Water droplets on the pasture grass fractured the sun into crimson sparks.

As Gurney walked to his car, the assault on his senses awakened something from his childhood, when the sweet smell of grass was the smell of peace and security. Then it was gone—erased by his plans for the day.

He was heading for the Institute for Spiritual Renewal. If Mark Mellery was going to resist getting the police involved, Gurney wanted to argue that decision with him face-to-face. It wasn't that he intended to wash his own hands of the matter. In fact, the more he pondered it, the more curious he was about his old classmate's prominent place in the world and how it might relate to who and what were now threatening him. As long as he was careful about boundaries, Gurney imagined there would be room in the investigation for both himself and the local police.

He'd called Mellery to let him know he was coming. It was a perfect morning for a drive through the mountains. The route to Peony took him first through Walnut Crossing, which, like many Catskill villages, had grown up in the nineteenth century around an intersection

of locally important roads. The intersection, with diminished importance, remained. The eponymous nut tree, along with the region's
prosperity, was long gone. But the depressed economy, serious as it
was, had a picturesque appearance—weathered barns and silos,
rusted plows and hay wagons, abandoned hill pastures overgrown
with fading goldenrod. The road from Walnut Crossing that led
eventually to Peony wound its way through a postcard river valley
where a handful of old farms were searching for innovative ways to
survive. Abelard's was one of these. Squeezed between the village of
Dillweed and the nearby river, it was devoted to the organic cultiva-
tion of "Pesticide-Free Veggies," which were then sold at Abelard's
General Store, along with fresh breads, Catskill cheeses, and very
good coffee—coffee that Gurney felt an urgent need for as he pulled
in to one of the little dirt parking spaces in front of the store's sag-
ging front porch.

Inside the door of the high-ceilinged space, against the right
wall, stood a steaming array of coffeepots, which Gurney headed for.
He filled a sixteen-ounce container, smiling at the rich aroma—
better than Starbucks at half the price.

Unfortunately, the thought of Starbucks brought with it the
image of a certain kind of young, successful Starbucks customer, and
that immediately brought Kyle to mind, along with a little mental
wince. It was his standard reaction. He suspected that it arose from a
frustrated desire for a son who thought a smart cop was worth looking up to, a son more interested in seeking his guidance than Kyle
was. Kyle—unteachable and untouchable in that absurdly expensive
Porsche that his absurdly high Wall Street income had paid for at
the absurdly young age of twenty-four. Still, he did owe the young
man a return phone call, even if all the kid wanted to talk about was
his latest Rolex or Aspen ski trip.

Gurney paid for his coffee and returned to his car. As he was
thinking about the prospective call, his phone rang. He disliked coincidences and was relieved to discover that it was not Kyle but Mark
Mellery.

"I just got today's mail. I called you at home, but you'd gone out.

Madeleine gave me your cell number. I hope you don't mind me calling."

"What's the problem?"

"My check came back. The guy who has the post-office box in Wycherly where I sent the $289.87 check to Arybdis—he sent it back to me with a note saying there's nobody there by that name, that I must have gotten the address wrong. But I checked it again. It was the right box number. Davey? Are you there?"

"I'm here. Just trying to make sense of that."

"Let me read you the note. 'I found the enclosed piece of mail in my post-office box. There must be a mistake in the address. There is no one here named X. Arybdis.' And it's signed 'Gregory Dermott.' The letterhead on the notepaper says 'GD Security Systems,' and there's an address and phone number in Wycherly."

Gurney was about to explain that it was now almost certain that X. Arybdis was not a real name but a curious play on the name of a mythological whirlpool, a whirlpool that tore its victims to pieces, but he decided that the issue was already disturbing enough. The revelation of this extra twist could wait until he got to the institute. He told Mellery he'd be there in an hour.

What the hell was going on? It made no sense. What could be the purpose of demanding a specific amount of money, having the check made out to an obscure mythological name, and then having it sent to the wrong address in the likelihood that it would be returned to the sender? Why such a complex and seemingly point-less preamble to the nasty poems that followed?

The baffling aspects of the case were increasing, and so was Gur-ney's interest.

Chapter 10

The perfect place

Peony was a town twice removed from the history it sought to reflect. Adjacent to Woodstock, it pretended to the same tie-dyed, psychedelic, rock-concert past—while Woodstock in turn nourished its own ersatz aura through its name association with the pot-fogged concert that had actually been held fifty miles away on a farm in Bethel. Peony's image was the product of smoke and mirrors, and upon this chimerical foundation had risen predictable commercial structures—New Age bookstores, tarot parlors, Wiccan and Druidical emporia, tattoo shops, performance-art spaces, vegan restaurants—a center of gravity for flower children approaching senility, Deadheads in old Volkswagen buses, and mad eclectics swathed in everything from leathers to feathers.

Of course, among these colorfully weird elements there were interspersed plenty of opportunities for tourists to spend money: stores and eateries whose names and decor were only a little outrageous and whose wares were tailored to the upscale visitors who liked to imagine they were exploring the cultural edge.

The loose web of roads radiating out from Peony's business district led to money. Real-estate prices had doubled and tripled after 9/11, when New Yorkers of substantial means and galloping paranoia were captivated by the fantasy of a rural sanctuary. Homes in the hills surrounding the village grew in size and number, the SUVs morphed from Blazers and Broncos into Hummers and Land Rovers, and the people who came for country weekends wore what Ralph Lauren told them people in the country wore.

Hunters, firemen, and teachers gave way to lawyers, investment bankers, and women of a certain age whose divorce settlements financed their cultural activities, skin treatments, and mind-expanding involvements with gurus of this and that. In fact, Gurney suspected that the local population's appetite for guru-based solutions to life's problems may have persuaded Mark Mellery to set up shop there.

He turned off the county highway just before the village center, following his Google directions onto Filchers Brook Road—which snaked up a wooded hillside. This brought him eventually to a road-side wall of native slate, laid nearly four feet high. The wall ran parallel to the road, set back about ten feet, for at least a quarter of a mile. The setback was thick with pale blue asters. Halfway along the stretch of wall, there were two formal openings about fifty feet apart, the entrance and exit of a circular drive. Affixed to the wall at the first of these openings was a discreet bronze sign: MELLERY INSTITUTE FOR SPIRITUAL RENEWAL.

Turning in to the driveway brought the aesthetic of the place into sharper focus. Everywhere Gurney looked, he was given an impression of unplanned perfection. Beside the gravel drive, autumn flowers seemed to grow in haphazard freedom. Yet he was sure this casual image, not unlike Mellery's, received careful tending. As in many haunts of the low-profile rich, the note intoned was one of meticulous informality, nature as it ought to be, with no wilting bloom left unpruned. Following the driveway brought Gurney's car to the front of a large Georgian manor house, as gently groomed as the gardens.

Standing in front of the house and eyeing him with interest was an imperious man with a ginger beard. Gurney rolled down his window and asked where the parking area might be found. The man replied with a plummy British accent that he should follow the drive to its end.

Unfortunately, this led Gurney out through the other opening in the stone wall onto Filchers Brook Road. He drove back around through the entrance and followed the drive again to the front of the house, where the tall Englishman again regarded him with interest.

"The end of the drive took me to the public road," said Gurney. "Did I miss something?"

"What a bloody fool I am!" the man cried with exaggerated chagrin that seemed in conflict with his natural bearing. "I think I know everything, but most of the time I'm wrong!"

Gurney had an inkling he might be in the presence of a madman. He also at that point noticed a second figure in the scene. Standing back in the shadow of a giant rhododendron, watching them intently, was a dark, stocky man who looked as if he might be waiting for a *Sopranos* audition.

"Ah," cried the Englishman, pointing with enthusiasm farther along the drive, "there's your answer! Sarah will take you under her protective wing. She's the one for you!" Saying this with high theatricality, he turned and strode off, followed at some distance by the comic-book gangster.

Gurney drove on to where a woman stood by the driveway, solicitude writ large on her pudgy face. Her voice exuded empathy.

"Dear me, dear me, we've got you driving around in circles. That's not a nice way to welcome you." The level of concern in her eyes was alarming. "Let me take your car for you. Then you can go right into the house."

"That's not necessary. Could you just tell me where the parking area is?"

"Of course! Just follow me. I'll make sure you don't get lost this time." Her tone made the task seem more daunting than one would imagine it to be.

She waved to Gurney to follow her. It was an expansive wave, as though she were commanding a caravan. In her other hand, at her side, she carried a closed umbrella. Her deliberate pace conveyed a concern that Gurney might lose sight of her. Reaching a break in the shrubbery, she stepped to the side, pointing Gurney into a narrow offshoot of the driveway that passed through the bushes. As he came abreast of her, she thrust the umbrella toward his open window.

"Take it!" she cried.

He stopped, nonplussed.

"You know what they say about mountain weather," she explained.

"I'm sure I'll be fine." He continued past her into the parking area, a place that looked able to accommodate twice the cars currently there, which Gurney numbered at sixteen. The neat rectangular space was nestled amid the ubiquitous flowers and shrubs. A lofty copper beech at the far end separated the parking area from a three-story red barn, its color vivid in the slanting sunlight.

He chose a space between two gargantuan SUVs. While he was parking, he became aware of a woman watching the process from behind a low bed of dahlias. When he got out of the car, he smiled politely at her—a dainty violet of a woman, small-boned and delicate of feature, with an old-fashioned look about her. If she were an actress, thought Gurney, she'd be a natural to play Emily Dickinson in *The Belle of Amherst.*

"I wonder if you could tell me where I might find Mark—" But the violet interrupted him with her own question.

"Who the fuck said you could park there?"

Chapter 11

A unique ministry

From the parking area, Gurney followed a cobblestone pathway around the Georgian mansion, which he guessed would be used as the institute's business office and lecture center, to a smaller Georgian house about five hundred feet behind it. A small gold-lettered sign by the path read PRIVATE RESIDENCE.

Mark Mellery opened the door before Gurney knocked. He wore the same sort of costly-casual attire he'd worn on his visit to Walnut Crossing. Against the background of the institute's architecture and landscape, the apparel lent him a squire-like aura.

"Good to see you, Davey!"

Gurney stepped into a spacious chestnut-floored entry hall furnished with antiques, and Mellery led the way to a comfortable study toward the rear of the house. A blaze crackling softly in the fireplace perfumed the room with a hint of cherry smoke.

Two wing chairs stood opposite each other to the right and left of the fireplace and, with the sofa that faced the hearth, formed a U-shaped sitting area. When they were settled in the chairs, Mellery asked whether he'd had any trouble finding his way around the property. Gurney recounted the three peculiar conversations he'd had, and Mellery explained that the three individuals were guests of the institute and their behavior constituted part of their self-discovery therapy.

"In the course of his or her stay," Mellery explained, "each guest plays ten different roles. One day he might be the Mistake Maker—that sounds like the role Worth Partridge, the British chap, was playing when you came upon him. Another day he might be the Helper—that's the role Sarah, who wanted to park your car, was playing. Another role is the Confronter. The last lady you encountered sounds like she was playing that part with extra relish."

"What's the point?"

Mellery smiled. "People act out certain roles in their lives. The content of the roles—the scripts, if you will—is consistent and predictable, although generally unconscious and rarely seen as a matter of choice." He was warming to his subject, despite the fact he must have spoken these explanatory sentences hundreds of times. "What we do here is simple, although many of our guests consider it profound. We make them aware of the roles they unconsciously play, what the benefits and costs of those roles are, and how they affect others. Once our guests see their patterns of behavior in the light of day, we help them see that each pattern is a choice. They can retain or discard it. Then—this is the most important part—we provide them a program of action to replace damaging patterns with healthier ones."

The man's anxiety, Gurney noted, receded as he spoke. The subject had put an evangelical brightness in his eyes.

"By the way, all this might sound familiar to you. *Pattern, choice,* and *change* are the three most overused words in the whole shabby world of self-help. But our guests tell us that what we do here is different—the heart of it is different. Just the other day, one of them said to me, 'This is the most perfect place on earth.'"

Gurney tried to keep skepticism out of his voice. "The therapeutic experience you provide must be very powerful."

"Some find it so."

"I've heard that some powerful therapies are quite confrontational."

"Not here," said Mellery. "Our approach is soft and welcoming.

Our favorite pronoun is *we*, not *you*. We speak about *our* failings and fears and limitations. We never point at anyone and accuse *them* of anything. We believe that accusations are more likely to strengthen the walls of denial than to break them down. After you look through one of my books, you'll understand the philosophy better."

"I just thought things might occasionally happen on the ground, so to speak, that weren't part of the philosophy."

"What we say is what we do."

"No confrontations at all?"

"Why do you belabor the point?"

"I was wondering if you'd ever kicked anyone hard enough in the balls to make him want to kick you back."

"Our approach rarely makes anyone angry. Besides, whoever my pen pal is, he's from a part of my life long before the institute."

"Maybe, maybe not."

A confused frown appeared on Mellery's face. "He's fixated on my drinking days, something I did drunk, so it has to be before I founded the institute."

"On the other hand, it could be someone involved with you in the present who read about your drinking in your books and wants to scare you."

As Mellery's gaze wandered through a new array of possibilities, a young woman entered. She had intelligent green eyes and red hair pulled back in a ponytail.

"Sorry to intrude. I thought you might want to see your phone messages."

She handed Mellery a small pile of pink message notes. His surprised expression gave Gurney the sense that he was not often interrupted this way.

"At least," she said, raising an eyebrow significantly, "you might want to look at the one on top."

Mellery read it twice, then bent forward and handed the message form across the table to Gurney, who also read it twice.

On the "To" line was written: Mr. Mellery.

On the "From" line was written: X. Arybdis.

In the space allocated to "Message" were the following lines of verse:

> *Of all the truths*
> *you can't remember,*
> *here are the truest two:*
> *Every act demands its price.*
> *And every price comes due.*
> *I'll call tonight to promise you*
> *I'll see you in November*
> *or, if not, in December.*

Gurney asked the young woman if she herself had taken the message. She glanced at Mellery.

He said, "I'm sorry, I should have introduced you. Sue, this is an old and good friend of mine, Dave Gurney. Dave, meet my wonderful assistant, Susan MacNeil."

"Nice to meet you, Susan."

She smiled politely and said, "Yes, I was the one who took the message."

"Man or woman?"

She hesitated. "Odd you should ask. My first impression was a man. A man with a high voice. Then I wasn't sure. The voice changed."

"How?"

"At first it sounded like a man trying to sound like a woman. Then I got the idea that it might be a woman trying to sound like a man. There was something unnatural about it, something forced."

"Interesting," said Gurney. "One more thing—did you write down everything this person said?"

She hesitated. "I'm not sure I know what you mean."

"It looks to me," he said, holding up the pink slip, "like this message was dictated to you carefully, even the line breaks."

"That's right."

"So he must have told you that the arrangement of the lines was important, that you should write them exactly as he dictated them."

"Oh, I see. Yes, he did tell me where to start each new line."

"Was anything else said that's not actually written here?"

"Well . . . yes, he did say one other thing. Before he hung up, he asked if I worked at the institute directly for Mr. Mellery. I said yes, I did. Then he said, 'You might want to look at new job opportunities. I've heard that spiritual renewal is a dying industry.' He laughed. He seemed to think it was very funny. Then he told me to make sure Mr. Mellery got the message right away. That's why I brought it over from the office." She shot a worried look at Mellery. "I hope that was okay."

"Absolutely," said Mellery, imitating a man in control of a situation.

"Susan, I notice you refer to the caller as 'he,'" said Gurney. "Does that mean that you're pretty sure it was a man?"

"I think so."

"Did he give any indication what time tonight he planned to call?"

"No."

"Is there anything else you remember, anything at all, no matter how trivial?"

Her brow furrowed a little. "I got a sort of creepy feeling—a feeling that he wasn't very nice."

"He sounded angry? Tough? Threatening?"

"No, not that. He was polite, but . . ."

Gurney waited while she searched for the right words.

"Maybe too polite. Maybe it was the odd voice. I can't say for sure what gave me the feeling. He scared me."

After she left to go back to her office in the main building, Mellery stared at the floor between his feet.

"It's time to go to the police," said Gurney, picking this moment to make his point.

"The Peony police? God, it sounds like a gay cabaret act."

Gurney ignored the shaky attempt at humor. "We're not just

dealing with a few crank letters and a phone call. We're dealing with someone who hates you, who wants to get even with you. You're in his sights, and he may be about to pull the trigger."

"X. Arybdis?"

"More likely the inventor of the alias X. Arybdis."

Gurney proceeded to tell Mellery what he had recalled, with Madeleine's help, about the deadly Charybdis of Greek myth. Plus the fact that he had been unable to find a record of any X. Arybdis in Connecticut or any adjoining state through any online directory or search engine.

"A whirlpool?" asked Mellery uneasily.

Gurney nodded.

"Jesus," said Mellery.

"What is it?"

"My worst phobia is about drowning."

Chapter 12

The importance
of honesty

Mellery stood at the fireplace with a poker, rearranging the burning logs.

"Why would the check come back?" he said, returning to the subject like a tongue to a sore tooth. "The guy seems so precise—Christ, look at the handwriting, like an accountant's—not a guy who'd get an address wrong. So he did it on purpose. What purpose?" He turned from the fire. "Davey, what the hell is going on?"

"Can I see the note it came back with, the one you read me on the phone?"

Mellery went over to a small Sheraton desk on the other side of the room, carrying the poker with him, not noticing it until he was there. "Christ," he muttered, looking around in frustration. He found a spot on the wall where he could lean it before taking an envelope from the desk drawer and bringing it to Gurney.

Inside a large outer envelope addressed to Mellery was the envelope Mellery had sent to X. Arybdis at P.O. Box 49449 in Wycherly, and inside that envelope was his personal check for $289.87. In the large outer envelope, there was a sheet of quality stationery with a GD SECURITY SYSTEMS letterhead including a phone number, with the brief typed message that Mellery had read over the phone to Gurney earlier. The letter was signed by Gregory Dermott, with no indication of his title.

"You haven't spoken to Mr. Dermott?" asked Gurney.

"Why should I? I mean, if it's the wrong address, it's the wrong address. What's it got to do with him?"

"Lord only knows," said Gurney. "But it would make sense to talk to him. Do you have a phone handy?"

Mellery unclipped the latest-model BlackBerry from his belt and handed it over. Gurney entered the number from the letterhead. After two rings he was connected to a recording: *"This is GD Security Systems, Greg Dermott speaking. Leave your name, number, the best time to return your call, and a brief message. You may begin now."* Gurney switched off the phone and passed it back to Mellery.

"Why I'm calling would be hard to explain in a message," said Gurney. "I'm not your employee or legal representative or a licensed PI, and I'm not the police. Speaking of which, it's the police you need—right here, right now."

"But suppose that's his goal—get me disturbed enough to call the cops, stir up a ruckus, embarrass my guests. Maybe having me call the cops and create a bunch of turmoil is what this sicko wants. Bring the bulls into the china shop and watch everything get smashed."

"If that's all he wants," said Gurney, "be thankful."

Mellery reacted as if he'd been slapped. "You really think he's planning to . . . do something serious?"

"It's quite possible."

Mellery nodded slowly, as though the deliberateness of the gesture could keep a lid on his fear.

"I'll talk to the police," he said, "but not until we get the phone call tonight from Charybdis, or whatever he calls himself."

Seeing Gurney's skepticism, he went on, "Maybe the phone call will clear this thing up, let us know who we're dealing with, what he wants. We may not have to involve the police after all, and even if we do, we'll have more to tell them. Either way it makes sense to wait."

Gurney knew that having the police present to monitor the actual call could be important, but he also knew that no rational argument at this point would budge Mellery. He decided to move on to a tactical detail.

"In the event that Charybdis does call tonight, it would be helpful to record the conversation. Do you have any kind of recording device—even a cassette player—that we could hook up to an extension phone?"

"We've got something better," said Mellery. "All our phones have recording capability. You can record any call just by pushing a button."

Gurney looked at him curiously.

"You're wondering why we have such a system? We had a difficult guest a few years back. Some accusations were made, and we found ourselves being harassed by phone calls that were increasingly unhinged. To make a long story short, we were advised to tape the calls." Something in Gurney's expression stopped him. "Oh, no, I can see what you're thinking! Believe me, that mess has nothing to do with what's happening now. It was resolved long ago."

"You sure of that?"

"The individual involved is dead. Suicide."

"Remember the lists I asked you to work on? Lists of relationships involving serious conflicts or accusations?"

"I don't have a single name I can write down in good conscience."

"You just mentioned a conflict, at the end of which someone killed him- or herself. You don't think that qualifies?"

"She was a troubled individual. There was no connection between her dispute with us, which was the product of her imagination, and her suicide."

"How do you know that?"

"Look, it's a complicated story. Not all of our guests are poster children for mental health. I'm not going to write down the name of every person who ever expressed a negative feeling in my presence. That's crazy!"

Gurney leaned back in his chair and gently rubbed his eyes, which were starting to feel dry from the fire.

When Mellery spoke again, his voice seemed to come from a different place inside himself, a less guarded place. "There's a word you used when you were describing the lists. You said I should write down the names of people with whom I had 'unresolved' problems. Well, I've been telling myself that the conflicts of the past have all been resolved. Maybe they haven't. Maybe by 'resolved' I just mean I don't think about them anymore." He shook his head. "God, Davey, what's the point of these lists, anyway? No offense, but what if some muscle-headed cop starts knocking on doors, stirring up old resentments? Christ! Did you ever feel the ground slipping from under your feet?"

"All we're talking about is putting names on paper. It's a way to get your feet *on* the ground. You don't have to show the names to anyone if you don't want to. Trust me, it's a useful exercise."

Mellery nodded in numb acquiescence.

"You said not all your guests are models of mental health."

"I didn't mean to imply that we're running a psychiatric facility."

"I understand that."

"Or even that our guests have an unusual number of emotional problems."

"So who *does* come here?"

"People with money, looking for peace of mind."

"Do they get it?"

"I believe they do."

"In addition to *rich* and *anxious*, what other words describe your clientele?"

Mellery shrugged. "Insecure, despite the aggressive personality that goes with success. They don't like themselves—that's the main thing we deal with here."

"Which of your current guests do you think is capable of physi-cally harming you?"

"What?"

"How much do you know for certain about each of the people currently staying here? Or the people who have reservations for the coming month?"

"If you're talking about background checks, we don't do them. What we know is what they tell us, or what the people who refer them tell us. Some of it is sketchy, but we don't pry. We deal with what they are willing to tell us."

"What sorts of people are here right now?"

"A Long Island real-estate investor, a Santa Barbara housewife, a man who may be the son of a man who may be the head of an organized-crime family, a charming Hollywood chiropractor, an incognito rock star, a thirty-something retired investment banker, a dozen others."

"These people are here for *spiritual renewal*?"

"In one way or another, they've discovered the limitations of success. They still suffer from fears, obsessions, guilt, shame. They've found that all the Porsches and Prozac in the world won't give them the peace they're looking for."

Gurney felt a little stab, being reminded of Kyle's Porsche. "So your mission is to bring serenity to the rich and famous?"

"It's easy to make it sound ridiculous. But I wasn't chasing the smell of money. Open doors and open hearts led me here. My clients found *me*, not the other way around. I didn't set out to be the guru of Peony Mountain."

"Still, you have a lot at stake."

Mellery nodded. "Apparently that includes my life." He stared into the sinking fire. "Can you give me any advice about handling tonight's phone call?"

"Keep him talking as long as you can."

"So the call can be traced?"

"That's not the way the technology works anymore. You've been watching old movies. Keep him talking because the more he says, the more he may reveal and the better chance you may have of recognizing his voice."

"If I do, should I tell him I know who he is?"

"No. Knowing something he doesn't think you know could be an advantage to you. Just stay calm and stretch out the conversation."

"Will you be home tonight?"

"I plan to be—for the sake of my marriage, if nothing else. Why?"

"Because I just remembered that our phones have another fancy feature we never use. The trade name is 'Ricochet Conferencing.' What it lets you do is bring another party into a conference call after someone has called you."

"So?"

"With ordinary teleconferencing, all the participants need to be dialed from one initiating source. But the Ricochet system gets around that. If someone calls you, you can add other participants by dialing them from your end without disconnecting the person who called you—in fact, without them even knowing you're doing it. The way it was explained to me, the call to the party to be added goes out on a separate line, and after the connection is made, the two signals are combined. I'm probably botching up the technical explanation—but the point is, when Charybdis calls tonight, I can dial you into it and you can hear the conversation."

"Good. I'll definitely be home."

"Great. I appreciate that." He smiled like a man experiencing momentary relief from chronic pain.

Out on the grounds, a bell rang several times. It had the strong, brassy ring of an old ship's bell. Mellery checked the slim gold watch on his wrist.

"I have to prepare for my afternoon lecture," he said with a little sigh.

"What's your topic?"

Mellery rose from his wing chair, brushed a few wrinkles out of his cashmere sweater, and set his face with some effort in a generic smile.

"The Importance of Honesty."

The weather had remained blustery, never gaining any warmth. Brown leaves swirled over the grass. Mellery had gone to the main building after thanking Gurney again, reminding him to keep his phone line free that evening, apologizing for his schedule, and extending a last-minute invitation. "As long as you're here, why don't you look over the grounds, get a feel for the place."

Gurney stood on Mellery's elegant porch and zipped up his jacket. He decided to take the suggestion and head for the parking lot by a roundabout route, following the broad sweep of the gardens that surrounded the house. A mossy path brought him around the rear of the house to an emerald lawn, beyond which a maple forest fell away toward the valley. A low drystone wall formed a demarcating line between the grass and the woods. Out at the midpoint of the wall, a woman and two men seemed to be engaged in some sort of planting and mulching activity.

As Gurney strolled toward them across the wide lawn, he could see that the men, wielding spades, were young and Latino and that the woman, wearing knee-high green boots and a brown barn jacket, was older and in charge. Several bags of tulip bulbs, each a different color, lay open on a flat garden cart. The woman was eyeing her workers impatiently.

"Carlos!" she cried. *"Roja, blanca, amarilla . . . roja, blanca, amarilla!"* Then she repeated to no one in particular, "Red, white, yellow . . . red, white, yellow. Not such a difficult sequence, is it?"

She sighed philosophically at the ineptitude of servants, then beamed benignly as Gurney approached.

"I believe that a flower in bloom is the most healing sight on earth," she announced in that tight-lipped, upper-class Long Island accent once known as Locust Valley Lockjaw. "Don't you agree?"

Before he could answer, she extended her hand and said, "I'm Caddy."

"Dave Gurney."

"Welcome to heaven on earth! I don't believe I've seen you before."

"I'm just here for the day."

"Really?" Something in her tone seemed to be demanding an explanation.

"I'm a friend of Mark Mellery."

She frowned slightly. "Dave Gurney, did you say?"

"That's right."

"Well, I'm sure he's mentioned your name, it just doesn't ring a bell. Have you known Mark long?"

"Since college. May I ask what it is that you do here?"

"What I do here?" Her eyebrows rose in amazement. "I live here. This is my home. I'm Caddy Mellery. Mark is my husband."

Chapter 13

Nothing to be guilty about

Although it was noon, the thickening clouds gave the enclosed valley the feeling of a winter dusk. Gurney turned on the car heater to take the chill off his hands. Each year his finger joints were becoming more sensitive, reminding him of his father's arthritis. He flexed them open and shut on the steering wheel.

The identical gesture.

He remembered once asking that taciturn, unreachable man if there was pain in his swollen knuckles. "Just age, nothing to be done about it," his father had replied, in a tone that prevented further discussion.

His mind drifted back to Caddy. Why hadn't Mellery told him about his new wife? Didn't he want him to talk to her? And if he left out having a wife, what else might he be leaving out?

And then, by some obscure mental linkage, he wondered why the blood was as red as a *painted* rose? He tried to recall the full text of the third poem: *I do what I've done / not for money or fun / but for debts to be paid, / amends to be made. / For blood that's as red / as a painted rose. / So every man knows / he reaps what he sows.* A rose was a symbol of redness. What was he adding by calling it a *painted* rose? Was that supposed to make it sound more red? Or more like blood?

Gurney's eagerness to get home was intensified by hunger. It was midafternoon, and his morning coffee from Abelard's was all he'd had all day.

While too much time between meals made Madeleine nauseous, it made him judgmental—a state of mind not easy to recognize in oneself. Gurney had discovered some barometers for assessing his mood, and one of them was located on the westbound side of the road just outside Walnut Crossing. The Camel's Hump was an art gallery that featured the work of local painters, sculptors, and other creative spirits. Its barometric function was simple. A glance at the window produced in him, in a good mood, appreciation of the eccentricity of his artistic neighbors, in a bad mood insight into their vacuity. Today was a vacuity day—fair warning, as he turned up the road toward hearth and wife, to think twice before voicing any strong opinions.

The residue of the morning flurries, long gone from the county highway and lower parts of the valley, was present in scattered patches along the dirt road that rose through a depression in the hills and ended at the Gurney barn and pasture. The slaty clouds gave the pasture a drab, wintry feel. He saw with a twinge of annoyance that the tractor had been driven up from the barn and parked by the shed that housed its attachments—the brush mower, the post-hole digger, the snow thrower. The shed door had been opened, hinting annoyingly at work to be done.

He entered the house through the kitchen door. Madeleine was sitting by the fireplace in the far corner of the room. The plate on the coffee table—with its apple core, grape stems and seeds, flecks of cheddar, and bread crumbs—suggested that a nice lunch had just been consumed, reminding him of his hunger and ratcheting his spring a bit tighter. She looked up from her book, offered him a small smile.

He went to the sink and let the water run until its temperature dropped to the frigid level he liked. He was aware of a feeling of aggression—a defiance of Madeleine's opinion that drinking very cold water was not a good thing to do—followed by a feeling of embarrassment that he could be petty enough, hostile enough, infantile enough to savor such delusional combat. He had an urge to change the subject, then realized there was no subject to change. He spoke anyway.

"I see you drove the tractor up to the shed."

"I wanted to attach the snow thrower to it."

"Was there a problem?"

"I thought we might want it on before we get a real snowstorm."

"I mean, was there a problem attaching it?"

"It's heavy. I thought if I waited, you could help me."

He nodded ambiguously, thinking, *There you go again, pressuring me into a job by starting it yourself, knowing I'll have to finish it.* Aware of the perils of his mood, he thought it wise to say nothing. He filled his glass with the very cold water now coming from the tap and drank it unhurriedly.

Looking down at her book, Madeleine said, "That woman from Ithaca called."

"Woman from Ithaca?"

She ignored the question.

"Do you mean Sonya Reynolds?" he asked.

"That's right." Her voice was as seemingly disinterested as his.

"What did she want?" he asked.

"Good question."

"What do you mean, 'good question'?"

"I mean she didn't specify what she wanted. She said you could call her anytime before midnight."

He detected a definite edge on the last word. "Did she leave a number?"

"Apparently she thinks you have it."

He refilled his glass with icy water and drank it, taking ruminative pauses between mouthfuls. The Sonya situation was emotionally problematical, but he saw no way of dealing with that, short of abandoning the Mug Shot Art project that formed the basis of his connection with her gallery, and he wasn't ready to do that.

Given some distance from these awkward exchanges with Madeleine, he found his awkwardness, his lack of confidence, perplexing. It was curious that a man as deeply rational as he was would get so hopelessly tangled up, so emotionally brittle. He knew from his hundreds of interviews with crime suspects that guilty feelings always lay at the root of that sort of tangle, that sort of confusion. But the truth was that he had done nothing to be guilty about.

Nothing to be guilty about. Ah, there was the problem—the absoluteness of that claim. Perhaps he had done nothing *recently* to feel guilty about—nothing substantial, nothing that came quickly to mind—but if the context were to be stretched back fifteen years, his protestation of innocence would ring painfully false.

He put his water glass down in the sink, dried his hands, walked to the French doors, and stared out at the gray world. A world between autumn and winter. Fine snow blew like sand across the patio. In a context that went back fifteen years, he could hardly claim to be guiltless, because that expanded world would include the accident. As if pressing down on an angry wound to judge the state of the infection, he forced himself to substitute for "the accident" the specific words he found so difficult:

The death of our four-year-old son.

He spoke the words ever so faintly, to himself, hardly more than a whisper. His voice in his own ears sounded eroded and hollow, like someone else's voice.

He couldn't bear the thoughts and feelings that came with the words, and he tried to push them away by seizing the nearest diversion.

Clearing his throat, turning from the glass door to Madeleine across the room, he said with an excess of enthusiasm, "How about we take care of the tractor before it gets dark?"

Madeleine looked up from her book. If she found the artificial cheeriness of his tone disturbing or revealing, she didn't show it.

Mounting the snow thrower took an hour of heaving, banging, yanking, greasing, and adjusting—after which Gurney went on to spend a second hour splitting logs for the woodstove while Madeleine prepared a dinner of squash soup and pork chops braised in apple juice. Then they built a fire, sat side by side on the sofa in the cozy living room adjoining the kitchen, and drifted into the kind of drowsy serenity that follows hard work and good food.

He yearned to believe that these small oases of peace foreshadowed a return of the relationship they'd once had, that the emotional evasions and collisions of recent years were somehow temporary, but it was a belief he found hard to sustain. Even now this fragile hope was being supplanted, bit by bit, moment by moment, by the kind of thoughts his detective mind focused on more comfortably—thoughts about the anticipated Charybdis phone call and the teleconferencing technology that would let him listen in.

"Perfect night for a fire," said Madeleine, leaning gently against him.

He smiled and tried to refocus himself on the orange flames and the simple, soft warmth of her arm. Her hair had a wonderful smell. He had a passing fancy that he could lose himself in it forever.

"Yes," he answered. "Perfect."

He closed his eyes, hoping that the goodness of the moment would counteract those mental energies that were always propelling him into puzzle solving. For Gurney, achieving even a little contentment was, ironically, a struggle. He envied Madeleine's keen attachment to the fleeting instant and the pleasure she found in it. For him, living in the moment was always a swim upstream, his analytic mind naturally preferring the realms of probability, possibility.

He wondered if it was genetic or a learned form of escape. Probably both, mutually reinforcing. Possibly . . .

Jesus!

He caught himself in the absurd act of analyzing his propensity for analysis. He ruefully tried again to be present in the room. *God help me to be here*, he said to himself, even though he had little faith in prayer. He hoped he hadn't said it aloud.

The phone rang. It felt like a reprieve, permission to take a break from the battle.

He heaved himself up from the couch and went to the den to answer it.

"Davey, it's Mark."

"Yes?"

"I was just speaking to Caddy, and she told me she met you in the meditation garden today."

"Right."

"Ah . . . well . . . the thing is, I feel kind of embarrassed, you know, for not introducing you earlier in the day." He paused, as if awaiting a response, but Gurney said nothing.

"Dave?"

"I'm here."

"Well . . . anyway, I wanted to apologize for not introducing you. That was thoughtless of me."

"No problem."

"You're sure?"

"I'm sure."

"You don't sound happy."

"I'm not unhappy—just a bit surprised that you didn't mention her."

"Ah . . . yes . . . I guess with so much on my mind, it didn't occur to me. Are you still there?"

"I'm here."

"You're right, it must seem peculiar I didn't mention her. It just never crossed my mind." He paused, then added with an awkward laugh, "I guess a psychologist would find that interesting—forgetting to mention I was married."

"Mark, let me ask you something. Are you telling me the truth?"

"What? Why would you ask me that?"

"You're wasting my time."

There was an extended silence.

"Look," said Mellery with a sigh, "it's a long story. I didn't want to involve Caddy in this . . . this mess."

"What exact mess are we talking about?"

"The threats, the insinuations."

"She doesn't know about the letters?"

"There's no point. It would just frighten her."

"She must know about your past. It's in your books."

"To a degree. But these threats are something else. I just want to save her from worrying."

That sounded almost plausible to Gurney. Almost.

"Is there any particular piece of your past you're especially eager to keep from Caddy, or from the police, or from me?"

This time the indecisive pause before Mellery said "No" so patently contradicted the denial that Gurney laughed.

"What's so funny?"

"I don't know if you're the worst liar I've ever heard, Mark, but you're in the finals."

After another long silence, Mellery began to laugh, too—a soft, rueful laugh that sounded like muted sobbing. He said in a deflated voice, "When all else fails, it's time to tell the truth. The truth is, shortly after Caddy and I were married, I had a brief affair with a woman who was a guest here. Pure lunacy on my part. It turned out badly—as any sane person could have predicted."

"And?"

"And that was that. I recoil from the mere thought of it. It attaches me to all the ego, lust, and lousy judgment of my past."

"Maybe I'm missing something," said Gurney. "What's that got to do with not telling me you were married?"

"You're going to think I'm paranoid. But I got to thinking that the affair might in some way be connected to this Charybdis business. I was afraid that if you knew about Caddy, you'd want to talk to her and . . . the last thing on earth I want is for her to be exposed to anything that might be connected to my ridiculous, hypocritical affair."

"I see. By the way, who owns the institute?"

"Owns? In what sense?"

"How many senses are there?"

"In spirit, I own the institute. The program is based on my books and tapes."

"'In spirit'?"

"Legally, Caddy owns everything—the real estate and other tangible assets."

"Interesting. So you're the star trapeze artist, but Caddy owns the circus tent."

"You could say that," Mellery replied coldly. "I should get off the phone now. The Charybdis call could come anytime."

It came exactly three hours later.

Chapter 14

Commitment

Madeleine had brought her bag of knitting to the sofa and was engrossed in one of the three projects she had in various stages of completion. Gurney had settled in an adjacent armchair and was leafing through the six-hundred-page user's manual for his photo-manipulation software but was having a hard time concentrating on it. The logs in the woodstove had burned down into embers from which wisps of flame rose, wavered, and disappeared.

When the phone rang, Gurney hurried into the den and picked it up.

Mellery's voice was low and nervous. "Dave?"

"I'm here."

"He's on the other line. The recorder is on. I'm going to switch you in. Ready?"

"Go ahead."

A moment later Gurney heard a strange voice in midsentence.

". . . away for a certain period of time. But I do want you to know who I am." The pitch of the voice was high and strained, the speech rhythm awkward and artificial. There was an accent, foreign-sounding but nonspecific, as if the words were being mispronounced as a way of disguising the voice. "Earlier this evening I left something for you. Do you have it?"

"Have what?" Mellery's voice was brittle.

"You don't have it yet? You'll get it. Do you know who I am?"

"Who are you?"

"Really want to know?"

"Of course. Where do I know you from?"

"The number six fifty-eight didn't tell you who I am?"

"It doesn't mean anything to me."

"Really? But it was your choice—of all the numbers you could have chosen."

"Who the hell are you?"

"There is one more number."

"What??" Mellery's voice rose in fear and exasperation.

"I said there is one more number." The voice was amused, sadistic.

"I don't understand."

"Think of any number at all, other than six fifty-eight."

"Why?"

"Think of any number other than six fifty-eight."

"All right, fine. I thought of a number."

"Good. We're making progress. Now, whisper the number."

"I'm sorry—what?"

"Whisper the number."

"Whisper it?"

"Yes."

"Nineteen." Mellery's whisper was loud and rasping.

It was greeted by a long humorless laugh. "Good, very good."

"Who *are* you?"

"You still don't know? So much pain, and you have no idea. I thought this might happen. I left something for you earlier. A little note. You sure you don't have it?"

"I don't know what you're talking about."

"Ah, but you knew that the number was nineteen."

"You said to think of a number."

"But it was the right number, wasn't it?"

"I don't understand."

"When did you last look in your mailbox?"

"My mailbox? I don't know. This afternoon?"

"You better look again. Remember, I'll see you in November or, if not, in December." The words were followed by a soft disconnect sound.

"Hello!" cried Mellery. "Are you there? Are you there?" When he spoke again, he sounded exhausted. "Dave?"

"I'm here," said Gurney. "Hang up, check your mailbox, call me back."

No sooner had Gurney put the phone down when it rang again. He picked it up.

"Yes?"

"Dad?"

"Excuse me?"

"Is that you?"

"Kyle?"

"Right. You okay?"

"Fine. I'm just in the middle of something,"

"Is everything all right?"

"Yes. Sorry to be so abrupt. I'm waiting for a call that's supposed to come within the next minute or two. Can I call you back?"

"No problem. Just wanted to bring you up to date with some stuff, some stuff that's happened, stuff I'm doing. We haven't spoken in a long time."

"I'll call you back as soon as I can."

"Sure. Okay."

"Sorry. Thanks. Talk to you soon."

Gurney closed his eyes and took a few deep breaths. Christ, things had a way of piling up. Of course, it was his own fault for letting them pile up. His relationship with Kyle was an area of clear dysfunction in his life, full of avoidance and rationalization.

Kyle was the product of his first marriage, his short-lived marriage to Karen—the memory of which still, twenty-two years after the divorce, made Gurney uneasy. Their incompatibility was obvious from the beginning to everyone who knew them, but a defiant determination (or emotional disability, as he saw it in the wee hours of sleepless nights) had driven them into that unfortunate union.

Kyle looked like his mother, had her manipulative instincts and material ambition—and, of course, the name she had insisted on giving him. *Kyle*. Gurney had never been able to get comfortable with that. Despite the young man's intelligence and precocious success in the financial world, *Kyle* still sounded to him like a self-absorbed pretty boy in a soap opera. Moreover, Kyle's existence was a constant reminder of the marriage, a reminder that there was some powerful part of himself that he failed to understand—the part that had wanted to marry Karen to begin with.

He closed his eyes, depressed by his blindness to his own motivations and by his negative reaction to his own son.

The phone rang. He picked it up, afraid it would be Kyle again, but it was Mellery.

"Davey?"

"Yes."

"There was an envelope in the mailbox. My name and address are typed on it, but there's no postage or postmark. Must have been delivered by hand. Shall I open it?"

"Does it feel like there's anything in it other than paper?"

"Like what?"

"Anything at all, anything more than just a letter."

"No. It feels perfectly flat, like nothing at all. No foreign objects in it, if that's what you mean. Shall I open it?"

"Go ahead, but stop if you see anything other than paper."

"Okay. Got it open. Just one sheet. Typed. Plain, no letterhead." There were a few seconds of silence. "What? What the hell . . . ?"

"What is it?"

"This is impossible. There's no way . . ."

"Read it to me."

Mellery read in an incredulous voice, "'I am leaving this note for you in case you miss my call. If you don't know yet who I am, just think of the number nineteen. Does it remind you of anyone? And remember, I'll see you in November or, if not, in December.'"

"That's it?"

"That's it. That's what it says—'just think of the number nineteen.' How the hell could he do that? It's not possible!"

"But that's what it says?"

"Yes. But what I'm saying is . . . I don't know what I'm saying . . . I mean . . . it isn't possible. . . . Christ, Davey, what the hell is going on?"

"I don't know. Not yet. But we're going to find out."

Something had clicked into place—not the solution, he was still far from that, but something inside him had moved. He was now committed 100 percent to the challenge. He looked up and saw Madeleine watching him from the den door with a poignant intensity, as though she could sense in the air the escalation of his commitment to the case. He could only guess at what she was feeling, but it looked something like a combination of awe and loneliness.

The intellectual challenge the new number mystery presented— and the surge of adrenaline it generated—kept Gurney awake well past midnight, although he'd been in bed since ten. He turned restlessly from side to side as his mind kept colliding with the problem, like a man in a dream who couldn't find his key, circling a house, repeatedly trying each locked door and window.

Then he began retasting the nutmeg from the squash soup they'd had for dinner, and that added to the bad-dream feeling.

If you don't know yet who I am, just think of the number nineteen. And that was the number Mellery thought of. The number he thought of before he opened the letter. Impossible. But it happened.

The nutmeg problem kept getting worse. Three times he got up for water, but the nutmeg refused to subside. And then the butter became a problem, too. Butter and nutmeg. Madeleine used a lot of both in her squash soup. He'd even mentioned it once to their therapist. Their former therapist. Actually, a therapist they'd seen only twice, back when they were wrestling over the issue of whether he should retire and thought (incorrectly, as it turned out) that a third party might bring a greater clarity to their deliberations. He tried to remember now how the soup issue had come up, what the context was, why he'd seen fit to mention something so picayune.

It was the session in which Madeleine had spoken about him as if he weren't in the room. She'd started by talking about how he slept. She'd told the therapist that once he was asleep, he rarely awoke until morning. Ah, yes, that was it. That's when he said that the only exception was on nights when she made squash soup and he kept tasting the butter and nutmeg. But she went on, ignoring his silly little interruption, addressing her comments to the therapist, as though they were adults discussing a child.

She said it didn't surprise her that once Dave was asleep, he rarely woke till morning, because just being who he was seemed to involve such a strenuous daily effort. He was so devoid of common ease and comfort. He was such a good man, so decent, yet so full of guilt for being human. So tortured by his mistakes, imperfections. A peerless record of successes in his profession, obscured in his mind by a handful of failures. Always thinking. Thinking his way relentlessly through problems—one after another—like Sisyphus rolling the stone up the hill again, again, again. Grasping life as an awkward puzzle to be solved. But not everything in life was a puzzle, she'd said, looking at him, speaking at last to him instead of to the therapist. There were things to be embraced in other ways. Mysteries, not puzzles. Things to be loved, not deciphered.

Recalling her comments as he lay there in bed had a strange effect on him. He was wholly absorbed by the memory, both disturbed and exhausted by it. It finally faded, along with the tastes of butter and nutmeg, and he slipped into an uneasy sleep.

Toward morning he was half awakened by Madeleine getting out of bed. She blew her nose gently, quietly. For a second he wondered if she'd been crying, but it was a hazy thought, easily supplanted by the more likely explanation that she was suffering from one of her autumn allergies. He was dimly aware of her going to the closet and putting on her terry-cloth robe. A little while later, he heard or imagined—he wasn't sure which—her footsteps on the basement stairs. Sometime after that she passed the bedroom door soundlessly. In the first touch of dawn light stretching across the bedroom into the hallway, she appeared, specterlike, to be carrying something, a box of some kind.

His eyes were still heavy with exhaustion, and he dozed for another hour.

Chapter 15

Dichotomies

When he got up, it was not because he felt rested, or even fully awake, but because getting up seemed preferable to sinking back into a dream that had left him without any recollection of its details yet with a distinct feeling of claustrophobia. It was like one of the hangovers he'd experienced in his college days.

He forced himself into the shower, which slightly improved his mood, then dressed and went out to the kitchen. He was relieved to see that Madeleine had made enough coffee for both of them. She was sitting at the breakfast table, looking out thoughtfully through the French doors and holding her large spherical cup—with steam rising from it—in both hands as if to warm them. He poured a cup of coffee for himself and sat across the table from her.

"Morning," he said.

She smiled a vague little smile in reply.

He followed her gaze out across the garden to the wooded hillside at the far edge of the pasture. An angry wind was stripping the trees of their few remaining leaves. High winds usually made Madeleine nervous—ever since a massive oak came crashing down across the road in front of her car the day they moved to Walnut Crossing—but this morning she seemed too preoccupied to notice.

After a minute or two, she turned toward him, and her expression sharpened as though something about his attire or demeanor had just struck her.

"Where are you going?" she asked.

He hesitated. "To Peony. To the institute."

"Why?"

"Why?" His voice was raspy with irritation. "Because Mellery is still refusing to report his problem to the local police, and I want to push him a little harder in that direction."

"You could do that on the phone."

"Not as well as I can face-to-face. Plus, I want to pick up copies of all the written messages and a copy of his recording of last night's phone call."

"Isn't that what FedEx is for?"

He stared at her. "What's the problem with me going to the institute?"

"The problem isn't *where* you're going, it's *why* you're going."

"To persuade him to go to the police? To pick up the messages?"

"You honestly believe that's why you're driving all the way to Peony?"

"Why the hell else?"

She gave him a long, almost pitying look before answering. "You're going," she said softly, "because you've grabbed onto this thing and you can't let go. You're going because you can't stay away." Then she closed her eyes slowly. It was like the fade-out at the end of a movie.

He didn't know what to say. Every so often Madeleine would end an argument just this way—by saying or doing something that seemed to leapfrog over his train of thought and render him silent.

This time he thought he knew the reason for the effect on him, or at least part of the reason. In her tone he'd heard an echo of her speech to the therapist, the speech he'd so vividly recollected a few hours earlier. He found the coincidence unsettling. It was as though Madeleine present and Madeleine past were ganging up on him, one whispering in each ear.

He was quiet for a long time.

She eventually took the coffee cups to the sink and washed them. Then, rather than laying them in the dish drainer as she usually did, she dried them and put them back in the cabinet above the sideboard.

Continuing to look into the cabinet, as though she'd forgotten why she was standing there, she asked, "What time are you going?"

He shrugged and looked around the room as though a clue to the right answer might be on one of the walls. As he did so, his gaze was attracted by an object resting on the coffee table in front of the fireplace at the far end of the room. It was a cardboard box, of the size and shape one might get at a liquor store. But what really caught his eye and held it was the white ribbon encircling the box and fastened on the top with a simple white bow.

Dear God. That's what she'd brought up from the basement.

Although the box seemed smaller than he remembered it from so many years ago and the cardboard a darker brown, the ribbon was unmistakable, unforgettable. The Hindus had definitely gotten it right: white, not black, was the natural color for mourning.

He felt a tugging emptiness in his lungs, as though gravity were dragging his breath, his soul, down into the earth. *Danny. Danny's drawings. My little Danny boy.* He swallowed and looked away, looked away from such immense loss. He felt too weak to move. He looked out through the French doors, coughed, cleared his throat, tried to replace stirred memories with immediate sensations, tried to redirect his mind by saying something, hearing his own voice, breaking the dreadful silence.

"I don't imagine I'll be late," he said. It took all his strength, all his will, to push himself up out of his chair. "I should be home in time for dinner," he added meaninglessly, hardly knowing what he was saying.

Madeleine watched him with a wan smile, not really a smile in the normal sense of the word, said nothing.

"Better go," he said. "Need to be on time for this thing."

Blindly, almost staggering, he kissed her on the cheek and went out to the car, forgetting his jacket.

The landscape was different that morning, more like winter, with virtually all of autumn's color gone from the trees. But he sensed this only dimly. He was driving automatically, almost unseeingly, consumed by the image of the box, his recollection of its contents, the significance of its presence on the table.

Why? Why now, after all these years? To what purpose? What was she thinking? He had driven through Dillweed, driven past Abelard's without even noticing. He felt sick to his stomach. He had to focus on something else, had to get a grip.

Focus on where you're going, why you're going there. He tried to force his mind in the direction of the messages, the poems, the number nineteen. Mellery thinking of the number nineteen. Then finding it in the letter. How could that have been done? This was the second time Arybdis or Charybdis—or whatever his name was—had performed this impossible feat. There were certain differences between the two instances, but the second was as baffling as the first.

The image of the box on the coffee table pressed relentlessly against the edges of his concentration—and then the contents of the box, as he remembered them being packed away so long ago. Danny's crayon scribbles. Oh, God. The sheet of little orange things that Madeleine had insisted were marigolds. And that funny little drawing that might have been a green balloon or maybe a tree, maybe a lollipop. Oh, Jesus.

Before he knew it, he was pulling in to the neatly graveled parking area at the institute, the drive hardly registering in his consciousness. He looked around at his surroundings, trying to center himself, trying to wrestle his mind into the same location as his body.

Gradually he relaxed, felt almost drowsy, the emptiness that so often followed intense emotion. He looked at his watch. Somehow he'd arrived exactly on time. Apparently that part of him operated without conscious intervention, like his autonomic nervous system. Wondering if the chill had driven the role players indoors, he locked the car and took the winding path to the house. The front door, as on his previous visit, was opened by Mellery before he knocked.

Gurney stepped in out of the wind. "Any new developments?"

Mellery shook his head and closed the heavy antique door, but not before half a dozen dead leaves skittered over the threshold.

"Come back to the den," he said. "There's coffee, juice . . ."

"Coffee would be fine," said Gurney.

Again they chose the wing chairs by the fire. On the low table between them was a large manila envelope. Gesturing toward it, Mellery said, "Xeroxes of the written messages and a recording of the call. It's all there for you."

Gurney took the envelope and placed it on his lap.

Mellery eyed him expectantly.

"You should go to the police," said Gurney.

"We've been through that already."

"We need to go through it again."

Mellery closed his eyes and massaged his forehead as though it ached. When he opened his eyes, he appeared to have made a decision.

"Come to my lecture this morning. It's the only way you'll understand." He spoke quickly, as if to forestall objection. "What goes on here is very subtle, very fragile. We teach our guests about conscience, peace, clarity. Earning their trust is critical. We're exposing them to something that can change their lives. But it's like sky-writing. In a calm sky, it's legible. A few gusts and it's all gibberish. Do you understand what I'm saying?"

"I'm not sure I do."

"Just come to the lecture," pleaded Mellery.

It was exactly 10:00 A.M. when Gurney followed him into a large room on the ground floor of the main building. It resembled the sitting room of an expensive country inn. A dozen armchairs and half a dozen sofas were oriented in the general direction of a grand fireplace. Most of the twenty attendees were already seated. A few lingered at a sideboard on which stood a silver coffee urn and a tray of croissants.

Mellery walked casually to a spot in front of the fireplace and faced his audience. Those at the sideboard hurried to their seats, and all fell expectantly silent. Mellery motioned Gurney to an armchair by the fireplace.

"This is David," announced Mellery with a smile in Gurney's direction. "He wants to know more about what we do, so I've invited him to sit in on our morning meeting."

Several voices offered pleasant greetings, and all the faces offered smiles, most of which looked genuine. He caught the eye of the birdlike woman who'd accosted him obscenely the day before. She looked demure, even blushed a little.

"The roles that dominate our lives," Mellery began without pre-amble, "are the ones we're unaware of. The needs that drive us most relentlessly are the ones we're least conscious of. To be happy and free, we must see the roles we play for what they are, and bring our hidden needs into the light of day."

He was speaking calmly and straightforwardly and had the complete attention of his audience.

"The first stumbling block in our search will be the assumption that we already know ourselves, that we understand our own motives, that we know why we feel the way we do about our circumstances and the people around us. In order to make progress, we will need to be more open-minded. To find out the truth about myself, I must stop insisting that I already know it. I'll never remove the boulder from my path if I fail to see it for what it is."

Just as Gurney was thinking that this last observation was expanding the envelope of New Age fog, Mellery's voice rose sharply.

"You know what that boulder is? That boulder is your image of yourself, who you think you are. The person you think you are is keeping the person you really are locked up without light or food or friends. The person you think you are has been trying to murder the person you really are for as long as you both have lived."

Mellery paused, seemingly overtaken by some desperate emotion. He stared at his audience, and they seemed hardly to breathe. When he resumed speaking, his voice had dropped to a conversational volume but was still full of feeling.

"The person I think I am is terrified of the person I really am, terrified of what others would think of that person. What would they do to me if they knew the person I really was? Better to be safe! Better to hide the real person, starve the real person, bury the real person!"

Again he paused, letting the erratic fire in his eyes subside.

"When does it all start? When do we become this set of dysfunctional twins—the invented person in our head and the real person locked up and dying? It starts, I believe, very early. I know in my own case the twins were well established, each in his own uneasy place, by the time I was nine. I'll tell you a story. My apologies to those who've heard me tell it before."

Gurney glanced around the room, noting among the attentive faces a few with smiles of recognition. The prospect of hearing one of Mellery's stories for a second or third time, far from boring or annoying anyone, seemed only to increase their anticipation. It was like the response of a small child to the promised retelling of a favorite fairy tale.

"One day as I was leaving for school, my mother gave me a twenty-dollar bill to pick up some groceries on my way home that afternoon—a quart of milk and a loaf of bread. When I got out of school at three o'clock, I stopped at a little luncheonette next to the school yard to buy a Coke before I went to the grocery store. It was a place where some of the kids hung out after class. I put the twenty-dollar bill on the counter to pay for the Coke, but before the counterman took the bill to make change, one of the other kids came over and saw it. 'Hey, Mellery,' he said, 'where'd you get the twenty bucks?' Now, this kid happened to be the toughest kid in the fourth grade, which is the grade I was in. I was nine, and he was eleven. He'd been left back twice, and he was a scary kid—not someone I was supposed to be hanging around with, or even speaking to. He got in a lot of fights, and there were stories that he used to break in to people's houses and steal things. When he asked me where I got the money, I was going to say that my mother gave it to me to buy milk and bread, but I was afraid he'd make fun of me, call me a mama's boy, and I wanted to say something that would impress him, so I said that I stole it. He looked interested, which made me feel good. Then he asked me who I stole it from, and I said the first thing that came into my mind. I said that I stole it from my mother. He nodded and smiled and walked away. Well, I was sort of relieved and uncomfortable at the same time. By the next day, I'd forgotten about it. But a week later he came up to me in the school yard and said, 'Hey, Mellery, you steal any more money from your mother?' I said no, I hadn't. And he said, 'Why don't you steal another twenty bucks?' I didn't know what to say. I just stared at him. Then he smiled a creepy little smile and said, 'You steal another twenty bucks and give it to me, or I'll tell your mother about the twenty you stole last week.' I felt the blood drain out of me."

"My God," said a horse-faced woman in a burgundy armchair on the far side of the fireplace, as other murmurings of empathic anger rippled across the room.

"What a prick!" growled a thickly built man with murder in his eyes.

"It threw me into a panic. I could picture him going to my mother, telling her I had stolen twenty dollars from her. The absurdity of that—the unlikelihood of this little gangster going to my mother about anything—never occurred to me. My mind was too overloaded with fear—fear that he would tell her and she would believe him. I had no confidence whatever in the truth. So, in this state of mindless panic, I made the worst possible decision. I stole twenty dollars from my mother's purse that night and gave it to him the next day. Of course, the next week he made the same demand. And the week after that. And so on, for six weeks, until I was finally caught in the act by my father—caught closing the top drawer of my mother's bureau, with a twenty-dollar bill clutched in my hand. I confessed. I told my parents the whole horrible, shameful story. But it only got worse. They called our pastor, Monsignor Reardon, and took me to the church rectory to tell the story all over again. The next night the monsignor had us come back and sit down with the little blackmailer and his mother and father, and again I had to tell the story. Even that wasn't the end of it. My parents cut off my allowance for a year to pay them back for the money I stole. It changed the way they looked at me. The blackmailer concocted a version of events to tell everyone in school that painted him as some kind of Robin Hood and me as a rat that snitched. And every once in a while, he'd give me an icy little smirk that suggested that someday soon I might get pushed off an apartment-house roof."

Mellery paused in the recounting of his tale and massaged his face with the palms of his hands, as though easing muscles that had been tightened by his recollections.

The burly man shook his head grimly and said again, "What a prick!"

"That's exactly what I thought," said Mellery. "What a manipulative little prick! Whenever that mess came to mind, the next thought in my head was always, 'What a prick!' That's all I could think."

"You were right," said the burly man in a voice that sounded used to being listened to. "That's exactly what he was."

"That's exactly what he was," Mellery agreed with rising intensity, "exactly what *he* was. But I never got past what *he* was, to ask myself what *I* was. It was so obvious what he was, I never asked myself what *I* was. Who on earth was this nine-year-old kid, and why did he do what he did? It's not enough to say he was afraid. Afraid of what, exactly? And who did he think he was?"

Gurney found himself surprisingly caught up in this. Mellery had captured his attention as completely as anyone else's in the room. Gurney had slipped from being an observer into being a participant in this sudden search for meaning, motive, identity. Mellery had begun pacing back and forth in front of the giant hearth as he spoke, as though driven by memories and questions that would not let him stand still. The words tumbled out of him.

"Whenever I thought of that boy—myself, at the age of nine— I thought of him as a victim, a victim of blackmail, a victim of his own innocent desire for love, admiration, acceptance. All he wanted was for the big kid to like him. He was a victim of a cruel world. Poor little kid, poor little sheep in the jaws of a tiger."

Mellery stopped his pacing and spun around to face his audience.

Now he spoke softly. "But that little boy was something else, as well. He was a liar and a thief."

The audience was divided between those who looked like they wanted to object and those who nodded.

"He lied when he was asked where he got the twenty dollars. He claimed to be a thief to impress someone he assumed was a thief. Then, faced with the threat of his mother's being told he was a thief, he actually became a thief rather than have her think he was one. What he cared about most was controlling what people thought of him. Compared to what they *thought*, it didn't matter much to him whether he actually *was* a liar or a thief, or what effect his behavior had on the people he lied to and stole from. Let me put it this way: It didn't matter enough to keep him from lying and stealing. It only mattered enough to eat away like acid at his self-esteem when he did lie and steal. It mattered just enough to make him hate himself and wish he was dead."

Mellery fell silent for several seconds, letting his comments sink in, then continued, "Here's what I want you to do. Make a list of people you can't stand, people you're angry at, people who've done you wrong—and ask yourself, 'How did I get into that situation? How did I get into that relationship? What were my motives? What would my actions in the situation have looked like to an objective observer?' Do not—I repeat, do not—focus on the terrible things the other person did. We are not searching for someone to blame. We did that all our lives, and it got us nowhere. All we got was a long, useless list of people to blame for everything that ever went wrong! A long, useless list! The real question, the only question that matters is '*Where was I in all of this?* How did I open the door that led into the room?' When I was nine, I opened the door by lying to win admiration. How did you open the door?"

The little woman who had cursed Gurney was looking increasingly disconcerted. She raised her hand uncertainly and asked, "Doesn't it sometimes happen that an evil person does something terrible to an innocent person, breaks in to their house and robs them, let's say? That wouldn't be the innocent person's fault, would it?"

Mellery smiled. "Bad things happen to good people. But those good people do not then spend the rest of their lives gnashing their teeth and replaying over and over their resentful mental videotape of the burglary. The personal collisions that upset us the most, the ones we seem powerless to let go of, are those in which we played a role that we are unwilling to acknowledge. That's why the pain lasts—because we refuse to look at its source. We cannot detach it, because we refuse to look at the point of attachment."

Mellery closed his eyes, seemingly gathering strength to go on. "The worst pain in our lives comes from the mistakes we refuse to acknowledge—the things we've done that are so out of harmony with who we are that we can't bear to look at them. We become two people in one skin, two people who can't stand each other. The liar and the person who despises liars. The thief and the person who despises thieves. There is no pain like the pain of that battle, raging below the level of consciousness. We run from it, but it runs with us. Wherever we run, we take the battle with us."

Mellery paced back and forth in front of the fireplace.

"Do what I said. Make a list of all the people you blame for the troubles in your life. The angrier you are with them, the better. Put down their names. The more convinced you are of your own blame-lessness, the better. Write down what they did and how you were hurt. Then ask yourself how you opened the door. If your first thought is that this exercise is nonsense, ask yourself why you are so eager to reject it. Remember, this is not about absolving the other people of whatever blame is theirs. You have no power to absolve them. Absolution is God's business, not yours. Your business comes down to one question: '*How did I open the door?*'"

He paused and looked around the room, making eye contact with as many of his guests as he could.

"'*How did I open the door?*' Your happiness for the rest of your life will depend on how honestly you answer that question."

He stopped, seemingly exhausted, and announced a break, "for coffee, tea, fresh air, restrooms, et cetera." As people rose from their couches and chairs and headed for the various options, Mellery looked inquiringly at Gurney, who'd remained seated.

"Did that help any?" he asked.

"It was impressive."

"In what way?"

"You're a hell of a good lecturer."

Mellery nodded—neither modestly nor immodestly. "Did you see how fragile it all is?"

"You mean the rapport you establish with your guests?"

"I guess *rapport* is as good a word as any, as long as you mean a combination of trust, identification, connection, openness, faith, hope, and love—and as long as you understand how delicate those flowers are, especially when they first begin to bloom."

Gurney was having a hard time making up his mind about Mark Mellery. If the man was a charlatan, he was the best he'd ever encountered.

Mellery raised his hand and called to a young woman by the coffeepot. "Ah, Keira, could you do me a huge favor and get Justin for me?"

"Absolutely!" she said without hesitation, pirouetted, and departed on her quest.

"Who's Justin?" asked Gurney.

"A young man whom I am increasingly unable to do without. He originally came here as a guest when he was twenty-one—that's the youngest we'll take anyone. He returned three times, and the third time he never left."

"What does he do?"

"I guess you could say he does what I do."

Gurney gave Mellery a quizzical look.

"Justin, from his first visit here, was on the right wavelength—always picked up what I was saying, nuances and all. An acute young man, wonderful contributor to everything we do. The institute's message was made for him, and he was made for the message. He has a future with us if he wants it."

"Mark Jr.," said Gurney, mostly to himself.

"Beg pardon?"

"Sounds like an ideal son. Absorbs and appreciates everything you have to offer."

A trim, intelligent-looking young man entered the room and came toward them.

"Justin, I'd like you to meet an old friend, Dave Gurney."

The young man extended his hand with a combination of warmth and shyness.

After they shook hands, Mellery took Justin to the side and spoke to him in a low voice. "I'd like you to take the next half-hour segment, give some examples of internal dichotomies."

"Love to," said the young man.

Gurney waited until Justin went to the sideboard for coffee, then said to Mellery, "If you have the time, there's a call I'd like you to make before I leave."

"We'll go back to the house." It was clear that Mellery wanted to put distance between his guests and anything that might be related to his current difficulties.

On the way, Gurney explained that he wanted him to call Gregory Dermott and ask for more details about the history and security of his post-office box and any additional recollections he might have concerning his receipt of the $289.87 check, made out to X. Arybdis, which he had returned to Mellery. Specifically, was there anyone else in Dermott's company authorized to open the box? Was the key always in Dermott's possession? Was there a second key? How long had he been the renter of that box? Had he ever before received mail misaddressed to that box? Had he ever received an unexplained check? Did the names Arybdis or Charybdis or Mark Mellery mean anything to him? Had anyone ever said anything to him about the Institute for Spiritual Renewal?

Just as Mellery was beginning to look overloaded, Gurney pulled an index card from his pocket and handed it to him. "The questions are all here. Mr. Dermott may not feel like answering them all, but it's worth a try."

As they walked on, amid beds of dead and dying flowers, Mellery seemed to be sinking deeper into his worries. When they reached the patio behind the elegant house, he stopped and spoke in the low tone of one fearful of prying ears.

"I didn't sleep at all last night. That 'nineteen' business has been driving me completely out of my mind."

"No connection occurred to you? No meaning it might have?"

"Nothing. Silly things. A therapist once gave me a twenty-question test to find out if I had a drinking problem, and I scored nineteen. My first wife was nineteen when we married. Stuff like that—random associations, nothing anyone could predict I'd think of, no matter how well they knew me."

"Yet they did."

"That's what's driving me crazy! Look at the facts. A sealed envelope is left in my mailbox. I get a phone call telling me it's there and asking me to think of any number I wish. I think of nineteen. I go to the mailbox and get the envelope, and the letter in the envelope mentions the number nineteen. Exactly the number I thought of. I could have thought of seventy-two thousand nine hundred and fifty-one. But I thought of nineteen, and that was the number in the letter. You say ESP is bullshit, but how can you explain it any other way?"

Gurney replied in a tone as calm as Mellery's was agitated. "Something is missing in our concept of what happened. We're looking at the problem in a way that's making us ask the wrong question."

"What's the right question?"

"When I figure it out, you'll be the first to know. But I guarantee you it won't have anything to do with ESP."

Mellery shook his head, the gesture resembling a tremor more than a form of expression. Then he glanced up at the back of his house and down at the patio on which he was standing. His blank look said he wasn't sure how he had gotten there.

"Shall we go inside?" Gurney suggested.

Mellery refocused himself and seemed to have a sudden recollection. "I forgot—I'm sorry—Caddy's home this afternoon. I can't . . . I mean, it might be better if . . . what I mean is, I won't be able to make the call to Dermott right away. I'll have to play it by ear."

"But you will do it today?"

"Yes, yes, of course. I'll just have to work out the right time. I'll call you as soon as I speak to him."

Gurney nodded, gazing into his companion's eyes, seeing in them the fear of a collapsing life.

"One question before I leave. I heard you ask Justin to talk about 'internal dichotomies.' I was wondering what that referred to."

"You don't miss much," said Mellery with a small frown. "'Dichotomy' refers to a division, a duality within something. I use it to describe the conflicts within us."

"You mean Jekyll-and-Hyde stuff?"

"Yes, but it goes beyond that. Human beings are loaded with inner conflicts. They shape our relationships, create our frustrations, ruin our lives."

"Give me an example."

"I could give you a hundred. The simplest conflict is the one between the way we view ourselves and the way we view others. For example, if we were arguing and you screamed at me, I would see the cause as your inability to control your temper. However, if I screamed at you, I would see the cause not as my temper but your provocation—something in you to which my scream is an appropriate response."

"Interesting."

"We each seem to be wired to believe *my situation causes my problems but your personality causes yours.* This creates trouble. My desire to have everything my way seems to make sense, while your desire to have everything your way seems infantile. A better day would be a day during which I felt better and you behaved better. The way I see things is the way they are. The way you see things is warped by your agenda."

"I get the point."

"That's just the beginning, hardly scratches the surface. The mind is a mass of contradictions and conflicts. We lie to make others trust us. We hide our true selves in the pursuit of intimacy. We chase happiness in ways that drive happiness away. When we're wrong we fight the hardest to prove we're right."

Caught up in the content of his program, Mellery spoke with verve and eloquence. Even in the midst of his current stress, it had the power to focus his mind.

"I get the impression," said Gurney, "that you're talking about a personal source of pain, not just the general human condition."

Mellery nodded slowly. "There's no pain worse than having two people living in one body."

Chapter 16

The end of the beginning

Gurney had an uncomfortable feeling. It had been with him on and off since Mellery's initial visit to Walnut Crossing. Now he realized with chagrin that the feeling was a longing for the relative clarity of an actual crime; for a crime scene that could be combed and sifted, measured and diagrammed; for fingerprints and footprints, hairs and fibers to be analyzed and identified; for witnesses to be questioned, suspects to be located, alibis to be checked, relationships to be investigated, a weapon to be found, bullets for ballistics. Never before had he been so frustratingly engaged in a problem so legally ambiguous, with so many obstructions to normal procedure.

During the drive down the mountain from the institute to the village, he speculated on Mellery's competing fears—on one side a malevolent stalker, on the other a client-alienating police intervention. Mellery's conviction that the cure would be worse than the disease kept the situation in limbo.

He wondered if Mellery knew more than he was saying. Was he aware of something he'd done in the distant past that could be the cause of the current campaign of threat and innuendo? Did Dr. Jekyll know what Mr. Hyde had done?

Mellery's lecture topic of two minds at war inside one body interested Gurney for other reasons. It resonated with his own perception over the years, reinforced now by his Mug Shot Art efforts, that divisions of the soul are often evident in the face, and most evident in the eyes. Time and again he had seen faces that were really two faces. The phenomenon was easiest to observe in a photograph. All you had to do was alternately cover each half of the face with a sheet of paper—along the center of the nose, so only one eye was visible each time. Then jot down a character description of the person you see on the left and another of the person you see on the right. It was amazing how different those descriptions could be. A man might appear peaceful, tolerant, wise on one side—and resentful, cold, manipulative on the other. In those faces whose blankness was pierced by a glint of the malice that led to murder, the glint often was present in one eye and absent from the other. Perhaps in real-life encounters our brains were wired to combine and average the disparate characteristics of two eyes, making the differences between them hard to see, but in photographs they were hard to miss.

Gurney remembered the photo of Mellery on the cover of his book. He made a mental note to take a closer look at the eyes when he arrived home. He also remembered that he needed to return the call from Sonya Reynolds—the one Madeleine had mentioned with a touch of ice. A few miles outside Peony, he pulled off onto a patch of weedy gravel separating the road from the Esopus Creek, took out his cell phone, and entered the number for Sonya's gallery. After four rings her smooth voice invited him to leave as long a message as he wished.

"Sonya, it's Dave Gurney. I know I promised you a portrait this week, and I hope to bring it to you Saturday, or at least e-mail you a graphics file you can print a sample from. It's almost finished, but I'm not satisfied yet." He paused, aware of the fact that his voice had dropped into that softer register triggered by attractive women—a habit Madeleine had once brought to his attention. He cleared his throat and continued, "The essence of this art is character. The face should be consistent with murder, especially the eyes. That's what I'm working on. That's what's taking time."

There was a click on the line, and Sonya's voice broke in, breathlessly.

"David, I'm here. I couldn't make it to the phone, but I heard what you said. And I understand perfectly your need to get it just right. But it would be really great if you could deliver it Saturday. There's a festival Sunday, lots of gallery traffic."

"I'll try. It might be late in the day."

"Perfect! I'll be closing at six, but I'll be here working for another hour. Come then. We'll have time to talk."

It struck him that Sonya's voice could make anything sound like a sexual overture. Of course, he knew he was bringing too damn much receptivity and imagination to the situation. He also knew he was being pretty damn silly.

"Six o'clock sounds good," he heard himself say—even as he remembered that Sonya's office, with its large couches and plush rugs, was furnished more like an intimate den than a place of business.

He dropped the phone back into the glove box and sat gazing up the grassy valley. As usual, Sonya's voice had disrupted his rational thoughts, and his mind was pinballing from object to object: Sonya's too-cozy office, Madeleine's uneasiness, the impossibility of anyone knowing in advance the number another person would think of, blood as red as a painted rose, you and I have a date Mr. 658, Charybdis, the wrong post-office box, Mellery's fear of the police, Peter Piggert the mass-murdering motherfucker, the charming young Justin, the rich aging Caddy, Dr. Jekyll and Mr. Hyde, and so on, without rhyme or reason, around and around. He lowered the window on the passenger side of the car by the creek, leaned back, closed his eyes, and tried to focus on the sound of the water tumbling over the rocky streambed.

A knock at the closed window by his ear roused him. He glanced up at an expressionless rectangular face, eyes concealed behind mirrored sunglasses, shaded by the rigid circular brim of a trooper's gray hat. He lowered the window.

"Everything all right, sir?" The question sounded more threatening than solicitous, the *sir* more perfunctory than polite.

"Yes, thank you, I just needed to close my eyes for a moment." He glanced at the dashboard clock. The moment, he saw, had lasted fifteen minutes.

"Where are you heading, sir?"

"Walnut Crossing."

"I see. Have you had anything to drink today, sir?"

"No, Officer, I haven't."

The man nodded and stepped back, looking over the car. His mouth, the only visible feature that might betray his attitude, was contemptuous—as though he considered Gurney's drink denial a transparent lie and would soon find evidence to that effect. He walked with exaggerated deliberation around to the rear of the car, then up along the passenger side, around the front, and finally back to Gurney's window. After a long, evaluative silence, he spoke with a contained menace more appropriate to a Harold Pinter play than a routine vehicle check.

"Were you aware that this is not a legal parking area?"

"I didn't realize that," said Gurney evenly. "I only intended to stop for a minute or two."

"May I see your license and registration, please?"

Gurney produced them from his wallet and handed them out the window. It was not his habit in such situations to present evidence of his status as a retired NYPD detective first grade, with the connections that might imply, but he sensed, as the trooper turned to walk back to his patrol car, an arrogance that was off the scale and a hostility that would be expressed in an unjustifiable delay, at the very least. He reluctantly withdrew another card from his wallet.

"Just a moment, Officer, this might be helpful as well."

The trooper took the card cautiously. Then Gurney saw the flicker of a change at the corners of his mouth, not in the direction of friendliness. It looked like a combination of disappointment and anger. Dismissively, he handed the card, license, and registration back through the window.

"Have a nice day, sir," he said in a tone that conveyed the opposite sentiment, returned to his vehicle, made a rapid U-turn, and drove off in the direction he'd come from.

No matter how sophisticated the psychological testing had become, thought Gurney, no matter how high the educational requirements, no matter how rigorous the academy training, there would always be cops who shouldn't be cops. In this case the trooper had committed no specific violation, but there was something hard and hateful in him—Gurney could feel it, see it in the lines in his face— and it was only a matter of time before it collided with its mirror image. Then something terrible would happen. In the meantime a lot of people would be delayed and intimidated to no good end. He was one of those cops who made people dislike cops.

Maybe Mellery had a point.

During the next seven days, winter came to the northern Catskills. Gurney spent most of his time in the den, alternating between the mug-shot project and a painstaking reexamination of the Charybdis communications—stepping deftly back and forth between those two worlds and repeatedly veering away from thoughts of Danny's drawings and the inner chaos that came with them. The obvious thing would be to talk to Madeleine about it, find out why she'd decided to raise the issue now—literally to bring it up from the basement—and why she was waiting with such peculiar patience for him to say something. But he couldn't seem to summon the necessary willingness. So he would push it out of his mind and return to the Charybdis matter. At least he could think about that without feeling lost, without his heart racing.

He frequently thought, for example, about the evening after his last visit to the institute. As promised, Mellery had called him at home that night and related the conversation he'd had with Gregory Dermott of GD Security Systems. Dermott had been obliging enough to answer all his questions—the ones Gurney had written out—but the information itself did not amount to much. The man had been renting the box for about a year, ever since he'd moved his consulting business from Hartford to Wycherly; there had never been a problem before, certainly no misaddressed letters or checks; he was the only person with access to the box; the names Arybdis, Charybdis, and Mellery meant nothing to him; he had never heard of the institute. Pressed on the question of whether anyone else in his company could have been using the box in some unauthorized way, Dermott had explained that it was impossible, since there *wasn't* anyone else in his company. GD Security Systems and Gregory Dermott were one and the same. He was a security consultant to companies with sensitive databases that required protection against hackers. Nothing he said cast any light on the matter of the misdirected check.

Neither had the Internet background searches Gurney had conducted. The sources concurred on the main points: Gregory Dermott had a science degree from M.I.T., a solid reputation as a computer expert, and a blue-clip client roster. Neither he nor GD Security was linked to any lawsuit, judgment, lien, or bad press, past or present. In short, he was a squeaky-clean presence in a squeaky-clean field. Yet someone had, for some still impenetrable reason, appropriated his post office box number. Gurney kept asking himself the same baffling question: *Why demand that a check be sent to someone who would almost certainly return it?*

It depressed him to keep thinking about it, to keep walking down that dead-end street as if the tenth time he'd find something there that wasn't there the ninth time. But it was better than thinking about Danny.

The first measurable snow of the season came the evening of the first Friday in November. From a few flakes drifting here and there at dusk, it increased over the next couple of hours, then tapered off, stopping around midnight.

As Gurney was coming to life over his Saturday-morning coffee, the pale disk of the sun was creeping over a wooded ridge a mile to the east. There had been no wind during the night, and everything outside from the patio to the roof of the barn was coated with at least three inches of snow.

He hadn't slept well. He'd been trapped for hours in an endless loop of linked worries. Some, dissolving now in the daylight, involved Sonya. He had at the last minute postponed their planned after-hours meeting. The uncertainty of what might happen there—his uncertainty about what he *wanted* to happen—made him put it off.

He sat, as he had for the past week, with his back turned to the end of the room where the ribbon-tied carton of Danny's drawings lay on the coffee table. He sipped his coffee and looked out at the blanketed pasture.

The sight of snow always brought to mind the smell of snow. On an impulse he went to the French doors and opened them. The sharp chill in the air touched off a chain of recollected moments—snowbanks shoveled up chest-high along the roads, his hands rosy and aching from packing snowballs, bits of ice stuck in the wool of his jacket cuffs, tree branches arcing down to the ground, Christmas wreaths on doors, empty streets, brightness wherever he looked.

It was a curious thing about the past—how it lay in wait for you, quietly, invisibly, almost as though it weren't there. You might be tempted to think it was gone, no longer existed. Then, like a pheasant flushed from cover, it would roar up in an explosion of sound, color, motion—shockingly alive.

He wanted to surround himself with the smell of the snow. He pulled his jacket from the peg by the door, slipped it on, and went out. The snow was too deep for the ordinary shoes he was wearing, but he didn't want to change them now. He walked in the general direction of the pond, closing his eyes, inhaling deeply. He had gone less than a hundred yards when he heard the kitchen door opening and Madeleine's voice calling to him.

"David, come back!"

He turned and saw her halfway out the door, alarm on her face. He started back.

"What is it?"

"Hurry!" she said. "It's on the radio—Mark Mellery is dead!"

"What?"

"Mark Mellery—he's dead, it was just on the radio. He was murdered!" She stepped back inside.

"Jesus," said Gurney, feeling a constriction in his chest. He ran the last few yards to the house, entering the kitchen without removing his snow-covered shoes. "When did it happen?"

"I don't know. This morning, last night, I don't know. They didn't say."

He listened. The radio was still on, but the announcer had gone on to another news item, something about a corporate bankruptcy.

"How?"

"They didn't say. They just said it was an apparent homicide."

"Any other information?"

"No. Yes. Something about the institute—where it happened. The Mellery Institute for Spiritual Renewal in Peony, New York. They said the police are on the scene."

"That's all?"

"I think. How awful!"

He nodded slowly, his mind racing.

"What are you going to do?" she asked.

A rapid mental review of the options eliminated all but one.

"Inform the officer-in-charge of my connection to Mellery. What happens after that is up to him."

Madeleine took a long breath and seemed to be attempting a brave smile, which fell a good deal short of success.

Part Two

Macabre
Games

Chapter 17

Quite a lot of blood

It was precisely 10:00 A.M. when Gurney called the Peony police station to give them his name, address, phone number, and a brief summary of his involvement with the victim. The officer he spoke to, Sergeant Burkholtz, told him that the information would be passed along to the State Police Bureau of Criminal Investigation team that had taken control of the case.

Assuming he might be contacted within twenty-four to forty-eight hours, he was taken aback when the call came in less than ten minutes. The voice was familiar but not instantly placeable, a problem prolonged by the man's nameless introduction of himself.

"Mr. Gurney, this is the senior investigator at the Peony crime scene. I understand you have some information for us."

Gurney hesitated. He was about to ask the officer to identify himself—a matter of normal procedure—when the voice's timbre suddenly generated a recollection of the face and the name that went with it. The Jack Hardwick he remembered from a sensational case they'd worked on together was a loud, obscene, red-faced man with a prematurely white crew cut and pale malamute eyes. He was a relentless banterer, and half an hour with him could seem like half a day—a day you kept wishing would end. But he was also smart, tough, tireless, and politically incorrect with a vengeance.

"Hello, Jack," said Gurney, hiding his surprise.

"How did you . . . Fuck! Someone fucking told you! Who told you?"

"You have a memorable voice, Jack."

"Memorable voice, my ass! It's been ten fucking years!"

"Nine." The Peter Possum Piggert arrest had been one of the biggest in Gurney's career, the one that secured his promotion to the coveted rank of detective first grade, and the date was one he remembered.

"Who told you?"

"Nobody told me."

"Bullshit!"

Gurney fell silent, recalling Hardwick's penchant for having the last word and the inane exchanges that would go on indefinitely until he got it.

After a long three seconds, Hardwick continued in a less combative tone. "Nine goddamn years. And all of a sudden you pop up out of nowhere, right in the middle of what might be the most sensational murder case in New York State since you fished the bottom half of Mrs. Piggert out of the river. That's some goddamn coincidence."

"Actually, it was the top half, Jack."

After a short silence, the phone exploded with the long braying laugh that was a Hardwick trademark.

"Ah!" he cried, out of breath at the end of the bray. "Davey, Davey, Davey, always a stickler for details."

Gurney cleared his throat. "Can you tell me how Mark Mellery died?"

Hardwick hesitated, caught in the awkward space between relationship and regulation where cops lived much of their lives and got most of their ulcers. He opted for the full truth—not because it was required (Gurney had no official standing in the case and was entitled to no information at all) but because it had a harsh edge. "Someone cut his throat with a broken bottle."

Gurney grunted as though he'd been punched in the heart. This first reaction, however, was quickly replaced by something more professional. Hardwick's answer had jarred into position one of the loose puzzle pieces in Gurney's mind.

"Was it by chance a whiskey bottle?"

"How the hell did you know that?" Hardwick's tone traveled in seven words from amazement to accusation.

"It's a long story. Would you like me to drop by?"

"I think you better."

The sun, which that morning was visible as a cool disk behind a gray wash of winter cloud cover, was now entirely obscured by a lumpy, leaden sky. The shadowless light seemed ominous—the face of a cold universe, uncaring as ice.

Finding this train of thought embarrassingly fanciful, Gurney put it aside as he brought his car to a stop behind the line of police vehicles parked jaggedly on the snow-covered roadside in front of the Mellery Institute for Spiritual Renewal. Most bore the blue and yellow New York State Police insignia, including a tech van from the regional forensics lab. Two were white sheriff's department cars, and two were green Peony police cruisers. Mellery's crack about its sounding like the name of a gay cabaret act came to mind, along with the expression he'd had on his face when he said it.

The aster beds, crowded between the cars and the stone wall, had been reduced by the hardening winter weather to tangled masses of brown stalks sporting weird cotton-ball blossoms of snow. He got out of the car and headed for the entrance. A crisply uniformed trooper with a paramilitary scowl stood at the open gate. He was probably a year or two younger, Gurney noted with an odd feeling, than his own son.

"Can I help you, sir?"

The words were polite, but the look wasn't.

"My name is Gurney. I'm here to see Jack Hardwick."

The young man blinked twice, once at the sound of each name. His expression suggested that at least one of them was giving him acid reflux.

"Hold on a minute," he said, removing a walkie-talkie from his belt. "You need to be escorted."

Three minutes later the escort arrived—a BCI investigator who looked like he was trying to look like Tom Cruise. Despite the winter chill, he wore only a black windbreaker hanging open over a black T-shirt and jeans. Knowing the strictness of the state police dress code, Gurney figured attire that informal would mean he'd been called directly to the scene from an off-duty or undercover activity. The edge of a nine-millimeter Glock in a matte black shoulder holster visible under the windbreaker seemed as much a statement of attitude as a tool of the trade.

"Detective Gurney?"

"Retired," said Gurney, as though appending an asterisk.

"Yeah?" said Tom Cruise without interest. "That must be nice. Follow me."

As Gurney followed his leader along the path around the main building toward the residence behind it, he was struck by the difference a three-inch snowfall had made in the appearance of the place. It had created a simplified canvas, removing extraneous details. Walking into the minimalism of the white landscape was like stepping onto a newly created planet—a thought at absurd variance with the messy reality at hand. They rounded the old Georgian house where Mellery had lived and stopped short at the edge of the snow-covered patio where he'd died.

The location of his death was obvious. The snow still bore the impression of a body, and spread out around the head-and-shoulders area of that impression was an enormous bloodstain. Gurney had seen that shocking red and white contrast before. The indelible memory was from Christmas morning of his rookie year on the job. An alcoholic cop whose wife had locked him out of their house shot himself in the heart, sitting on a snowbank.

Gurney forced the old image out of his mind and focused his keen professional gaze on the scene before him.

A prints specialist was kneeling by a row of footprints in the snow next to the main bloodstain, spraying them with something.

From where he was standing, Gurney couldn't see the label on the can, but he guessed it was snow-print wax, a chemical used to stabilize snow prints sufficiently for the application of a dental casting compound. Prints in snow were extremely fragile, but when treated with care they provided an extraordinary level of detail. Although he'd witnessed the process often enough before, he couldn't help but admire the specialist's steady hand and intense concentration.

Yellow police tape had been strung in an irregular polygon around most of the patio, including the back door of the house. Corridors of the same tape had been established on opposite sides of the patio—to enclose and preserve the arrival and departure routes of a distinct set of footprints that came from the direction of the large barn beside the house, proceeded to the area of the bloodstain, then headed away from the patio over the snow-blanketed lawn toward the woods.

The back door of the house was open. A member of the crime-scene team was standing in the doorway studying the patio from the perspective of the house. Gurney knew exactly what the man was doing. When you were at a crime scene, you tended to spend a lot of time just trying to absorb the feel of it—often trying to see it as the victim might have seen it in his final moments. There were clear, well-understood rules for locating and collecting evidence—blood, weapons, fingerprints, footprints, hairs, fibers, paint chips, out-of-place mineral or plant material, and so forth—but there was also a fundamental focus problem. Simply put, you needed to remain open-minded about what had happened, exactly where it had happened, and how it had happened, because if you jumped to conclusions too quickly, it would be easy to miss evidence that didn't fall within your view of the situation. At the same time, you had to begin developing at least a loose hypothesis that would guide your evidence search. You can make painful mistakes by getting too sure too fast about the apparent crime scenario, but you can also waste a lot of precious time and manpower fine-tooth-combing a square mile of ground looking for God-knows-what.

What good detectives did—what Gurney was sure the detective in the doorway was doing—was a kind of unconscious flipping back and forth between inductive and deductive mind-sets. What do I see here, and what sequence of events do these data points suggest? And, if that scenario is valid, what additional evidence should I be seeing and where should I be looking for it?

The key to the process, Gurney had become convinced through much trial and error of his own, was maintaining the right balance between observation and intuition. The greatest danger to the process was ego. A supervising detective who remains undecided about the possible explanation for crime-scene data might waste some time by not focusing his team's efforts in a particular direction soon enough, but the guy who knows, and aggressively announces, at first glance exactly what happened in that blood-spattered room and sets everyone to proving he's right can end up causing very serious problems— wasted time being the least of them.

Gurney wondered which approach might be prevailing at the moment.

Outside the yellow tape barrier, on the far side of the bloodstain, Jack Hardwick was giving instructions to two serious-looking young men, one of whom was the Tom Cruise wannabe who'd just delivered Gurney to the site, and the other appeared to be his twin. The nine intervening years since they worked together on the infamous Piggert case seemed to have added twice that many years to Hardwick's age. The face was redder and fatter, the hair thinner, and the voice had developed the kind of roughness that comes from too much tobacco and tequila.

"There are twenty guests," he was saying to the *Top Gun* doubles. "Each of you take nine of them. Get preliminary statements, names, addresses, phone numbers. Get verification. Leave Patty Cakes and the chiropractor to me. I'll also talk to the widow. Check back with me by four P.M."

More comments went back and forth among them in voices too low for Gurney to hear, punctuated by Hardwick's grating laugh. The young man who'd escorted Gurney from the front gate said a final word, tilting his head significantly in Gurney's direction. Then the duo set off toward the main building.

Once they were out of sight, Hardwick turned and offered Gurney a greeting halfway between a grin and a grimace. His strange blue eyes, once brightly skeptical, seemed fraught with a tired cynicism.

"I'll be damned," he rasped, walking around the taped area toward Gurney, "if it isn't Professor Dave."

"Just a humble instructor," corrected Gurney, wondering what else Hardwick had taken the trouble to find out about his post-NYPD stint teaching criminology at the state university.

"Don't give me that humility shit. You're a star, my boy, and you know it."

They shook hands without much warmth. It struck Gurney that the bantering attitude of the old Hardwick had curdled into something toxic.

"Not a lot of doubt about the location of death," said Gurney, nodding at the bloodstain. He was eager to get to the point, brief Hardwick on what he knew, and get out of there.

"There's doubt about everything," proclaimed Hardwick. "Death and doubt are the only two certainties in life." Getting no response from Gurney, he went on, "I'll grant you there may be less doubt about the location of death than about some other things here. God-damn loony bin. People here go on about the victim like he was that Deepdick Chopup guy on TV."

"You mean Deepak Chopra?"

"Yeah, Dipcock or whatever. Christ, gimme a break!"

Despite the uncomfortable reaction building inside him, Gurney said nothing.

"What the hell do people come to places like this for? Listen to some New Age asshole with a Rolls-Royce talk about the meaning of life?" Hardwick shook his head at the foolishness of his fellow man—frowning at the back of the house all the while, as though eighteenth-century architecture might bear a large part of the blame.

Irritation overcame Gurney's reticence. "As far as I know," he said evenly, "the victim was not an asshole."

"I didn't say he was."

"I thought you did."

"I was making a general observation. I'm sure your buddy was an exception."

Hardwick was getting under Gurney's skin like a sharp sliver. "He wasn't my buddy."

"I got the impression from the message you left with the Peony police, which they kindly passed along to me, that your relationship went way back."

"I knew him in college, had no contact with him for twenty-five years, and got an e-mail from him two weeks ago."

"What about?"

"Some letters he got in the mail. He was upset."

"What kind of letters?"

"Poems, mostly. Poems that sounded like threats."

This made Hardwick stop and think before going on. "What did he want from you?"

"My advice."

"What advice did you give him?"

"I advised him to call the police."

"I gather he didn't."

The sarcasm irked Gurney, but he held his temper.

"There was another poem," said Hardwick.

"What do you mean?"

"A poem, on a single sheet of paper, laid on the body, with a rock on it for a paperweight. All very neat."

"He's very precise. A perfectionist."

"Who?"

"The killer. Possibly very disturbed, definitely a perfectionist."

Hardwick stared at Gurney with interest. The mocking attitude was gone, at least temporarily. "Before we go any further, I need to know how you knew about the broken bottle."

"Just a wild guess."

"Just a wild guess that it was a whiskey bottle?"

"Four Roses, specifically," said Gurney, smiling with satisfaction when he saw Hardwick's eyes widen.

"Explain how you know that," demanded Hardwick.

"It was a bit of a leap, based on references in the poems," said Gurney. "You'll see when you read them." In response to the question forming on the other man's face, he added, "You'll find the poems, along with a couple of other messages, in the desk drawer in the den. At least, that's the last place I saw Mellery put them. It's the room with the big fireplace off the center hall."

Hardwick continued staring at him as though doing so would resolve some important issue. "Come with me," he finally said. "I want to show you something."

He led the way in uncharacteristic silence to the parking area, situated between the massive barn and the public road, and came to a halt where it was connected to the circular driveway and where a corridor of yellow police tape began.

"This is the nearest place to the road where we can clearly distinguish the footprints we believe belong to the perp. The road and the drive were plowed after the snow stopped around two A.M. We don't know whether the perp entered the property before or after the plowing. If before, any tracks on the road outside or on the drive would have been obliterated by the plow. If after, no tracks would have been made to begin with. But from this point right here, around the back of the barn, to the patio, across the open area to the woods, through the woods, to a pine thicket by Thornbush Lane, the tracks are perfectly clear and easy to follow."

"No effort made to conceal them?"

"No," said Hardwick, sounding bothered by this. "None at all. Unless I'm missing something."

Gurney gave him a curious glance. "What's the problem?"

"I'll let you see for yourself."

They walked along the yellow-taped corridor, following the tracks to the far side of the barn. The imprints, sharply indented in the otherwise featureless three-inch layer of snow, were of large

(Gurney estimated size ten or eleven, D width) hiking boots. Who-ever had come this way in the wee hours of the morning hadn't cared that his route would later be noted.

As they rounded the back of the barn, Gurney saw that a wider area there had been taped off. A police photographer was taking pic-tures with a high-resolution camera while a crime-scene specialist in a protective white bodysuit and hair enclosure awaited his turn with an evidence-collection kit. Every shot was taken at least twice, with and without a ruler in the frame to establish scale, and objects were photographed at various focal-length settings—wide to establish position relative to other objects in the scene, normal to present the object itself, and close-up to capture detail.

The center of their attention was a folding lawn chair of the flimsy sort that might be sold in a discount store. The footprints led directly to the chair. In front of it, stamped out in the snow, were half a dozen cigarette butts. Gurney squatted to take a closer look and saw they were Marlboros. The footprints then continued from the chair around a thicket of rhododendrons toward the patio where the murder had apparently occurred.

"Jesus," said Gurney. "He just sat there smoking?"

"Yeah. A little relaxation before cutting the victim's throat. At least that's the way it looks. I assume your raised eyebrow is a way of asking where the crappy little lawn chair came from? That was my question, too."

"And?"

"Victim's wife claimed she'd never seen it before. Seemed appalled at its low quality."

"What?" Gurney flicked the word out like a whip. Hardwick's supercilious comments had become nails on a blackboard.

"Just a little levity." He shrugged. "Can't let a cut throat get you down. But seriously, it was probably the first time in her posh life that Caddy Smythe-Westerfield Mellery came that close to a chair that cheap."

Gurney knew all about cop humor and how necessary it was in

coping with the routine horrors of the job, but there were occasions it got on his nerves.

"Are you telling me that the killer brought his own lawn chair with him?"

"Looks that way," said Hardwick, grimacing at the absurdity.

"And after he finished smoking—what, half a dozen Marlboros?—he walked over to the back door of the house, got Mellery to come out on the patio, and slit his throat with a broken bottle? That's the reconstruction so far?"

Hardwick nodded reluctantly, as though beginning to feel that the crime scenario suggested by the evidence sounded a bit off the wall. And it only got worse.

"Actually," he said, "'slit his throat' is putting it mildly. Victim was stabbed through the throat at least a dozen times. When the medical examiner's assistants were transferring the body to the van to take it for autopsy, the fucking head almost fell off."

Gurney looked in the direction of the patio, and although it was entirely obscured by the rhododendrons, the image of the huge bloodstain came back to his mind as colorfully and sharply as if he were staring at it under arc lights.

Hardwick watched him for a while, chewing thoughtfully on his lip. "As a matter of fact," he said finally, "that's not the really weird part. The really weird part comes later, when you follow the footprints."

Chapter 18

Footprints to nowhere

ardwick led Gurney from the back of the barn around the hedges, past the patio to where the tracks of the presumed assailant left the scene of the attack and proceeded across the snow-covered lawn that extended from the back of the house to the edge of the maple forest several hundred feet away.

Not far from the patio, as they were following the footprints in the direction of the woods, they came upon another evidence tech, dressed in the hermetic plastic jumpsuit, surgical cap, and face mask of his trade—designed to protect DNA or other trace evidence from contamination by the collector.

He was squatting about ten feet from the footprints, lifting what appeared to be a shard of brown glass out of the snow with stainless-steel tongs. He'd already bagged three other pieces of similar glass and one large-enough segment of a quart whiskey bottle to be recognizable as such.

"The murder weapon, most likely," said Hardwick. "But you, ace detective, already knew that. Even knew it was Four Roses."

"What's it doing out on the lawn?" asked Gurney, ignoring Hardwick's needling tone.

"Jeez, I figured you'd know that, too. If you already knew the fucking brand . . ."

Gurney waited wearily, like he was waiting for a slow computer program to open, and eventually Hardwick answered, "It looks like he carried it away from the body and dropped it over here on his way to the woods. Why did he do that? That's an excellent question. Maybe he didn't realize he still had it in his hand. I mean, he just stabbed the victim in the neck a dozen times. That could have absorbed his attention. Then, as he's walking away across the lawn, he notices he still has it and tosses it aside. At least that makes some kind of sense."

Gurney nodded, not wholly convinced but unable to offer a better explanation. "Is that the 'really weird' element you mentioned?"

"That?" said Hardwick with a laugh that was more of a bark. "You ain't seen nothin' yet."

Ten minutes and half a mile later, the two men arrived at a spot in the maple forest just short of a small copse of white pines. The sound of a passing car indicated they were close to a road, but any sight of it was blocked by the low pine branches.

At first he wasn't sure why Hardwick had brought him there. Then he saw it—and began studying the ground in the vicinity with growing bewilderment. What he saw made no sense. The footprints they had been following simply stopped. The clear progression of prints in the snow, one after another, proceeding for half a mile or more, simply came to an end. There was no sign of what had happened to the individual who'd made the prints. The snow all around was pristine, untouched by a human foot or by anything else. The trail of footprints stopped a good ten feet from the nearest tree, and, if the sound of that passing vehicle was any indication, at least a hundred yards from the nearest road.

"Am I missing something?" asked Gurney.

"Same thing we're all missing," said Hardwick, sounding relieved that Gurney had not come up with a simple explanation that had eluded him and his team.

Gurney examined the ground around the final print more carefully. Just beyond this well-defined impression was a small area of multiple overlapping impressions, all appearing to have been made by the same pair of hiking boots that had created the clear tracks they'd been following. It was as if the killer had walked purposefully to this spot, stood about shifting from foot to foot for a few minutes, perhaps waiting for someone or something, and then . . . evaporated.

The lunatic possibility that Hardwick was playing a practical joke on him flashed through his mind, but he dismissed it. Tampering with a major murder scene for a laugh would be too far over the edge even for an outrageous character like Hardwick.

So what they were looking at was the way it was.

"The tabloids find out about this, they'll turn it into an alien abduction," said Hardwick, as though the words tasted like metal in his mouth. "Reporters will be on this like flies on a barrel of cow shit."

"You have a more presentable theory?"

"My hopes are riding on the razor-sharp mind of the most revered homicide detective in the history of the NYPD."

"Cut the crap," said Gurney. "Has the processing team come up with anything?"

"Nothing that makes sense of this. But they took snow samples from that packed-down spot where it looks like he was standing. Didn't seem to be any visible foreign matter there, but maybe the lab techs can find something. They also checked the trees and the road behind those pines. Tomorrow they'll grid out everything within a hundred feet of this spot and take a closer look."

"But so far they've come up with zero?"

"You got it."

"So what are you left with—asking all the institute guests and neighbors if anyone saw a helicopter lowering a rope into the woods?"

"Nobody did."

"You asked?"

"Felt like an idiot, but yes. The fact is, someone walked out here this morning—almost certainly the killer. He stopped right here. If a helicopter or the world's largest crane didn't lift him out, where the fuck is he?"

"So," Gurney began, "no helicopters, no ropes, no secret tunnels . . ."

"Right," said Hardwick, cutting him off. "And no evidence that he hopped away on a pogo stick."

"Which leaves us with what?"

"Which leaves us with nothing. Zilch, zippo. Not one goddamn real possibility. And don't tell me that once the killer walked all the way out here, he walked all the way back—stepping backwards, perfectly, into each footprint, without messing up a single one—just to drive us crazy." Hardwick looked challengingly at Gurney, as though he might propose this very thing. "Even if that were possible, which it isn't, the killer would have bumped into the two people who were on the scene by that time, Caddy the wife and Patty the gangster."

"So it's all impossible," said Gurney lightly.

"What's impossible?" said Hardwick, ready for a fight.

"Everything," said Gurney.

"What the hell are you talking about?"

"Calm down, Jack. We need to find a starting point that makes sense. What seems to have happened can't have happened. Therefore, what seems to have happened *didn't* happen."

"Are you telling me those aren't footprints?"

"I'm telling you there's something wrong with the way we're looking at them."

"Is that or is that not a footprint?" said Hardwick, exasperated.

"It looks very much like a footprint to me," said Gurney agreeably.

"So what are you saying?"

Gurney sighed. "I don't know, Jack. I just have a feeling we're asking the wrong questions."

Something in the softness of his tone took the edge off Hardwick's attitude. Neither man looked at the other or said anything for several long seconds. Then Hardwick raised his head as though remembering something.

"I almost forgot to show you the icing on the cake." He reached into the side pocket of his leather jacket and pulled out an evidence-collection envelope.

Through the clear plastic, on a plain sheet of white stationery, Gurney could see neat handwriting in red ink.

"Don't remove it," said Hardwick, "just read it."

Gurney did as he was told. Then he read it again. And a third time, committing it to memory.

> *I ran through the snow.*
> *Fool, look high and low.*
> *Ask where did I go.*
> *You scum of the earth,*
> *here witness my birth:*
> *Revenge is reborn*
> *for children who mourn,*
> *for all the forlorn.*

"That's our boy," said Gurney, handing the envelope back. "Revenge theme, eight lines, consistent meter, elite vocabulary, perfect punctuation, delicate handwriting. Just like all the others—up to a point."

"Up to a point?"

"There's a new element in this one—an indication that the killer hates someone else in addition to the victim."

Hardwick glanced over the encased note, frowning at the suggestion that he'd missed something significant. "Who?" he asked.

"You," said Gurney, smiling for the first time that day.

Chapter 19

Scum of the earth

It was unfair, of course, a bit of dramatic license, to say that the killer had set his sights equally on Mark Mellery and Jack Hardwick. What Gurney meant, he explained as they strode back toward the crime scene from the dead-end trail in the woods, was that the killer seemed to be aiming some part of his hostility at the police investigating the murder. Far from disturbing Hardwick, the implied challenge energized him. The combative glint in his eye shouted, "Bring the fucker on!"

Then Gurney asked him if he remembered the case of Jason Strunk.

"Why should I?"

"Does the Satanic Santa ring a bell? Or, as another media genius called him, Cannibal Claus?"

"Yeah, yeah, sure, I remember. Wasn't really a serious cannibal, though. Just chewed off the toes."

"Right, but that wasn't all, was it?"

Hardwick grimaced. "I seem to recollect that after he chewed their toes off, he cut the bodies up with a band saw, sealed the pieces in plastic bags—very neat—put them in Christmas-gift boxes, and mailed them. That's how he got rid of them. No burial problems."

"You happen to remember who he mailed them to?"

"That was twenty years ago. I wasn't even on the job then. I read about it in the papers."

"He mailed them to the home addresses of homicide detectives in the precincts where the victims had lived."

"Home addresses?" Hardwick shot Gurney an appalled look. Murder, moderate cannibalism, and dissection with a band saw might be forgivable, but not this final twist.

"He hated cops," Gurney continued. "Loved upsetting them."

"I can see how getting a foot mailed to you might do that."

"It's especially upsetting when your wife opens the box."

The odd note caught Hardwick's attention. "Holy shit. That was your case. He sent you a body part, and she opened the box?"

"Yep."

"Holy shit. Is that why she divorced you?"

Gurney glanced at him curiously. "You remember that my first wife divorced me?"

"Some things I remember. Not so much things I read—but if somebody tells me something about themselves, that kind of stuff I never forget. Like, I know you were an only child, your father was born in Ireland, he hated it, he would never tell you anything about it, and he drank too much."

Gurney stared at him.

"You told me while we were working on the Piggert case."

Gurney wasn't sure whether he was more distressed by having revealed those quirky little family facts, by forgetting that he had, or by Hardwick's recalling them.

They walked on toward the house through the powdery snow, which had begun eddying in intermittent breezes under a darkening sky. Gurney tried to shake off the chill that was enveloping him and refocus himself on the matter at hand.

"Getting back to my point," he said, "this killer's last note is a challenge to the police, and that could be a significant development."

Hardwick was the sort of man who'd get back to someone else's point when he damn well felt like it.

"So is that why she divorced you? She got some guy's dick in a box?"

It was none of his business, but Gurney decided to answer.

"We had plenty of other problems. I could give you a list of my complaints, and a longer list of hers. But I think, bottom line, she was shocked to discover what it's like to be married to a cop. Some wives discover that slowly. Mine had a revelation."

They had reached the back patio. Two evidence techs were sifting through the snow around the bloodstain, now more brown than red, and examining the flagstones they were uncovering in the process.

"Well, anyway," said Hardwick, as though brushing aside an unnecessary complication, "Strunk was a serial killer, and this doesn't look like that."

Gurney nodded his tentative agreement. Yes, Jason Strunk was a typical serial killer, and whoever killed Mark Mellery seemed to be anything but that. Strunk had little or no prior acquaintance with his victims. It was safe to say that he didn't have anything resembling a "relationship" with them. He chose them on the basis of their fitting the parameters of a certain physical type and their availability when the pressure to act overwhelmed him—the coinciding of urge and opportunity. Mellery's killer, however, knew him well enough to torture him with allusions to his past—even knew him well enough to predict what numbers might come to his mind under certain circumstances. He gave indications of having shared the kind of intimate history with his victim that was not typical of serial killers. Moreover, there were no known reports of similar recent murders—although that would have to be researched more carefully.

"It doesn't look like a serial case," agreed Gurney. "I doubt you'll start finding thumbs in your mailbox. But there is something disconcerting about his addressing you, the chief investigating officer, as 'scum of the earth.'"

They walked around the house to the front door to avoid disrupting the crime-scene processors on the patio. A uniformed officer from the sheriff's department was stationed there to control access to the house. The wind was sharper there, and he was stamping his feet and clapping his gloved hands together to generate some warmth. His obvious discomfort twisted the smile with which he greeted Hardwick.

"Any coffee on the way, you think?"

"No idea. But I hope so," said Hardwick, sniffling loudly to keep his nose from running. He turned to Gurney. "I won't keep you much longer. I just want you to show me the notes you told me were in the den—and make sure they're all there."

Inside the beautiful old chestnut-floored house, all was quiet. More than ever, the place smelled of money.

Chapter 20

A family friend

A picturesque fire was burning in the stone-and-brick fireplace, and the air in the room was sweetened by grace notes of cherry smoke. A pale but composed Caddy Mellery was sharing the sofa with a well-tailored man in his early seventies.

As Gurney and Hardwick entered, the man rose from his place on the sofa with an ease surprising for his age. "Good afternoon, gentlemen," he said. The words had a courtly, vaguely southern intonation. "I'm Carl Smale, an old friend of Caddy's."

"I'm Senior Investigator Hardwick, and this is Dave Gurney, a friend of Mrs. Mellery's late husband."

"Ah, yes, Mark's friend. Caddy was telling me."

"We're sorry to bother you," said Hardwick, glancing around the room as he spoke. His eyes settled on the small Sheraton desk set against the wall opposite the fireplace. "We need access to some papers, possibly related to the crime, which we have reason to believe may be located in that desk. Mrs. Mellery, I'm sorry to be bothering you with questions like this, but do you mind if I take a look?"

She closed her eyes. It was unclear whether she'd understood the question.

Smale reseated himself on the couch next to her, placing his hand on her forearm. "I'm sure Caddy has no objection to that."

Hardwick hesitated. "Are you ... speaking as Mrs. Mellery's representative?"

Smale's reaction was nearly invisible—a slight wrinkling of the nose, like a sensitive woman's response to a rude word at a dinner party.

The widow opened her eyes and spoke through a sad smile. "I'm sure you can appreciate that this is a difficult time. I'm relying on Carl completely. Whatever he says is wiser than anything I would say."

Hardwick persisted. "Mr. Smale is your attorney?"

She turned toward Smale with a benevolence Gurney suspected was fueled by Valium and said, "He's been my attorney, my representative in sickness and in health, in good times and bad, for over thirty years. My God, Carl, isn't that frightening?"

Smale mirrored her nostalgic smile, then spoke to Hardwick with a new crispness in his tone. "Feel free to examine this room for whatever materials may be related to your investigation. We'd naturally appreciate receiving a list of any materials you wish to remove."

The pointed reference to "this room" did not escape Gurney. Smale was not granting the police a blanket exemption from a search warrant. Apparently it hadn't escaped Hardwick, either, judging from the hard look he gave the dapper little man on the sofa.

"All evidence we take possession of is fully inventoried." Hardwick's tone conveyed the unspoken part of the message as well: "We don't give you a list of things we *wish* to take. We give you a list of things we have *actually taken.*"

Smale, who obviously had the ability to hear unspoken communication, smiled. He turned to Gurney and asked in his languorous drawl, "Tell me, are you *the* Dave Gurney?"

"I'm the only one my parents had."

"Well, well, well. A detective of legend! A pleasure to meet you."

Gurney, who inevitably found this sort of recognition uncomfortable, said nothing.

The silence was broken by Caddy Mellery. "I must apologize, but I have a blinding headache and must lie down."

"I sympathize," said Hardwick. "But I do need your help with a few details."

Smale regarded his client with concern. "Couldn't it wait for an hour or two? Mrs. Mellery is in obvious pain."

"My questions will only take two or three minutes. Believe me, I'd rather not intrude, but a delay could create problems."

"Caddy?"

"It's fine, Carl. Now or later makes no difference." She closed her eyes. "I'm listening."

"I'm sorry to make you think about these things," said Hardwick. "Do you mind if I sit here?" He pointed to the wing chair nearest Caddy's end of the sofa.

"Go right ahead." Her eyes were still shut.

He perched on the edge of the cushion. Questioning the recently bereaved was uncomfortable for any cop. Hardwick, though, looked like he wasn't terribly bothered by the task.

"I want to go over something you told me this morning to make sure I've got it right. You said the phone rang a little after one A.M.—that you and your husband were asleep at the time?"

"Yes."

"And you knew the time because . . . ?"

"I looked at the clock. I wondered who would be calling us at that hour."

"And your husband answered it?"

"Yes."

"What did he say?"

"He said hello, hello, hello—three or four times. Then he hung up."

"Did he tell you if the caller said anything at all?"

"No."

"And a few minutes later, you heard an animal screaming in the woods?"

"Screeching."

"Screeching?"

"Yes."

"What distinction do you make between 'screeching' and 'screaming'?"

"Screaming—" She stopped and bit hard on her lower lip.

"Mrs. Mellery?"

"Will there be much more of this?" asked Smale.

"I just need to know what she heard."

"Screaming is more human. Screaming is what I did when I . . ." She blinked as if to force a speck out of her eye, then continued. "This was some kind of animal. But not in the woods. It sounded close to the house."

"How long did this screaming—*screeching*—go on?"

"A minute or two, I'm not sure. It stopped after Mark went downstairs."

"Did he say what he was going to do?"

"He said he was going to see what it was. That's all. He just—" She stopped speaking and began taking slow, deep breaths.

"I'm sorry, Mrs. Mellery. This won't take much longer."

"He just wanted to see what it was, that's all."

"Did you hear anything else?"

She put her hand over her mouth, holding her cheeks and jaw in an apparent effort to keep control of herself. Red and white splotches appeared under her fingernails from the tightness of her grip.

When she spoke, the words were muffled by her hand.

"I was half asleep, but I did hear something, something like a clap—as though someone had clapped their hands together. That's all." She continued holding on to her face as though the pressure were her sole comfort.

"Thank you," said Hardwick, rising from the wing chair. "We'll keep our intrusions to a minimum. For now, all I need to do is go through that desk."

Caddy Mellery raised her head and opened her eyes. Her hand fell to her lap, leaving livid finger marks on her cheeks. "Detective," she said in a frail but determined voice, "you may take anything relevant, but please respect our privacy. The press is irresponsible. My husband's legacy is of supreme importance."

Chapter 21

Priorities

"Get bogged down in this poetry and we'll be chasing ourselves up our own asses for the next year," said Hardwick. He articulated the word *poetry* as though it were the messiest sort of mire.

The messages from the killer were arrayed on a large table in the middle of the institute's boardroom, occupied by the BCI team as their on-site location for the intensive start-up phase of the investigation.

There was the initial two-part letter from "X. Arybdis" making the uncanny prediction that the number Mellery would think of would be 658 and asking for $289.87 to cover the expense of having located him. There were the three increasingly menacing poems that had subsequently arrived by mail. (The third of these was the one Mellery had placed in a small plastic food-storage bag, he had told Gurney, to preserve any fingerprints.) Also laid out in sequence were Mellery's returned $289.87 check along with the note from Gregory Dermott indicating that there was no "X. Arybdis" at that address; the poem dictated by the killer on the phone to Mellery's assistant; a cassette tape of the killer's phone conversation later that evening with Mellery, during which Mellery mentioned the number nineteen; the letter found in the institute mailbox predicting that Mellery would pick nineteen; and the final poem found on the corpse. It was a remarkable amount of evidentiary material.

"You know anything about the plastic bag?" Hardwick asked. He sounded as unenthusiastic about plastic as he did about poetry.

"By that point Mellery was seriously frightened," said Gurney. "He told me he was trying to save possible fingerprints."

Hardwick shook his head. "It's that *CSI* bullshit. Plastic looks higher-tech than paper. Keep evidence in plastic bags, and it rots from trapped moisture. Assholes."

A uniformed cop with a Peony police badge on his hat and a harried expression on his face was standing at the door.

"Yeah?" Hardwick said, daring the visitor to bring him another problem.

"Your tech team needs access. That okay?"

Hardwick nodded, but his attention had returned to the collection of rhyming threats spread out across the table.

"Neat handwriting," he said, his face wrinkling up in distaste. "What do you think, Dave? You think maybe we got a homicidal nun on our hands?"

Half a minute later, the techs appeared in the boardroom with their evidence bags, a laptop, and a portable bar-code printer to secure and label all the items temporarily displayed on the table. Hardwick requested that photocopies be made of each of the materials before they were sent to the forensics lab in Albany for latent-fingerprint inspection and for handwriting, paper, and ink analysis—with special attention to the note left on the body.

Gurney kept a low profile, observing Hardwick at work in his crime-scene supervisor role. The way a case turned out months, or even years, down the road often depended on how well the guy in charge of the scene did his job in the early hours of the process. In Gurney's opinion Hardwick was doing a very good job indeed. He watched him go over the photographer's documentation of his shots and locations to make sure all relevant areas of the property had been covered, including key parts of the perimeter, entries and exits, all the footprints and visible physical evidence (lawn chair, cigarette butts, broken bottle), the body itself in situ, and the blood-drenched snow around it. Hardwick also asked the photographer to arrange for aerial shots of the entire property and its environs—not a normal part of the process, but under the circumstances, particularly the circumstance of a set of footprints that led nowhere, it made sense.

In addition, Hardwick conferred with the pair of younger detectives to verify that the interviews assigned to them earlier had been conducted. He met with the senior evidence tech to review the trace-evidence collection list, then had one of his detectives arrange for a scent-tracking dog to be brought to the scene the following morning—a sign to Gurney that the footprint problem was very much on Hardwick's mind. Finally he'd examined the crime-scene arrival and departure log maintained by the trooper at the front gate to make sure there had been no inappropriate personnel on site. Having watched Hardwick absorb and evaluate, prioritize and direct, Gurney concluded that the man was still as competent under pressure as he'd been during their former collaboration. Hardwick might be a bristly bastard, but there was no denying he was efficient.

At a quarter past four, Hardwick said to him, "Long day, and you're not even getting paid. Why don't you head home to the farm?" Then he did a little double take, as if a thought had ambushed him, and added, "I mean, we're not paying you. Were you getting paid by the Mellerys? Shit, I bet you were. Famous talent doesn't come cheap."

"I don't have a license. I couldn't charge if I wanted to. Besides, working as a paid PI is the last thing on earth I'd want to do."

Hardwick shot him a disbelieving look.

"In fact, right now I think I'll take your suggestion and call it a day."

"Think you could drop by regional headquarters around noon tomorrow?"

"What's the plan?"

"Two things. First, we need a statement—your history with the victim, the piece from long ago and the current piece. You know the drill. Second, I'd like you to sit in on a meeting—an orientation to get everyone on the same page. Preliminary reports on cause of death, witness interviews, blood, prints, murder weapon, et cetera. Initial theories, priorities, next steps. Guy like you could be a big help, get us on the right track, keep us from wasting taxpayer money. Be a crime not to share your big-city genius with us shitkickers. Noon tomorrow. Be good if you could bring your statement along with you."

The man needed to be a wise-ass. It defined his place in the world: Wise-Ass Hardwick, Major Crimes Unit, Bureau of Criminal Investigation, New York State Police. But Gurney sensed that underneath the bullshit, Hardwick really did want his help with a case that was growing stranger by the hour.

Gurney drove most of the way home oblivious to his surroundings. Not until he had driven up into the high end of the valley past Abelard's General Store in Dillweed did he become aware the clouds that had gathered earlier in the day were gone, and in their place a remarkable glow from the setting sun was illuminating the western face of the hills. The snowy cornfields that bordered the meandering river were bathed in a pastel so rich that his eyes widened at the sight. Then, with surprising speed, the coral sun descended below the opposing ridge, and the glow was extinguished. Again the leafless trees were black, the snow a vacant white.

As he slowed approaching his turnoff, his attention was drawn to a crow on the shoulder of the road. The crow was standing on something that elevated it a few inches above the level of the pavement. As he came abreast of it, he looked more closely. The crow was standing on a dead possum. Strangely, considering the normal caution of crows, it neither flew away nor showed any sign of disturbance at the passing car. Motionless, it had about it an expectant air—giving the odd tableau the quality of a dream.

Gurney turned onto his road and downshifted for the slow, winding ascent—his mind full of the image of the black bird atop the dead animal in the fading dusk, watchful, waiting.

It was two miles—and five minutes—from the intersection to Gurney's property. By the time he came to the narrow farm track that led from the barn to the house, the atmosphere had grown grayer and colder. A ghostlike snow devil reeled across the pasture, almost reaching the dark woods before dissolving.

He pulled in closer to the house than usual, turned up his collar against the chill, and hurried to the back door. As soon as he entered the kitchen, he was aware of the uniquely vacant sound that signaled Madeleine's absence. It was as if she had about her the faint hum of an electric current, an energy that filled a space when it was present and left a palpable void when it was not.

There was something else in the air as well, the emotional residue of that morning, the dark presence of the box from the basement, the box that still sat on the coffee table at the shadowed end of the room, its delicate white ribbon untouched.

After a brief detour to the bathroom off the pantry, he went directly into the den and checked the phone messages. There was just one. The voice was Sonya's—satiny, cello-like. *"Hello, David. I have a customer who is enthralled by your work. I told him you're completing another piece, and I'd like to tell him when it will be available.* Enthralled *is not too strong a term, and money does not seem to be an issue. Give me a call as soon as you can. We need to get our heads together on this one. Thanks, David."*

He was starting to replay the message when he heard the back door opening and shutting. He pressed the "stop" button on the machine to abort the Sonya replay and called out, "Is that you?"

There was no answer, which annoyed him.

"Madeleine," he called, more loudly than he needed to.

He heard her voice answer, but it was too low to make out what she said. It was a voice level that, in his hostile moments, he labeled "passive-aggressively low." His first inclination was to stay in the den, but that seemed infantile, so he went out to the kitchen.

Madeleine turned to him from the coat pegs on the far side of the room where she'd hung her orange parka. It still had sprinkles of snow on the shoulders, which meant she'd been walking through the pines.

"It's so-o-o beautiful out," she said, running her fingers through her thick brown hair, fluffing it up where the parka hood had pressed it down. She walked into the pantry, came out a minute later, and glanced around at the countertops.

"Where did you put the pecans?"

"What?"

"Didn't I ask you to get pecans?"

"I don't think so."

"Maybe I didn't. Or maybe you didn't hear me?"

"I have no idea," he said. He was having a hard time fitting the subject into the current shape of his mind. "I'll get some tomorrow."

"Where?"

"Abelard's."

"On Sunday?"

"Sun— Oh, right, they're closed. What is it you need them for?"

"I'm the one making dessert."

"What dessert?"

"Elizabeth is making the salad and baking the bread, Jan is making the chili, and I'm making the dessert." Her eyes darkened. "You forgot?"

"They're coming here tomorrow?"

"That's right."

"What time?"

"Is that an issue?"

"I have to deliver a written statement to the BCI team at noon."

"On Sunday?"

"It's a murder investigation," he said dully, he hoped not sarcastically.

She nodded. "So you'll be gone all day."

"Part of the day."

"How big a part?"

"Christ, you know the nature of these things."

The sadness and anger that contended with each other in her eyes disturbed Gurney more than a slap would have. "So I guess you'll get home tomorrow whatever time you get home, and maybe you'll join us for dinner and maybe not," she said.

"I have to deliver a signed statement as a witness-before-the-fact in a murder case. That is not something I *want* to do." His voice rose abruptly, shockingly, spitting the words at her. "There are some things in life we are *required* to do. This is a legal obligation—not a matter of preference. I didn't write the goddamn law!"

She stared at him with a weariness as sudden as his fury. "You still don't see it, do you?"

"See what?"

"That your brain is so tied up with murder and mayhem and blood and monsters and liars and psychopaths, there's simply nothing left for anything else."

Chapter 22

Getting it straight

He spent two hours that night writing and editing his statement. It recounted simply—without adjectives, emotions, opinions—the facts of his acquaintance with Mark Mellery, including their casual association in college and their recent contacts, beginning with Mellery's e-mail requesting a meeting and ending with his adamant refusal to take the matter to the police.

He drank two mugs of strong coffee while composing the statement and, as a result, slept poorly. Cold, sweaty, itchy, thirsty, with a transient ache that drifted inexplicably from one leg to the other—the night's succession of discomforts provided a malignant nursery for troubled thoughts, especially concerning the pain he'd glimpsed in Madeleine's eyes.

He knew that it came from her sense of his priorities. She was complaining that when the roles in his life collided, Dave the Detective always superseded Dave the Husband. His retirement from the job had made no difference. It was clear she'd hoped it would, maybe believed it would. But how could he stop being what he was? However much he cared for her, however much he wanted to be with her, however much he wanted her to be happy, how could he become someone he wasn't? His mind worked exceptionally well in a certain way, and the greatest satisfactions in his life had come from applying that intellectual gift. He had a supremely logical brain and a finely tuned antenna for discrepancy. These qualities made him an outstanding detective. They also created the cushion of abstraction that allowed him to maintain a tolerable distance from the horrors of his profession. Other cops had other cushions—alcohol, frat-boy solidarity, heart-deadening cynicism. Gurney's shield was his ability to grasp situations as intellectual challenges, and crimes as equations to be solved. That was who he was. It was not something he could cease to be, simply by retiring. At least that's the way he was thinking about it when he finally fell asleep an hour before dawn.

Sixty miles east of Walnut Crossing, ten miles beyond Peony, on a bluff within sight of the Hudson, State Police Regional Headquarters had the look and feel of a newly erected fortress. Its massive gray stone exterior and narrow windows seemed designed to withstand the apocalypse. Gurney wondered if the architecture was influenced by the 9/11 hysteria, which had bred projects even sillier than impregnable trooper stations.

Inside, fluorescent lighting maximized the harsh look of the metal detectors, remote cameras, bulletproof guard booth, and polished concrete floor. There was a microphone for communicating with the guard in the booth—which was really more like a control room, containing a bank of monitors for the security cameras. The lights, which cast a cold glare on all the hard surfaces, gave the guard an exhausted pallor. Even his colorless hair was rendered sickly by the unnatural illumination. He looked like he was about to throw up.

Gurney spoke into the microphone, resisting an urge to ask the guard if he was all right. "David Gurney. I'm here for a meeting with Jack Hardwick."

The guard pushed a temporary facility pass and a visitor's sign-in sheet through a narrow slot at the base of the formidable glass wall running from the ceiling down to the counter that separated them. He picked up the phone, consulted a list that was Scotch-taped to his side of the counter, dialed a four-digit extension, said something Gurney couldn't hear, then replaced the phone on its cradle.

A minute later a gray steel door in the wall next to the booth opened to reveal the same plainclothes trooper who'd escorted him the previous day at the institute. He motioned to Gurney without any indication of recognizing him and led him down a featureless gray corridor to another steel door, which he opened.

They stepped into a large, windowless conference room—windowless no doubt to keep conferees safe from the flying glass of a terrorist attack. Gurney was a bit claustrophobic, hated windowless spaces, hated the architects who thought they were a good idea.

His laconic guide made straight for the coffee urn in the far corner. Most of the seats at the oblong conference table had already been claimed by people not yet in the room. Jackets were hanging over the backs of four of the ten chairs, and three other chairs had been reserved by tilting them forward against the table. Gurney removed the light parka he was wearing and placed it over the back of one of the free chairs.

The door opened, and Hardwick entered, followed by a wonkish red-haired woman in a genderless suit, carrying a laptop and a fat file folder, and the other Tom Cruise look-alike, who headed for his buddy at the coffee urn. The woman proceeded to an unclaimed chair and put her things on the table in front of it. Hardwick approached Gurney, his face stuck in an odd spot between anticipation and disdain.

"You're in for a treat, my boy," he whispered gratingly. "Our precocious DA, youngest in the history of the county, is gracing us with his presence."

Gurney felt that reflexive antagonism toward Hardwick that he realized was out of proportion to the man's aimless acidity. Despite his effort not to react, his lips stiffened as he spoke. "Wouldn't his involvement be expected in something like this?"

"I didn't say I didn't expect it," hissed Hardwick. "I just said you were in for a treat." He glanced at the three chairs tilted in at the center of the table and, with the curled lip that was becoming part of his face, commented to no one in particular, "Thrones for the Three Wise Men."

On the heels of his remark, the door opened and three men entered.

Hardwick identified them sotto voce at Gurney's shoulder. It struck Gurney that Hardwick's missed vocation was ventriloquism, considering his ability to speak without moving his lips.

"Captain Rod Rodriguez, officious prick," said the disembodied whisper, as a squat, salon-tanned man with a loose smile and malevolent eyes stepped into the room and held the door for the taller man behind him—a lean, alert type whose gaze swept the room, alighting for no more than a second on each individual. "DA Sheridan Kline," said the whisper. "Wants to be Governor Kline."

The third man, sidling in behind Kline, prematurely bald and radiating all the charm of a bowl of cold sauerkraut, was "Stimmel, Kline's chief assistant."

Rodriguez ushered them to the tilted chairs, pointedly offering the center one to Kline, who took it as a matter of course. Stimmel sat at his left, Rodriguez at his right. Rodriguez eyed the other faces in the room through glasses with thin wire frames. The immaculately coiffed mass of thick black hair rising from his low forehead was obviously dyed. He gave the table a few sharp raps with his knuckles, looking around to be sure he had everyone's attention.

"Our agenda says this meeting starts at twelve noon, and twelve noon is what it says on the clock. If you don't mind taking your seats . . . ?"

Hardwick sat next to Gurney. The coffee-urn group came to the table, and within half a minute all had settled into their chairs. Rodriguez looked around sourly, as if to suggest that true professionals would not have taken so long to accomplish this. Seeing Gurney, his mouth twitched in a way that could have been a quick smile or a wince. His sour expression deepened at the sight of one empty chair. Then he continued.

"I don't need to tell you that a high-profile homicide has landed in our laps. We're here to make sure that we're all here." He paused, as if checking to see who might appreciate this Zen witticism. Then he translated it for the dull of mind. "We're here to make sure that we're all on the same page from day one of this case."

"Day two," muttered Hardwick.

"Excuse me?" said Rodriguez.

The Cruise twins exchanged matching looks of confusion.

"Today is day *two*, sir. Yesterday was day one, sir, and it was a bitch."

"Obviously, I was using a figure of speech. My point is that we need to be on the same page from the very beginning of this case. We all need to be marching to the same drum. Am I making myself clear?"

Hardwick nodded innocently. Rodriguez made a show of turning away from him to direct his comments to the more serious people at the table.

"From what little we know at this point, the case promises to be difficult, complex, sensitive, potentially sensational. I am told the victim was a successful author and lecturer. His wife's family is reputed to be extremely wealthy. The clientele of the Mellery Institute includes some rich, opinionated, troublesome characters. Any one of these factors could create a media circus. Put all three together and you have an enormous challenge. The four keys to success will be organization, discipline, communication, and more communication. What you see, what you hear, what you conclude is all worthless unless it is properly recorded and reported. Communication and more communication." He glanced around, letting his eyes dwell longest on Hardwick, identifying him not so subtly as a prime violator of the recording and reporting rules. Hardwick was studying a large freckle on the back of his right hand.

"I don't like people who bend the rules," Rodriguez went on. "Rule benders cause more trouble in the long run than rule breakers. Rule benders always claim they do it to get things done. The fact is, they do it for their own convenience. They do it because they lack discipline, and the lack of discipline destroys organizations. So hear me, people, loud and clear. We are going to follow the rules on this one. All the rules. We will use our checklists. We will fill out our reports in detail. We will submit them on time. Everything will go through proper channels. Every legal question will be addressed with District Attorney Kline's office before—I repeat, before—any questionable action is taken. Communication, communication, communication." He lobbed the words like a succession of artillery shells at an enemy position. Judging all resistance quelled, he turned with saccharine deference to the district attorney, who had been growing restless during the harangue, and said, "Sheridan, I know how personally involved you intend to be in this case. Is there anything you want to say to our team?"

Kline smiled broadly with what, at a greater distance, might have been mistaken for warmth. Up close, what came through was the radiant narcissism of a politician.

"The only thing I want to say is that I'm here to help. Help any way I can. You guys are pros. Trained, experienced, talented pros. You know your business. It's your show." The hint of a chuckle reached Gurney's ear. Rodriguez blinked. Might Rodriguez be that attuned to Hardwick's frequency? "But I agree with Rod. It could be a very big show, a very difficult show to manage. It's sure as hell going to be on TV, and a lot of people are going to be watching. Get ready for sensational headlines—'Gory Murder of New Age Guru.' Like it or not, gentlemen, this one's a candidate for the tabloids. I do not want us to look like the assholes in Colorado who screwed up the JonBenét case or the assholes in California who screwed up the Simpson case. We're going to have a lot of balls in the air with this one, and if they start dropping, we're going to have a mess on our hands. Those balls—"

Gurney's curiosity regarding their final disposition was left unsatisfied. Kline was silenced by a cell phone's intrusive chime, which drew everyone's attention with varying degrees of irritation. Rodriguez glared as Hardwick reached into his pocket, produced the offending instrument, and earnestly recited the captain's mantra: "Communication, communication, communication." Then he pressed the "talk" button and spoke into the phone.

"Hardwick here. . . . Go ahead. . . . Where? . . . They match the footprints? . . . Any indication how they got there? . . . Any idea why he did that? . . . All right, get them to the lab ASAP. . . . No problem." He pressed the "disconnect" button and stared thoughtfully at the phone.

"Well?" said Rodriguez, his glare warped by curiosity.

Hardwick addressed his answer to the redheaded woman in the genderless suit who had her laptop open on the table and was watching him expectantly.

"News from the crime scene. They found the killer's boots—or at least some hiking boots that match the boot prints leading away from the body. The boots are in transit to your people in the lab."

The redhead nodded and began typing on her keyboard.

"I thought you told me the prints went off into the middle of nowhere and stopped," said Rodriguez, as though he'd caught Hardwick in some sort of lie.

"Yes," said Hardwick, without looking at him.

"So where were these boots found?"

"In the middle of the same nowhere. In a tree near where the tracks ended. Hanging from a branch."

"Are you telling me your killer climbed a tree, took his boots off, and left them there?"

"Looks that way."

"Well . . . where . . . I mean, what did he do then?"

"We don't have the faintest goddamn idea. Maybe the boots will point us in the right direction."

Rodriguez uttered a harsh bark of a laugh. "Let's hope something does. In the meantime we need to get back to our agenda. Sheridan, I believe you were interrupted."

"With his balls in the air," said the ventriloquist's whisper.

"Not really interrupted," said Kline with an I-can-turn-anything-to-my-advantage grin. "The truth is, I'd rather listen—especially to news coming in from the field. The better I understand the problem, the more I can help."

"As you wish, Sheridan. Hardwick, you seem to have everyone's attention. You might as well give us the rest of the facts—as briefly as possible. The district attorney is being generous with his time, but he has a lot on his plate. Bear that in mind."

"Okay, kids, you heard the man. Here's the compressed-file version, one time only. No daydreaming, no stupid questions. Listen up."

"Whoa!" Rodriguez raised both hands. "I don't want anyone to feel they can't ask questions."

"Figure of speech, sir. Just don't want to tie up the district attorney any longer than necessary." The level of respect with which he articulated Kline's title was just exaggerated enough to suggest an insult while remaining safely ambiguous.

"Fine, fine," said Rodriguez with an impatient wave. "Go ahead."

Hardwick began a flat recitation of the available data. "Over a three- to four-week period prior to the murder, the victim received several written communications of a disturbing or threatening nature, as well as two phone calls, one taken and transcribed by Mellery's assistant, the other taken and recorded by the victim. Copies of these communications will be distributed. Victim's wife, Cassandra (aka Caddy), reports that on the night of the murder she and her husband were awakened at one A.M. by a phone call from a caller who hung up."

As Rodriguez was opening his mouth, Hardwick answered the anticipated question. "We are in touch with the phone company to access landline and cell records for the night of the murder and for the times of the two previous calls. However, given the level of planning involved in the execution of this crime, I would be surprised if the perp left a followable phone trail."

"We'll see," said Rodriguez.

Gurney decided that the captain was a man whose greatest imperative was to appear to be in control of any situation or conversation he might find himself in.

"Yes, sir," said Hardwick with that touch of exaggerated deference, too subtle to be pounced on, that he was adept at. "In any event, a couple of minutes later they were disturbed by sounds close to the house—sounds she describes as animals screeching. When I went back and asked her about it again, she said she thought it might be raccoons fighting. Her husband went to investigate. A minute later she heard what she describes as a muffled slap, shortly after which *she* went to investigate. She found her husband lying on the patio just outside the back door. Blood was spreading into the snow from wounds to his throat. She screamed—at least she thinks she screamed—tried to stop the bleeding, wasn't able to, ran back into the house, called 911."

"Do you know whether she changed the position of the body when she tried to stop the bleeding?" Rodriguez made it sound like a trick question.

"She says she can't remember."

Rodriguez looked skeptical.

"I believe her," said Hardwick.

Rodriguez shrugged in a way that assigned a low value to other men's beliefs. Glancing at his notes, Hardwick continued his emotionless narrative.

"Peony police were first on the scene, followed by a sheriff's department car, followed by Trooper Calvin Maxon from the local barracks. BCI was contacted at one fifty-six A.M. I arrived on the scene at two-twenty A.M., and the ME arrived at three twenty-five A.M."

"Speaking of Thrasher," said Rodriguez angrily, "did he call anyone to say he'd be late?"

Gurney glanced along the row of faces at the table. They seemed so inured to the medical examiner's odd name that no one reacted to it. Nor did anyone show any interest in the question—suggesting that the doctor was one of those people who was perennially late. Rodriguez stared at the conference-room door, through which Thrasher should have entered ten minutes earlier, doing a slow burn at the violation of his schedule.

As if he'd been lurking behind it, waiting for the captain's temper to boil, the door popped open and a gangly man lurched into the room with a briefcase pinned under his arm, a container of coffee in his hand, and seemingly in the middle of a sentence.

" . . . construction delays, men working. Hah! So say the signs." He smiled brightly at several people in succession. "Apparently the word *working* means standing around scratching your crotch. Lots of that. Not much digging or paving going on. None that I could see.

Pack of incompetent louts blocking the road." He peered at Rodriguez over the top of a pair of reading glasses that were askew. "Don't suppose the state police could do anything about that, eh, Captain?"

Rodriguez reacted with the weary smile of a serious man forced to deal with fools. "Good *afternoon*, Dr. Thrasher."

Thrasher put his briefcase and coffee on the table in front of the one unoccupied chair. His gaze darted around the room, coming to rest on the district attorney.

"Hello, Sheridan," he said with some surprise. "Getting in early on this one, are you?"

"You have some interesting information for us, Walter?"

"Yes, as a matter of fact. At least one small surprise."

Patently eager to keep his grip on the helm of the meeting, Rodriguez made a show of steering it where it was already going.

"Look, people, I see an opportunity here to turn the doctor's lateness to our advantage. We've been listening to a rundown of the events surrounding the discovery of the body. The last fact I heard concerned the arrival of the medical examiner at the scene. Well, the medical examiner has just arrived here—so why don't we incorporate his report right now into the narrative?"

"Great idea," said Kline without taking his eyes off Thrasher.

The ME began speaking as if it had been his intention all along to make his presentation the moment he arrived.

"You get the full written report in one week, gentlemen. Today you get the bare bones."

If that was a witticism, mused Gurney, it went by unappreciated. Perhaps it was so often repeated that the audience had grown deaf to it.

"Interesting homicide," Thrasher went on, reaching for his coffee container. He took a long, thoughtful swig and replaced the container on the table. Gurney smiled. This rumpled, sandy-haired stork had a taste for timing and drama. "Things are not exactly as they first appeared."

He paused until the room was on the verge of exploding with impatience.

"Initial examination of the body in situ led to the hypothesis that cause of death had been the severing of the carotid artery by multiple slash and puncture wounds, inflicted by a broken bottle later discovered at the scene. Initial autopsy results indicate, however, that cause of death was the severing of the carotid artery by a single bullet fired at close range into the victim's neck. The wounds from the broken bottle were subsequent to the gunshot and were inflicted after the victim had fallen to the ground. There were a minimum of fourteen puncture wounds, perhaps as many as twenty, several of which left shards of glass in the neck tissue and four of which passed completely through the neck muscles and trachea, emerging at the back of the neck."

There was silence at the table, accompanied by a variety of puzzled and intrigued looks. Rodriguez placed his fingertips together to create a steeple. He was the first to speak.

"Shot, eh?"

"Shot," said Thrasher, with the relish of a man who loved discovering the unforeseen.

Rodriguez looked accusingly at Hardwick. "How come none of your witnesses heard this gunshot? You told me there were at least twenty guests on the property, and for that matter, how come his wife didn't hear it?"

"She did."

"What? How long have you known this? Why wasn't I told?"

"She heard it, but she didn't know she heard it," said Hardwick. "She said she heard something like a muffled slap. The significance of that didn't occur to her at the time, and it didn't occur to me until this minute."

"Muffled?" said Rodriguez incredulously. "Are you telling me the victim was shot with a silencer?"

Sheridan Kline's attention level shot up a notch.

"That explains it!" cried Thrasher.

"Explains what?" Rodriguez and Hardwick asked in unison.

Thrasher's eyes glinted triumphantly. "The traces of goose down in the wound."

"And in the blood samples from the area around the body." The redhead's voice was as gender-unspecific as her suit.

Thrasher nodded. "Of course it would be there, too."

"This is all very tantalizing," said Kline. "Could one of you who understands what's being said take a moment to fill me in?"

"Goose down!" boomed Thrasher as though Kline were hard of hearing.

Kline's expression of cordial confusion began to freeze over.

Hardwick spoke as the truth dawned on him. "The muffling of the gunshot, combined with the presence of goose down, suggests that the silencing effect might have been produced by wrapping the gun in some sort of quilted material—maybe a ski jacket or a parka."

"You're saying that a gun could be silenced just by holding it inside a ski jacket?"

"Not exactly. What I'm saying is that if I held the gun in my hand and wrapped it around and around—especially around the muzzle—with a thick enough quilted material, it's possible that the report could be reduced to something that might sound like a slap, if you were listening from inside a well-insulated house with the windows closed."

The explanation seemed to satisfy everyone except Rodriguez. "I'd want to see the results of some tests before buying into that."

"You don't think it was an actual silencer?" Kline sounded disappointed.

"It could have been," said Thrasher. "But then you'd need to explain all those microscopic down particles some other way."

"So," said Kline, "the murderer shoots the victim point-blank—"

"Not point-blank," interjected Thrasher. "Point-blank implies virtual contact between the muzzle and the victim, and there was no evidence of that."

"From how far, then?"

"Hard to say. There were a few distinct single-point powder burns on the neck, which would put the gun within five feet, but the burns were not numerous enough to form a pattern. The gun may have been even closer, with the powder burns minimized by the material around the muzzle."

"I don't suppose you recovered a bullet." Rodriguez addressed the criticism to a spot in the air between Thrasher and Hardwick.

Gurney's jaw tightened. He had worked for men like Rodriguez—men who mistook their control obsession for leadership and their negativity for tough-mindedness.

Thrasher responded first. "The bullet missed the vertebrae. There's not much in the neck tissue itself that could stop it. We have an entry wound and an exit wound—neither one easy to find, by the way, with all the puncture damage inflicted later." If he was fishing for compliments, thought Gurney, this was a dead pond. Rodriguez shifted his querying gaze to Hardwick, whose tone was again just short of insubordinate.

"We didn't look for a bullet. We had no reason to believe there was a bullet."

"Well, now you do."

"Excellent point, sir," said Hardwick with a hint of mockery. He pulled out his cell phone and entered a number, walking away from the table. Despite his lowered voice, it was clear that he was talking to an officer at the crime scene and requesting a search for the bullet on a priority basis. When he returned to the table, Kline asked if there was any hope of recovering a bullet fired outdoors.

"Usually not," said Hardwick. "But in this case there's a chance. Considering the position of the body, he was probably shot with his back to the house. If it wasn't deflected in a major way, we might find it in the wood siding."

Kline nodded slowly. "Okay, then, as I started to say a minute ago, just to get this straight—the murderer shoots the victim at close range, the victim falls to the ground, carotid artery severed, blood spurting from his neck. Then the murderer produces a broken bottle and squats down next to the body and stabs it fourteen times. Is that the picture?" he asked incredulously.

"At least fourteen, possibly more," said Thrasher. "When they overlap, an accurate count becomes difficult."

"I understand, but what I'm really getting at is, why?"

"Motive," said Thrasher, as though the concept were on a scientific par with dream interpretation, "is not my area of expertise. Ask our friends here from BCI."

Kline turned to Hardwick. "A broken bottle is a weapon of convenience, a weapon of the moment, a barroom substitute for a knife or a gun. Why would a man who already has a loaded gun feel the need to carry a broken bottle, and why would he use it after he had already killed his victim with the gun?"

"To make sure he was dead?" offered Rodriguez.

"Then why not just shoot him again? Why not shoot him in the head? Why not shoot him in the head to begin with? Why in the neck?"

"Maybe he was a lousy shot."

"From five feet away?" Kline turned back to Thrasher. "Are we sure about the sequence? Shot, then stabbed?"

"Yes, to a reasonable level of professional certainty, as we say in court. The powder burns, although limited, are clear. If the neck area had already been covered with blood from stab wounds at the time of the shot, it is unlikely that distinct burns could have occurred."

"And you would have found the bullet." The redhead said this in such a soft, matter-of-fact way that only a few people heard her. Kline was one of them. Gurney was another. He'd been wondering when this point would occur to someone. Hardwick was unreadable but did not appear surprised.

"What do you mean?" asked Kline.

She answered without taking her eyes off her laptop screen. "If he was stabbed fourteen times in the neck as part of the initial assault, with four of the wounds passing completely through, he could hardly have remained standing. And if he was then shot from above while lying on his back, the bullet would have been on the ground underneath him."

Kline cast her an assessing glance. Unlike Rodriguez, mused Gurney, he was intelligent enough to respect intelligence.

Rodriguez made an effort to retake the reins. "What caliber bullet are we looking for, Doctor?"

Thrasher glared over the top of the half-glasses that were making their way down his long nose. "What do I have to do to get you people to grasp the simplest facts of pathology?"

"I know, I know," said Rodriguez peevishly, "the flesh is pliable, it shrinks, it expands, you can't be exact, et cetera, et cetera. But would you say it was closer to a .22 or a .44? Make an educated guess."

"I'm not paid to guess. Besides, no one remembers for more than five minutes that it was only a guess. What they remember is that the ME said something about a .22 and he turned out to be wrong." There was a cold gleam of recollection in his eyes, but all he said was, "When you dig the bullet out of the back of the house and give it to ballistics, then you'll know—"

"Doctor," interrupted Kline like a little boy questioning Mr. Wizard, "is it possible to estimate the exact interval between the gunshot and the subsequent stabbings?"

The tone of the question seemed to mollify Thrasher. "If the interval between the two were substantial, and both wounds bled, we would find blood in two different stages of coagulation. In this case I would say that that the two types of wounds occurred in close enough sequence to make that sort of comparison impossible. All we can say is that the interval was relatively short, but whether it was ten seconds or ten minutes would be hard to say. That's a good pathology question, though," he concluded, distinguishing it from the captain's question.

The captain's mouth twitched. "If that's all you have for us at the moment, Doctor, we won't keep you. I'll get the written report no later than one week from today?"

"I believe that's what I said." Thrasher picked up his bulging case from the table, nodded to the district attorney with a thin-lipped smile, and left the room.

Chapter 23

Without a trace

"There goes one pathological pain in the ass," said Rodriguez, surveying the faces at the table for appreciation of his wit in so describing a pathologist, but only the perennial smirks of the twin Cruises came close to providing it. Kline ended the silence by asking Hardwick to continue the crime-scene narrative he'd been providing when the ME arrived.

"Exactly what I was thinking, Sheridan," Rodriguez chimed in. "Hardwick, pick up where you left off, and stay with the key facts." The warning suggested that this was not something Hardwick normally did.

Gurney noted the predictability of the captain's attitudes—hostile to Hardwick, sycophantic to Kline, self-important in general.

Hardwick spoke rapidly. "The most visible trace of the murderer was a set of footprints, entering the property through the front gate, proceeding through the parking area around to the rear of the barn, where they stopped at a lawn chair—"

"In the snow?" asked Kline.

"Correct. Cigarette butts were found on the ground in front of the chair."

"Seven," said the redhead at the laptop.

"Seven," repeated Hardwick. "The footprints proceed from the chair—"

"Excuse me, Detective, but did the Mellerys normally keep lawn chairs out in the snow?" asked Kline.

"No, sir. It appears that the murderer brought the chair with him."

"Brought it with him?"

Hardwick shrugged.

Kline shook his head. "Sorry to interrupt you. Go ahead."

"Don't be sorry, Sheridan. Ask him anything you want. A lot of this stuff doesn't make sense to me, either," said Rodriguez, with a look that attributed the lack of sense to Hardwick.

"The footprints proceed from the chair to the location of the encounter with the victim."

"The spot where Mellery was killed, you mean?" asked Kline.

"Yes, sir. And from there they proceed through an opening in the hedge, out across the lawn, and into the woods, where they finally terminate half a mile from the house."

"How do you mean, 'terminate'?"

"They stop. They go no farther. There is a small area there where the snow is tamped down, as if the individual was standing there for a while—but no more footprints, either coming to or leaving that spot. As you heard a little while ago, the boots that made the prints were found hanging in a nearby tree—with no sign of what happened to the individual who was wearing them."

Gurney was watching Kline's face and saw there a combination of bafflement at the puzzle and surprise at his inability to see any solution. Hardwick was opening his mouth to press forward when the redhead spoke again in her quiet, uninflected voice, perfectly pitched halfway between male and female.

"At this point we should say the sole patterns of the boots are *consistent with* the prints in the snow. Whether, in fact, they made the prints will be determined in the lab."

"You can be that definite with footprints in snow?" asked Kline.

"Oh, yes," she said with her first bit of enthusiasm. "Snow prints are the best of all. Compressed snow can capture details too fine to see with the naked eye. Never kill anyone in the snow."

"I'll remember that," said Kline. "Sorry again for the interruption, Detective. Please go on."

"This might be a good time for a status report on items of

evidence collected so far. If that's all right with you, Captain?" Again Hardwick's tone struck Gurney as a subtle mockery of respect.

"I'd welcome some hard facts," said Rodriguez.

"Let me just bring the file up," said the redhead, stroking a few keys on her computer. "You want the items in any particular order?"

"How about order of importance?"

Showing no reaction to the captain's patronizing tone, she began reading from her computer screen.

"Evidence item number one—one lawn chair, made of light aluminum tubing and white plastic webbing. Initial examination for foreign material discovered a few square millimeters of Tyvek caught in the folding joint between the seat and the arm support."

"You mean the stuff they insulate houses with?" asked Kline.

"It's a moisture barrier used over plywood sheathing, but also used in other products—notably in painters' coveralls. That was the only foreign material discovered, the only indication that the chair had ever been used."

"No prints, hair, sweat, saliva, abrasions, nothing at all?" queried Rodriguez, as though he suspected that her people hadn't been looking hard enough.

"No prints, hair, sweat, saliva, or abrasions—but I wouldn't say nothing at all," she said, letting the tone of his question breeze by her like a drunk's punch. "Half the webbing in the chair had been replaced—all the horizontal strips."

"But you said it had never been used."

"There's no sign of use, but the webbing had definitely been replaced."

"What possible reason could there be for that?"

Gurney was tempted to offer an explanation, but Hardwick put it into words first. "She said the webbing was all white. That kind of chair commonly has two colors of webbing interlaced to create a pattern—blue and white, green and white, something like that. Maybe he didn't want any color on it."

Rodriguez chewed on this like a stale gumdrop. "Proceed, Sergeant Wigg. We have a lot to get through before lunch."

"Item number two—seven Marlboro cigarette butts, also without human traces."

Kline leaned forward. "No traces of saliva? No partial fingerprints? Not even a trace of skin oil?"

"Zero."

"Isn't that odd?"

"Extremely. Item number three—a broken whiskey bottle, incomplete, brand label Four Roses."

"Incomplete?"

"Approximately half of the bottle was present in one piece. That and all remaining shards recovered add up to somewhat less than two-thirds of a complete bottle."

"No prints?" said Rodriguez.

"No prints—not a surprise, really, considering their absence from the chair and cigarettes. There was one substance present, in addition to the victim's blood—a minuscule trace of detergent in a fissure along the broken edge of the glass."

"Meaning what?" said Rodriguez.

"The presence of the detergent and the absence of a portion of the bottle suggest that the bottle was broken elsewhere and washed before being brought to the scene."

"So the frenzied stabbing was as premeditated as the gunshot?"

"So it appears. Shall I continue?"

"Please," said Rodriguez, making the word sound rude.

"Item number four—the victim's clothing, including underwear, bathrobe, and moccasins, all stained with his own blood. Three foreign hairs found on the bathrobe, possibly from the victim's wife, yet to be verified. Item number five—blood samples taken from the ground around the body. Tests in progress—so far all samples match the victim. Item number six—bits of broken glass taken from the flagstone under the back of the victim's neck. This is consistent with the initial autopsy finding that four puncture wounds from the bottle glass passed through the neck from front to back and that the victim was on the ground at the time of the stabbing."

Kline had the pained squint of a man driving into the sun. "I'm getting the impression here that someone has committed an extremely violent crime, a crime involving shooting, stabbing— more than a dozen deep stab wounds, some of them delivered with great force—and yet the killer managed to do this without leaving a single unintentional trace of himself."

One of the Cruise twins spoke up for the first time, in a voice surprisingly high-pitched for the macho look of the body it came from. "How about the lawn chair, the bottle, the footprints, the boots?"

Kline's face twitched impatiently. "I said *unintentional* trace. Those things look like they were left behind on purpose."

The young man shrugged as though this were a tricky bit of sophistry.

"Item number seven is divided into subcategories," said the genderless Sergeant Wigg (but perhaps not sexless, observed Gurney, noting the interesting eyes and finely sculpted mouth). "Item seven includes communications received by the victim which may be relevant to the crime, including the note found on the body."

"I've had copies made of all that," announced Rodriguez. "I'll hand them out at the appropriate time."

Kline asked Wigg, "What are you looking for in the communications?"

"Fingerprints, paper indentations . . ."

"Like impressions from a writing pad?"

"Correct. We're also doing ink-identification tests on the handwritten letters and printer-identification tests on the letter that was generated through a word processor—the last one received prior to the murder."

"We'll also have experts look at the handwriting, vocabulary, and syntax," interjected Hardwick, "and we're getting a sound-print analysis of the phone conversation the victim taped. Wigg already has a preliminary take on it, and we'll review that today."

"We'll also go over the boots that were found today, as soon as they get to the lab. That's all for now," concluded Wigg, tapping a key on her computer. "Any questions?"

"I have one," said Rodriguez. "Since we discussed presenting these evidence items in order of importance, I was wondering why you placed the lawn chair first."

"Just a hunch, sir. We can't know how it all fits together until it all fits together. At this point it's impossible to say which piece of the puzzle—"

"But you did put the lawn chair first," interrupted Rodriguez. "Why?"

"It seemed to illustrate the most striking feature of the case."

"What's that supposed to mean?"

"The planning," said Wigg softly.

She had the ability, thought Gurney, to respond to the captain's interrogation as though it were a series of objective questions on paper, devoid of supercilious facial expressions and insulting intonations. There was a curious purity in this lack of emotional entanglement, this immunity to petty provocation. And it got people's attention. Gurney noticed everyone at the table, except Rodriguez, unconsciously leaning forward.

"Not just the planning," she went on, "but the weirdness of the planning. Bringing a lawn chair to a murder. Smoking seven cigarettes without touching them with your fingers or your lips. Breaking a bottle, washing it, and bringing it to the scene to stab a dead body with. Not to mention the impossible footprints and how the perp disappeared from the woods. It's like the guy is some kind of genius hit man. It's not just a lawn chair, but a lawn chair with half the webbing removed and replaced. Why? Because he wanted it all white? Because it would be less visible in the snow? Because it would be less visible against the white Tyvek painter's suit he may have been wearing? But if visibility was such a big issue, why would he sit there in a lawn chair, smoking cigarettes? I'm not sure why, but I wouldn't be surprised if the chair turned out to be the key to unraveling the whole thing."

Rodriguez shook his head. "The key to solving this crime will be police discipline, procedure, and communication."

"My money's on the lawn chair," whispered Hardwick with a wink at Wigg.

The comment registered on the captain's face, but before he could speak, the conference-room door opened and a man entered holding a gleaming computer disk. "What is it?" Rodriguez snapped.

"You told me to bring you any fingerprint results as soon as we had them, sir."

"And?"

"We have them," he said, holding up the disk. "You'd better have a look. Maybe Sergeant Wigg could . . . ?"

He extended the disk tentatively toward her laptop. She inserted it and clicked a couple of keys.

"Interesting," she said.

"Prekowski, would you mind telling us what you have there?"

"Krepowski, sir."

"What?"

"My name is Krepowski."

"Fine, good. Now, would you please tell us whether you found any prints."

The man cleared his throat. "Well, yes and no," he said.

Rodriguez sighed. "You mean they're too smudged to be useful?"

"They're a hell of a lot more than smudged," said the man. "In fact, they're not really prints at all."

"Well, what are they?"

"I guess you could call them smears. It looks like the guy used his fingertips to write with—using the skin oil in his fingertips like it was invisible ink."

"To write? Write what?"

"Single-word messages. One on the back of each of the poems he mailed to the victim. Once we made the words chemically visible, we photographed them and copied the images to disk. It shows up pretty clearly on the screen."

With a faint touch of amusement playing at her lips, Sergeant Wigg slowly rotated her laptop until the screen directly faced

Rodriguez. There were three sheets of paper shown in the photo, side by side—the reverse sides of the sheets on which the three poems had been written arranged in the sequence in which they'd been received. On each of the three sheets, a single four-letter word appeared in smudgy block letters:

DUMB EVIL COPS

Chapter 24

Crime of the year

"What the fuck . . . ?" said the Cruise boys, aroused in unison.

Rodriguez frowned.

"Damn!" cried Kline. "This is getting more interesting by the minute. This guy is declaring war."

"An obvious nutcase," said Cruise One.

"A smart, ruthless nutcase who wants to do battle with the police." It was clear that Kline found the implications exciting.

"So what?" said Cruise Two.

"I said earlier that this crime was likely to generate some media interest. Scratch that. This could be the crime of the year, maybe the crime of the decade. Every element of this thing is a media magnet." Kline's eyes glittered with the possibilities. He was leaning so far forward in his chair that his ribs pressed against the edge of the table. Then, as suddenly as his enthusiasm had flared, he reined it in, sitting back with a pensive expression—as though a private alarm had warned him that murder was a tragic affair and needed to be treated as such. "The anti-police element could be significant," he said soberly.

"No doubt about it," concurred Rodriguez. "I'd like to know if any of the institute's guests had anti-police attitudes. How about it, Hardwick?"

The senior investigator uttered a single-syllable bark of a laugh.

"What's so funny?"

"Most of the guests we interviewed rank the police somewhere between IRS agents and garden slugs."

Somehow, Gurney marveled, Hardwick had managed to convey that this was exactly what he himself thought of the captain.

"I'd like to see their statements."

"They're in your in-box. But I can save you some time. The statements are useless. Name, rank, and serial number. Everyone was asleep. No one saw anything. No one heard anything—except for Pasquale Cachese, aka Patty Cakes. Says he couldn't sleep. Opened his window to get some air and heard the so-called muffled slap—and he guessed what it was." Hardwick riffled through a stack of papers in his file folder and removed one, as Kline again came forward in his seat. "'It sounded like someone got popped,' he said. He said it very matter-of-factly, like it was a sound he was familiar with."

Kline's eyes were glittering again. "Are you telling me there was a mob guy present at the time of the murder?"

"Present on the property, not at the scene," said Hardwick.

"How do you know that?"

"Because he woke Mellery's assistant instructor, Justin Bale, a young man who has a room in the same building with the guest rooms. Cachese told him he'd heard a noise from the direction of Mellery's house, thought it might be an intruder, suggested they take a look. By the time they got some clothes on and got across the gardens to the back of the Mellery house, Caddy Mellery had already discovered her husband's body and gone back inside to call 911."

"Cachese didn't tell this Bale person that he'd heard a shot?" Kline was starting to sound like he was in a courtroom.

"No. He told us when we interviewed him the next day. By that time, though, we'd found the bloody bottle and all the obvious stab wounds but no noticeable bullet wounds and no other weapon, so we didn't pursue the gunshot thing right away. We figured Patty was the kind of guy who might have guns on his mind—that it might be a conclusion he'd jump to."

"Why didn't he tell Bale he thought it was a shot?"

"He said he didn't want to scare him."

"Very considerate," said Kline with a sneer. He glanced at the stoic Stimmel seated next to him. Stimmel mirrored the sneer. "If he'd—"

"But he told *you*," Rodriguez broke in. "Too bad you didn't pay attention."

Hardwick stifled a yawn.

"What the hell was a mob guy doing at a place that sells 'spiritual renewal'?" asked Kline.

Hardwick shrugged. "Says he loves the place. Comes once a year to calm his nerves. Says it's a little piece of heaven. Says Mellery was a saint."

"He actually said that?"

"He actually said that."

"This case is amazing! Any other interesting guests on the grounds?"

That ironic glint Gurney found so inexplicably distasteful came into Hardwick's eyes. "If you mean arrogant, infantile, drug-addled nutcases, yeah, there are a fair number of 'interesting guests'—plus the richer-than-God widow."

As he pondered, perhaps, the media ramifications of so sensational a crime scene, Kline's gaze settled on Gurney, who happened to be sitting diagonally across the table from him. At first his expression remained as disconnected as if he were regarding an empty chair. Then he cocked his head curiously.

"Wait a minute," he said. "Dave Gurney, NYPD. Rod told me who'd be attending this meeting, but the name just registered. Aren't you the guy *New York* magazine did the article on a few years back?"

Hardwick answered first. "That's our boy. Headline was 'Super Detective.'"

"I remember now," exclaimed Kline. "You solved those big serial-killer cases—the Christmas lunatic with the body parts, and Porky Pig or whatever the hell his name was."

"Peter Possum Piggert," said Gurney mildly.

Kline stared at him with open awe. "So this Mellery guy who got murdered just happens to be the best friend of the NYPD's serial-murder star?" The media ramifications were obviously getting richer by the minute.

"I was involved to some extent in both cases," Gurney said in a voice as devoid of hype as Kline's was full of it. "So were a lot of other people. As for Mellery being my best friend, that would be sad if it were true, considering we hadn't spoken to each other in twenty-five years, and even back then——"

"But," Kline interrupted, "when he found himself in trouble, you were the man he turned to."

Gurney took in the faces at the table, displaying various shades of respect and envy, and marveled at the seductive power of an over-simplified narrative. BLOODY MURDER OF TOP COP'S BUDDY instantly appealed to that part of the brain that loves cartoons and hates complexity.

"I suspect he came to me because I was the only cop he knew."

Kline looked like he was not ready to let the point go, might revisit it later, but for now was willing to move on. "Whatever your exact relationship was, your contact with the victim gives you a window on the affair no one else has."

"That's why I wanted him here today," said Rodriguez in his I'm-in-charge-here style.

A short hack of a laugh came out of Hardwick's throat, followed by a whisper that just reached Gurney's ear: "He hated the idea until Kline liked it."

Rodriguez went on, "I have him scheduled to give us his statement next and answer whatever questions it raises—which could be quite a few. To avoid interruptions, let's take five minutes now for a restroom break."

"Piss on you, Gurney," said the disembodied whisper, lost amid the sounds of chairs being pushed back from the table.

Chapter 25

Questioning Gurney

Gurney had a theory that men behaved in bathrooms as if they were either locker rooms or elevators—which is to say, with either rowdy familiarity or uneasy aloofness. This was an elevator crowd. It was not until they all returned to the conference room that anyone spoke.

"So how did such a modest guy get to be so famous?" asked Kline, grinning with a practiced charm that both concealed and revealed the ice behind it.

"I'm not that modest, and I'm sure as hell not that famous," said Gurney.

"If everyone will have a seat," said Rodriguez brusquely, "you'll each find in front of you a set of the messages received by the victim. As our witness presents his account of his communications with the victim, you can refer to the messages they were discussing." With a curt nod toward Gurney, he concluded, "Whenever you're ready."

Gurney was no longer surprised at the man's officiousness, but it still rankled. He glanced around the table, achieving eye contact with all but his guide at the murder site, who was flipping noisily through his packet of papers, and Stimmel, the DA's chief assistant, who sat gazing into space like a contemplative toad.

"As the captain indicated, there's a lot to cover. It might be best to let me give you a summary of the events in the order in which they occurred, and to hold your questions until you have the whole story." He saw Rodriguez's head rising to object, then subsiding the instant Kline nodded approvingly at the proposed procedure.

In his clear, concise way (he'd been told more than once that he could have been a professor of logic) Gurney gave a twenty-minute summary of the affair—beginning with Mellery's e-mail asking to see him, proceeding through the series of disconcerting communications and Mellery's reactions, concluding with the phone call from the killer and the note in the mailbox (the one mentioning the number nineteen).

Kline was a rapt listener throughout and the first to speak when it ended. "It's an epic revenge story! The killer was obsessed with getting even with Mellery for something horrible he did years ago when he was drunk."

"Why wait so long?" asked Sergeant Wigg, whom Gurney was finding more interesting each time she spoke.

Kline's eyes were bright with possibilities. "Maybe Mellery revealed something in one of his books. Maybe that's how the killer discovered he was responsible for some tragic event he hadn't connected with him before. Or maybe Mellery's success was the last straw, the thing the killer couldn't stand. Or maybe, like the first note said, the killer just happened to see him on the street one day. A smoldering resentment comes back to life. The enemy steps into the crosshairs and . . . bang!"

"Bang, my ass," said Hardwick.

"You have a different opinion, Senior Investigator Hardwick?" inquired Kline with an edgy smile.

"Carefully composed letters, number mysteries, directions to send a check to the wrong address, a series of increasingly threatening poems, hidden messages to the police that could only be discovered through latent-prints chemistry, surgically clean cigarette butts, a concealed gunshot wound, an impossible trail of footprints, and a fucking lawn chair for Chrissake! That's a hell of a dragged-out bang."

"My sketch of the situation was not meant to exclude premeditation," said Kline. "But at this point I'm more interested in the basic motive than in details. I want to understand the connection between the murderer and his victim. Understanding the connection is usually the key to a conviction."

This lecturing response generated an unpleasant silence, broken by Rodriguez.

"Blatt!" he barked at Gurney's guide, who was staring at his copies of the first two messages as though they'd dropped into his lap from outer space. "You look lost."

"I don't get it. The perp sends a letter to the victim, tells him to think of a number and then look in a sealed envelope. He thinks of six fifty-eight, looks in the envelope, and there it is—six fifty-eight. You saying that actually happened?"

Before anyone could answer, his partner broke in, "And two weeks later the perp does it again—this time on the phone. He tells him to think of a number and look in his mailbox. Victim thinks of the number nineteen, looks in his mailbox, and there's the number nineteen in the middle of a letter from the perp. That's some pretty weird shit, dude."

"We have the recording the victim made of the actual phone call," said Rodriguez, making it sound like a personal achievement. "Play the part about the number, Wigg."

Without comment the sergeant tapped a few keys, and after a two- or three-second interval the call between Mellery and his stalker—the one Gurney had audited via Mellery's conference-call gizmo—began at its midpoint. The faces at the table were riveted by the bizarre accent of the caller's voice, the taut fear in Mellery's.

"Now, whisper the number."

"Whisper it?"

"Yes."

"Nineteen."

"Good, very good."

"Who are you?"

"You still don't know? So much pain, and you have no idea. I thought this might happen. I left something for you earlier. A little note. You sure you don't have it?"

"I don't know what you're talking about."

"Ah, but you knew that the number was nineteen."

"You said to think of a number."

"But it was the right number, wasn't it?"

"I don't understand."

After a moment Sergeant Wigg tapped two keys and said, "That's it."

The brief playback left Gurney feeling bereaved, angry, sick.

Blatt turned his palms up in a gesture of confusion. "What the hell was that, a man or a woman?"

"Almost certainly a man," said Wigg.

"How the hell can you tell?"

"We did a voice-pitch analysis this morning, and the printout shows more stress as the frequency rises."

"So?"

"The pitch varies considerably from phrase to phrase, even word to word, and in every case the voice is measurably less stressed at the lower frequencies."

"Meaning the caller was straining to speak in a high register and the lower pitches came more naturally?" asked Kline.

"Exactly," said Wigg in her ambiguous but not unattractive voice. "It's not conclusive evidence, but it's strongly suggestive."

"What about the background noise?" asked Kline. It was a question on Gurney's mind as well. He'd been aware of a number of vehicle sounds on the recording that placed the source of the call in an open area—perhaps a busy street or an outdoor mall.

"We'll know more after we do an enhancement, but right now there seem to be three categories of sound—the conversation itself, traffic, and the hum of some sort of engine."

"How long will the enhancement take?" asked Rodriguez.

"Depends on the complexity of the data captured," said Wigg. "I'd estimate twelve to twenty-four hours."

"Make it twelve."

After an awkward silence, something Rodriguez had a talent for initiating, Kline asked a question of the room in general. "What about that whispering business? Who wasn't supposed to hear Mellery say the number nineteen?" He turned to Gurney. "You have any ideas?"

"No. But I doubt it has anything to do with not being overheard."

"Why would you say that?" challenged Rodriguez.

"Because whispering is a lousy way of not being overheard," whispered Gurney, quite audibly, to underline his point. "It's like other peculiar elements in the case."

"Like what?" Rodriguez persisted.

"Well, for example, why the uncertainty in the note referring to November or December? Why a gun and a broken bottle? Why the mystery with the footprints? And one other small matter that no one's mentioned—why no animal tracks?"

"What?" Rodriguez looked baffled.

"Caddy Mellery said that she and her husband heard the shrieking sounds of animals fighting behind the house—that was why he went downstairs and looked out the back door. But there were no animal tracks anywhere near there—and they would have been quite obvious in the snow."

"We're getting bogged down. I don't see how the presence or absence of raccoon tracks, or whatever the hell we're talking about, matters."

"Christ," said Hardwick, ignoring Rodriguez and shooting Gurney an admiring grin. "You're right. There wasn't a single mark in that snow that wasn't made by the victim or the killer. Why didn't I notice that?"

Kline turned to Stimmel. "I've never seen a case with so many items of evidence and so few that made sense." He shook his head. "I mean, how on earth did the killer pull off that business with the numbers? And why twice?" He looked at Gurney. "You sure the numbers meant nothing to Mellery?"

"Ninety percent sure—about as sure as I get about anything."

"Getting back to the big picture," said Rodriguez, "I was thinking about the issue of motive you mentioned earlier, Sheridan—"

Hardwick's cell phone rang. He had it out of his pocket and at his ear before Rodriguez could object.

"Shit," he said, after listening for about ten seconds. "You're sure?" He looked around the table. "No bullet. They went over every inch of the rear wall of the house. Nothing."

"Have them check inside the house," said Gurney.

"But the shot was fired outside."

"I know, but Mellery probably didn't close the door behind him. An anxious person in a situation like that would want to leave it open. Tell the techs to consider the possible trajectories and check any interior wall that could have been in the line of fire."

Hardwick relayed the instructions quickly and ended the call.

"Good idea," said Kline.

"Very good," said Wigg.

"About those numbers," said Blatt, abruptly changing the subject. "It pretty much has to be some kind of hypnosis or ESP, right?"

"I wouldn't think so," said Gurney.

"But it's got to be. What else could it be?"

Hardwick shared Gurney's sentiments on this subject and responded first. "Christ, Blatt, when was the last time the state police investigated a crime involving mystical mind control?"

"But he knew what the guy was thinking!"

This time Gurney answered first, in his conciliatory way. "It does look like somebody knew exactly what Mellery was thinking, but my bet is we're missing something, and it will turn out to be a lot simpler than mind-reading."

"Let me ask you something, Detective Gurney." Rodriguez was sitting back in his chair, his right fist cupped in the left palm in front of his chest. "There was rapidly accumulating evidence, through a series of threatening letters and phone calls, that Mark Mellery was the target of a homicidal stalker. Why didn't you bring this evidence to the police prior to the murder?"

The fact that Gurney had anticipated the question and was prepared to answer it did not diminish its sting.

"I appreciate the 'Detective' title, Captain, but I retired that title
with my shield and weapon two years ago. As for reporting the matter to the police as it was developing, nothing practical could be done
without Mark Mellery's cooperation, and he made it clear that he
would provide no cooperation whatsoever."

"Are you saying you couldn't bring the situation to the attention
of the police without his permission?" Rodriguez's voice was rising,
his attitude stiffening.

"He made it clear to me that he did not want the police involved, that he regarded the idea of police intrusion into the affair
as more destructive than helpful, and that he would take whatever
steps were necessary to prevent it. If I had reported the matter, he
would have stonewalled you and refused any further communication with me."

"His further communication with you didn't do him much good,
did it?"

"Unfortunately, Captain, you're right about that."

The softness, the absence of resistance, in Gurney's reply left
Rodriguez momentarily off balance. Sheridan Kline stepped into
the empty space. "Why was he opposed to involving the police?"

"He considered the police too clumsy and incompetent to achieve
a positive result. He believed they were unlikely to make him safer
but very likely to create a public-relations mess for his institute."

"That's ridiculous," said Rodriguez, affronted.

"'Bulls in a china shop' is what he kept saying. He was determined there would be no cooperation with the police—no police
allowed on his property, no police contact with his guests, no information from him personally. He seemed willing to take legal action
at the slightest hint of police interference."

"Fine, but what I'd like to know——" began Rodriguez, but he
was again cut short by the familiar chime of Hardwick's phone.

"Hardwick here. . . . Right. . . . Where? . . . Fantastic. . . . Okay, good.
Thanks." He pocketed the phone and announced to Gurney, in a

voice loud enough for all to hear, "They found the bullet. In an inside wall. In fact, in the center hall of the house, on a direct line from the back door, which was apparently open when the shot was fired."

"Congratulations," said Sergeant Wigg to Gurney, and then to Hardwick, "Any idea what caliber?"

"They think it's a .357, but we'll wait on ballistics for that."

Kline looked preoccupied. He addressed a question to no one in particular. "Could Mellery have had other reasons for not wanting the police around?"

Blatt, his face screwed up in befuddlement, added his own question: "What the hell are 'balls in a china shop'?"

Chapter 26

A blank check

By the time Gurney had driven the width of the Catskill Mountains and arrived at his farmstead outside Walnut Crossing, exhaustion had enveloped him—an emotional fog that muddled together hunger, thirst, frustration, sadness, and self-doubt. November's progress toward winter was making days distressingly shorter—especially in the valleys, where the enclosing mountains made for early dusks. Madeleine's car was gone from its place by the garden shed. The snow, partly melted by the midday sun and refrozen by the evening chill, crunched underfoot.

The house was deadly silent. Gurney switched on the hanging fixture over the butcher-block island. He remembered Madeleine saying something that morning about their planned dinner party's being canceled because of some sort of meeting the women all wanted to attend, but the details eluded him. *So there was no need for the god-damn pecans after all.* He put a Darjeeling tea bag in a cup, filled it at the tap, and put it in the microwave. Moved by habit, he headed for his armchair on the far side of the country kitchen. He sank into it and propped his feet on a wooden stool. Two minutes later the beep of the microwave was absorbed into the texture of a shadowy dream.

He awoke at the sound of Madeleine's footsteps.

It was an oversensitive perception, perhaps, but something

in the footsteps sounded angry. It seemed to him that their direction and proximity indicated that she must have seen him in the chair yet had chosen not to speak to him.

He opened his eyes in time to see her leaving the kitchen, heading for their bedroom. He stretched, pushed himself up from the depths of the chair, went to the sideboard for a tissue, and blew his nose. He heard a closet door close, a bit too affirmatively, and a minute later she returned to the kitchen. She had replaced her silk blouse with a shapeless sweatshirt.

"You're awake," she said.

He heard it as a criticism of the fact that he'd been asleep.

She switched on a row of track lights over the main countertop and opened the refrigerator. "Have you eaten?" It sounded like an accusation.

"No, I had a very tiring day, and when I got home, I just made a cup of— Oh, damn, I forgot about it." He went to the microwave, removed a cup of dark, cold tea and emptied it, bag and all, into the sink.

Madeleine went to the sink, picked his tea bag out of it, and pointedly dropped it into the garbage container.

"I'm pretty tired myself." She shook her head silently for a moment. "I don't understand why these local morons believe that building a hideous prison, surrounded by razor wire, in the middle of the most beautiful county in the state is a good idea."

Now he remembered. She'd told him that morning she planned to attend a town meeting at which the controversial proposal was slated to be discussed yet again. At issue was whether the town should compete to become the location of a facility its opponents referred to as a prison and its supporters called a treatment center. The nomenclature battle arose from the ambiguous bureaucratic language authorizing this pilot project for a new class of institution. It was to be known as a SCATE—State Correctional and Therapeutic Environment—and its dual purpose was the incarceration and rehabilitation of felony drug offenders. In fact, the bureaucratic language was quite impenetrable and left a lot of room for interpretation and argument.

It was a touchy subject between them—not because he didn't share her desire to keep the SCATE out of Walnut Crossing but because he wasn't joining the battle as sharply as she thought he should. "There are probably half a dozen people who'll make out like bandits," she said grimly, "and everyone else in the valley—and everyone who has to drive through the valley—will be stuck with a wretched eyesore for the rest of their lives. And for what? For the so-called rehabilitation of a pack of drug-dealing creeps? Give me a break!"

"Other towns are competing for it. With any luck, one will win."

She smiled bleakly. "Sure, if their town boards are even more corrupt than ours, that might happen."

Feeling the heat of her indignation as a form of pressure on himself, he decided to try changing the subject.

"Shall I make us a couple of omelets?" He watched her hunger vying briefly with her residual anger. Her hunger won.

"No green peppers," she warned. "I don't like them."

"Why do you buy them?"

"I don't know. Certainly not for omelets."

"You want any scallions?"

"No scallions."

She set the table while he beat the eggs and heated the pans.

"You want anything to drink?" he asked.

She shook her head. He knew she never drank anything with her meals, but he asked anyway. Peculiar little quirk, he thought, to keep asking that question.

Neither of them spoke more than a few words until they'd finished eating and both had given their empty plates a ritual nudge toward the center of the table.

"Tell me about your day," she said.

"My day? You mean my meeting with the ace homicide team?"

"You weren't impressed?"

"Oh, I was impressed. If you wanted to write a book about dysfunctional team dynamics, run by the Captain from Hell, you could set up a tape recorder in that place and transcribe it word for word."

"Worse than what you retired from?"

He was slow in answering, not because he was unsure of the answer but because of the fraught intonation he detected in the word *retired*. He decided to respond to the words instead of the tone.

"There were some difficult people in the city, but the Captain from Hell operates on a whole other level of arrogance and insecurity. He's desperate to impress the DA, has no respect for his own people, no real feeling for the case. Every question, every comment, was either hostile or off the point, usually both."

She eyed him speculatively. "I'm not surprised."

"What do you mean?"

She shrugged lightly. It looked like she was trying to compose her expression to convey as little as possible. "Just that I'm not surprised. I think if you came home and said you'd spent the day with the best homicide team you'd ever met, that would have surprised me. That's all."

He knew damn well that wasn't all. But he was smart enough to know that Madeleine was smarter than he was and there was no way he was going to cajole her into talking about something she wasn't inclined to talk about.

"Well," he said, "the fact is, it was exhausting and unencouraging. Right now I intend to put it out of my mind and do something completely different."

It was a statement made without forethought and followed by a mental blank. Moving on to something completely different was not as easy as it sounded. The difficulties of the day continued to swirl before him, along with Madeleine's enigmatic reaction. At that moment the option which for the past week had been tugging at the edges of his resistance, the option he'd desperately kept out of sight but not entirely out of mind, again intruded. This time, unexpectedly, along with it came a surge of determination to take the action he'd been avoiding.

"The box . . ." he said. His throat was constricted, his voice raspy, as he forced the subject into the open before his fear of it could recapture him, before he even knew how he would finish the sentence.

She looked up at him from her empty plate—calm, curious, attentive—waiting for him to go on.

"His drawings . . . What . . . I mean, why . . . ?" He struggled to coax from the conflict and confusion in his heart a rational question.

The effort was unnecessary. Madeleine's ability to see his thoughts in his eyes always exceeded his ability to articulate them.

"We need to say good-bye." Her voice was gentle, relaxed.

He stared down at the table. Nothing in his mind was forming into words.

"It's been a long time," she said. "Danny is gone, and we never said good-bye to him."

He nodded, almost imperceptibly. His sense of time was dissolving, his mind strangely empty.

When the phone rang, he felt as if he were being awakened, yanked back into the world—a world of familiar, measurable, describable problems. Madeleine was still at the table with him, but he wasn't sure how long they'd been sitting there.

"Do you want me to answer it?" she asked.

"That's all right. I'll get it." He hesitated, like a computer reloading information, then stood up, a little unsteadily, and went to the den.

"Gurney." Answering the phone that way—the way he'd answered it for so many years in homicide—was a habit he'd found difficult to break.

The voice that greeted him was bright, aggressive, artificially warm. It brought to mind that old rule of salesmanship: Always smile when you're speaking on the phone, because it makes you sound friendlier.

"Dave, I'm glad you're there! This is Sheridan Kline. I hope I didn't interrupt your dinner."

"What can I do for you?"

"I'll get right to the point. I believe you're the kind of man I can be perfectly frank with. I know your reputation. This afternoon I had a glimpse of the reason for it. I was impressed. I hope I'm not embarrassing you."

Gurney was wondering where this was leading. "You're being very kind."

"Not kind. Truthful. I'm calling because this case cries out for someone of your ability, and I'd love to find a way to take advantage of your talent."

"You know I'm retired, right?"

"So I was told. And I'm sure that going back to the old routine is the last thing you'd want to do. I'm not suggesting anything like that. I have a feeling this case is going to be very big, and I'd love to have access to your thinking."

"I'm not sure what you're asking me to do."

"Ideally," said Kline, "I'd like you to find out who killed Mark Mellery."

"Isn't that what the BCI Major Crimes Unit is for?"

"Sure. And with some luck they may eventually succeed."

"But?"

"But I want to improve my odds. This case is too important to leave to the mercy of our usual procedures. I want an ace up my sleeve."

"I don't see how I'd fit in."

"You don't see yourself working for BCI? Don't worry. I figured Rod wasn't your kind of guy. No, you'd report to me personally. We could set you up as some kind of adjunct investigator or consultant to my office, whatever would work for you."

"How much of my time are we talking about?"

"That's up to you." When Gurney did not respond, he went on, "Mark Mellery must have admired and trusted you. He asked you to help him deal with a predator. I'm asking you to help me deal with that same predator. Whatever you can give me I'd be grateful for."

This guy is good, thought Gurney. *He's got the sincerity thing down pat.* He said, "I'll talk to my wife about it. I'll get back to you in the morning. Give me a number where I can reach you."

The smile in the voice was huge. "I'll give you my home number. I have a feeling you're an early riser like me. Call anytime after six A.M."

When he returned to the kitchen, Madeleine was at the table, but her mood had changed. She was reading the *Times*. He sat opposite her at a right angle so he was facing the old Franklin woodstove. He looked toward it without really seeing it and began massaging his forehead as if the decision confronting him were a muscle kink to be worked out.

"It's not that difficult, is it?" said Madeleine without looking up from her paper.

"What?"

"What you're thinking about."

"The DA seems eager for my help."

"Why wouldn't he be?"

"An outsider wouldn't normally be brought into something like this."

"But you're not just any outsider, are you?"

"I guess my connection with Mellery makes a difference."

She cocked her head, peering at him with her X-ray vision.

"He was very flattering," said Gurney, trying not to sound flattered.

"Probably just describing your talents accurately."

"Compared to Captain Rodriguez, anyone would look good."

She smiled at his awkward humility. "What did he offer you?"

"A blank check, really. I'd operate through his office. Have to be very careful not to step on toes, though. I told him I'd decide by tomorrow morning."

"Decide what?"

"Whether or not I want to do this."

"Are you joking?"

"You think it's that bad an idea?"

"I mean, are you joking about not having decided yet?"

"There's a lot involved."

"More than you may think, but it's obvious you're going to do it."

She went back to reading her paper.

"What do you mean, more than I may think?" he asked after a long minute.

"Choices sometimes have consequences we don't anticipate."

"Like what?"

Her sad stare told him it was a stupid question.

After a pause he said, "I feel I owe something to Mark."

A flicker of irony was added to the stare.

"Why the funny look?"

"That's the first time I've heard you call him by his first name."

Chapter 27

Getting to know the DA

The County Office Building, which had carried that bland designation since 1935, had formerly been called the Bumblebee Lunatic Asylum—founded in 1899 through the generosity (and temporary insanity, his disowned heirs argued to no avail) of the eponymous British transplant, Sir George Bumblebee. The murky redbrick edifice, infused with a century of soot, loomed darkly over the town square. It was about a mile from state police headquarters and the same hour-and-a-quarter drive from Walnut Crossing.

The inside was even less appealing than the outside, for the opposite reason. In the 1960s it had been gutted and modernized. Begrimed chandeliers and oak wainscoting were replaced by glaring fluorescent fixtures and white drywall. The thought crossed Gurney's mind that the harsh modern light might serve to keep at bay the mad ghosts of its former residents—an odd thing for a man to be thinking on his way to negotiate the details of an employment contract, so he focused instead on what Madeleine had said that morning on his way out: "He needs you more than you need him." He pondered that as he waited to pass through the elaborate lobby security apparatus. Once past that barrier, he followed a series of arrows to a door whose frosted-glass panel bore the words DISTRICT ATTORNEY in elegant black lettering.

Inside, a woman at a reception desk met his eyes as he entered. It was Gurney's observation that a man's choice of a female assistant is based on competence, sex, or prestige. The woman at the desk seemed to offer all three. Despite a possible age of fifty or so, her hair, skin, makeup, clothes, and figure were so well tended they suggested a focus on things physical that was almost electric. The assessing look in her eyes was cool as well as sensual. A little brass rectangle propped up on her desk announced that her name was Ellen Rackoff.

Before either of them spoke, a door to the right of her desk opened and Sheridan Kline stepped into the reception room. He grinned with an approximation of warmth.

"Nine o'clock on the dot! I'm not surprised. You strike me as a person who does exactly what he says he's going to do."

"It's easier than the alternative."

"What? Oh, yes, yes, of course." Bigger grin, but less warmth. "Do you prefer coffee or tea?"

"Coffee."

"Me, too. Never understood tea. You a dog man or a cat man?"

"Dog, I guess."

"Ever notice that dog people prefer coffee? Tea is for cat people?"

Gurney didn't think that was worth thinking about. Kline gestured for him to follow him into his office, then extended the gesture in the direction of a contemporary leather sofa, settling himself into a matching armchair on the other side of a low glass table and replacing his grin with a look of almost comical earnestness.

"Dave, let me say how happy I am that you're willing to help us."

"Assuming there's an appropriate role for me."

Kline blinked.

"Turf is a touchy issue," said Gurney.

"Couldn't agree more. Let me be frank—speak with an open kimono, as the saying goes."

Gurney hid a grimace under a polite smile.

"People I know at the NYPD tell me impressive things about you. You were the lead investigator on some very big cases, the key man, the man who put it all together, but when the time came for congratulations, you always gave the credit to someone else. Word is, you had the biggest talent and smallest ego in the department."

Gurney smiled, not at the compliment, which he knew was calculated, but at Kline's expression, which seemed truly baffled by the notion of reluctance to take credit.

"I like the work. I don't like being the center of attention."

Kline looked for a long moment as if he were trying to identify an elusive flavor in his food, then gave it up.

He leaned forward. "Tell me how you think you can have an impact on this case."

This was the critical question. Anticipating how it might be answered had occupied much of Gurney's drive from Walnut Crossing.

"As a consulting analyst."

"What does that mean?"

"The investigation team at BCI is responsible for gathering, inspecting, and preserving evidence, interviewing witnesses, following up leads, checking alibis, and formulating a working hypothesis regarding the identity, movements, and motives of the killer. That last piece is crucial, and it's the one I believe I can help with."

"How?"

"Looking at the facts in a complex situation and developing a reasonable narrative is the only part of my job I was any good at."

"I doubt that."

"Other people are better at questioning suspects, discovering evidence at the scene—"

"Like bullets no one else knew where to look for?"

"That was a lucky guess. There's usually someone better than I am at each little piece of an investigation. But when it comes to fitting the pieces together, seeing what matters and what doesn't, I can do that. On the job I wasn't always right, but I was right often enough to make a difference."

"So you have an ego after all."

"If you want to call it that. I know my limitations, and I know my strengths."

He also knew from his years of interrogations how certain personalities would respond to certain attitudes, and he wasn't wrong about Kline. The man's gaze reflected a more comfortable understanding of that exotic flavor he'd been trying to label.

"We should discuss compensation," said Kline. "What I have in mind is an hourly rate that we've established for certain consultant categories in the past. I can offer you seventy-five dollars an hour, plus expenses—expenses within reason—starting now."

"That's fine."

Kline extended his politician's hand. "I look forward to working with you. Ellen has put together a packet of forms, releases, affidavits, confidentiality agreements. It may take you some time if you want to read what you're signing. She'll give you an office you can use. There are details we'll need to work out as we go along. I'll personally bring you up to date on any new information I receive from BCI or from my own people, and I'll include you in general briefings like the one yesterday. If you need to talk to investigative staff, arrange that through my office. To talk to witnesses, suspects, persons of interest—ditto, through my office. That okay with you?"

"Yes."

"You don't waste words. I don't, either. Now that we're working together, let me ask you something." Kline sat back and steepled his fingers, lending his question added weight. "Why would you shoot someone first, then stab them fourteen times?"

"That large a number would normally suggest an act of rage or a cold-blooded effort to create an appearance of rage. The exact number may be meaningless."

"But shooting him first . . ."

"It suggests that the purpose of the stabbing was something other than homicide."

"I don't follow you," said Kline, cocking his head like a curious bird.

"Mellery was shot at very close range. The bullet severed the carotid artery. There was no sign in the snow that the gun was dropped or thrown to the ground. Therefore the killer must have taken the time to remove the material he'd wrapped around it to deaden the sound and then replace the gun in a pocket or holster before switching to the broken bottle and getting in position to stab the victim—now lying in the snow unconscious. The arterial wound would have been spurting blood dramatically at that point. So why bother with the stabbing? It wasn't to kill the victim—who was, for all practical purposes, already dead. No, the perpetrator's objective must have been either to obliterate the evidence of the gunshot—"

"Why?" asked Kline, moving forward in his chair.

"I don't know why. It's just a possibility. But it's more likely, given the content of the notes preceding the attack and the trouble he took to bring the broken bottle, the stabbing has some ritual significance."

"Satanic?" Kline's expression of conventional horror poorly concealed his appetite for the media potential of such a motive.

"I doubt it. As crazy as the notes seem, they don't strike me as being crazy in that particular way. No, I mean 'ritual' in the sense that doing the murder in a specific way was important to him."

"A revenge fantasy?"

"Could be," said Gurney. "He wouldn't be the first killer to have spent months or years imagining how he was going to get even with someone."

Kline looked troubled. "If the key part of the attack was the stabbing, why bother with the gun?"

"Instant incapacity. He wanted it to be a sure thing, and a gun is a surer way than a broken bottle to incapacitate a victim. After all the planning that went into this business, he didn't want anything to go wrong."

Kline nodded, then jumped to another piece of the puzzle. "Rodriguez insists the murderer is one of the guests."

Gurney smiled. "Which one?"

"He's not ready to say, but that's where he's putting his money. You don't agree?"

"The idea is not completely crazy. The guests are housed on the institute grounds, which puts them all, if not at the scene, at least conveniently close to the scene. They're definitely an odd lot—druggy, emotionally erratic, at least one with major-league criminal connections."

"But?"

"There are practical problems."

"Like what?"

"Footprints and alibis, to begin with. Everyone agrees the snow began around dusk and continued until after midnight. The murderer's footprints entered the property from the public road after the snow had stopped completely."

"How can you be sure of that?"

"The prints are in the snow, but there's no new snow in the prints. For one of the guests to have made those prints, he would have to have left the main house before the snow fell, since there are no prints in the snow leading away from the house."

"In other words . . ."

"In other words, someone would have to have been missing from dusk to midnight. But no one was."

"How do you know that?"

"Officially, I don't. Let's just say I heard a rumor from Jack Hardwick. According to the interview summaries, every individual was seen by at least six other individuals at various times in the evening. So unless everyone is lying, everyone was present."

Kline looked reluctant to brush aside the possibility that everyone might be lying.

"Maybe someone in the house had help," he said.

"You mean maybe someone in the house hired a hit man?"

"Something like that."

"Then why be there at all?"

"I don't follow you."

"The only reason the current guests are under any suspicion at all is their physical proximity to the murder. If you were hiring an outsider to come in and do the murder, why put yourself in that proximity to begin with?"

"Excitement?"

"I guess that's conceivable," said Gurney with an obvious lack of enthusiasm.

"All right, let's forget about the guests for the moment," said Kline. "How about a mob hit set up by someone other than one of the guests?"

"Is that Rodriguez's backup theory?"

"He thinks it's a possibility. I gather from your expression that you don't."

"I don't see the logic of it. I don't think it would even come to mind if Patty Cakes didn't happen to be one of the guests. First, there's nothing currently known about Mark Mellery that could make him a mob target—"

"Wait a minute. Suppose the persuasive guru got one of his guests—someone like Patty Cakes—to confess something to him, you know, in the interest of inner harmony or spiritual peace or whatever bullshit Mellery was selling these people."

"And?"

"And maybe later, when he's home, the bad guy gets to thinking that he might have been a little rash with all that honesty and openness. Harmony with the universe might be a swell thing, but maybe not worth the risk of someone's having information that could cause you serious problems. Maybe when he's away from the charm of the guru, the bad guy reverts to thinking in more practical terms. Maybe he hires someone to eliminate the risk he's concerned about."

"Interesting hypothesis."

"But?"

"But there isn't a contract guy on earth who'd bother with the kind of mind games involved in this particular murder. Men who kill for money don't hang their boots from tree limbs and leave poems on corpses."

Kline looked like he might debate this but stopped when the door opened after a perfunctory knock. The sleek creature from the reception desk entered with a lacquered tray on which there were two china cups and saucers, an elegantly spouted pot, a delicate

sugar bowl and creamer, and a Wedgwood plate bearing four bis-
cotti. She set the tray on the coffee table.

"Rodriguez called," she said, glancing at Kline, then added, as if
answering a telepathic question, "He's on his way, said he'd be here
in a few minutes."

Kline looked at Gurney as if he were trying to read his reaction.
"Rod called me earlier," he explained. "He seemed eager to express
some opinions on the case. I suggested he drop by while you were
here. I like everyone to know everything at the same time. The more
we all know, the better. No secrets."

"Good idea," said Gurney, suspecting that Kline's motivation for
having them both there at the same time had nothing to do with
openness and everything to do with a penchant for managing by
conflict and confrontation.

Kline's assistant left the room, but not before Gurney caught the
knowing Mona Lisa smile on her face that confirmed his own view
of the situation.

Kline poured both coffees. The china looked antique and expensive, yet he handled it with neither pride nor concern, reinforcing
Gurney's impression that the wunderkind DA had been to the manner born, and law enforcement was a step toward something more
consistent with patrician birth. What was it Hardwick had whispered to him at yesterday's meeting? Something about a desire to be
governor? Maybe cynical old Hardwick was right again. Or maybe
Gurney was reading too much into how a man held a cup.

"By the way," said Kline, leaning back in his chair, "that bullet
in the wall, the one they thought was a .357—it wasn't. That was
just a guess based on the size of the hole in the wall before they dug
it out. Ballistics says it's actually a .38 Special."

"That's odd."

"Pretty common, actually. Standard sidearm in most police
departments until the 1980s."

"Common caliber, but an odd choice."

"I don't follow."

"The killer went to some trouble to muffle the sound of the shot, make it as quiet as possible. If noise was a major concern, a .38 Special was an odd weapon to choose. A .22 pistol would have made a lot more sense."

"Maybe it's the only weapon he had."

"Maybe."

"But you don't think so?"

"He's a perfectionist. He'd make absolutely sure he had the right gun."

Kline gave Gurney a cross-examiner's stare. "You're contradicting yourself. First you said that the evidence shows he wanted to keep the shot as quiet as possible. Then you said he picked the wrong gun to do that. Now you're saying he's not the kind of guy who'd pick the wrong gun."

"Keeping the shot quiet was important. But maybe something else was more important."

"Like what?"

"If there's a ritual aspect to this affair, then the choice of gun could be part of that. The obsession with carrying out the murder in a certain way could take precedence over the sound problem. He'd do it the way he felt compelled to do it and deal with the noise as best he could."

"When you say ritual, I hear psycho. Just how crazy do you think this guy is?"

"*Crazy* is not a term I find useful," said Gurney. "Jeffrey Dahmer was judged legally sane, and he ate his victims. David Berkowitz was judged legally sane, and he killed people because a satanic dog told him to."

"Is that what you think we're dealing with here?"

"Not exactly. Our killer is vengeful and obsessed—obsessed to the point of emotional derangement, but probably not to the point of eating body parts or taking orders from a dog. He's obviously very sick, but there's nothing in the notes that reflect the *DSM* criteria for psychosis."

There was a knock on the door.

Kline frowned thoughtfully, pursed his lips, seemed to be weighing Gurney's assessment—or perhaps he was just trying to look like a man not easily distracted by a mere knock on the door.

"Come in," he finally said in a loud voice.

The door opened, and Rodriguez entered. He couldn't entirely conceal his displeasure at seeing Gurney.

"Rod!" boomed Kline. "Good of you to come over. Have a seat."

Conspicuously avoiding the couch on which Gurney sat, he chose an armchair facing Kline.

The DA smiled heartily. Gurney guessed it was at the prospect of witnessing a clash of viewpoints.

"Rod wanted to drop by to share his current perspective on the case." He sounded like a referee introducing one fighter to another.

"I look forward to hearing it," said Gurney mildly.

Not mildly enough to keep Rodriguez from interpreting it as a provocation in disguise. He required no further urging to share his perspective.

"Everybody's focused on the trees," he said, loudly enough to be heard in a much larger room than Kline's office. "We're forgetting the forest!"

"The forest being . . . ?" asked Kline.

"The forest being the huge issue of opportunity. Everybody's getting tangled up in motive speculation and the crazy little details of the method. We're being distracted from Issue Number One—a houseful of drug addicts and other criminal slimebags with easy access to the victim."

Gurney wondered if this reaction was the result of the captain's feeling his control of the case threatened or if there was more to it.

"What are you suggesting should be done?" Kline asked.

"I'm having all the guests reinterviewed, and I'm having deeper background checks done. We're going to turn over some rocks in the lives of these cokehead creeps. I'm telling you right now—one of them did it, and it's only a matter of time until we find out which one."

"What do you think, Dave?" Kline's tone was almost too casual,

as though he were trying to hide the pleasure he derived from pro-
voking a battle.

"Reinterviews and background checks could be helpful," said
Gurney blandly.

"Helpful but not necessary?"

"We won't know until they're done. It could also be helpful to
address the question of opportunity, or access to the victim, in a
broader context—for example, inns or bed-and-breakfasts in the
immediate vicinity that might be almost as convenient as the guest
quarters of the institute."

"I'll lay odds it was a guest," said Rodriguez. "When a swimmer
disappears in shark-infested waters, it isn't because he was kid-
napped by a passing water-skier." He glared at Gurney, whose smile
he interpreted as a challenge. "Let's get real about this!"

"Are we looking into the bed-and-breakfasts, Rod?" asked Kline.

"We're looking into everything."

"Good. Dave, is there anything else that would be on your priority list?"

"Nothing that's not already in the pipeline. Lab work on the
blood; foreign fibers on and around the victim; brand, availability, and any peculiarities of the boots; ballistics matches on the bullet; analysis of the audio recording of the perp's call to Mellery,
with enhancements of the background sounds, and originating
transmission-tower ID if it was a cell call; landline and cell records
of the current guests; handwriting analysis of the notes, with paper
and ink IDs; psych profile based on communications and murder
MO; cross-check of the FBI's threatening-letters database. I think
that would cover it. Am I forgetting anything, Captain?"

Before Rodriguez could answer, which he seemed in no rush to do,
Kline's assistant opened the door and stepped into the office. "Excuse
me, sir," she said with a deference that seemed designed for public
consumption. "There is a Sergeant Wigg here to see the captain."

Rodriguez frowned.

"Send her in," said Kline, whose appetite for confrontation
seemed boundless.

The genderless redhead from the BCI headquarters meeting entered, wearing the same plain blue suit and carrying the same laptop.

"What do you want, Wigg?" asked Rodriguez, more annoyed than curious.

"We discovered something, sir, that I thought was important enough to bring to your attention."

"Well?"

"It's about the boots, sir."

"Boots?"

"The boots in the tree, sir."

"What about them?"

"May I place this on the coffee table?" asked Wigg, indicating her laptop.

Rodriguez looked at Kline. Kline nodded.

Thirty seconds and a few keystrokes later, the three men were looking at a split-screen pair of photos of apparently identical boot prints.

"The ones on the left are actual prints from the scene. The ones on the right are prints we made in the same snow with the boots recovered from the tree."

"So the boots that made the trail are the boots we found at the end of the trail. You didn't need to come all the way to this meeting to tell us that."

Gurney couldn't resist interrupting. "I think Sergeant Wigg came to tell us just the opposite."

"Are you saying the boots in the tree weren't the boots the killer wore?" asked Kline.

"That doesn't make any sense," said Rodriguez

"Very little in this case does," said Kline. "Sergeant?"

"The boots are the same brand, same style, same size. Both pairs are brand new. But they are definitely two separate pairs. Snow, especially snow within ten degrees of the freezing point, provides an excellent medium for registering detail. The relevant detail in this instance is this tiny deformity in this portion of the tread." She pointed with a sharp pencil to an almost invisible raised speck on the heel of the boot on the right, the one from the tree. "That deformity, which probably occurred during the manufacturing process, shows up on every print we made with this boot, but not on any of the prints at the scene. The only plausible explanation is that they were made by different boots."

"Surely there could be other explanations," said Rodriguez.

"What did you have in mind, sir?"

"I'm just pointing out the likelihood that something is being overlooked."

Kline cleared his throat. "For the sake of argument, let's assume Sergeant Wigg is right and we're dealing with two pairs—one worn by the perp and one left hanging in the tree at the end of the trail. What on earth does that mean? What does it tell us?"

Rodriguez eyed the computer screen resentfully. "Not a damn thing of any use in catching the killer."

"How about you, Dave?"

"It tells me the same thing as the note left on the body. It's just another kind of note. It says, 'Catch me if you can, but you can't, because I'm too smart for you.'"

"How the hell does a second pair of boots tell you that?" There was anger in Rodriguez's voice.

Gurney replied with an almost sleepy calmness—his characteristic reaction to anger as long as he could remember. "Alone, they wouldn't tell me anything. But add them to the other peculiar details and the whole picture looks more and more like an elaborate game."

"If it's a game, the goal is to distract us, and it's succeeding," sneered Rodriguez.

When Gurney did not respond, Kline prodded him. "You look like you might not agree with that."

"I think the game is more than a distraction. I think it's the whole point."

Rodriguez rose from his chair in disgust. "Unless you need me for anything else, Sheridan, I have to get back to my office."

After giving Kline a grim handshake, he left, followed after a short pause by Wigg. Kline concealed whatever reaction he had to the departure.

"So tell me," he said after a moment, leaning toward Gurney, "what should we be doing that we're not doing? Clearly you don't see the situation the way Rod does."

Gurney shrugged. "There's no harm in taking a closer look at the guests. It would need to be done at some point. But the captain has higher hopes than I do that it will lead to an arrest."

"You're saying it's essentially a waste of time?"

"It's a necessary process of elimination. I just don't think the murderer is one of the guests. The captain keeps emphasizing the importance of opportunity—the supposed convenience of the killer's being on the property. But I see it as an inconvenience—too great a chance of being seen leaving or returning to his room, too much stuff to be concealed. Where would he keep the lawn chair, boots, bottle, gun? The risks and complications would be unacceptable to this kind of individual."

Kline raised a curious eyebrow, and Gurney went on.

"On a disorganized-to-organized personality axis, this guy is off the scale on the organized end. His attention to detail is extraordinary."

"You mean like reweaving the webbing on the lawn chair to make it all white and reduce its visibility in the snow?"

"Yes. He's also very cool under pressure. He didn't run from the crime scene, he walked. The footprints from the patio to the woods are so unhurried you'd think he was out for a stroll."

"That frenzy of stabbing the victim with a shattered whiskey bottle doesn't sound cool to me."

"If it happened in a bar, you'd be right. But remember that the bottle was carefully prepared beforehand, even washed and wiped clean of fingerprints. I'd say the appearance of frenzy was as planned as everything else."

"Okay," agreed Kline slowly. "Cool, calm, organized. What else?"

"A perfectionist in the way he communicates. Well read—with a feeling for language and meter. Just between us, I'll go way out on a limb and say that the poems have an odd formality that feels to me like the affected gentility you sometimes see in first-generation sophistication."

"What on earth are you talking about?"

"The educated child of uneducated parents, desperate to set himself apart. But as I said, I'm out on a limb with that—way past any solid evidence."

"Anything else?"

"Mild-mannered on the outside, full of hate on the inside."

"And you don't think he's one of the guests?"

"No. From his point of view, the advantage of increased proximity would be trumped by the disadvantage of increased risk."

"You're a very logical man, Detective Gurney. Do you think the killer is that logical?"

"Oh, yes. As logical as he is pathological. Off the scale on both counts."

Chapter 28

Back to the scene
of the crime

Gurney's route home from Kline's office passed through Peony, so he decided to make a stop at the institute.

The temporary ID Kline's assistant had provided him with got him past the cop at the gate, no questions asked. As Gurney breathed in the chilly air, he reflected that the day was eerily similar to the morning after the murder. The layer of snow, which in the intervening days had partly melted away, was now restored. Nighttime flurries, common in the higher elevations of the Catskills, had freshened and whitened the landscape.

Gurney decided to rewalk the killer's route, thinking he might notice something about the surroundings he'd missed. He proceeded along the driveway, through the parking area, around to the back of the barn where the lawn chair was found. He looked about him, trying to understand why the killer chose that spot to sit. His concentration was broken by the sounds of a door opening and slamming and a harsh, familiar voice.

"Jesus Christ! We ought to call in an airstrike and level the fucking place."

Thinking it best to make his presence known, Gurney stepped through the high hedge that separated the barn area from the rear patio of the house. Sergeant Hardwick and Investigator Tom Cruise Blatt greeted him with unwelcoming stares.

"What the hell are you doing here?" asked Hardwick.

"Temporary arrangement with the DA. Just wanted to take another look at the scene. Sorry to interrupt, but I thought you might want to know I was here."

"In the bushes?"

"Behind the barn. I was standing where the killer was sitting."

"What for?"

"Better question would be what was *he* there for?"

Hardwick shrugged. "Lurking in the shadows? Taking a smoke break in his fucking lawn chair? Waiting for the right moment?"

"What would make the moment right?"

"What difference does it make?"

"I'm not sure. But why wait here? And why arrive at the scene so early you have to bring a chair with you?"

"Maybe he wanted to wait until the Mellerys went to sleep. Maybe he wanted to watch until all the lights went out."

"According to Caddy Mellery, they went to bed and turned out the lights hours earlier. And the phone call that woke them was almost certainly from the murderer—meaning that he wanted them awake, not asleep. And if he wanted to know whether the lights were out, why station himself in one of the few spots where he couldn't see the upstairs windows? In fact, from the position of that chair, he could barely have seen the house at all."

"What the hell is all that supposed to mean?" blustered Hardwick, his tone belied by an uneasy look in his eyes.

"It means either that a very smart, very careful perp went to great lengths to do something senseless or that our reconstruction of what happened here is wrong."

Blatt, who'd been following the conversation as if it were a tennis game, stared at Hardwick.

Hardwick looked like he was tasting something unpleasant. "Any chance you could track down some coffee?"

Blatt pursed his lips by way of complaint but retreated into the house, presumably to do what he was told.

Hardwick took his time lighting a cigarette. "There's something else that doesn't make sense. I was looking at a report on the footprint data. The spacing between the prints coming from the public road to the chair location behind the barn averages three inches greater than between the prints going from the body to the woods."

"Meaning that the perp was walking faster when he arrived than when he left?"

"Meaning exactly that."

"So he was in a bigger hurry to get to the barn and sit and wait than to get away from the scene after the murder?"

"That's Wigg's interpretation of the data, and I can't come up with another one."

Gurney shook his head. "I'm telling you, Jack, our lens is out of focus. And by the way, there's another odd bit of data bothering me. Where exactly was that whiskey bottle found?"

"About a hundred feet from the body, alongside the departing prints."

"Why there?"

"Because that's where he dropped it. What's the problem?"

"Why carry it there? Why not leave it by the body?"

"An oversight. In the heat of the moment, he didn't realize he still had it in his hand. When he noticed it, he tossed it. I don't see the problem."

"Maybe there isn't any. But the footprints are very regular, relaxed, unhurried—like everything was proceeding according to plan."

"What the hell are you getting at?" Hardwick was showing the frustration of a man trying to hold his groceries inside a ripped bag.

"Everything about the case feels super cool, super planned—very cerebral. My gut tells me that everything is where it is for a reason."

"You're telling me he carried the weapon a hundred feet away and dropped it there for a premeditated reason?"

"That would be my guess."

"What goddamn reason could he have?"

"What effect did it have on us?"

"What are you talking about?"

"This guy is as much focused on the police as he was on Mark Mellery. Has it occurred to you that the oddities of the crime scene might be part of a game he's playing with us?"

"No, that did not occur to me. Frankly, it's kind of far out."

Gurney restrained an urge to argue the point and said instead, "I gather Captain Rod still thinks our man is one of the guests."

"Yeah, 'one of the lunatics in the asylum' is how he puts it."

"You agree?"

"That they're lunatics? Absolutely. That one of them is the murderer? Maybe."

"And maybe not?"

"I'm not sure. But don't tell Rodriguez that."

"Does he have any favorite candidates?"

"Any of the drug addicts would be okay with him. He was going on yesterday about the Mellery Institute for Spiritual Renewal being nothing but a pricey spa for rich scumbags."

"I don't get the connection."

"Between what?"

"What exactly does drug addiction have to do with Mark Mellery's murder?"

Hardwick took a final thoughtful drag from his cigarette, then flicked the butt into the damp earth beneath the holly hedge. Gurney reflected that this was not the sort of thing one was supposed to do at a crime scene, even after it had been fine-combed, but it was exactly the sort of thing he'd gotten used to during their former collaboration. Nor was he surprised when Hardwick walked over to the hedge to extinguish the smoldering butt with the toe of his shoe. That was the way the man gave himself time to think about what he was going to say, or not say, next. When the butt was thoroughly extinguished and buried a good three inches in the soil, Hardwick spoke.

"Probably not much to do with the murder, but a lot to do with Rodriguez."

"Anything you can talk about?"

"He has a daughter in Greystone."

"The mental hospital down in New Jersey?"

"Yeah. She did some permanent damage. Club drugs, crystal meth, crack. Fried a few brain circuits, tried to kill her mother. The way Rodriguez sees it, every other drug addict in the world is responsible for what happened to her. It's not a subject he's rational about."

"So he thinks an addict killed Mellery?"

"That's the way he wants it to be, so that's what he thinks."

A damp, isolated gust of wind swept across the patio from the direction of the snow-covered lawn. Gurney shivered and stuck his hands deep into his jacket pockets. "I thought he just wanted to impress Kline."

"That, too. For a dickhead he's pretty complicated. Control freak. Nasty little bundle of ambition. Totally insecure. Obsessed with punishing addicts. Not too happy about you, by the way."

"Any specific reason?"

"Doesn't like deviations from standard procedure. Doesn't like smart guys. Doesn't like anyone closer to Kline than he is. Who the fuck knows what else?"

"Doesn't sound like the ideal frame of mind for leading an investigation."

"Yeah, well, what else is new in the wonderful world of criminal justice? But just because a guy is a fucked-up asshole doesn't mean he's always wrong."

Gurney contemplated this bit of Hardwickian wisdom without comment, then changed the subject. "Does the focus on the guests mean other avenues are being ignored?"

"Like what?"

"Like talking to people in the area. Motels, inns, B&Bs . . ."

"Nothing is being *ignored*," said Hardwick with sudden defensiveness. "The households in the vicinity—there aren't that many, less than a dozen on the road from the village up to the institute—were contacted within the first twenty-four hours, an effort that produced zero information. Nobody heard anything, saw anything, remembered anything. No strangers, no noises, no vehicles at odd hours, nothing out of the ordinary. Couple of people thought they heard coyotes. Couple more thought they heard a screech owl."

"What time was that?"

"What time was what?"

"The screech owl."

"I have no idea, because they had no idea. Middle of the night was as close as they could get."

"Lodging facilities?"

"What?"

"Did someone check the lodging facilities in the area?"

"There's one motel just outside the village—run-down place that caters to hunters. Empty that night. Only other places within a three-mile radius are two bed-and-breakfasts. One is closed for the winter. The other one, if I'm remembering right, had one room booked the night of the murder—some bird-watcher guy and his mother."

"Bird-watching in November?"

"Seemed odd to me, too, so I checked some bird-watching websites. Turns out the serious ones love the winter—foliage off the trees, better visibility, lots of pheasants, owls, grouse, chickadees, blah-blah-blah."

"You talked to the people?"

"Blatt spoke to one of the owners—pair of fags, silly names, no useful information."

"Silly names?"

"Yeah, one of them was Peachpit, something like that."

"Peachpit?"

"Something like that. No, Plumstone, that was it. Paul Plumstone. You believe that?"

"Anyone speak to the bird-watchers?"

"I think they'd left before Blatt stopped by, but don't quote me on that."

"No one followed up?"

"Jesus Christ! What the hell would they know about anything? You want to visit the Peachpits, be my guest. Name of the place is The Laurels, mile and a half down the mountain from the institute.

I have a certain amount of manpower assigned to this case, and I can't goddamn waste it chasing after every warm body that ever passed through Peony."

"Right."

The meaning of Gurney's reply was vague at best, but it seemed to somehow appease Hardwick, who said in a tone that was almost cordial, "Speaking of manpower, I need to get back to work. What did you say you were doing here?"

"I thought if I walked around the grounds again, something might occur to me."

"That's the methodology of the NYPD's ace crime solver? That's pathetic!"

"I know, Jack, I know. But right now it's the best I can do."

Hardwick went back into the house shaking his head in exaggerated disbelief.

Gurney inhaled the moist smell of the snow, and, as always, it displaced for a moment all rational thoughts, stirring a powerful childhood emotion for which he had no words. He set out across the white lawn toward the woods, the snow smell flooding him with memories—memories of stories his father had read to him when he was five or six years old, stories that were more vivid to him than anything in his actual life—stories about pioneers, cabins in the wilderness, trails in the forest, good Indians, bad Indians, snapped twigs, moccasin impressions in the grass, the broken stem of a fern offering crucial evidence of the enemy's passage, and the cries of the forest birds, some real, some mimicked by the Indians as coded communications—images so concrete, so richly detailed. It was ironic, he thought, how the memories of the stories his father had told him in early childhood had replaced most of his memories of the man himself. Of course, other than telling him those stories, his father had never had much to do with him. Mainly his father worked. Worked and kept to himself.

Worked and kept to himself. This life-summarizing phrase, it struck Gurney, described his own behavior as accurately as it did his father's. The barriers he'd once erected against recognizing such similarities seemed lately to be developing large leaks. He suspected not just that he was becoming his father but that he had done so long ago. *Worked and kept to himself.* What a small and chilly sense of his life it conveyed. How humiliating it was to see how much of one's time on earth could be captured in so short a sentence. What sort of husband was he if his energies were so circumscribed? And what sort of father? What sort of father is so absorbed in his professional priorities that . . . No, enough of that.

Gurney walked into the woods, following what he recalled to be the route of the footprints, now obscured by the new snow. When he came to the evergreen thicket where the trail had, implausibly, ended, he inhaled the piney fragrance, listened to the deep silence of the place, and waited for inspiration. None came. Chagrined at expecting otherwise, he forced himself to review for the twentieth time what he actually knew about the events of the night of the murder. That the killer had entered the property on foot from the public road? That he was carrying a .38 Police Special, a broken Four Roses bottle, a lawn chair, an extra pair of boots, and a mini tape player with the animal screeches that got Mellery out of bed? That he was wearing Tyvek coveralls, gloves, and a thick goose-down jacket he could use to muffle the gunshot? That he sat behind the barn smoking cigarettes? That he got Mellery to come out onto the patio, shot him dead, then stabbed the body at least fourteen times? That he then walked calmly across the open lawn and half a mile into the woods, hung an extra pair of boots from a tree branch, and disappeared without a trace?

Gurney's face had worked itself into a grimace—partly because of the damp, darkening chill of the day and partly because now, more clearly than ever, he realized that what he "knew" about the crime didn't make a damn bit of sense.

Chapter 29

Backwards

November was his least favorite month, a month of waning light, an uncertain month shambling between autumn and winter.

This sense of the season seemed to exacerbate the feeling that he was stumbling around in a fog on the Mellery case, blind to something right in front of him.

When he arrived home from Peony that day, he decided, uncharacteristically, to share his confusion with Madeleine, who was sitting at the pine table over the remains of tea and cranberry cake.

"I'd love to get your input on something," he said, immediately regretting his word choice. Madeleine was not fond of terms like *input*.

She tilted her head curiously, which he took as an invitation.

"The Mellery Institute sits on a hundred acres between Filchers Brook Road and Thornbush Lane in the hills above the village. There are about ninety acres of woods, maybe ten acres of lawns, flower beds, a parking area, and three buildings—the main lecture center, which also includes the offices and guest rooms, the private Mellery residence, and a barn for maintenance equipment."

Madeleine raised her eyes to the clock on the kitchen wall, and he hurried on. "The responding officers found a set of footprints that entered the property from Filchers Brook Road and led to a chair behind the barn. From the chair they led to the spot where Mellery was killed and from there to a location half a mile away in the woods, where they stopped. No more footprints. No hint of how the individual who left the prints up to that point could have gotten away without leaving any further prints."

"Is this a joke?"

"I'm describing the actual evidence at the scene."

"What about the other road you mentioned?"

"Thornbush Lane is over a hundred feet from the last footprint."

"The bear came back," said Madeleine after a short silence.

"What?" Gurney stared at her, uncomprehending.

"The bear." She nodded toward the side window.

Between the window and their dormant, rime-encrusted garden beds, a steel shepherd's-crook support for a finch feeder had been bent to the ground, and the feeder itself had been broken in half.

"I'll take care of it later," said Gurney, annoyed at the irrelevant comment. "Do you have any reaction to the footprint problem?"

Madeleine yawned. "I think it's silly, and the person who did it is crazy."

"But how did he do it?"

"It's like the number trick."

"What do you mean?"

"I mean, what difference does it make how he did it?"

"Tell me more," said Gurney, his curiosity slightly greater than his irritation.

"*How* doesn't matter. The question is *why*, and the answer is obvious."

"And the obvious answer is . . . ?"

"He wants to prove that you're a pack of idiots."

Her answer put Gurney in two emotional places at once—pleased that she agreed with him that the police were targets in the case, but not so pleased with how much emphasis she put on *idiots*.

"Maybe he walked backwards," she suggested with a shrug. "Maybe where you think the footprints went is where they came from, and where you think they came from is where they went."

It was among the possibilities that Gurney had considered and dismissed. "There are two problems. First, it just moves the question of how the prints could stop in the middle of nowhere to how they could start in the middle of nowhere. Second, the tracks are very evenly spaced. It's hard to imagine someone walking backwards half a mile through the woods without stumbling even once."

Then it occurred to him that even the smallest sign of interest from Madeleine was something he'd like to encourage, so he added warmly, "But actually, it's a pretty interesting thought—so please keep thinking."

At two o'clock the following morning, gazing at the rectangle of his bedroom window, faintly illuminated by a quarter moon behind a cloud, Gurney was the one who was still thinking—and still pondering Madeleine's observation that the direction in which the footprints pointed and the direction in which they had actually traveled were separate matters. That was true, but how did it help in the interpretation of the data? Even if someone could walk that far backwards over uneven terrain without a single misstep, which no one could, that hypothesis only served to turn the inexplicable ending of the trail into an inexplicable beginning.

Or did it?

Suppose . . .

But that would be unlikely. Still, just suppose for the moment . . .

To quote Sherlock Holmes, "When you have eliminated the impossible, whatever remains, however improbable, must be the truth."

"Madeleine?"

"Hmm?"

"Sorry to wake you. It's important."

Her answer was a long sigh.

"Are you awake?"

"I am now."

"Listen. Suppose the killer enters the property not from the main road but from the back road. Suppose he arrives several hours before the crime—in fact, just before it starts to snow. Suppose he walks into the little pine grove from the back road with his little lawn chair and other paraphernalia, puts on his Tyvek jumpsuit and his latex gloves, and waits."

"In the woods?"

"In the pine grove, at the spot where we thought the footprints ended. He sits there and waits until the snow stops—a little after midnight. Then he gets up, takes his chair, whiskey bottle, gun, and mini tape player with the animal screeches, and walks the half mile to the house. On the way he calls Mellery on his cell phone to make sure he's awake enough to hear the animal noises—"

"Wait a minute. I thought you said he couldn't walk backwards through the woods."

"He didn't. He didn't have to. You were right to separate the toe-heel orientation of the footprints from their actual direction—but we need to make one more separation. Suppose the soles of the shoes were separated from the uppers."

"How?"

"All the killer had to do was cut the soles off one pair of boots and glue them on another pair—backwards. Then he could walk forward easily and leave a neat trail of impressions behind him that seemed to be going in the direction he was coming from."

"And the lawn chair?"

"He takes it to the patio. Maybe lays his various items on it while he wraps the goose-down parka around his gun as a partial silencer. The chair marks could easily be obscured by his own footprints, so no one would see them later. Then he plays his tape of the screeching animals to bring Mellery to the back door. There are variations in exactly how all this could be done, but the bottom line is he gets Mellery out onto the patio at gunpoint and shoots him. When Mellery goes down, the killer takes the broken bottle and stabs him repeatedly. Then he tosses the bottle back toward the footprints he made on his way to the patio—footprints that, of course, point away from the patio."

"Why not just leave it by the body—or take it with him?"

"He didn't take it because he wanted us to find it. The whiskey bottle is part of the game, part of what this whole thing is about. And it would be my guess that he threw it alongside the seemingly departing footprints to put the icing on the cake of that particular little deception."

"That's a pretty subtle detail."

"Like the subtle detail of leaving a pair of boots at what seemed to be the end of the trail—but, of course, he left them there as he was starting out."

"So they weren't the boots that made the tracks?"

"No, but we already knew that. There's a tech at the BCI lab who found a tiny difference between the tread of one of the boots and the imprints left in the snow. At first it made no sense. But it fits this revised version of the facts—perfectly."

Madeleine said nothing for a few moments, but he could almost feel her mind absorbing, evaluating, testing the new scenario for weak points.

"So after he tosses the bottle, what then?"

"Then he goes from the patio to the back of the barn, sets the lawn chair there, and tosses a handful of cigarette butts on the ground in front of it to make it look like he'd been sitting there before the murder. He takes off the Tyvek suit and latex gloves, puts his parka on, walks around the far side of barn—leaving those goddamn backwards footprints—heads out onto Filchers Brook Road, which the town has plowed, so no prints are left there, and walks to his car on Thornbush Lane, or down to the village, or wherever."

"Did the Peony police see anyone when they were on their way up the road?"

"Apparently not, but he could easily have stepped into the woods, or . . ." He paused to consider the options.

"Or . . . ?"

"It's not the most likely possibility, but I've been told there's a bed-and-breakfast place on the mountain that BCI was supposed to be checking. It sounds bizarre after nearly hacking his victim's head off, but our homicidal maniac may simply have strolled back to a cozy little B&B."

They lay silently side by side in the dark for several long minutes, Gurney's mind racing back and forth over his reconstruction of the crime like a man who has just launched a homebuilt boat and is checking it intently for possible leaks. When he was confident there were no major holes, he asked Madeleine what she thought.

"The perfect adversary," she said.

"What?"

"The perfect adversary."

"Meaning?"

"You love puzzles. So does he. A marriage made in heaven."

"Or hell?"

"Whichever. By the way, there's something wrong with those notes."

"Wrong with . . . what?"

Madeleine had a way of skipping through a chain of associations that sometimes left him a long step behind.

"The notes you showed me, from the killer to Mellery—the first two, and then the poems. I was trying to remember exactly what was in each one."

"And?"

"And I was having a hard time, even though I have a good memory. Then I realized why. There's nothing real in them."

"What do you mean?"

"There are no specifics. No mention of what Mellery actually did or who was hurt. Why so vague? No names, dates, places, no concrete references to anything. Peculiar, isn't it?"

"The numbers six fifty-eight and nineteen were pretty specific."

"But they didn't mean anything to Mellery, other than the fact that he'd thought of them. And that had to be a trick."

"If it was, I haven't been able to figure it out."

"Ah, but you will. You're very good at connecting the dots." She yawned. "No one's better at it than you." There was no detectable irony in her voice.

He lay there in the dark next to her, relaxing ever so briefly in the comfort of her praise. Then his mind began combing restlessly through the killer's notes, reviewing their language in the light of her observation.

"They were specific enough to scare the shit out of Mellery," he said.

She sighed sleepily. "Or unspecific enough."

"Meaning what?"

"I don't know. Maybe there was no specific event to be specific about."

"But if Mellery didn't do anything, why was he killed?"

She made a little sound in her throat that was the equivalent of a shrug. "I don't know. I just know there's something wrong with those notes. Time to go back to sleep."

Chapter 30

Emerald cottage

He awoke at dawn feeling better than he had for weeks, maybe months. It might be an exaggeration to say that his explanation of the boot mystery meant that the first domino had fallen, but that was the way it felt as he drove across the county, eastward into the rising sun, on his way to the B&B on Filchers Brook Road in Peony.

It occurred to him that interviewing "the fags" without clearing it with Kline's office or with BCI might be stretching the rules. But what the hell—if someone wanted to slap his wrist later, he'd survive. Besides, he had a feeling that things were starting to go his way. *"There is a tide in the affairs of men . . ."*

With less than a mile to go to the Filchers Brook intersection, his phone rang. It was Ellen Rackoff.

"District Attorney Kline got some news he wanted you to know about. He said to tell you that Sergeant Wigg from the BCI lab did an enhancement of the tape Mark Mellery made of the phone call he got from the killer. Are you familiar with the call?"

"Yes," said Gurney, recalling the disguised voice and Mellery thinking of the number nineteen, then finding that number in the letter the killer had left in his mailbox.

"Sergeant Wigg's report says that the sound-wave analysis shows that the background traffic noises on the tape were prerecorded."

"Say that again?"

"According to Wigg, the tape contains two generations of sounds. The caller's voice and the background sound of a motor, which she says was definitely an automobile engine, were first generation. That is, they were live sounds at the time of the call transmission. But the other background sounds, primarily of passing traffic, were second generation. That is, they were being played on a tape machine during the live call. Are you there, Detective?"

"Yes, yes, I was just . . . trying to make some sense out of that."

"Would you like me to repeat it?"

"No, I heard you. It's . . . very interesting."

"District Attorney Kline thought you might think so. He'd like you to give him a call when you figure out what it means."

"I'll be sure to do that."

He turned up Filchers Brook Road and a mile later spotted a sign on his left proclaiming the manicured property behind it to be THE LAURELS. The sign was a graceful oval plaque, with the lettering in a delicate calligraphy. A little past the sign, there was an arched trellis set in a row of high mountain laurels. A narrow driveway passed through the trellis. Although the blossoms had been gone for months, as Gurney drove through the opening, some trick of the mind conjured up a flowery scent, and a further leap brought to mind King Duncan's comment on Macbeth's estate, where that night he would be murdered: *"This castle hath a pleasant seat . . ."*

Beyond the trellis there was a small parking area of gravel raked as cleanly as a Zen garden. A path of the same pristine gravel led from the parking area to the front door of a spotless, cedar-shingled Cape. In place of a doorbell, there was an antique iron knocker. As Gurney reached for it, the door opened to reveal a small man with alert, assessing eyes. Everything about him looked freshly laundered, from his lime polo shirt to his pink skin to the hair a shade too blond for his middle-aged face.

"Ahh!" he said with the edgy satisfaction of a man whose pizza order, twenty minutes late, has finally arrived.

"Mr. Plumstone?"

"No, I'm not Mr. Plumstone," said the small man. "I'm Bruce

Wellstone. The apparent harmony between the names is purely coincidental."

"I see," said Gurney, baffled.

"And you, I assume, are the policeman?"

"Special Investigator Gurney, district attorney's office. Who told you I was coming?"

"The policeman on the phone. I have absolutely no memory for names. But why are we standing in the doorway? Do come in."

Gurney followed him through a short hallway into a sitting room furnished with fussy Victoriana. Wondering who the policeman on the phone might have been put a quizzical look in his eyes.

"I'm sorry," said Wellstone, evidently misinterpreting Gurney's expression. "I'm not familiar with the procedure in cases like this. Would you prefer to go directly to Emerald Cottage?"

"Excuse me?"

"Emerald Cottage."

"What emerald cottage?"

"The scene of the crime."

"What crime?"

"Didn't they tell you anything?"

"About what?"

"About why you're here."

"Mr. Wellstone, I don't mean to be rude, but perhaps you should start at the beginning and tell me what you're talking about."

"This is exasperating! I told everything to the sergeant on the phone. In fact, I told him everything twice, since he didn't seem to grasp what I was saying."

"I see your frustration, sir, but perhaps you could tell me what you told him?"

"That my ruby slippers were stolen. Do you have any idea what they're worth?"

"Your ruby slippers?"

"My God, they didn't tell you a blessed thing, did they?" Wellstone began taking deep breaths as though he might be trying to ward off some kind of fit. Then he closed his eyes. When he reopened them, he seemed reconciled to the ineptitude of the police and spoke to Gurney in the voice of an elementary-school teacher.

"My ruby slippers, which are worth a great deal of money, were stolen from Emerald Cottage. Although I have no proof, I have no doubt they were stolen by the last guest who occupied it."

"This Emerald Cottage is part of this establishment?"

"Of course it is. The entire property is called 'The Laurels,' for obvious reasons. There are three buildings—the main house in which we stand, plus two cottages: Emerald Cottage and Honeybee Cottage. The decor of Emerald Cottage is based on *The Wizard of Oz*—the greatest film ever made." A glint in his eyes seemed to dare Gurney to disagree. "The focal point of the decor was a remarkable reproduction pair of Dorothy's magic slippers. I discovered this morning that they were missing."

"And you reported this to . . . ?"

"To you people, obviously, because here you are."

"You called the Peony police department?"

"Well, I certainly didn't call the Chicago police department."

"We have two separate problems here, Mr. Wellstone. The Peony police will no doubt get back to you regarding the theft. That's not why I'm here. I'm investigating a different matter, and I need to ask some questions. A state police detective who came by the other day was told—by a Mr. Plumstone, I believe—that three nights ago you had a pair of bird-watchers as guests here—a man and his mother."

"That's the one!"

"What one?"

"The one who stole my ruby slippers!"

"The bird-watcher stole your slippers?"

"The bird-watcher, the burglar, the pilfering little bastard—yes, him!"

"And the reason this was not mentioned to the detective from the state police . . . ?"

"It wasn't mentioned because it wasn't known. I told you I only discovered the theft this morning."

"So you weren't in the cottage since the man and his mother checked out?"

"'Checked out' is a rather too-formal way of saying it. They simply departed at some point during the day. They'd paid in advance, so there was no need, you see, for any 'checking-out' procedure. We strive for a certain civilized informality here, which of course makes the betrayal of our trust all the more galling." Talking about it had brought Wellstone close to gagging on the gall.

"Was it normal to wait so long before . . . ?"

"Before making up a room? Normal at this time of year. November is our slowest month. The next booking for Emerald Cottage is Christmas week."

"The BCI man didn't go through the cottage?"

"BCI man?"

"The detective who was here two days ago was from the Bureau of Criminal Investigation."

"Ah. Well, he spoke to Mr. Plumstone, not to me."

"Who exactly is Mr. Plumstone?"

"That's an awfully good question. That's a question I've been asking myself." He said this with an arch bitterness, then shook his head. "I'm sorry, I mustn't let extraneous emotional issues intrude into official police business. Paul Plumstone is my business partner. We are joint owners of The Laurels. At least we are partners as of this moment."

"I see," said Gurney. "Getting back to my question—did the BCI man go through the cottage?"

"Why would he? I mean, he was apparently here about that ghastly business up the mountain at the institute, wanting to know if we'd seen any suspicious characters lurking about. Paul—Mr. Plumstone—told him that we hadn't, and the detective left."

"He didn't press you for any specific information on your guests?"

"The bird-watchers? No, of course not."

"Of course not?"

"The mother was a semi-invalid, and the son, although he turned out to be a thief, was hardly a mayhem-and-carnage sort of person."

"What sort of person would you say he was?"

"I would have said he was on the frail side. Definitely on the frail side. Shy."

"Would you say he was gay?"

Wellstone looked thoughtful. "Interesting question. I'm almost always sure, one way or the other, but in this case I'm not. I got the impression that he wanted to give me the impression he was gay. But that doesn't make much sense, does it?"

Not unless the whole persona was an act, thought Gurney. "Other than frail and shy, how else would you describe him?"

"Larcenous."

"I mean from a physical point of view."

Wellstone frowned. "A mustache. Tinted glasses."

"Tinted?"

"Like sunglasses, dark enough so you couldn't really see his eyes—I hate talking to someone when I can't see their eyes, don't you?—but light enough so he could wear them indoors."

"Anything else?"

"Woolly hat—one of those Peruvian things pulled down around his face—scarf, bulky coat."

"How did you get the impression he was frail?"

Wellstone's frown tightened into a kind of consternation. "His voice? His manner? You know, I'm not really sure. All I remember seeing—actually *seeing*—was a big puffy coat and hat, sunglasses, and a mustache." His eyes widened with sudden umbrage. "Do you think it was a disguise?"

Sunglasses and a mustache? To Gurney it sounded more like a parody of a disguise. But even that little extra twist could fit the weirdness of the pattern. Or was he over-thinking it? Either way, if it was a disguise, it was an effective one, leaving them with no useful physical description. "Can you recall anything else about him? Anything at all?"

"Obsessed with our little feathered friends. Had an enormous pair of binoculars—looked like those infrared things you see commandos in the movies creeping around with. Left his mother in the cottage and spent all his time in the woods, searching for grosbeaks—rose-breasted grosbeaks."

"He told you that?"

"Oh, yes."

"That's surprising."

"Why?"

"There aren't any rose-breasted grosbeaks in the Catskills in the winter."

"But he even said . . . That lying bastard!"

"He even said what?"

"The morning before he left, he came into the main house, and he couldn't stop raving about the damn grosbeaks. He kept repeating over and over that he had seen four rose-breasted grosbeaks. Four rose-breasted grosbeaks, he kept saying, as though I were doubting him."

"Maybe he wanted to be sure you'd remember," said Gurney, half to himself.

"But you're telling me he couldn't have seen them, because there aren't any to be seen. Why would he want me to remember something that didn't happen?"

"Good question, sir. May I take a quick look at the cottage now?"

From the sitting room, Wellstone led him through an equally Victorian dining room, full of ornate oak chairs and mirrors, out a side door onto a pathway whose spotless cream-colored pavers, while not exactly the yellow brick road of Oz, did bring it to mind. The path ended at a storybook cottage covered with English ivy, bright green despite the season.

Wellstone unlocked the door, swung it open, and stood to the side. Instead of entering, Gurney looked in from the threshold. The front room was partly a living room and partly a shrine to the film—with its collection of posters, a witch hat, a magic wand, Cowardly Lion and Tin Man figurines, and a stuffed replica of Toto.

"Would you like to go in and see the display case the slippers were taken from?"

"I'd rather not," said Gurney, stepping back onto the path. "If you're the only person who's been inside since your guests left, I'd like to keep it that way until we can get an evidence-processing team on site."

"But you said you weren't here for—Wait a minute, you said you were here for 'a different matter'—isn't that what you said?"

"Yes, sir, that's correct."

"What sort of 'evidence processing' are you talking about? I mean, what . . . Oh, no, surely you can't think that my light-fingered bird-watcher is your Jack the Ripper?"

"Frankly, sir, I have no reason to think he is. But I have to cover every possibility, and it would be prudent for us to have the cottage examined more closely."

"My, oh, my. I don't know what to say. If it's not one crime, it's another. Well, I suppose I can't impede police progress—outlandish as it seems. And there's a silver lining. Even if all this has nothing to do with the horror on the hill, you may end up finding a clue to my missing slippers."

"Always a possibility," said Gurney with a polite smile. "You can expect an evidence team here sometime tomorrow. Meanwhile keep the door locked. Now, let me ask you once more—because this is very important—are you sure no one but yourself has been inside the cottage during the past two days, not even your partner?"

"Emerald Cottage was my creation and my exclusive responsibility. Mr. Plumstone is responsible for Honeybee Cottage, including its unfortunate decor."

"Sorry?"

"The theme of Honeybee Cottage is a bore-you-blind illustrated history of beekeeping. Need I say more?"

"One last question, sir. Do you have the bird-watcher's name and address in your guest register?"

"I have the name and the address he gave me. Considering the theft, I rather doubt their authenticity."

"I'd better look at the register and make a note of them, anyway."

"Oh, there's no need to look at the register. I can see it now with perfect, painful clarity. Mr. and Mrs.—odd way, don't you think, for a gentleman to describe himself and his mother?—Mr. and Mrs. Scylla. The address was a post-office box in Wycherly, Connecticut. I can even give you the box number."

Chapter 31

A routine call from
the Bronx

Gurney was sitting in the spotless gravel parking area. He'd completed his call to BCI for an evidence team to be sent to The Laurels ASAP and was just slipping his cell phone into his pocket when it rang. It was Ellen Rackoff again. First he gave her the news about the Scylla couple and the peculiar theft to pass along to Kline. Then he asked why she'd called. She gave him a phone number.

"It's a homicide detective from the Bronx who wants to talk to you about a case he's working on."

"He wants to talk to me?"

"He wants to talk to someone on the Mellery case, which he read about in the paper. He called the Peony police, who referred him to BCI, who referred him to Captain Rodriguez, who referred him to the district attorney, who referred him to you. His name is Detective Clamm. Randy Clamm."

"Is that a joke?"

"I wouldn't know about that."

"How much information did he volunteer about his own case?"

"Zero. You know how cops are. Mostly he wanted to know about our case."

Gurney called the number. It was answered on the first ring.

"Clamm."

"Dave Gurney, returning your call. I'm with the district attor—"

"Yes, sir, I know. Appreciate the quick response."

Although he was basing it on next to nothing, Gurney had a vivid impression of the cop on the other end—a fast-thinking, fast-talking multitasker who, with better connections, might have ended up at West Point instead of the police academy.

"I understand you're on the Mellery homicide," the crisp young voice raced on.

"Correct."

"Multiple stab wounds to the victim's throat?"

"Correct."

"Reason for my call is a similar homicide down here, and we wanted to rule out the possibility of any connection."

"By similar, you mean—"

"Multiples to the throat."

"My recollection of Bronx stabbing statistics is that there are over a thousand reported incidents a year. Have you looked for connections closer to home?"

"We're looking. But so far your case is the only one with over a dozen wounds, all to the same part of the body."

"What can I do for you?"

"Depends on what you're willing to do. I was thinking it might help both of us if you were able to come down here for a day, look at the crime scene, sit in on an interview with the widow, ask questions, see if anything rings a bell."

It was the definition of a long shot—more far-fetched than many a tenuous lead he'd wasted his time chasing down in his years at the NYPD. But it was a constitutional impossibility for Dave Gurney to ignore a possibility, however flimsy it might be.

He agreed to meet Detective Clamm in the Bronx the following morning.

Part Three

Back to the Beginning

Chapter 32

The cleansing to come

The young man leaned back into the deliciously soft pillows propped against the headboard and smiled placidly at the screen of his laptop.

"Where's my little Dickie Duck?" asked the old woman next to him in the bed.

"He's in his happy beddy-bye, planning how the monsters die."

"Are you writing a poem?"

"Yes, Mother."

"Read it out loud."

"It isn't finished."

"Read it out loud," she said again, as though she'd forgotten she'd said it before.

"It's not very good. It needs something more." He adjusted the angle of the screen.

"You have such a beautiful voice," she said as if by rote, absently touching the blond ringlets of her wig.

He closed his eyes for a moment. Then, as though he were about to play a flute, he licked his lips lightly. When he began to speak, it was in a lilting half-whisper.

"These are some of my favorite things:
the magic change a bullet brings,
the blood that spurts out on the floor
until there isn't any more,

their eyes for an eye, their teeth for a tooth,
the end of it all, their moment of truth,
the good that I've done with that drunkard's gun—
all nothing compared to the cleansing to come."

He sighed and stared at the screen, wrinkling his nose. *"The meter isn't right."*

The old woman nodded with serene incomprehension and asked in a coy little-girl voice, *"What will my little Dickie do?"*

He was tempted to describe "the cleansing to come" in all the detail in which he imagined it. The death of all the monsters. It was so colorful, so exciting, so . . . satisfying! But he also prided himself on his realism, his grasp of his mother's limitations. He knew that her questions required no specific answers, that she forgot most of them as soon as she uttered them, that his words were mainly sounds, sounds she liked, found soothing. He could say anything—count to ten, recite a nursery rhyme. It really made no difference what he said, so long as he said it with feeling and rhythm. He always strove for a certain richness of inflection. He enjoyed pleasing her.

Chapter 33

A hell of a night

Every so often Gurney would have a dream that was achingly sad, a dream that seemed to be the heart of sadness itself. In these dreams he saw with a clarity beyond words that the wellspring of sadness was loss, and the greatest loss was the loss of love.

In the most recent version of the dream, little more than a vignette, his father was dressed as he'd been dressed for work forty years ago and in all respects looked exactly as he had then. The nondescript beige jacket and gray pants, the fading freckles on the backs of his large hands and on his rounded receding forehead, the mocking look in the eyes that seemed focused on a scene occurring somewhere else, the subtle suggestion of a restlessness to be on his way, to be anywhere but where he was, the odd fact that he said so little yet managed to convey with his silence so much dissatisfaction—all these buried images were resurrected in a scene that lasted no more than a minute. And then Gurney was part of the scene as a child, looking at that distant figure pleadingly, pleading with him not to leave, warm tears streaming down his face in the intensity of the dream—as he was sure they'd never done in the actual presence of his father, for he could not remember a single expression of strong emotion ever passing between them—and then awakening suddenly, his face still bathed in tears, his heart hurting.

He was tempted to wake Madeleine, tell her about the dream, let her see his tears. But it had nothing to do with her. She'd barely known his father. And dreams, after all, were only dreams. Ultimately they meant nothing. Instead he asked himself what day it was. It was Thursday. With this thought came that quick, practical transformation of his mental landscape that he'd come to rely on to sweep away the residue of a disturbing night and replace it with the reality of things to be done in the daylight. Thursday. Thursday would be occupied mainly with his trip to the Bronx—to a neighborhood not far from the neighborhood where he'd grown up.

Chapter 34

A dark day

The three-hour drive was a journey into ugliness, a perception amplified by the cold drizzle that required continual adjustment of the intermittent wiper speed. Gurney was depressed and edgy—partly because of the weather and partly, he suspected, because his dream had left him with a raw, oversensitive perspective.

He hated the Bronx. He hated everything about the Bronx—from the buckled pavements to the burned-out carcasses of stolen cars. He hated the garish billboards touting four-day, three-night escapes to Las Vegas. He hated the smell—a shifting miasma of diesel fumes, mold, tar, and dead fish, with an insinuating undertone of something metallic. Even more than what he saw, he hated the memory from his childhood that invaded his mind whenever he was in the Bronx—hideous, prehistorically armored horseshoe crabs with spearlike tails, lurking in the mudflats of Eastchester Bay.

Having spent half an hour creeping across the clogged "expressway" to the last exit, he was relieved to negotiate the few city blocks to the agreed-upon meeting place—the parking lot of Holy Saints Church. The lot was enclosed by a chain-link fence with a sign warning that parking was reserved for those engaged in church business. The lot was empty except for a nondescript Chevy sedan, beside which a young man with a fashionably gelled crew cut was speaking into a cell phone. As Gurney parked his car on the other side of the Chevy, the man concluded his call and clipped the phone to his belt.

The drizzle that had shrouded most of his drive that morning had diminished to a mist too fine to see, but as Gurney stepped from his car, he could feel its cold pinpricks on his forehead. Perhaps the young man was feeling it, too; perhaps that accounted for his expression of anxious discomfort.

"Detective Gurney?"

"Dave," said Gurney, extending his hand.

"Randy Clamm. Thanks for making the trip. Hope it's not a waste of your time. Just trying to cover all the bases, and we've got this crazy MO that sounded like what you guys are working on. Could be unrelated—I mean, it doesn't make much sense that the same guy would want to kill some hotshot guru upstate and an unemployed night watchman in the Bronx—but all those stab wounds in the throat, I couldn't just let it go. You get a feeling about these things—you think, 'Christ, if I let it go, it'll turn out to be the same guy,' you know what I mean?"

Gurney wondered whether the breathless pace of Clamm's speech was propelled by caffeine, cocaine, the pressures of the job, or just the way his personal spring happened to be wound.

"I mean, a dozen stab wounds to the throat isn't all that common. There might be other connections we could find between the cases. Maybe we could have sent reports back and forth between here and upstate, but I thought maybe if you were on the scene and you could talk to the victim's wife, you might see something or ask something that might not occur to you if you weren't here. That's what I was hoping. I mean, I hope there might be something in it. I hope it's not a waste of your time."

"Slow down, son. Let me tell you something. I drove here today because it seemed like a reasonable thing to do. You want to check out every possibility. So do I. The worst-case scenario here is that we eliminate one of those possibilities, and eliminating possibilities is not a waste of time, it's part of the process. So don't worry about my time."

"Thank you, sir, I just meant . . . I mean, I know it was a long drive for you. I do appreciate that." Clamm's voice and manner had settled down a notch or two. He still had a revved-up, nervous look, but at least it wasn't off the charts.

"Speaking of time," said Gurney, "would now be a good time to take me to the scene?"

"Now would be great. Better leave your car here, come in mine. Victim's house is in a cramped little area—some of the streets give you like two inches clearance each side of the car."

"Sounds like Flounder Beach."

"You know Flounder Beach?"

Gurney nodded. He'd been there once, when he was a teenager, at a girl's birthday party—a friend of a girl he was going steady with.

"How do you know Flounder Beach?" asked Clamm as he turned out of the parking lot in the opposite direction from the main avenue.

"I grew up not far from here—out by City Island."

"No shit. I thought you were from upstate."

"At the moment," said Gurney. He heard the temporariness of the phrase he'd chosen and realized he wouldn't have put it that way in front of Madeleine.

"Well, it's still the same nasty little bungalow colony. At high tide with a blue sky, you could almost think you were at a real beach. Then the tide goes out, the mud stinks, and you remember it's the Bronx."

"Right," said Gurney.

Five minutes later they slowed to a stop on a dusty side street facing an opening in another chain-link fence like the one that enclosed the church parking lot. A painted metal sign on the fence announced that this was the FLOUNDER BEACH CLUB and parking was by permit only. A line of bullet holes had cut the sign nearly in half.

The image of the party three decades earlier came to Gurney's mind. He wondered if that was the same entrance he'd used then. He could see the face of the girl whose birthday it was—a fat girl with pigtails and braces.

"Better to park here," said Clamm, commenting again on the grubby enclave's impossible streets. "Hope you don't mind the walk."

"Christ, how old do I look?"

Clamm responded with an awkward laugh and a tangential question as they got out of the car. "How long have you been on the job?"

Having no appetite for discussing his retirement and ad hoc reemployment, he said simply, "Twenty-five years."

"It's a weird case," said Clamm, as though the observation followed naturally. "Not just all the knife wounds. It's more than that."

"You're sure they're knife wounds?"

"Why do you ask?"

"In our case it was a broken bottle—a broken whiskey bottle. Did you recover any weapon?"

"Nope. Guy from the ME's office said 'probable knife wounds'— double-edged, though, like a dagger. Guess a pointed piece of glass could make a cut like that. They were kinda backed up. We don't have the autopsy report yet. But like I was saying, it's more than that. The wife . . . I don't know, there's something weird about the wife."

"Weird like how?"

"Lot of ways. First, she's some kind of religious nut. In fact, that's her alibi. She was at some kind of hallelujah prayer meeting."

Gurney shrugged. "What else?"

"She's on heavy-duty medication. Has to take some big pills to remember that this is her native planet."

"I hope she keeps taking them. Anything else troubling you about her?"

"Yeah," said Clamm, stopping in the middle of the narrow street they were walking along—more of an alley than a street. "She's lying about something." He looked like he had a pain in his eyes. "There's something she isn't telling us. Or maybe something she is telling us is bullshit. Maybe both. That's the house." Clamm pointed to a squat bungalow just ahead on the left, set back about ten feet from the little street. The peeling paint on the siding was a bilious green. The door was a reddish brown that reminded Gurney of dried blood. Yellow crime-scene tape, tied to portable stanchions, encircled the shabby little property. All it needed was a bow in the front, thought Gurney, to make it the gift from hell.

Clamm knocked on the door. "Oh, one other thing," he said. "She's big."

"Big?"

"You'll see."

The warning had not fully prepared Gurney for the woman who opened the door. Well over three hundred pounds, with arms like thighs, she seemed misplaced in the little house. Even more misplaced was the face of a child on this very broad body—an off-balance, dazed sort of child. Her short black hair was parted and combed like a little boy's.

"Can I help you?" she asked, looking as if help were the last thing on earth she was capable of providing.

"Hello, Mrs. Rudden, I'm Detective Clamm. Remember me?"

"Hello." She said the word like she was reading it from a foreign phrase book.

"I was here yesterday."

"I remember."

"We need to ask you a few more questions."

"You want to know more about Albert?"

"That's part of it. May we come in?"

Without answering, she turned away from the door, walked across the small living room into which it opened, and sat on a sofa—which seemed to shrink under her great bulk.

"Sit down," she said.

The two men looked around. There were no chairs. The only other objects in the room were an absurdly ornate coffee table with a cheap vase of pink plastic flowers in the center of it, an empty bookcase, and a television big enough for a ballroom. The bare plywood floor was clean except for a scattering of synthetic fibers—meaning, Gurney assumed, that the carpet on which the body was found had been taken to the lab for forensic examination.

"We don't need to sit," said Clamm. "We won't be long."

"Albert liked sports," said Mrs. Rudden, smiling blankly at the gargantuan TV.

An archway on the left side of the little living room led to three doors. From behind one came the sound effects of a combat video game.

"That's Jonah. Jonah is my son. That's his bedroom."

Gurney asked how old he was.

"Twelve. In some ways older, in some ways younger," she said, as if this were something that had just for the first time occurred to her.

"Was he with you?" asked Gurney.

"What do you mean, was he *with* me?" she asked, with a weird suggestiveness that gave Gurney a chill.

"I mean," said Gurney, trying to keep whatever it was he was feeling out of his voice, "was he with you at your religious service the night your husband was killed?"

"He's accepted Jesus Christ as his Lord and Savior."

"Does that mean he was with you?"

"Yes. I told the other policeman."

Gurney smiled sympathetically. "Sometimes it helps us to go over these things more than once."

She nodded as if in deep agreement and repeated, "He's accepted Jesus Christ."

"Did your husband accept Jesus Christ?"

"I believe he did."

"You're not sure?"

She closed her eyes tightly as if searching the insides of her eyelids for the answer. She said, "Satan is powerful, and devious are his ways."

"Devious indeed, Mrs. Rudden," said Gurney. He pulled the coffee table with the pink flowers on it back a little from the couch, walked around, and sat on the edge of it, facing her. He'd learned that the best way to talk to someone who talked like that was to talk the same way, even if he had no idea where the conversation was going.

"Devious and terrible," he said, watching her closely.

"'The Lord is my shepherd,'" she said. "'I shall not want.'"

"Amen."

Clamm cleared his throat and shifted his feet.

"Tell me," said Gurney, "in what devious way did Satan reach out to Albert?"

"It is the upright man that Satan pursueth!" she cried with sudden insistence. "For the evil man he hath already in his power."

"And Albert was an upright man?"

"Jonah!" she cried even louder, rising from the couch and moving with surprising speed through the archway on the left to one of the doors beyond it, which she began slapping with the palm of her hand. "Open the door! Now! Open the door!"

"What the fuck . . . ?" said Clamm.

"I said now, Jonah!"

A lock clicked, and the door opened halfway, revealing an obese boy almost as large as the mother he resembled to a disturbing degree—right up to the odd sense of detachment in the eyes, making Gurney wonder whether the cause was genetics or medication or both. His crew cut was bleached pure white.

"I told you not to lock that door when I'm home. Turn down the sound. It sounds like someone being murdered in there." If either of them had any feeling about the awkwardness of this comment under the circumstances, neither showed it. The boy looked at Gurney and Clamm without interest. No doubt, mused Gurney, this was one of those families so accustomed to social-services interventions that official-looking strangers in the living room didn't merit a second thought. The boy looked back at his mother.

"Can I have my Popsicle now?"

"You know you can't have it now. Keep the sound down or you won't have it at all."

"I'll have it," he said flatly, and shut the door in her face.

She came back into the living room and sat back down on the couch. "He was devastated by Albert's death."

"Mrs. Rudden," said Clamm in his let's-move-right-along way, "Detective Gurney here needs to ask you some questions."

"Isn't that a funny coincidence? I have an Aunt Bernie. I was just thinking about her this morning."

"Gurney, not Bernie," said Clamm.

"It's close, though, isn't it?" Her eyes seemed to gleam with the significance of the similarity.

"Mrs. Rudden," said Gurney, "during the past month, did your husband tell you anything he was worried about?"

"Albert never worried."

"Did he seem in any way different to you?"

"Albert was always the same."

Gurney suspected that these perceptions could as likely be due to the cushioning and fogging effect of her medication as to any consistency on Albert's part.

"Did he ever receive any mail with a handwritten address or with any writing in red ink?"

"The mail is all bills and ads. I never look at it."

"Albert took care of the mail?"

"It was all bills and ads."

"Do you know if Albert paid any special bills lately or wrote any unusual checks?"

She shook her head emphatically, making her immature face appear shockingly childish.

"One last question. After you found your husband's body, did you change or move anything in the room before the police arrived?"

Again she shook her head. It might have been his imagination, but he thought he caught a glimpse of something new in her expression. Had there been a ripple of alarm in that blank stare? He decided to take a chance.

"Does the Lord speak to you?" he asked.

There was something else in her expression now, not so much alarm as vindication.

"Yes, He does."

Vindication and pride, thought Gurney.

"Did the Lord speak to you when you found Albert?"

"'The Lord is my shepherd,'" she began—and went on to

recite the entire Twenty-third Psalm. The impatient tics and blinks that peppered Clamm's face were visible even in Gurney's peripheral vision.

"Did the Lord give you specific instructions?"

"I don't hear voices," she said. Again that flicker of alarm.

"No, not voices. But the Lord did speak to you, to help you?"

"We are here on earth to do what He would have us do."

Gurney leaned toward her from his perch on the edge of the coffee table. "And you did as the Lord directed?"

"I did as the Lord directed."

"When you found Albert, was there something that needed to be changed, something not the way it should be, something the Lord wanted you to do?"

The big woman's eyes filled with tears, and they ran down her round, girlish cheeks. "I had to save it."

"Save it?"

"The policemen would have taken it away."

"Taken what away?"

"They took everything else—the clothes he was wearing, his watch, his wallet, the newspaper he was reading, the chair he was sitting in, the rug, his eyeglasses, the glass he was drinking . . . I mean, they took everything."

"Not quite everything—right, Mrs. Rudden? They didn't take what you saved."

"I couldn't let them. It was a gift. It was Albert's last gift to me."

"May I see the gift?"

"You already saw it. There—behind you."

Gurney swiveled around and followed her gaze to the vase of pink flowers in the middle of the table—or what, upon closer inspection, turned out to be a vase with one pink plastic flower whose bloom was so large and showy it gave the initial impression of a bouquet.

"Albert gave you that flower?"

"That was his intention," she said after a hesitation.

"He didn't actually give it to you?"

"He couldn't, could he?"

"Do you mean because he was killed?"

"I know he got it for me."

"This could be very important, Mrs. Rudden," said Gurney softly. "Please tell me exactly what you found and what you did."

"When Jonah and I came home from Revelation Hall, we heard the television, and I didn't want to disturb Albert. Albert loved television. He didn't like it if someone walked in front of him. So Jonah and I walked around to the back door that goes into the kitchen, rather than come in the front and have to walk in front of him. We sat in the kitchen, and Jonah had his bedtime Popsicle."

"How long did you sit in the kitchen?"

"I couldn't tell you that. We got to talking. Jonah is very deep."

"Talking about what?"

"Jonah's favorite subject—the tribulation of the End Times. It says in the Scriptures that in the End Times there will be tribulation. Jonah always asks if I believe that, and how much tribulation I believe there will be, and what kind of tribulation. We talk a lot about that."

"So you talked about tribulation, and Jonah ate his Popsicle?"

"Like always."

"Then what?"

"Then it was time for him to go to bed."

"And?"

"And he went through the kitchen door into the living room to get to his bedroom, but it wasn't five seconds before he was back in the kitchen, backing up like, and pointing at the living room. I tried to get him to say something, but all he would do was point. So I went in there myself. I mean, I came in here," she said, looking around the room.

"What did you see?"

"Albert."

Gurney waited for her to go on. When she didn't, he prompted, "Albert was dead?"

"There was a lot of blood."

"And the flower?"

"The flower was on the floor next to him. You see, he must have been holding it in his hand. He must have wanted to give it to me when I got home."

"What did you do then?"

"Then? Oh. I went next door. We don't have a phone. I think they called the police. Before the police came, I picked up the flower. It was for me," she said with the sudden, raw insistence of a child. "It was a gift. I put it in our nicest vase."

Chapter 35

Stumbling into the light

Although it was time for lunch when they finally left the Rudden house, Gurney was in no mood for it. It wasn't that he wasn't hungry, and it wasn't that Clamm hadn't suggested a convenient place to eat. He was too frustrated, mostly with himself, to say yes to anything. As Clamm drove him back to the church parking lot where he'd left his car, they made a last halfhearted attempt to align the facts of the cases to see if there was anything at all that might connect them. The attempt led nowhere.

"Well," said Clamm, straining to give the exercise a positive interpretation, "at least there's no proof at this point that they're *not* connected. The husband could have gotten mail the wife never saw, and it doesn't look like the kind of marriage where there was much communication, so he might not have told her anything. And with whatever the hell she's on, she wasn't likely to notice any subtle emotional changes in him on her own. Might be worth having another talk with the kid. I know he's as spacey as she is, but it's possible he might remember something."

"Sure," said Gurney with zero conviction. "And you might want to see if Albert had a checking account, and if there's a stub made out to anyone named Charybdis or Arybdis or Scylla. That's a long shot, but at this point what the hell."

*   *   *

On the drive home, the weather deteriorated further in a kind of morbid sympathy with Gurney's frame of mind. The drizzle of the morning developed into a steady rain, reinforcing his dismal assessment of the trip. If there were any connections between the murders of Mark Mellery and Albert Rudden, beyond the large number and location of the stab wounds, they were not apparent. None of the distinctive features of the Peony crime scene were present at Flounder Beach—no tricky footprints, no lawn chair, no broken whiskey bottle, no poems—no sign of game playing at all. The victims appeared to have nothing in common. That a murderer would choose as his twin targets Mark Mellery and Albert Rudden made no sense.

These thoughts, along with the unpleasantness of driving in an increasing downpour, no doubt contributed to his strained expression as he entered the kitchen door of the old farmhouse, dripping.

"What happened to you?" asked Madeleine, looking up from the onion she was dicing.

"What's that supposed to mean?"

She shrugged and made another slice through the onion.

The edginess of his reply hung in the air. After a moment he mumbled apologetically, "I had an exhausting day, a six-hour round-trip in the rain."

"And?"

"And? And the whole damn thing was probably a dead end."

"And?"

"Isn't that enough?"

She shot him a disbelieving little smile.

"To give it an extra twist, it was the Bronx," he added morosely. "There's no human experience that the Bronx can't make a little uglier."

She began chopping the onion into tiny pieces. She spoke as if she were addressing the cutting board.

"You have two messages on the phone—your friend from Ithaca and your son."

"Detailed messages, or just asking me to call back?"

"I didn't pay that much attention."

"By my 'friend from Ithaca,' do you mean Sonya Reynolds?"

"Are there others?"

"Other what?"

"Friends you have in Ithaca, yet to be announced."

"I have no 'friends' at all in Ithaca. Sonya Reynolds is a business associate—and barely that. What did she want, anyway?"

"I told you, the message is on the phone." Madeleine's knife, which had been hovering above the pile of onion bits, sliced down through them with particular force.

"Jesus, watch your fingers!" The words erupted from him with more anger than concern.

With the sharp edge of the knife still pressed against the cutting board, she looked at him curiously. "So what really happened today?" she asked, rewinding the conversation to the point before it ran into the ditch.

"Frustration, I guess. I don't know." He went to the refrigerator and took out a bottle of Heineken, opened it, and set it on the table in the breakfast nook by the French doors. Then he took off his jacket, draped it over the back of one of the chairs, and sat down.

"You want to know what happened? I'll tell you. At the request of an NYPD detective by the ridiculous name of Randy Clamm, I made a three-hour drive to a sad little house in the Bronx where an unemployed man had been stabbed in the throat."

"Why did he call you?"

"Ah. Good question. Seems that Detective Clamm heard about the murder up here in Peony. The similarity of the method prompted him to call the Peony police, who passed him along to the state police regional HQ, who passed him along to the captain overseeing the case, a nasty little ass-licking moron by the name of Rodriguez, whose brain is just large enough to recognize a lousy lead."

"So he passed it along to you?"

"To the DA, who he knew would automatically pass it along to me."

Madeleine said nothing, but the obvious question was in her eyes.

"Yeah, I knew it was an iffy lead. Stabbing in that part of the world is just another form of arguing, but for some reason I thought I might find something to tie the two cases together."

"Nothing?"

"No. For a while it looked hopeful, though. The widow seemed to be holding something back. Finally she admits tampering with the crime scene. There was a flower on the floor that her husband apparently brought home for her. She was afraid the evidence techs would take it, and she wanted to keep it—understandably. So she picked it up and put it in a vase. End of story."

"You were hoping she'd admit covering up some footprints in the snow or hiding a white lawn chair?"

"Something like that. But all it turned out to be was a plastic flower."

"Plastic?"

"Plastic." He took a long, slow swallow from the Heineken bottle. "Not a very tasteful gift, I guess."

"Not really a gift at all," she said with some conviction.

"What do you mean?"

"Real flowers could be gifts—they almost always are, aren't they? Artificial flowers are something else."

"What?"

"Items of home decor, I'd say. A man wouldn't be any more likely to buy a woman a plastic flower than a roll of floral wallpaper."

"What are you telling me?"

"I'm not sure. But if this woman found a plastic flower at the murder scene and assumed that her husband had bought it for her, I think she's wrong."

"Where do you think it came from?"

"I have no idea."

"She seemed pretty sure he'd gotten it as a gift for her."

"She would want to think that, wouldn't she?"

"Maybe so. But if he didn't bring it into the house, and assuming the son was out all evening with her as she claims, that would leave the murderer as a possible source."

"I suppose," said Madeleine with diminishing interest. Gurney knew that she drew a definite line between understanding what a real person would do under certain circumstances and airy hypothesizing about the source of an object in a room. He sensed he'd just crossed that line, but he pressed on, anyway.

"So why might a murderer leave a flower by his victim?"

"What kind of flower?"

He could always trust her to make the question more specific.

"I'm not sure what it was. I know what it wasn't. It wasn't a rose, it wasn't a carnation, it wasn't a dahlia. But it was sort of similar to all of them."

"In what way?"

"Well, the first thing I was reminded of was a rose, but it was larger, with a lot more petals, more crowded together. It was almost the size of a big carnation or a dahlia, but the individual petals were broader than dahlia or carnation petals—a bit like crinkly rose petals. It was a very busy, showy sort of flower."

For the first time since he'd arrived home, Madeleine's face was alive with real interest.

"Has something occurred to you?" he asked.

"Maybe . . . hmm . . ."

"What? You know what kind of flower it is?"

"I think so. It's quite a coincidence."

"Jesus! Are you going to tell me?"

"Unless I'm mistaken, the flower you just described sounds very much like a peony."

The Heineken bottle slipped out of his hand. "Holy Christ!"

After asking Madeleine a few pertinent questions about peonies, he went to the den to make some calls.

Chapter 36

One thing leads to another

By the time he got off the phone, Gurney had persuaded Detective Clamm that it had to be more than coincidence that the eponymous flower of the first murder's location had shown up at the second murder.

He also suggested that several actions be taken without delay—conduct an all-out search of the Rudden house for any odd letters or notes, anything in verse, anything handwritten, anything in red ink; alert the medical examiner's office to the gunshot-and-broken-bottle combination used in Peony, in case they might want to take a second look at Rudden's body; comb the house for evidence of a gunshot or material that may have been used to muffle one; re-search the property and adjoining properties and roadway between the house and the community fence for broken bottles, especially whiskey bottles; and start compiling a biographical profile of Albert Rudden to mine for potential links to Mark Mellery, conflicts or enemies, legal problems, or trouble involving alcohol.

Eventually becoming aware of the peremptory tone of his "suggestions," he slowed down and apologized.

"I'm sorry, Randy. I'm getting out of order here. The Rudden case is all yours. You're the man responsible, which makes the next move entirely your call. I know I'm not in charge, and I'm sorry for behaving like I am."

"No problem. By the way, I've got a Lieutenant Everly down

here who says he went through the academy with a Dave Gurney. Would that be you?"

Gurney laughed. He'd forgotten that Bobby Everly had ended up in that precinct. "Yeah, that would be me."

"Well, sir, in that case I'd welcome any input from you at any time. And anytime you'd like to question Mrs. Rudden again, please be my guest. I thought you were good with her."

If this was sarcasm, it was well concealed. Gurney decided to take it as a compliment.

"Thank you. I don't need to talk to her directly, but let me make one small suggestion. If I happened to be face-to-face with her again, I would ask her in a very matter-of-fact way what the Lord told her to do with the whiskey bottle."

"What whiskey bottle?"

"The one she may have removed from the scene for reasons best known to herself. I'd ask about it in a way that suggests you already know that the bottle was there and that she removed it at the Lord's urging, and you're just curious to know where it is. Of course, there may not have been any whiskey bottle at all, and if you get the sense that she really doesn't have a clue what you're talking about, just move on to something else."

"You're sure this whole deal is going to follow the pattern of the Peony thing—so there ought to be a whiskey bottle somewhere?"

"That's what I'm thinking. If you don't feel comfortable approaching her that way, that's okay. It's your call."

"Might be worth a try. Not much to lose. I'll let you know."

"Good luck."

The next person Gurney needed to talk to was Sheridan Kline. The truism that your boss should never find out from someone else what he should have found out from you was true-times-two in law enforcement. He reached Kline as he was en route to a regional conference of district attorneys in Lake Placid, and the frequent interruptions caused by the spotty cell-phone coverage in the upstate mountains made the "peony" connection more difficult to explain than Gurney would have liked. When he was finished, Kline took so long to respond that Gurney was afraid he'd driven into another dead transmission area.

He finally said, "This flower thing—you're comfortable with that?"

"If it's just a coincidence," said Gurney, "it's a remarkable one."

"But it's not really solid. If I were playing devil's advocate here, I'd have to point out that your wife didn't actually see the flower— the plastic flower—you were describing to her. Suppose it's not a peony at all. Where are we then? Even if it *is* a peony, it's not exactly proof of anything. God knows it's not the kind of breakthrough I could stand up and talk about at a press conference. Christ, why couldn't it be a real flower, so there'd be less doubt about what it was? Why plastic?"

"That bothered me, too," said Gurney, trying to conceal his irritation at Kline's reaction. "Why not a real one? A few minutes ago, I asked my wife about it, and she told me that florists don't like to sell peonies. It has a top-heavy bloom that won't remain upright on its stem. They're available in nurseries for planting, but not at this time of year. So a plastic one might be the only way he could send us his little message. I'm thinking it was an opportunistic thing—he saw it in a store and was struck by the idea, by the playfulness of it."

"Playfulness?"

"He's taunting us, testing us, playing a game with us. Remember the note he left on Mellery's body—come and get me if you can. That's what the backwards footprints were all about. This maniac is dangling messages in front of our faces, and they all say the same thing: 'Chase me, chase me, betcha can't catch me!'"

"Okay, I get it, I see what you're saying. You may be right. But there's no way I can publicly connect these cases based on one guy's guess about the meaning of a plastic flower. Get me something real—ASAP."

After he hung up the phone, Gurney sat by the den window gazing out at the late-afternoon gloom. Suppose, as Kline had conjectured, the flower wasn't a peony after all. Gurney was shocked to realize how fragile his new "link" was—and how much confidence he'd had in it. Overlooking the glaring flaw in a theory was a sure sign of excessive emotional attachment to it. How many times had he made that point to the criminology students in the course he taught at the state university, and here he was blundering into the same trap. It was depressing.

The dead ends of the day ran around in his head in a fatiguing loop for maybe half an hour, maybe longer.

"Why are you sitting in there in the dark?"

He swiveled in his chair and saw Madeleine silhouetted in the doorway.

"Kline wants connections more tangible than a debatable peony," he said. "I gave the Bronx guy a few places to look. Hopefully he'll come up with something."

"You sound doubtful."

"Well, on the one hand, we have the peony, or at least what we think is a peony. On the other hand, we have the difficulty of imagining the Ruddens and the Mellerys being connected to each other in any way. If ever there were people who lived in different worlds . . ."

"What if it's a serial killer and there are no connections?"

"Even serial killers aren't random killers. Their victims tend to have something in common—all blondes, all Asians, all gays— some characteristic with special meaning for the killer. So even if Mellery and Rudden were never directly involved in anything together, we'd still be looking for some common ground or similarity between them."

"What if . . ." Madeleine began, but the ringing of the phone interrupted her.

It was Randy Clamm.

"Sorry to bother you, sir, but I thought you'd like to know you were right. I took a drive over to see the widow, and I asked that question just like you said I should—sort of matter-of-fact. All I said was, 'Can I have the whiskey bottle that you found?' I didn't even have to bring the Lord into it. I'll be damned if she didn't say, just as matter-of-factly as myself, 'It's in the garbage.' So we go out in the kitchen and there it is, sitting there in the garbage pail, a broken Four Roses bottle. I'm staring at it, speechless. Not that I was surprised that you were right—don't get me wrong—but, Jesus, I didn't expect it to be so easy. So damn obvious. As soon as I collect my thoughts, I ask her to show me exactly where she'd found it. But then the whole situation suddenly catches up with her—maybe because now I'm not sounding so casual—and she looks very upset. I tell her to relax, don't worry about it, could she just tell me where it was, because that would be really helpful to us, and maybe, like, you know, would she mind telling me why the hell she moved it. I didn't put it that way, of course, but that's what I'm thinking. So she looks at me, and you know what she says? She says Albert's been so good about the drinking problem, he didn't have a drink for almost a year. He's going to AA, he's doing great—and when she sees the bottle, which was on the floor next to him, next to the plastic flower, the first thing she thinks is that he started drinking again and fell on the bottle, and it cut his throat, and that's how he died. It doesn't immediately occur to her that he's been murdered—it doesn't even cross her mind until the cops come and they start talking about it. But before they come, she hides the bottle because she's thinking it's his bottle, and she doesn't want anyone to know he had a relapse."

"And even after it sank into her head that he was killed, she still didn't want anyone to know about the bottle?"

"No. Because she still thinks it was his bottle and she doesn't want anyone to know he was drinking, especially his nice new friends from AA."

"Jesus Christ."

"So the whole thing turns out to be a pathetic mess. On the other hand, you got your proof that the murders are connected."

Clamm was upset, full of the conflicted feelings that Gurney was all too familiar with—the feelings that made being a good cop so hard, so ultimately wearying.

"You did a great job there, Randy."

"Just did what you told me to do," said Clamm in his rapid, agitated way. "After securing the bottle, I called for the evidence team to make a return visit, go over the whole house for letters, notes, anything. I asked Mrs. Rudden for their checkbook. You mentioned that to me this morning. She gave it to me, but she didn't know anything about it—handled it like it might be radioactive, said Albert took care of all the bills. Said she doesn't like checks because there are numbers on them, and you got to be careful about numbers, numbers can be evil—some crap about Satan, crazy religious bullshit. Anyway, I took a look through the checkbook, and the bottom line on that is it's going to take more time to figure it out. Albert might have paid the bills, but he wasn't much of a record keeper. There was no reference on any of the check stubs to anyone named Arybdis or Charybdis or Scylla—that's what I looked for first—but that doesn't mean much, because most of the stubs had no names, just amounts, and some of them didn't even have that. As for monthly statements, she had no idea if there were any in the house, but we'll do a thorough search, and we'll get her permission to get photostats from the bank. In the meantime, now that we know we're holding two corners of the same triangle, is there anything else you want to share with me about the Mellery murder?"

Gurney thought about it. "The series of threats Mellery received prior to his murder included vague references to things he did when he was drunk. Now it turns out that Rudden had drinking problems, too."

"You saying we're looking for a guy who's running around knocking off drunks?"

"Not exactly. If that's all he wanted to do, there'd be easier ways to do it."

"Like toss a bomb into an AA meeting?"

"Something simple. Something that would maximize his opportunity and minimize his risk. But this guy's approach is complicated and inconvenient. Nothing easy or direct about it. Any part of it you look at raises questions."

"Like what?"

"To start with, why would he pick victims who are so far apart geographically—and in every other way, for that matter?"

"To keep us from connecting them?"

"But he wants us to connect them. That's the point of the peony. He wants to be noticed. Wants credit. This is not your average perp on the run. This guy wants to do battle—not just with his victims. With the police, too."

"Speaking of that, I need to bring my lieutenant up to date. He wouldn't be happy if he found out I called you first."

"Where are you?"

"On my way back to the station house."

"That would put you on Tremont Avenue?"

"How'd you know that?"

"That roar of Bronx traffic in the background. Nothing quite like it."

"Must be nice to be somewhere else. You got any message you want me to pass along to Lieutenant Everly?"

"Better hold the messages till later. He's going to be a lot more interested in what you have to tell him."

Chapter 37

Bad things come in threes

Gurney had an urge to call Sheridan Kline with the decisive new evidence supporting the peony linkage, but he wanted to make one other call first. If the two cases were as parallel as they now seemed to be, it was possible not only that Rudden had been asked for money but that he had been asked to send it to that same post-office box in Wycherly, Connecticut.

Gurney took his slim case folder out of his desk drawer and located his photocopy of the brief note Gregory Dermott had sent along with the check he'd returned to Mellery. The GD Security Systems letterhead—businesslike, conservative, even a little old-fashioned—included a Wycherly-area phone number.

The call was answered on the second ring by a voice consistent with the style of the letterhead.

"Good afternoon. GD Security. May I help you?"

"I'd like to speak to Mr. Dermott, please. This is Detective Gurney from the district attorney's office."

"Finally!" The vehemence that transformed the voice was startling.

"Excuse me?"

"You're calling about the misaddressed check?"

"Yes, as a matter of fact, but . . . ?"

"I reported it six days ago—six days ago!"

"Reported what six days ago?"

"Didn't you just say you were calling about the check?"

"Let's start over, Mr. Dermott. It's my understanding that Mark Mellery spoke to you approximately ten days ago about a check you'd returned to him, a check made out to 'X. Arybdis' and sent to your post-office box. Is that true?"

"Of course it's true. What kind of question is that?" The man sounded furious.

"When you say that you reported it six days ago, I'm afraid I don't—"

"The second one!"

"You received a second check?"

"Isn't that why you're calling?"

"Actually, sir, I was calling to ask you that very question."

"What question?"

"Whether you'd also received a check from a man by the name of Albert Rudden."

"Yes, Rudden was the name on the second check. That's what I called to report. Six days ago."

"Who did you call?"

Gurney heard a couple of long, deep breaths being taken, as though the man were trying to keep himself from exploding.

"Look, Detective, there's a level of confusion here that I'm not happy with. I called the police six days ago to report a troubling situation. Three checks had been sent to my post-office box, addressed to an individual I've never heard of. Now you call me back, ostensibly regarding these checks, but you don't seem to know what I'm talking about. What am I missing? What the hell is going on?"

"What police department did you call?"

"Mine, of course—my local Wycherly precinct. How could you not know that if you're calling me back?"

"The fact is, sir, I'm not calling you *back*. I'm calling from New York State regarding the original check you returned to Mark Mellery. We weren't aware of any additional checks. You said there were two more after the first?"

"That's what I said."

"One from Albert Rudden and one from someone else?"

"Yes, Detective. Is that clear now?"

"Perfectly clear. But now I'm wondering why three misaddressed checks disturbed you enough to call your local police."

"I called my local police because the postal police whom I first notified exhibited a colossal lack of interest. Before you ask me why I called the postal police, let me say that for a policeman you have a rather dull sense of security issues."

"Why do you say that, sir?"

"I'm in the security business, Officer—or Detective, or whatever you are. The computer-data security business. Do you have any idea how common identity theft is—or how often identity theft involves the misappropriation of addresses?"

"I see. And what did the Wycherly police do?"

"Less than the postal police, if that's possible."

Gurney could imagine Dermott's phone calls receiving a lackadaisical response. Three unfamiliar people sending checks to someone's post-office box might sound like something less than a high-priority peril.

"You did return the second and third checks to their senders, like you returned Mark Mellery's?"

"I certainly did, and I enclosed notes asking who gave them my box number, but neither individual had the courtesy to reply."

"Did you keep the name and address from the third check?"

"I certainly did."

"I need that name and address right now."

"Why? Is there something going on here I don't know about?"

"Mark Mellery and Albert Rudden are both dead. Possible homicides."

"Homicides? What do you mean, homicides?" Dermott's voice had become shrill.

"They may have been murdered."

"Oh, my God. You think this is connected with the checks?"

"Whoever gave them your post-office box address would be a person of interest in the case."

"Oh, my God. Why my address? What connection is there to me?"

"Good question, Mr. Dermott."

"But I never heard of anyone named Mark Mellery or Albert Rudden."

"What was the name on the third check?"

"The third check? Oh, my God. I've gone completely blank."

"You said you made a note of the name."

"Yes, yes, of course I did. Wait. Richard Kartch. Yes, that was it. Richard Kartch. K-a-r-t-c-h. I'll get the address. Wait, I have it here. It's 349 Quarry Road, Sotherton, Massachusetts."

"Got it."

"Look, Detective, since I seem to be involved in this in some way, I'd appreciate knowing whatever you can tell me. There must be a reason my post-office box was chosen."

"Are you sure you're the only one who has access to that box?"

"As sure as I can be. But God knows how many postal workers have access to it. Or who might have a duplicate key that I'm not aware of."

"The name Richard Kartch means nothing to you?"

"Nothing. I'm quite sure of that. It's the sort of name I'd remember."

"Okay, sir. I'd like to give you a couple of phone numbers where you can reach me. I would appreciate hearing from you immediately if anything at all occurs to you about the names of those three people, or about any access anyone else might have to your mail. And one last question. Do you recall the amounts of the second and third checks?"

"That's easy. The second and third were the same as the first— $289.87."

Chapter 38

A difficult man

Madeleine turned on one of the den lamps from a switch at the door. During Gurney's conversation with Dermott, the dusk had deepened and the room was nearly dark.

"Making progress?"

"Major progress. Thanks to you."

"My Great-Aunt Mimi had peonies," she said.

"Which one was Mimi?"

"My father's mother's sister," she said, not quite concealing her exasperation at the fact that a man so adept at juggling the details of the most complex investigation couldn't remember half a dozen family relationships. "Your dinner is ready."

"Well, actually . . ."

"It's on the stove. Don't forget about it."

"You're going out?"

"Yes."

"Where to?"

"I've told you about it twice in the past week."

"I remember something about Thursday. The details . . ."

". . . escape you at the moment? Nothing new there. See you later."

"You're not going to tell me where . . . ?"

Her footsteps were already receding through the kitchen to the back door.

There was no phone listing for Richard Kartch at 349 Quarry Road in Sotherton, but an Internet map search of contiguous addresses turned up names and phone numbers for 329 and 369.

The thick male voice that finally answered the call to 329 monosyllabically denied knowing anyone by the name of Kartch, knowing which house on the street 349 might be, or even knowing how long he himself had lived in the area. He sounded half comatose on alcohol or opiates, was probably lying as a matter of habit, and was clearly not going to be of any help.

The woman at 369 Quarry Road was more talkative.

"You mean the hermit?" Her way of saying it gave the epithet a creepy pathology.

"Mr. Kartch lives alone?"

"Oh, indeed he does, unless you count the rats his garbage attracts. His wife was lucky to escape. I'm not surprised you're calling—you said you're a police officer?"

"Special investigator with the district attorney's office." He knew that he ought, in the interest of full disclosure, to mention the state and county of jurisdiction, but he rationalized that the details could be filled in later.

"What's he done now?"

"Nothing that I'm aware of, but he may be able to help with an investigation, and we need to get in touch with him. Would you happen to know where he works or what time he gets home from work?"

"Work? That's a joke!"

"Is Mr. Kartch unemployed?"

"Try unemployable." There was venom in her voice.

"You seem to have a real problem with him."

"He's a pig, he's stupid, he's dirty, he's dangerous, he's crazy, he stinks, he's armed to the teeth, and he's usually drunk."

"Sounds like quite a neighbor."

"The neighbor from hell! Do you have any idea what it's like trying to show your home to a prospective buyer while the shirtless, beer-swilling ape next door blasts holes in a garbage can with his shotgun?"

Knowing what the answer was likely to be, he decided to ask his next question, anyway. "Would you be willing to give Mr. Kartch a message for me?"

"Are you kidding? All I'd be willing to give him is the sharp end of a stick."

"When would he be most likely to be at home?"

"Pick a time, any time. I've never seen that lunatic leave his property."

"Is there a visible house number?"

"Hah! You don't need any number to recognize the house. It wasn't finished when his wife left—still isn't. No siding. No lawn. No steps to the front door. The perfect house for a total nutcase. Whoever goes there better bring a gun."

Gurney thanked her and ended the conversation.

Now what?

Various individuals needed to be brought up to speed. First and foremost, Sheridan Kline. And, of course, Randy Clamm. Not to mention Captain Rodriguez and Jack Hardwick. The question was whom to call first. He decided they could all wait another few minutes. Instead he got the number of the Sotherton, Massachusetts, police department from information.

He spoke to the duty sergeant, a gravelly man by the name of Kalkan, kind of like the dog food. After identifying himself, Gurney explained that a Sotherton man by the name of Richard Kartch was a person of interest in a New York State murder investigation, that he might be in imminent danger, that he apparently had no phone, and that it was important that a phone be brought to him, or he brought to a phone, so that he could be warned about his situation.

"We're familiar with Richie Kartch," said Kalkan.

"Sounds like you may have had problems with him."

Kalkan didn't answer.

"He has a record?"

"Who did you say you were?"

Gurney told him again, with a little more detail.

"And this is part of your investigation of what?"

"Two murders—one in upstate New York, one in the Bronx—same pattern. Before they were killed, both victims received certain communications from the killer. We have evidence that Kartch has received at least one of those same communications, making him a possible third target."

"So you want Crazy Richie to get in touch with you?"

"He needs to call me immediately, preferably in the presence of one of your officers. After speaking with him on the phone, we'll probably want a follow-up interview with him in Sotherton—with the cooperation of your department."

"We'll send a car out to his place as soon as we can. Give me a number where you can be reached."

Gurney gave him his cell number in order to leave the house phone free for the calls he intended to make to Kline, BCI, and Clamm.

Kline was gone for the day, as was Ellen Rackoff, and the call was automatically rerouted to a phone that was answered on the sixth ring as Gurney was about to hang up.

"Stimmel."

Gurney remembered the man who'd come with Kline to the BCI meeting, the man with the personality of a mute war criminal.

"It's Dave Gurney. I have a message for your boss."

There was no response.

"You there?"

"I'm here."

Gurney figured that was as near an invitation to proceed as he was going to get. So he went ahead and gave Stimmel the evidence confirming the link between murders one and two; the discovery, through Dermott, of a third potential victim; and the steps he was taking through the Sotherton PD to reach him. "You got all that?"

"Got it."

"After you inform the DA, you want to pass the information along to BCI, or shall I speak with Rodriguez directly?"

There was a short silence during which Gurney assumed that the dour, unforthcoming man was calculating the consequences both ways. Knowing the penchant for control built into most cops, he was about 90 percent sure he'd get the answer he finally got.

"We'll handle it," said Stimmel.

Having disposed of the need to call BCI, Gurney was left with Randy Clamm.

As usual, he answered on the first ring.

"Clamm."

And as usual, he sounded like he was in a hurry and doing three other things as he spoke. "Glad you called. Just making a triple list of gaps in Rudden's checking account—check stubs with amounts but no names, checks issued but not cashed, check numbers skipped—going from most recent backwards."

"The amount $289.87 appear on any of your lists?"

"What? How'd you know that? It's one of the 'checks issued but not cashed.' How did you . . . ?"

"It's the amount he always asks for."

"Always? You mean more than twice?"

"A third check was sent to the same post-office box. We're in the process of getting in touch with the sender. That's why I'm calling—to let you know we have an ongoing pattern here. If the pieces of the pattern hold, the slug you're looking for in the Rudden bungalow is a .38 Special."

"Who's the third guy?"

"Richard Kartch, Sotherton, Mass. Apparently a difficult character."

"Massachusetts? Jesus, our boy's all over the place. This third guy's still alive?"

"We'll know in a few minutes. Local PD sent a car to his house."

"Okay. I'd appreciate your letting me know whatever you can whenever you can. I'll make some more noise about getting our evidence team back to the Ruddens'. I'll keep you posted. Thanks for the call, sir."

"Good luck. I'll talk to you soon."

Gurney's respect for the young detective was growing. The more he heard, the more he liked what he was hearing—energy, intelligence, dedication. And something else. Something earnest and unspoiled. Something that touched his heart.

He shook his head like a dog shaking off water and took several deep breaths. The day, he thought, must have been more emotionally draining than he'd realized. Or perhaps some residue of his dream about his father was still with him. He leaned back in his chair and closed his eyes.

He was awakened by the phone, mistaking it at first for his alarm clock. He found himself still in his den chair, with a painfully stiff neck. According to his watch, he'd been asleep for nearly two hours. He picked up the phone and cleared his throat.

"Gurney."

The DA's voice on the other end burst like a horse from the starting gate.

"Dave, I just got the news. God, this thing just keeps getting bigger. A third potential victim in Massachusetts? This could be the biggest damn murder case since Son of Sam, not to mention your own Jason Strunk. This is big! I just want to hear it from your own lips, before I talk to the media: We do have hard evidence that the same guy whacked the first two victims, is that right?"

"The evidence strongly suggests that, sir."

"Suggests?"

"Strongly suggests."

"Could you be more definite?"

"We don't have fingerprints. We don't have DNA. I'd say it's definite that the cases are connected, but we can't prove yet that the same individual cut both throats."

"The probability is high?"

"Very high."

"Your judgment on that is good enough for me."

Gurney smiled at this transparent pretense of trust. He knew damn well that Sheridan Kline was the sort of man who valued his own judgment far above anyone else's but would always leave a door open for blame shifting in case a situation went south.

"I'd say it's time to talk to our friends at Fox News—which means I need to touch base with BCI tonight and put together a statement. Keep me up to the minute on this, Dave, especially any developments on the Massachusetts angle. I want to know everything." Kline hung up without bothering to say good-bye.

So apparently he was planning to go public in a big way—rev up a media circus with himself as the ringmaster—before it occurred to the Bronx DA, or to the DA in any other jurisdiction where the murder spree might spread, to seize the personal publicity opportunity. Gurney's lips drew back in distaste as he imagined the press conferences to come.

"Are you all right?"

Startled at the voice so close to him, he looked up and saw Madeleine at the den door.

"Jesus, how the hell . . . ?"

"You were so engrossed in your conversation you didn't hear me come in."

"Apparently not." Blinking, he looked at his watch. "So where did you go?"

"Remember what I said on my way out?"

"You said you wouldn't tell me where you were going."

"I said I'd already told you twice."

"Okay, fine. Well, I have work to do."

As if it were his ally, the phone rang.

The call was from Sotherton, but it wasn't from Richard Kartch. It was from a detective by the name of Gowacki.

"We got a situation," he said. "How soon do you think you can get here?"

Chapter 39

You and I have a date,
Mr. 658

By the time Gurney got off the phone with the flat-voiced Mike Gowacki, it was nine-fifteen. He found Madeleine already in bed, propped against her pillows, with a book. *War and Peace.* She'd been reading it for three years, shuttling back and forth between it and, incongruously, Thoreau's *Walden*.

"I have to head out to a crime scene."

She looked up at him from the book—curious, worried, lonely.

He felt able to respond only to the curiosity. "Another male victim. Stabbed in the throat, footprints in the snow."

"How far?"

"What?"

"How far do you have to go?"

"Sotherton, Massachusetts. Three, four hours, maybe."

"So you won't be back until sometime tomorrow."

"For breakfast, I hope."

She smiled her who-do-you-think-you're-kidding? smile.

He started to leave, then stopped and sat on the edge of the bed. "This is a strange case," he said, letting his unsureness about it come through. "Getting stranger by the day."

She nodded, somehow placated. "You don't think it's your standard serial killer?"

"Not the standard version, no."

"Too much communication with the victims?"

"Yes. And too much diversity among the victims—personally and geographically. Typical serial killer doesn't bounce around from the Catskills to the East Bronx to the middle of Massachusetts pursuing famous authors, retired night watchmen, and nasty loners."

"They must have something in common."

"They all have drinking histories, and the evidence indicates the killer is focused on that issue. But they must have something else in common—otherwise why go to the trouble of choosing victims two hundred miles apart from one another?"

They fell silent. Gurney absently smoothed wrinkles out of the quilt in the space between them. Madeleine watched him for a while, her hands resting on her book.

"I better get going," he said.

"Be careful."

"Right." He rose slowly, almost arthritically. "See you in the morning."

She looked at him with an expression he could never put into words, couldn't even say if it was good or bad, but he knew it well. He felt its almost physical touch in the center of his chest.

It was well after midnight when he exited from the Mass. Turnpike and one-thirty when he drove through the deserted main street of Sotherton. Ten minutes later, on the rutted lane called Quarry Road, he arrived at a haphazard assembly of police vehicles, one of which had its strobes flashing. He pulled in alongside it. As he got out of his car, an irritated-looking uniformed cop emerged from the light machine.

"Hold it. Where do you think you're going?" He sounded not only irritated but exhausted.

"Name is Gurney—here to see Detective Gowacki."

"About what?"

"He's expecting me."

"What's it about?"

Gurney wondered whether the guy's edge was coming from a

long day or from a naturally lousy attitude. He had a low tolerance for naturally lousy attitudes.

"It's about him asking me to come here. You want some identification?"

The cop clicked his flashlight on and shined it in Gurney's face. "Who'd you say you were?"

"Gurney, district attorney's office, special investigator."

"The fuck didn't you say so?"

Gurney smiled without any emotion resembling friendliness. "You going to tell Gowacki I'm here?"

After a final hostile pause, the man turned and walked up the outer edge of a long, rising driveway toward a house that seemed, in the portable arc lights illuminating the property for the crime-scene techs, only half finished. Uninvited, Gurney followed him.

As the driveway neared the house, it made a left cut into the bank of the hill and arrived at the opening to a two-car basement garage, currently housing one car. At first Gurney thought the garage doors were open; then he realized there weren't any doors. The half inch of snow that coated the driveway continued inside. The cop stopped at the opening, blocked by crime-scene tape, and shouted, "Mike!"

There was no response. The cop shrugged as if an honest effort had been made, had failed, and that was the end of the matter. Then a tired voice came from the yard behind the house. "Back here."

Without waiting, Gurney headed around the perimeter of the tape in that direction.

"Make sure you stay outside the tape." The cop's warning struck Gurney as the final bark of a testy dog.

Rounding the rear corner of the house, he saw that the area, bright as day in the glare of the lights, was not exactly the "yard" he had expected. Like the house, it exhibited an odd blend of incompletion and decrepitude. A heavily built man with thinning hair was standing on a crude set of steps, cobbled together from two-by-tens, at the back door. The man's eyes scanned the half acre of open ground that separated the house from a thicket of sumac.

The ground was lumpy, as though it had never been graded after the foundation was backfilled. Scraps of framing lumber, heaped here and there, had taken on a weathered grayness. The house was only partially sided, and the plastic moisture barrier over the plywood sheathing was faded from exposure. The impression was not of construction in progress but construction abandoned.

When the stout man's gaze reached Gurney, he studied him for a few seconds before asking, "You the man from the Catskills?"

"That's right."

"Walk another ten feet along the tape, then step under it and come around here to the back door. Make sure you steer clear of that line of footprints from the house to the driveway."

Presumably this was Gowacki, but Gurney had an aversion to presuming, so he asked the question and got back an affirmative grunt.

As he made his way across the wasteland that should have been a backyard, he came close enough to the footprints to note their similarity to those at the institute.

"Look familiar?" asked Gowacki, eyeing Gurney curiously.

There was nothing thick about the thick-bodied detective's perception, thought Gurney. He nodded. Now it was his own turn to be perceptive.

"Those footprints bother you?"

"Little bit," said Gowacki. "Not the footprints, exactly. More the location of the body in relation to the footprints. You know something I don't?"

"Would the location of the body make more sense if the direction of the footprints were reversed?"

"If the direction were ... Wait a minute. ... Yes, goddamn it, perfect sense!" He stared at Gurney. "What the hell are we dealing with here?"

"First of all, we're dealing with someone who has killed three people—three that we know of—in the past week. He's a planner and a perfectionist. He leaves a lot of evidence behind, but only evidence he wants us to see. He's extremely intelligent, probably well educated, and may hate the police even more than he hates his victims. By the way, is the body still here?"

Gowacki looked like he was making a mental recording of Gurney's response. Finally he said, "Yeah, the body's here. I wanted you to see it. Thought something might register, based on what you know about the other two. Ready to take a look?"

The back door of the house led into a small, unfinished area probably intended to be a laundry room, given the position of the roughed-in plumbing, but there was no washing machine and no dryer. There wasn't even any drywall over the insulation. Illumination was provided by a bare bulb in a cheap white fixture nailed to an exposed ceiling joist.

In the raw, unwelcoming light, the body lay on its back, half in the would-be laundry area and half in the kitchen beyond the untrimmed doorway separating them.

"Can I take a closer look?" asked Gurney, grimacing.

"That's what you're here for."

The closer look revealed a pool of coagulated blood that had spread from multiple throat wounds out across the kitchen floor and under a thrift-shop breakfast table. The victim's face was full of anger, but the bitter lines etched into the large, hard face were the product of a lifetime and revealed nothing about the terminal assault.

"Unhappy-looking man," said Gurney.

"Miserable son of a bitch is what he was."

"I gather you've had some past trouble with Mr. Kartch."

"Nothing but trouble. Every damn bit of it unnecessary." Gowacki glared at the body as though its violent, bloody end had been insufficient punishment. "Every town has troublemakers— angry drunks, slobs who turn their places into pigsties to piss off the neighbors, creeps whose ex-wives have to get orders of protection, jerks who let their dogs bark all night, weirdos who mothers don't want their kids within a mile of. Here in Sotherton all those assholes were wrapped up in one guy—Richie Kartch."

"Sounds like quite a guy."

"Matter of curiosity, were the other two victims anything like that?"

"The first was the opposite of that. The second I don't have personal details on yet, but I doubt he was anything like this guy." Gurney took another look at the face staring up from the floor, as ugly in death as it had apparently been in life.

"Just thought maybe we had a serial killer trying to rid the world of assholes. Anyway, to get back to your comments about the footprints in the snow—how did you know they'd make more sense if they went the other way?"

"That's the way it was at the first murder."

Gowacki's eyes showed interest. "The position of this body is consistent with facing an attacker entering through the back door. But the footprints show someone coming in the front door and exiting by the back door. Doesn't make sense."

"Mind if I take a look around the kitchen?"

"Be my guest. Photographer, medical examiner, blood-prints-and-fibers guys were all here. Just don't move anything. We're still going through his personal possessions."

"ME say anything about powder burns?"

"Powder burns? Those are knife wounds."

"I suspect there's a bullet wound somewhere in that bloody mess."

"You see something I missed?"

"I think I see a small round hole in the corner of that ceiling above the refrigerator. Any of your people comment on that?"

Gowacki followed Gurney's gaze to the spot. "What are you telling me here?"

"That Kartch may have been shot first, then stabbed."

"And the footprints actually go in the opposite direction?"

"Right."

"Let me get this straight. You're saying the killer comes in the back door, shoots Richie in the throat, Richie goes down, then the killer stabs him a dozen times in the throat like he's tenderizing a fucking steak?"

"That's pretty much what happened in Peony."

"But the footprints . . ."

"The footprints could have been made by attaching a second sole to the boot—backwards—to make it look like he came in the front and went out the back, when in fact he came in the back and went out the front."

"Shit, that's ridiculous! What the hell's he playing at?"

"That's the word for it."

"What?"

"*Playing.* Hell of a game, but that's what he's doing, and now he's done it three times. 'Not only are you wrong, you're ass-backwards wrong. I hand you clue after clue, but you still can't get me. That's how fucking useless you cops are.' That's the message he's giving us at every crime scene."

Gowacki gave Gurney a slow, assessing look. "You see this guy pretty vividly."

Gurney smiled, stepping around the body to get to a heap of papers on the kitchen countertop. "You mean I sound a little intense?"

"Not for me to say. We don't get a lot of murders in Sotherton. Even those, and we only get one maybe every five years, they're the kind that plead down to manslaughter. They tend to involve baseball bats and tire irons in the parking lots of bars. Nothing planned. Definitely nothing playful."

Gurney grunted in sympathy. He'd seen more than his share of unsophisticated mayhem.

"That's mostly crap," said Gowacki, nodding toward the pile of junk mail that Gurney was gingerly poking through.

He was about to agree when, at the very bottom of the disorganized heap of *Pennysaver*s, flyers, gun magazines, collection-agency notices, and military-surplus catalogs, he came upon a small, empty envelope, torn open roughly at the flap, addressed to Richard Kartch. The handwriting was beautifully precise. The ink was red.

"You find something?" asked Gowacki.

"You might want to put this in an evidence bag," said Gurney, taking the envelope by its corner and moving it to a clear space on the countertop. "Our killer likes to communicate with his victims."

"There's more upstairs."

Gurney and Gowacki turned to the source of the new voice—a large young man standing in the doorway on the opposite side of the kitchen.

"Underneath a bunch of porno magazines on the table by his bed—there's three of them envelopes with red writing on them."

"Guess I ought to go up, take a look," said Gowacki with the reluctance of a man stocky enough to think twice about a flight of stairs. "Bobby, this here is Detective Gurney from Delaware County, New York."

"Bob Muffit," said the young man, extending his hand nervously to Gurney, keeping his eyes averted from the body on the floor.

The upstairs had the same half-done and half-abandoned appearance as the rest of the house. The landing provided access to four doors. Muffit led the way into the one on the right. Even by the shabby standard already established, it was a wreck. On those portions of the carpet not covered by dirty clothes or empty beer cans, Gurney observed what appeared to be dried vomit stains. The air was sour, sweaty. The blinds were closed. The light came from the sole working bulb in a three-bulb fixture in the middle of the ceiling.

Gowacki made his way to the table by the disarranged bed. Next to a pile of porno magazines were three envelopes with red handwriting, and next to them a personal check. Gowacki did not touch anything directly but slid the four items onto a magazine called *Hot Buns*, which he used as a tray.

"Let's go downstairs and see what we have here," he said.

The three men retraced their steps to the kitchen, where Gowacki deposited the envelopes and the check on the breakfast table. With a pen and a tweezers from his shirt pocket, he lifted back the ripped flap of each envelope and extracted the contents. The three envelopes held poems that looked identical, down to their nunlike penmanship, to the corresponding poems received by Mellery.

Gurney's first glance fell on the lines *"What you took you will give / when you get what you gave.... You and I have a date / Mr. 658.*"

The item that held his attention the longest, however, was the check. It was made out to "X. Arybdis," and it was signed "R. Kartch." It was evidently the check returned by Gregory Dermott to Kartch uncashed. It was made out for the same amount as Mellery's and Rudden's—$289.87. The name and address "*R. Kartch, 349 Quarry Road, Sotherton, Mass. 01055*" appeared in the upper left corner of the check.

R. Kartch. There was something about that name that bothered Gurney.

Perhaps it was just that same peculiar experience he always had when he looked at the printed name of a deceased person. It was as though the name itself had lost the breath of life, had become smaller, cut loose from that which had given it stature. It was strange, he reflected, how you can believe you have come to terms with death, even believe that its presence no longer has much effect on you, that it is just part of your profession. Then it comes at you in such a weird way—in the unsettling, shrunken quality of a dead man's name. No matter how hard one tries to ignore it, death finds a way to be noticed. It seeps into your feelings like water through a basement wall.

Perhaps that's why the name R. Kartch seemed odd to him. Or was there another reason?

Chapter 40

A shot in the dark

Mark Mellery. Albert Rudden. Richard Kartch. Three men. Targeted, mentally tortured, shot, and so forcibly and repeatedly stabbed that their heads were nearly hacked off. What had they done, separately or in concert, to engender such a macabre revenge?

Or was it revenge at all? Might the suggestion of revenge conveyed by the notes be—as Rodriguez had once proposed—a smoke screen to hide a more practical motive?

Anything was still possible.

It was nearly dawn when Gurney began his return drive to Walnut Crossing, and the air was raw with the scent of snow. He'd entered that strained state of consciousness in which a deep weariness struggles with an agitated wakefulness. Thoughts and pictures cascade through the brain without progress or logic.

One such image was the dead man's check, the name R. Kartch, something lurking beneath an inaccessible trapdoor of memory, something not quite right. Like a faint star, it eluded a direct search and might appear in his peripheral vision once he stopped looking for it.

He made an effort to focus on other aspects of the case, but his mind refused to proceed in an orderly way. Instead, he saw the half-dried pool of blood across Kartch's kitchen floor, the far edge spreading into the shadow of the rickety table. He stared hard at the highway ahead, trying to exorcise the image but succeeding only in replacing it with the bloodstain of similar size on Mark Mellery's stone patio—which in turn gave way to an image of Mellery in an Adirondack chair, leaning forward, asking for protection, deliverance.

Leaning forward, asking . . .

Gurney felt the pressure of tears welling.

He pulled in to a rest stop. There was only one other car in the little parking area, and it looked more abandoned than parked. His face felt hot, his hands cold. Not being able to think straight frightened him, made him feel helpless.

Exhaustion was a lens through which he had a tendency to see his life as a failure—a failure made more painful by the professional accolades heaped upon him. Knowing that this was a trick his tired mind played on him made it no less convincing. After all, he had his litany of proofs. As a detective, he'd failed Mark Mellery. As a husband, he'd failed Karen, and now he was failing Madeleine. As a father, he'd failed Danny, and now he was failing Kyle.

His brain had its limits, and after enduring another quarter hour of this laceration, it shut down. He fell into a brief, restorative sleep.

He wasn't sure how long it lasted, almost certainly less than an hour, but when he woke up, the emotional upheaval had passed and in its place was an uncluttered clarity. He also had a terribly stiff neck, but it seemed a small price to pay.

Perhaps because there was now room for it, a new vision of the Wycherly post-office box mystery began to form in his mind. The two original hypotheses had never seemed entirely satisfactory: namely, that the victims were directed by mistake to send their checks to the wrong box number (unlikely, given the killer's attention to detail) or that it was the right box but something had gone awry, allowing Dermott to receive and innocently return the checks before the killer could remove them through whatever method he'd devised.

But now Gurney saw a third explanation. Suppose it was the right box and nothing had gone awry. Suppose the purpose of asking for the checks had been something other than to cash them. Suppose the killer had managed to gain access to the box, open the envelopes, look at the checks or make copies of them, and then reseal them in their envelopes and replace them in the box before Dermott got to them.

If this new scenario was closer to the truth—if the killer was in fact using Dermott's post-office box for his own purposes—it opened a fascinating new avenue. *It might be possible for Gurney to communicate with the killer directly.* Despite its wildly hypothetical foundation, and despite the confusion and depression in which he'd just been immersed, this thought so excited him that several minutes passed before he realized that he'd pulled out of the rest stop and was racing homeward at eighty miles an hour.

Madeleine was out. He put his wallet and keys on the breakfast table and picked up the note lying there. It was in Madeleine's quick, clean handwriting and, as usual, challengingly concise: *"Went to 9 AM yoga. Back before storm. 5 messages. Was the fish a flounder?"*

What storm?

What fish?

He wanted to go into the den and listen to the five phone messages he assumed she was talking about, but there was something else he wanted to do first, something of greater urgency. The notion that he might be able to write to the killer—to send him a note via Dermott's mailbox—had given him an overwhelming desire to do so.

He could see that the scenario was shaky, with assumptions resting upon assumptions, but it had great appeal. The chance to *do* something was very exciting compared to the frustration of the investigation and that creepy sense that any progress they were making might be part of the enemy's plan. Impulsive and unreasonable as it was, the chance to toss a grenade over a wall where the enemy might be lurking was irresistible. The only thing remaining was to construct the grenade.

He really should listen to his messages. There could be something urgent, important. He started for the den. But a sentence came to mind—one he didn't want to forget, a rhyming couplet, the perfect beginning of a statement to the killer. Excitedly, he picked up the pad and pen Madeleine had left on the table and began to write. Fifteen minutes later he put down the pen and read the eight lines written in an elaborate, decorative script.

> *I see how all you did was done,*
> *from backwards boots to muffled gun.*
> *The game you started soon will end,*
> *your throat cut by a dead man's friend.*
> *Beware the snow, beware the sun,*
> *the night, the day, nowhere to run.*
> *With sorrow first his grave I'll tend*
> *and then to hell his killer send.*

Satisfied, he wiped the paper clean of fingerprints. It felt odd doing that—shady, evasive—but he brushed the feeling aside, got an envelope, and addressed it to X. Arybdis at Dermott's box number in Wycherly, Connecticut.

Chapter 41

Back to the real world

Gurney just made it down to the mailbox in time to hand the envelope to Rhonda, who filled in for Baxter, the regular mailman, two days a week. By the time he got back up through the pasture to the house, the excitement was already being gnawed at by the remorse that inevitably followed his rare acts of impulse.

He remembered his five messages.

The first was from the gallery in Ithaca.

"David, it's Sonya. We need to talk about your project. Nothing bad, all good, but we need to talk very, very soon. I'll be at the gallery until six this evening, or you can call me later at home."

The second was from Randy Clamm, and he sounded excited.

"Tried you at your cell phone, but it seems to be dead. We found some letters in the Rudden house we'd like you to look at—see if they look familiar. Seems Al was getting some weird little poems in the mail he didn't want his wife to see. Had them hidden in the bottom of his toolbox. Give me a number, and I'll fax them. Appreciate it."

The third was from Jack Hardwick at BCI, his supercilious attitude running amok.

"Hey, Sherlock, word is out that your guy has a couple more notches on his gun. You were probably too busy to give your old buddy a heads-up. I was, for one crazy moment, tempted to think that it was below the dignity of Mr. Sherlock Fucking Gurney to place a call to the humble Jack Hardwick. But of course that's not the kind of guy you are, right? Shame on me! Just to show you there's no hard feelings, I'm calling to give you a heads-up on a get-together being planned for tomorrow—a BCI progress report on the Mellery case, including a discussion of how recent events in the Bronx and in Sotherton should affect the direction of the investigation. Captain Rod will be hosting this clusterfuck. DA Kline is being invited, and he in turn will no doubt invite you. I just thought you'd like to know in advance. After all, what are friends for?"

The fourth message was the predicted call from Kline. It was not especially "invitational." The energy in his voice had curdled into agitation.

"Gurney, what the hell's the matter with your cell phone? We tried to reach you directly, then through the Sotherton police. They told me you left Sotherton two and a half hours ago. They also told me we are now dealing with murder number three by the same individual. That's an important fact, wouldn't you say? Something you should have called me about? We need to talk ASAP. Decisions have to be made, and we need every available piece of information. There's a meeting at BCI tomorrow noon. That's a priority. Call me as soon as you get this!"

The final message was from Mike Gowacki.

"Just wanted you to know, we dug a slug out of that hole in the kitchen wall. A .38 like you said. Also, one more little discovery after you left. We were checking the mailbox for any more of them red-ink love notes, and we found a dead fish. In the mailbox. You didn't mention a dead fish being part of the MO. Let me know if it means anything. I'm no psychologist, but I'd say our perp is a definite wacko. That's it for now. I'm going home to get some sleep."

A fish?

He went back out to the kitchen—to the breakfast table, to take another look at Madeleine's note.

"Went to 9 AM yoga. Back before storm. 5 messages. Was the fish a flounder?"

Why would she ask that? He checked the time on the old Regulator clock over the sideboard. Nine-thirty. Seemed more like dawn, the light coming in the French doors was such a chilly gray. *Back before storm.* It did look like it was about to do something, probably snow, hopefully not freezing rain. So she'd be home by ten-thirty, maybe ten if she got to worrying about the roads. Then he could ask about the flounder. Madeleine wasn't a worrier, but she had a thing about slippery roads.

He was going back to the den to return his calls when it struck him. The location of the first murder was the town of Peony, and the killer left a peony by the body of the second victim. The location of the second murder was the little Bronx enclave of Flounder Beach, making Madeleine's guess about the fish at the third crime scene characteristically insightful and almost certainly right.

His first callback was to Sotherton. The desk sergeant put him through to Gowacki's voice mail. He left two requests: for confirmation that the fish was a flounder and for ballistics photos so they could confirm that the slugs in Kartch's wall and in Mellery's wall came from the same gun. He didn't have much doubt on either point, but certainty was a holy thing.

Then he called Kline.

Kline was in court that morning. Ellen Rackoff reiterated the DA's complaints, scolding Gurney about the difficulty they'd had reaching him and his failure to keep them informed. She told him he'd better not miss the big meeting the following noon at BCI. But even into this lecture she managed to breathe an erotic undertone. Gurney wondered if his lack of sleep might be making him a little crazy.

He called Randy Clamm, thanked him for the update, and gave him a number at the DA's office to fax Rudden's letters, plus a number at BCI so a set could go to Rodriguez. Then he filled him in on the Richard Kartch situation, including the flounder connection and the fact that an alcohol element was now obvious in all three cases.

As for Sonya's call, that could wait. He was in no great rush to call Hardwick, either. His mind kept jumping to the following day's meeting at BCI. Not jumping there with joy—far from it. He hated meetings in general. His mind worked best alone. Groupthink made him want to leave the room. And his hasty poetic grenade tossing was making him uncomfortable about this meeting in particular. He didn't like having secrets.

He sank down in the soft leather armchair in the corner of the den to organize the key facts of the three cases, figure out what over-all hypothesis they best supported, and how to test it. But his sleep-deprived brain would not cooperate. He closed his eyes, and all semblance of linear thought dissolved. How long he sat there he wasn't sure, but when he opened his eyes, heavily falling snow had begun whitening the landscape, and in the singular stillness he could hear a car far down the road, coming closer. He pushed himself up out of the chair and went to the kitchen, arriving at the window in time to see Madeleine's car disappearing behind the barn at the end of the public road, presumably to check their mailbox. A minute later the phone rang. He picked up the extension on the kitchen counter.

"Good—you're there. Do you know if the mailman has been here yet?"

"Madeleine?"

"I'm down by the box. I have something to mail, but if he's been here already, I'll drop it off in town."

"Actually, it was Rhonda, and she was here a while ago."

"Damn. All right, no matter, I'll deal with it later."

Slowly her car emerged from behind the barn and turned up the pasture road to the house.

She entered through the side door of the kitchen with the strained look that driving in snow put on her face. Then she noted the very different look on his face.

"What's up?"

Engrossed in a thought that had occurred to him during her call from the mailbox, it wasn't until she'd taken off her coat and shoes that he answered.

"I think I just figured something out."

"Good!" She smiled and awaited the details, shaking snowflakes out of her hair.

"The number mystery—the second one. I know how he did it—or how he could have done it."

"The second one was?"

"The one with the number nineteen, the one Mellery recorded. I showed you the letter."

"I remember."

"The killer asked Mellery to think of a number and then to whisper it to him."

"Why did he ask him to whisper? By the way, that clock is wrong," she said, looking up at the Regulator.

He stared at her.

"Sorry," she said lightly. "Go on."

"I think he asked him to whisper because it added an odd element to the request that would lead him further from the truth than a simple 'Tell me the number.'"

"I don't follow you."

"The killer had no idea what number Mellery had in mind. The only way to find out was to ask him. He was just trying to blow some smoke around that issue."

"But wasn't the number mentioned in a letter the killer had already left in Mellery's mailbox?"

"Yes and no. Yes, the number was mentioned in the letter Mellery found in the box a few minutes later, but no, it wasn't *already* in the box. In fact, the letter hadn't been printed yet."

"You lost me."

"Suppose the killer had one of those mini printers attached to his laptop, with the text of the letter to Mellery complete except for the right number. And suppose the killer was sitting in his car by Mellery's mailbox on that dark country road that runs past the institute. He calls Mellery on his cell phone—like you just called me from our mailbox—persuades him to think of a number and then 'whisper' it, and the instant Mellery says the number, the killer enters it in the letter text and hits the print button. Half a minute later, he sticks the letter in an envelope, pops it in the mailbox, and drives off—creating the impression that he's a diabolical mind reader."

"Very clever," said Madeleine.

"Him or me?"

"Obviously both of you."

"I think it makes sense. And it makes sense that he recorded traffic noise—to give the impression that he was somewhere other than a quiet country road."

"Traffic noise?"

"Recorded traffic noise. Smart lab tech at BCI ran a sound-analysis program on the tape Mellery made of the phone call and discovered that there were two background sounds behind the killer's voice—a car engine and traffic. The engine was first generation—that is, the sound was actually occurring at the same time as the sound of the voice—but the traffic was second generation, meaning that a tape of traffic sounds was being played behind the live voice. Didn't make sense at first."

"Now it does," said Madeleine, "now that you've figured it out. Very good."

He looked closely at her, searching for the sarcasm that so often underlay her comments on his involvement in the case but finding none. She was regarding him with real admiration.

"I mean it," she said, as if detecting his doubt. "I'm impressed."

A recollection came to him with surprising poignancy: *how frequently she'd once looked at him that way in the early years of their marriage, how wonderful it had been to receive so often in so many ways the loving approval of such a fiercely intelligent woman, how priceless was the bond between them. And there it was again, or at least a delightful hint of it, alive in her eyes.* And then she turned a little sideways toward the window, and the gray light dimmed her expression. She cleared her throat.

"By the way, did we ever get a new roof rake? They're talking about ten to twelve inches of snow before midnight, and I'm not looking forward to another leak in the upstairs closet."

"Ten to twelve inches?"

He seemed to remember there was an old roof rake in the barn, maybe repairable with enough duct tape. . . .

She uttered a small sigh and headed for the stairs. "I'll just empty the closet."

He couldn't think of anything sensible to say. The phone ringing on the countertop saved him from saying something stupid. He picked it up on the third ring. "Gurney."

"Detective Gurney, this is Gregory Dermott." The voice was polite but fraught.

"Yes, Mr. Dermott?"

"Something happened. I want to make sure I'm alerting the proper authorities."

"Happened?"

"I received a peculiar communication. I think it may be connected to the letters you told me were received by the crime victims. Can I read it to you?"

"First tell me how you got it."

"How I got it is more disturbing than what it says. God, it makes my skin crawl! It was taped to the outside of my window—my kitchen window next to the little table where I have my breakfast every morning. Do you see what that means?"

"What?"

"It means he was there, right there touching the house, no more than fifty feet from where I was sleeping. And he knew what window to tape it to. That's what makes it so creepy."

"What do you mean, what window to tape it to?"

"The window where I sit every morning. That's no accident—he must know that I have breakfast at that table, which means he's been watching me."

"Have you called the police?"

"That's why I'm calling you now."

"I mean your local police."

"I know what you mean. Yes, I did call them—they're just not taking the situation seriously. I was hoping a call from you might help. Can you do that for me?"

"Tell me what the note says."

"Just a second. Here it is. Just two lines, written in red ink. 'Come one, come all. / Now all fools die.'"

"You read this to the police?"

"Yes. I explained there might be a connection to two murders, and they said a detective would be out to see me tomorrow morning, which doesn't sound to me like they think it's urgent."

Gurney weighed the pros and cons of telling him that there were now three murders but decided that the news wouldn't add anything except more fear, and Dermott sounded like he already had plenty of that.

"What does the message mean to you?"

"Mean?" Dermott's voice was panicky. "Just what it says. It says that someone is going to *die*. *Now*, it says. And the message was delivered to *me*. That's what it means, for Godsake! What's the matter with you people? How many dead bodies does it take to get your attention?"

"Try to stay calm, sir. Do you have the name of the police officer you spoke to?"

Upside down

By the time Gurney finished a tough phone conversation with Lieutenant John Nardo, Wycherly PD, he'd received grudging assurance that an officer would be dispatched that afternoon to provide Gregory Dermott with protection, at least temporarily, subject to a final decision by the chief.

The snowstorm, meanwhile, had grown into a swirling blizzard. Gurney had been up for nearly thirty hours and knew that he needed to sleep, but he decided to push himself a little further and put on a pot of coffee. He called upstairs to ask Madeleine if she wanted any. He couldn't decipher her monosyllabic answer, although he should have known what it would be. He asked again. This time the "No!" was loud and clear—louder and clearer than necessary, he thought.

The snow wasn't having its customary tranquilizing effect on him. The events in the case were piling up too rapidly, and launching his own poetic missive at the Wycherly post-office box in the hope of it reaching the killer was starting to feel like a mistake. He'd been given a degree of investigative autonomy, but it might not cover such "creative" interventions. As he waited for his coffee to brew, images of the Sotherton crime scene, including the flounder—which he pictured as vividly as if he'd seen it—competed with the note on Dermott's window for space in his mind. *Come one, come all. / Now all fools die.*

Searching for a route out of his emotional morass, it occurred to him that he could either repair the fractured roof rake or take a closer look at the "nineteen" business to see if it could lead him anywhere. He chose the latter.

Assuming that the deception had worked the way he believed it had, what conclusions could be drawn? That the killer was clever, imaginative, cool under pressure, playfully sadistic? That he was a control freak, obsessed with making his victims feel helpless? All of the above, but those qualities were already obvious. What wasn't obvious was why he'd chosen to go about it in that particular way. It dawned on Gurney that the outstanding fact about the "nineteen" trick was that it was a *trick*. And the effect of the trick was to create an impression that the perpetrator knew the victim well enough to know what he was thinking—without requiring any knowledge of him at all.

Christ!

What was that sentence in the second poem sent to Mellery?

Gurney almost ran from the kitchen into the den, grabbed his case file, and riffled through it. There it was! For the second time that day, he felt the thrill of touching a part of the truth.

> *I know what you think,*
> *when you blink,*
> *where you've been,*
> *where you'll be.*

What was it Madeleine had said that night in bed? Was that last night or the night before? Something about the messages being peculiarly nonspecific—having no facts in them, no names, no places, nothing real?

In Gurney's excitement he could feel major pieces of the puzzle clicking into place. The central piece was one he'd been holding upside down all along. The killer's intimate knowledge of his victims and their pasts was, it now seemed clear, a pretense. Again Gurney read through his file of the notes and phone calls Mellery and the others had received, and he wasn't able to find a scrap of evidence that the killer had any specific knowledge of them beyond their names and addresses. He did seem to know that at one time they all drank too much, but even there, there was no detail—no incident, person, place, time. It was all consistent with a killer trying to give his victims the impression that he knew them intimately when in fact he didn't know them at all.

This raised a new question. Why kill strangers? If the answer was that he had a pathological hatred for everyone with a drinking problem, then why not (as Randy Clamm had said to Gurney in the Bronx) just toss a bomb into the nearest AA meeting?

Again his thoughts began running in a circle, as weariness flooded his mind and body. With weariness came self-doubt. The elation of realizing how the number trick was done and what that meant about the relationship between the killer and his victims was replaced by that old self-critical feeling that he should have realized it sooner—and then by the fear that even this would turn out to be another dead end.

"What's wrong now?"

Madeleine was standing in the den doorway, holding a bulging black plastic garbage bag, her hair disarranged by her closet-clearing mission.

"Nothing."

She gave him an I-don't-believe-you look and deposited the garbage bag at the door. "This stuff was on your side of the closet."

He stared at the bag.

She went back upstairs.

The wind made a thin whistling sound at a window that needed new weather stripping. Damn. He'd meant to fix that. Every time the wind hit the house at that angle . . .

The phone rang.

It was Gowacki from Sotherton.

"Yeah, as a matter of fact, it's a flounder," he said without bothering to say hello. "How the hell did you know that?"

*   *   *

The fish confirmation gave Gurney's sleep-deprived psyche a quick lift out of the pit. It gave him enough energy to call the irritating Jack Hardwick about a point that had been bothering him all along. It was the first line of the third poem—which he extricated from his file as he dialed Hardwick's number.

> *I do what I've done*
> *not for money or fun*
> *but for debts to be paid,*
> *amends to be made.*
> *For blood that's as red*
> *as a painted rose.*
> *So every man knows*
> *he reaps what he sows.*

As usual, he had to endure a long minute of random abuse before he could get the BCI detective to listen to his concern and respond to it. The response was typical Hardwick.

"You figure the past tense means the perp already left a few severed heads behind him by the time he knocked off your buddy?"

"That would be the obvious meaning," said Gurney, "since the three victims we know of were alive when that was written."

"So what do you want me to do?"

"Might be a good idea to send out an MO inquiry for similars."

"How detailed you want the *modus operandi* spelled out?" Hardwick's arch intonation made the Latin term sound like a joke. His chauvinistic tendency to find foreign languages laughable always got under Gurney's skin.

"Up to you. In my opinion the throat wounds are the key piece."

"Hmm. You thinking this inquiry goes out to Pennsylvania, New York, Connecticut, Rhode Island, Massachusetts, maybe New Hampshire and Vermont?"

"I don't know, Jack. You decide."

"Time frame?"

"Last five years? Whatever you think."

"Last five years is as good as anything else." He made it sound as bad as anything else. "You all set for Captain R's get-together?"

"Tomorrow? Sure, I'll be there."

There was a pause. "So you think this fucking lunatic has been at this for a while?"

"Looks like a possibility, doesn't it?"

Another pause. "You getting anywhere on your end?"

Gurney gave Hardwick a summary of the facts and his new interpretation of them, ending with a suggestion. "I know that Mellery was in rehab fifteen years ago. You might want to check for any criminal or public-record data on him—anything involving alcohol. Ditto for Albert Rudden, ditto Richard Kartch. The homicide guys on the Rudden and Kartch cases are working on victim bios. They may have dug up something relevant. While you're at it, it wouldn't hurt to poke a little further into the background of Gregory Dermott. He's entangled in this mess somehow. The killer chose that Wycherly post-office box for some reason, and now he's threatening Dermott himself."

"He's what?"

Gurney told Hardwick about the "*Come one, come all. / Now all fools die*" note taped to Dermott's window and about his conversation with Lieutenant Nardo.

"What are you thinking we'll find in the background checks?"

"Something that makes sense out of three facts. First, the killer is focused on victims with drinking histories. Second, there is no evidence that he knew any of them personally. Third, he selected victims who lived far apart geographically, which suggests some factor in their selection other than just excessive alcohol consumption—a factor that connects them to each other, to the killer, and probably to Dermott. I have no idea what it is, but I'll know it when I see it."

"Is that a fact?"

"See you tomorrow, Jack."

Chapter 43

Madeleine

T omorrow came with a peculiar suddenness. After his conversation with Hardwick, Gurney had taken off his shoes and sprawled on the den couch. He slept deeply, without interruption, through the remainder of the afternoon and on through the night. When he opened his eyes, it was morning.

He stood, stretched, looked out the window. The sun was creeping up over the brown ridge on the eastern side of the valley, which he figured would make it about 7:00 A.M. He didn't have to leave for his BCI meeting until 10:30. The sky was perfectly blue, and the snow glittered as though it had been mixed with shattered glass. The beauty and peace of the scene mingled with the aroma of fresh coffee to make life for the moment seem simple and fundamentally good. His long rest had been thoroughly restorative. He felt ready to make the phone calls he'd been postponing—to Sonya and to Kyle—and was stopped only by the realization that they'd both still be asleep. He lingered for a few seconds over the image of Sonya in bed, then went out to the kitchen, resolving to make the calls right after nine.

The house had the empty feeling it always had when Madeleine was out. Her absence was confirmed by the note he found on the countertop: "*Dawn. Sun about to come up. Incredibly beautiful. Snowshoeing to Carlson's Ledge. Coffee in pot. M.*" He went to the bathroom, washed, brushed his teeth. As he was combing his hair, the thought occurred to him that he could set out after her. Her reference to the imminent sunrise meant she'd left within the past ten minutes or so. If he used his cross-country skis and followed in her snowshoe tracks, he could probably overtake her in about twenty minutes.

He put ski pants and boots on over his jeans, pulled on a thick wool sweater, snapped on his skis, and stepped out the back door into a foot of powdery snow. The ridge, which offered a long view of the north valley and the rows of hills beyond it, was about a mile distant and reachable by an old logging trail that rose up a gentle incline starting at the back end of their property. It was impassible in summer with its tangles of wild raspberry bushes, but in late fall and winter the thorny undergrowth subsided.

A family of cautious crows, their harsh cries the only sound in the cold air, took flight from bare treetops a hundred yards ahead of him and soon disappeared over the ridge, leaving behind an even deeper silence.

As Gurney emerged from the woods onto the promontory above Carlson's hillside farm, he saw Madeleine. She was sitting motionless on a stone slab, perhaps fifty feet from him, looking out over the rolling landscape that receded to the horizon with only two distant silos and a meandering road to suggest any human presence. He stopped, transfixed by the stillness of her pose. She seemed so . . . so absolutely solitary . . . yet so intensely *connected* to her world. A kind of beacon, beckoning him to a place just beyond his reach.

Without warning, without words to contain the feeling, the sight tore at his heart.

Dear God, was he having some kind of breakdown? For the third time in a week, his eyes filled with tears. He swallowed and wiped his face. Feeling light-headed, he moved his skis farther apart to steady himself.

Perhaps it was this motion at the corner of her vision, or the sound of the skis in the dry snow, that caused her to turn. She watched as he approached her. She smiled a little but said nothing. He had the rather peculiar feeling that she could see his soul as clearly as his body—peculiar, because "soul" was not a notion he'd ever found meaning in, not a term he ever used. He sat beside her on the flat boulder and stared out, unseeing, at the vista of hills and valleys. She took his arm in hers and held it against her.

He studied her face. He was at a loss for words to capture what he saw. It was as if all the radiance of the snow-covered landscape were reflected in her expression and the radiance of her expression were reflected in the landscape.

After a while—he couldn't be sure how long it was—they headed back by a roundabout route to the house.

About halfway there he asked, "What are you thinking?"

"Not thinking at all. It gets in the way."

"Of what?"

"The blue sky, the white snow."

He didn't speak again until they were back in the kitchen.

"I never did have that coffee you left for me," he said.

"I'll make a fresh pot."

He watched as she got a bag of coffee beans out of the refrigerator and measured some into the electric grinder.

"Yes?" She regarded him curiously, her finger on the button.

"Nothing," he said. "Just watching."

She pressed the button. There was a sharp barrage of noise from the little machine, which grew softer as the beans were pulverized. She looked at him again.

"I'll check the closet," he said, feeling a need to do something.

He started upstairs, but before reaching the closet he stopped on the landing at the window that faced the rear field and the woods beyond it and the trail to the ledge. He pictured her sitting on the rock in her solitary peace, and that nameless emotional intensity filled him again, achingly. He struggled to identify the pain.

Loss. Separation. Isolation.

Each rang true, each a facet of the same sensation.

The therapist he'd seen in his late teens as the result of a panic attack—the therapist who'd told him that the panic arose from a deep hostility he carried toward his father and that his complete lack of any conscious emotion for his father was proof of the hidden strength and negativity of the emotion—that same therapist had one day confided to him what he believed to be the purpose of life.

"The purpose of life is to get as close as we can to other people." He'd said it in a surprisingly straightforward way, as though he were pointing out that trucks were for transportation.

On another occasion he revealed, in the same matter-of-fact tone, the corollary: "An isolated life is a wasted life."

At the age of seventeen, Gurney hadn't been sure what the man was talking about. It sounded deep, but its depth was shadowy, and he couldn't see anything in it. He still didn't entirely grasp it at the age of forty-seven—at least not the way he grasped the purpose of trucks.

Forgetting about the closet, he went back down to the kitchen. Entering from the darker hallway, he found the room intensely bright. The sun, now well above the trees in a cloudless sky, shone directly through the southeast-facing French doors. The pasture had been transformed by the new snow into a dazzling reflector, throwing light up into corners of the room rarely illuminated.

"Your coffee is ready," said Madeleine. She was carrying a balled-up sheet of newspaper and a handful of kindling to the woodstove. "The light is so magical. Like music."

He smiled and nodded. Sometimes he envied her ability to be enthralled by nature's glittering bits and pieces. Why, he wondered, had such a woman, such an enthusiast, such a natural aesthete in the admirable sense of the word, a woman so in touch with the *glory* of things, married an unspontaneous and cerebral detective? Had she imagined that one day he'd cast aside the gray cocoon of his profession? Had he colluded in that fantasy, imagining that in a pastoral retirement he'd become a different person?

They made an odd couple, he thought, but surely no odder than his parents. His mother with all her artistic inclinations, all her little flight-of-fancy hobbies—papier-mâché sculpture, fantastical water-color painting, origami—had married his father, a man whose essential drabness was interrupted only by sparks of sarcasm, whose attention was always elsewhere, whose passions were unknown, and whose departure for work in the morning seemed to please him far more than did his return home in the evening. A man who in his quest for peace was forever *leaving*.

"What time do you have to leave for your meeting?" asked Madeleine, displaying her impossibly precise sensitivity to his passing thoughts.

Chapter 44

Final arguments

Déjà vu.

The sign-in procedure was the same as it had been before. The building's reception area—ironically designed to repel—was as antiseptic as a morgue but less peaceful. There was a new guard in the security booth, but the lighting gave him the same chemotherapy pallor as it had the last one. And, once again, Gurney's guide to the claustrophobic conference room was the hair-gelled, charming-as-dirt Investigator Blatt.

He preceded Gurney into the room, which was as Gurney remembered it, except it seemed shabbier. There were stains he hadn't noticed before on the colorless carpeting. The clock, not quite vertical and too small for the wall, read twelve noon. As usual, Gurney was exactly on time—less a virtue than a neurosis. Earliness and lateness both made him uncomfortable.

Blatt took a seat at the table. Wigg and Hardwick were already there in the same chairs they'd had in the first meeting. A woman with an edgy expression was standing by the coffee urn in the corner, obviously unhappy that Gurney hadn't been accompanied by whomever she was waiting for. She looked so much like Sigourney Weaver that Gurney wondered if she was making a conscious effort.

The three chairs nearest the center of the oblong table had been tilted against it, as before. As Gurney headed for the coffee, Hardwick grinned like a shark.

"Detective First Class Gurney, I've got a question for you."

"Hello, Jack."

"Or, better yet, I've got an answer for you. Let's see if you can guess what the question is. The answer is 'a defrocked priest in Boston.' To win the grand prize, all you got to do is figure out the question."

Instead of responding, Gurney picked up a cup, noticed it wasn't quite clean, put it back, tried another, then a third, then went back to the first.

Sigourney was tapping her foot and checking her Rolex, a parody of impatience.

"Hi," he said, resignedly filling his stained cup with what he hoped was antiseptically hot coffee. "I'm Dave Gurney."

"I'm Dr. Holdenfield," she said, as if she were laying down a straight flush to his pair of deuces. "Is Sheridan on his way?"

Something complex in her tone got his attention. And "Holdenfield" rang a bell.

"I wouldn't know." He wondered what sort of relationship might exist between the DA and the doctor. "If you don't mind my asking, what sort of doctor are you?"

"Forensic psychologist," she said absently, looking not at him but at the door.

"Like I said, Detective," said Hardwick, too loudly for the size of the room, "if the answer is a defrocked Boston priest, what's the question?"

Gurney closed his eyes. "For Christ's sake, Jack, why don't you just tell me?"

Hardwick wrinkled his face in distaste. "Then I'd have to explain it twice—for you and for the executive committee." He tilted his head at the tilted chairs.

The doctor looked again at her watch. Sergeant Wigg looked at whatever was happening on her laptop screen in response to the keys she was tapping. Blatt looked bored. The door opened, and Kline entered, looking preoccupied, followed by Rodriguez, carrying a fat file folder and looking more malevolent than ever, and Stimmel, looking like a pessimistic frog. When they were seated, Rodriguez gave Kline a questioning glance.

"Go ahead," said Kline.

Rodriguez fixed his gaze on Gurney, his lips tightening into a thin line.

"There's been a tragic development. A Connecticut police officer, dispatched to the home of Gregory Dermott, reportedly at your insistence, has been killed."

All eyes in the room, with various degrees of unpleasant curiosity, turned toward Gurney.

"How?" He asked the question calmly, despite a twinge of anxiety.

"Same way as your friend." There was something sour and insinuating in his tone, which Gurney chose not to respond to.

"Sheridan, what the hell is going on here?" The doctor, who was standing at the far end of the table, sounded so much like the hostile Sigourney of *Alien* that Gurney decided it must be on purpose.

"Becca! Sorry, didn't see you there. We got a little tied up. Last-minute complication. Apparently another murder." He turned to Rodriguez. "Rod, why don't you bring everyone up to date on this Connecticut cop thing." He gave his head a quick little shake, like there was water in one of his ears. "Damnedest case I've ever seen!"

"Damn right," echoed Rodriguez, opening his file folder. "Call was received at eleven twenty-five this morning from Lieutenant John Nardo of the Wycherly, Connecticut, PD regarding a homicide on the property of one Gregory Dermott, known to us as the postal-box holder in the Mark Mellery case. Dermott had been provided with temporary police protection at the insistence of Special Investigator David Gurney. At eight A.M. this morning—"

Kline raised his hand. "Hold on a second, Rod. Becca, have you met Dave?"

"Yes."

The cool, clipped affirmative seemed designed to ward off any expanded introduction, but Kline went on, anyway.

"You two should have a lot to talk about. The psychologist with the most accurate profiling record in the business and the detective with the most homicide arrests in the history of the NYPD."

The praise seemed to make everyone uncomfortable. But it also made Holdenfield look at Gurney with some interest for the first time. And although he was no fan of professional profilers, now he knew why her name sounded familiar.

Kline went on, determined, it seemed, to highlight his two stars. "Becca reads their minds, Gurney tracks them down—Cannibal Claus, Jason Strunk, Peter Possum Whatshisname . . ."

The doctor turned to Gurney, her eyes widening just a little. "Piggert? That was your case?"

Gurney nodded.

"Quite a celebrated arrest," she said with a hint of admiration.

He managed a small, distracted smile. The situation in Wycherly—and the question of whether his own impulsive intervention with the mailed poem had any bearing on the death of the police officer—was eating at him.

"Keep going, Rod," said Kline abruptly, as though the captain had caused the interruption.

"At eight A.M. this morning, Gregory Dermott made a trip to the Wycherly post office, accompanied by Officer Gary Sissek. According to Dermott, they returned at eight-thirty, at which time he made some coffee and toast and went through his mail, while Officer Sissek remained outside to check the perimeters of the property and the external security of the house. At nine A.M. Dermott went to look for Officer Sissek and discovered his body on the back porch. He called 911. First responders secured the scene and found a note taped to the back door above the body."

"Bullet and multiple stab wounds like the others?" asked Holdenfield.

"Stab wounds confirmed, no determination yet regarding the bullet."

"And the note?"

Rodriguez read from a fax in his folder. "'*Where did I come from? / Where did I go? / How many will die / because you don't know?'"*

"Same weirdo stuff," said Kline. "What do you think, Becca?"

"The process may be accelerating."

"The process?"

"Everything up till now was carefully premeditated—the choice of victims, the series of notes, all of it. But this one is different, more reactive than planned."

Rodriguez looked skeptical. "It's the same stabbing ritual, same kind of note."

"But it was an unplanned victim. It looks like your Mr. Dermott was the original target, but this policeman was opportunistically killed instead."

"But the note—"

"The note may have been brought to the scene to place on Dermott's body, if all had gone well, or it may have been composed on the spot in response to the altered circumstances. It may be significant that it is only four lines long. Weren't the others eight lines?" She looked at Gurney for confirmation.

He nodded, still half lost in guilty speculation, then forced himself back into the present. "I agree with Dr. Holdenfield. I hadn't thought about the possible significance of the four lines versus eight, but that makes sense. One thing I would add is that although it couldn't have been planned the same way the others were, the element of cop hatred that is part of this killer's mind-set at least partially integrates this killing into the pattern and may account for the ritual aspects the captain referred to."

"Becca said something about the pace accelerating," said Kline. "We already have four victims. Does that mean there are more to come?"

"Five, actually."

All eyes turned to Hardwick.

The captain held up his fist and extended a finger as he enunciated each name: "Mellery. Rudden. Kartch. Officer Sissek. That makes four."

"The Reverend Michael McGrath makes five," said Hardwick.

"Who?" The question erupted in jangled unison from Kline (excited), the captain (vexed), and Blatt (baffled).

"Five years ago a priest in the Boston diocese was relieved of his pastoral duties due to allegations involving a number of altar boys. He made some kind of deal with the bishop, blamed his inappropriate behavior on alcoholism, went to a long-term rehab, dropped out of sight, end of story."

"What the hell was it with the Boston diocese?" sneered Blatt. "Whole goddamn place was crawling with kid-fuckers."

Hardwick ignored him. "End of story until a year ago, when McGrath was found dead in his apartment. Multiple stab wounds to the throat. A revenge note was taped to the body. It was an eight-line poem in red ink."

Rodriguez's face was flushing. "How long have you known this?"

Hardwick looked at his watch. "Half an hour."

"What?"

"Yesterday Special Investigator Gurney requested a northeast-states regional inquiry to all departments for MOs similar to the Mellery case. This morning we got a hit—the late Father McGrath."

"Anyone arrested or prosecuted for his murder?" asked Kline.

"Nope. Boston homicide guy I spoke to wouldn't come out and say it, but I got the impression they hadn't exactly prioritized the case."

"What's that supposed to mean?" The captain sounded petulant.

Hardwick shrugged. "Former pederast gets himself stabbed to death, killer leaves a note referring vaguely to past misdeeds. Looks like someone decided to get even. Maybe the cops figure what the hell, they got other shit on their plates, plenty of other perps to catch with motives less noble than delayed justice. So maybe they don't pay too much attention."

Rodriguez looked like he had indigestion. "But he didn't actually say that."

"Of course he didn't say that."

"So," said Kline in his summation voice, "whatever the Boston police did or didn't do, the fact is, Father Michael McGrath is number five."

"*Sí, número cinco*," said Hardwick inanely. "But really *número uno*—since the priest got himself sliced up a year before the other four."

"So Mellery, who we thought was the first, was really the second," said Kline.

"I doubt that very strongly," said Holdenfield. When she had everyone's attention, she went on, "There's no evidence that the priest was the first—he may have been the tenth for all we know—but even if he *was* the first, there's another problem. One killing a year ago, then four in less than two weeks, is not a pattern you normally see. I would expect others in between."

"Unless," Gurney interjected softly, "some factor other than the killer's psychopathology is driving the timing and the selection of victims."

"What did you have in mind?"

"I believe it's something the victims have in common other than alcoholism, something we haven't found yet."

Holdenfield rocked her head speculatively from side to side and made a face that said she wasn't about to agree with Gurney's supposition but couldn't find a way to shoot it down, either.

"So we may or may not discover links to some old corpses," said Kline, looking unsure of how he felt about this.

"Not to mention some new ones," said Holdenfield.

"What's that supposed to mean?" It was becoming Rodriguez's favorite question.

Holdenfield showed no reaction to the testy tone. "The pace of the killings, as I started to say earlier, suggests that the endgame has begun."

"Endgame?" Kline intoned the word as though he liked the sound of it.

Holdenfield continued, "In this most recent instance, he was driven to act in an unplanned way. The process may be spinning out of his control. My feeling is that he won't be able to hold it together much longer."

"Hold what together?" Blatt posed the question, as he posed most of his questions, with a kind of congenital hostility.

Holdenfield regarded him for moment without expression, then looked at Kline. "How much education do I need to provide here?"

"You might want to touch on a few key points. Correct me if I'm wrong," he said, glancing around the table and clearly not expecting to be corrected, "but with the exception of Dave, I don't think the rest of us have had much practical experience with serial murder."

Rodriguez looked like he was about to object to something but said nothing.

Holdenfield smiled unhappily. "Is everyone at least familiar in a general way with the Holmes typology of serial murder?"

The assortment of murmurs and nods around the table was generally affirmative. Only Blatt had a question. "Sherlock Holmes?"

Gurney wasn't sure whether this was a stupid joke or just stupid.

"Ronald M. Holmes—a bit more contemporary, and an actual person," said Holdenfield in an exaggeratedly benign tone that Gurney couldn't quite place. Was it possible she was mimicking Mister Rogers addressing a five-year-old?

"Holmes categorized serial killers by their motivations—the type driven by imagined voices; the type on a mission to rid the world of some intolerable group of people—blacks, gays, you name it; the type seeking total domination; the thrill seeker who gets his greatest rush from killing; and the sex murderer. But they all have one thing in common—"

"They're all fucking nuts," said Blatt with a smug grin.

"Good point, Investigator," said Holdenfield with a deadly sweetness, "but what they really have in common is a terrible inner tension. Killing someone provides them with temporary relief from that tension."

"Sort of like getting laid?"

"Investigator Blatt," said Kline angrily, "it might be a good idea to keep your questions to yourself until Rebecca finishes her comments."

"His question is actually quite apt. An orgasm does relieve sexual tension. However, it does not in a normal person create a dysfunctional downward spiral demanding increasingly frequent orgasms at greater and greater cost. In that respect I believe serial killing has more in common with drug dependency."

"Murder addiction," said Kline slowly, speculatively, as though he were trying out a headline for a press release.

"Dramatic phrase," said Holdenfield, "and there's some truth in it. More than most people, the serial killer lives in his own fantasy world. He may appear to function normally in society. But he derives no satisfaction from his public life, and he has no interest in the real lives of other people. He lives only for his fantasies—fantasies of control, domination, punishment. For him these fantasies constitute a superreality—a world in which he feels important, omnipotent, alive. Any questions at this point?"

"I have one," said Kline. "Do you have an opinion yet on which of the serial-killer types we're looking for?"

"I do, but I'd love to hear what Detective Gurney has to say about that."

Gurney suspected that her earnest, collegial expression was as phony as her smile.

"A man on a mission," he said.

"Ridding the world of alcoholics?" Kline sounded half curious, half skeptical.

"I think 'alcoholic' would be part of the target-victim definition, but there may be more to it—to account for his specific choice of victims."

Kline responded with a noncommittal grunt. "In terms of a more expanded profile, something more than 'a man on a mission,' how would you describe our perp?"

Gurney decided to play tit for tat. "I have a few ideas, but I'd love to hear what Dr. Holdenfield has to say about that."

She shrugged, then spoke quickly and matter-of-factly. "Thirty-

year-old white male, high IQ, no friendships, no normal sexual relationships. Polite but distant. He almost certainly had a troubled
childhood, with a central trauma that influences his choice of victims. Since his victims are middle-aged men, it's possible the trauma
involved his father and an oedipal relationship with his mother—"

Blatt broke in. "You're not saying that this guy was literally . . . I
mean, are you saying . . . with his mother?"

"Not necessarily. This is all about fantasy. He lives in and for his
fantasy life."

Rodriguez's voice was jagged with impatience. "I'm having a real
problem with that word, Doctor. Five dead bodies are not fantasies!"

"You're right, Captain. To you and me, they're not fantasies at
all. They're real people, individuals with unique lives, worthy of
respect, worthy of justice, but that's not what they are to a serial
murderer. To him they're merely actors in his play—not human
beings as you and I understand the term. They are only the two-
dimensional stage props he imagines them to be—pieces of his fantasy, like the ritual elements found at the crime scenes."

Rodriguez shook his head. "What you're saying may make some
kind of sense in the case of a lunatic serial murderer, but so what? I
mean, I have other problems with this whole approach. I mean, who
decided this was a serial-murder case? You're racing down that road
without the slightest . . ." He hesitated, seeming suddenly aware of
the stridency of his voice and the impolitic nature of attacking one
of Sheridan Kline's favorite consultants. He went on in a softer register. "I mean, sequential murders are not always the work of a serial
murderer. There are other ways to look at this."

Holdenfield looked honestly baffled. "You have alternative
hypotheses?"

Rodriguez sighed. "Gurney keeps talking about some factor in
addition to drinking that accounts for the choice of victims. An obvious factor might be their common involvement in some past action,
accidental or intentional, which injured the killer, and all we're seeing now is revenge on the group responsible for the injury. It could
be as simple as that."

"I can't say a scenario like that is impossible," said Holdenfield, "but the planning, the poems, the details, the ritual all seem too pathological for simple revenge."

"Speaking of pathological," rasped Jack Hardwick like a man enthusiastically dying of throat cancer, "this might be the perfect time to bring everyone up to date on the latest piece of batshit evidence."

Rodriguez glared at him. "Another little surprise?"

Hardwick continued without reaction, "At Gurney's request, a team of techs was sent out to the B&B where he thought the killer might have stayed the night before the Mellery murder."

"Who approved that?"

"I did, sir," said Hardwick. He sounded proud of his transgression.

"Why didn't I see any paperwork on that?"

"Gurney didn't think there was time," lied Hardwick. Then he raised his hand to his chest with a curiously stricken I-think-I'm-having-a-heart-attack look and let loose with an explosive belch. Blatt, startled out of a private reverie, jerked back from the table so energetically his chair nearly toppled backwards.

Before Rodriguez, jangled by the interruption, could refocus on his paperwork concern, Gurney took the ball from Hardwick and launched into an explanation of why he'd wanted an evidence team at The Laurels.

"The first letter the killer sent to Mellery used the name X. Arybdis. In Greek, an x is equivalent to a *ch*, and Charybdis is the name of a murderous whirlpool in Greek mythology, linked to another fatal peril named Scylla. The night before the morning of Mellery's murder, a man and an older woman using the name Scylla stayed at that B&B. I would be very surprised if that were a coincidence."

"A man and an older woman?" Holdenfield looked intrigued.

"Possibly the killer and his mother, although the register, oddly enough, was signed 'Mr. and Mrs.' Maybe that supports the oedipal piece of your profile?"

Holdenfield smiled. "It's almost too perfect."

Again the captain's frustration seemed about to burst open, but Hardwick spoke first, picking up where Gurney had left off.

"So we sent the evidence team out there to this weird-ass little cottage that's decorated like a shrine to *The Wizard of Oz*. They go over it—inside, outside, upside down—and what do they find? Zip. Nada. Not a goddamn thing. Not a hair, not a smudge, not one iota that would tell you a human being had ever been in the room. Team leader couldn't believe it. She called me, told me there wasn't a hint of a fingerprint in places where there are always fingerprints—desktops, countertops, doorknobs, drawer pulls, window sashes, phones, shower handles, sink faucets, TV remotes, lamp switches, a dozen other places where you always find prints. Zilch. Not even one. Not even a partial. So I told her to dust everything—everything—walls, floors, the fucking ceiling. The conversation got a little testy, but I was persuasive. Then she starts calling me every half hour to tell me how she's still not finding anything and how much of her precious time I'm wasting. But the third time she calls, there's something different about her voice—it's a little quieter. She tells me they found something."

Rodriguez was too careful to let his disappointment show, but Gurney could feel it. Hardwick went on after a dramatic pause. "They found a word on the outside of the bathroom door. One word. *Redrum.*"

"What?" barked Rodriguez, not quite so careful about hiding his disbelief.

"*Redrum.*" Hardwick repeated the word slowly, with a knowing look, as though it were the key to something.

"*Redrum?* Like in the movie?" asked Blatt.

"Wait a second, wait a second," said Rodriguez, blinking with frustration. "You're telling me it took your evidence team, what, three, four hours to find a word written in plain sight on a door?"

"Not in plain sight," said Hardwick. "He wrote it the same way he left the invisible messages for us on the notes to Mark Mellery. DUMB EVIL COPS. Remember?"

The captain's only acknowledgment of the recollection was a silent stare.

"I saw that in the case file," said Holdenfield. "Something about words he rubbed onto the backs of the notes with his own skin oil. Is that actually feasible?"

"No problem at all," said Hardwick. "Fingerprints, in fact, are nothing but skin oil. He just utilized that resource for his own purpose. Maybe rubbed his fingers on his forehead to make them a little oilier. But it definitely worked then, and he did it again at The Laurels."

"But we *are* talking about the *redrum* from the movie, right?" repeated Blatt.

"Movie? What movie? Why are we talking about a movie?" Rodriguez was blinking again.

"*The Shining,*" said Holdenfield with growing excitement. "A famous scene. The little boy writes the word *redrum* on a door in his mother's bedroom."

"*Redrum* is *murder* spelled backwards," announced Blatt.

"God, it's all so perfect!" said Holdenfield.

"I assume all this enthusiasm means we'll have an arrest within the next twenty-four hours?" Rodriguez seemed to be straining for maximum sarcasm.

Gurney ignored him and addressed Holdenfield. "It's interesting that he wanted to remind us of *redrum* from *The Shining.*"

Her eyes glittered. "The perfect word from the perfect movie."

Kline, who for a long while had been observing the interplay at the table like a fan at one of his club's squash matches, finally spoke up. "Okay, guys, it's time to let me in on the secret. What the hell is so perfect?"

Holdenfield looked at Gurney. "You tell him about the word. I'll tell him about the movie."

"The word is backwards. It's as simple as that. It's been a theme since the beginning of the case. Just like the backwards trail of footprints in the snow. And, of course, it's the word *murder* that's backwards. He's telling us we've got the whole case backwards. DUMB EVIL COPS."

Kline fixed Holdenfield with his cross-examiner's gaze. "You agree with that?"

"Basically, yes."

"And the movie?"

"Ah, yes, the movie. I'll try to be as concise as Detective Gurney." She thought for a few moments, then spoke as if choosing each word carefully. "The movie is about a family in which a mother and son are terrorized by a crazy father. A father who happens to be an alcoholic with a history of violent binges."

Rodriguez shook his head. "Are you telling us that some crazy, violent, alcoholic father is our killer?"

"Oh, no, no. Not the father. The son."

"The son!?" Rodriguez's expression was twisted into new extremes of incredulity.

As she continued, Holdenfield slipped into something close to her Mister Rogers voice. "I believe that the killer is telling us that he had a father like the father in *The Shining*. I believe he may be explaining himself to us."

"Explaining himself?" Rodriguez's voice was close to sputtering.

"Everyone wants to present himself on his own terms, Captain. I'm sure you encounter that all the time in your line of work. I certainly do. We all have a rationale for our own behavior, however bizarre it may be. Everyone wants to be recognized as justified, even the mentally disturbed—perhaps especially the mentally disturbed."

This observation led to a general silence, which was eventually broken by Blatt.

"I've got a question. You're a psychiatrist, right?"

"A consulting forensic psychologist." Mister Rogers had morphed back into Sigourney Weaver.

"Right, whatever. You know how the mind works. So here's the question. This guy knew what number someone would think of before they thought of it. How did he do that?"

"He didn't."

"He sure as hell did."

"He appeared to do it. I assume you're referring to the incidents I read about in the case file involving the numbers six fifty-eight and nineteen. But he didn't actually do what you're saying. It's simply not possible to know in advance what number would occur to another individual in uncontrolled circumstances. Therefore he didn't."

"But the fact is that he did," Blatt persisted.

"There's at least one explanation," said Gurney. He went on to outline the scenario that had occurred to him when Madeleine was calling him on her cell phone from their mailbox—namely, how the killer could have used a portable printer in his car to create the letter with the number nineteen in it after Mark Mellery had mentioned it on the phone.

Holdenfield looked impressed.

Blatt looked deflated—a sure sign, thought Gurney, that lurking somewhere in that crude brain and overexercised body was a romantic in love with the weird and impossible. But the deflation was only momentary.

"What about the six fifty-eight?" Blatt asked, his combative gaze flicking back and forth between Gurney and Holdenfield. "There was no phone call that time, just a letter. So how did he know Mellery would think of that number?"

"I don't have an answer for that," said Gurney, "but I have an odd little story that might help someone think of an answer."

Rodriguez showed some impatience, but Kline leaned forward, and this demonstration of interest seemed to hold the captain in check.

"The other day I had a dream about my father," Gurney began. He hesitated, involuntarily. His own voice sounded different to him. He heard in it an echo of the profound sadness the dream had generated in him. He saw Holdenfield looking at him curiously but not unpleasantly. He forced himself to continue. "After I woke up, I found myself thinking about a card trick my father used to do when we had people to the house for New Year's and he'd had a few drinks, which always used to energize him. He'd fan out a deck and go around the room, asking three or four people to each pick a card. Then he'd narrow the focus down to one of those people and tell him to take a good look at the card he'd picked and put it back in the deck. Then he'd hand him the deck and tell him to shuffle it. After that he'd go into his mumbo-jumbo 'mind-reading' act, which could go on for another ten minutes, and it would finally end with him dramatically revealing the name of the card—which, of course, he knew from the moment it was picked."

"How?" asked Blatt, mystified.

"When he was getting the deck ready in the beginning, just before he fanned the cards out, he'd manage to identify at least one card and then control its position in the fan."

"Suppose no one picked it?" asked Holdenfield, intrigued.

"If no one picked it, he'd find a reason to discontinue the trick by creating some sort of distraction—suddenly remembering he had the kettle on for tea or something like that—so no one would realize there was a problem with the trick itself. But he almost never had to do that. The way he presented the fan-out, the first or second or third person he offered it to almost always picked the card he wanted them to. And if not, he'd just do his little kitchen routine, then come back and start the trick over. And of course he always had some perfectly plausible way of eliminating the people who'd picked the wrong cards, so no one would realize what was actually going on."

Rodriguez yawned. "Is this somehow related to the six fifty-eight business?"

"I'm not sure," said Gurney, "but the idea of someone thinking he's picking a card at random, while the randomness is actually being controlled—"

Sergeant Wigg, who had been listening with increasing interest, broke in. "Your card trick story reminds me of that private-eye direct-mail scam back in the late nineties."

Whether it was due to her unusual voice, pitched in the register where male and female overlap, or to the unusual fact that she was speaking at all, she captured everyone's instant attention.

"The recipient gets a letter, supposedly from a private-investigation company, apologizing for invading the recipient's privacy. The company 'confesses' that in the course of a botched surveillance assignment they mistakenly followed this individual for several weeks and photographed him in various situations. They claim that they are required by privacy legislation to give him all the existing prints of these photos. Then comes the curveball question: Since some of the photos seem to be of a compromising nature, would the recipient like them sent to a post-office box rather than to his home? If so, he will need to send them a fifty-dollar fee to cover the additional record keeping."

"Anyone stupid enough to fall for that deserves to lose fifty dollars," sneered Rodriguez.

"Oh, some people lost a lot more than that," said Wigg placidly. "It wasn't about getting the fifty-dollar payment. That was only a test. The scammer mailed out over a million of those letters, and the only purpose of the fifty-dollar request was to develop a refined list of people guilty enough about their behavior that they wouldn't want photos of their activities to fall into the hands of their spouses. Those individuals were then subjected to a series of far more exorbitant requests for payments related to the return of the compromising photographs. Some ended up paying as much as fifteen thousand dollars."

"For photos that never existed!" exclaimed Kline with an amalgam of indignation and admiration for the scammer's ingenuity.

"The stupidity of people never ceases to amaze—" began Rodriguez, but Gurney interrupted him.

"Jesus! That's it! That's what the two-hundred-eighty-nine-dollar request is. It's the same thing. It's a test!"

Rodriguez looked baffled. "A test of what?"

Gurney closed his eyes to help him visualize the letter Mellery had received asking for the money.

Frowning, Kline turned to Wigg. "That con artist—you said he mailed out a million letters?"

"That's the number I recall from the press reports."

"Then obviously this is a very different situation. That was basically a fraudulent direct-mail campaign—a big net thrown out to catch a few guilty fish. That's not what we're talking about here. We're talking about handwritten notes to a handful of people—people for whom the number six fifty-eight must have had some personal meaning."

Gurney slowly opened his eyes and stared at Kline. "But it didn't. At first I assumed it did, because why else would it come to mind? So I kept asking Mark Mellery that question—what did the number mean to him, what did it remind him of, had he ever thought of it before, had he ever seen it written, was it the price of something, an address, a safe combination? But he kept insisting the number meant nothing to him, that he never remembered thinking of it before, that it simply popped into his mind—a perfectly random event. And I believe he was telling the truth. So there has to be another explanation."

"So that means you're back where you started," said Rodriguez, rolling his eyes with exaggerated weariness.

"Maybe not. Maybe Sergeant Wigg's con game is closer to the truth here than we think."

"Are you trying to tell me that our killer sent out a million letters—a million handwritten letters? That's ridiculous—not to mention impossible."

"I agree that a million letters would be impossible, unless he had an awful lot of help, which isn't likely. But what number would be possible?"

"What do you mean?"

"Let's say our killer had a scheme that involved sending out letters to a lot of people—handwritten, so each recipient would get the impression that his letter was a one-of-a-kind personal communication. How many letters do you think he could write in, say, one year?"

The captain threw up his hands, intimating that the question was not only unanswerable but frivolous. Kline and Hardwick looked more serious—as if they might be attempting some kind of calculation. Stimmel, as always, projected amphibian inscrutability. Rebecca Holdenfield was watching Gurney with growing fascination. Blatt looked like he was trying to determine the source of a foul odor.

Wigg was the only one to speak. "Five thousand," she said. "Ten, if he were highly motivated. Conceivably fifteen, but that would be difficult."

Kline squinted at her with lawyerly skepticism. "Sergeant, these numbers are based on what, exactly?"

"To begin with, a couple of reasonable assumptions."

Rodriguez shook his head—implying that nothing on earth was more fallible than other people's reasonable assumptions. If Wigg noticed, she didn't care enough to let it distract her.

"First is the assumption that the model of the private-eye scam is applicable. If it is, it follows that the first communication—the one asking for money—would be sent to the most people and subsequent communications only to people who responded. In our own case, we know that the first communication consisted of two eight-line notes—a total of sixteen fairly short lines, plus a three-line address on the outer envelope. Except for the addresses, the letters would all be the same, making the writing repetitive and rapid. I would estimate that each mailing piece would take about four minutes to complete. That would be fifteen per hour. If he devoted just one hour a day to it, he'd have over five thousand done in a year. Two hours a day would result in close to eleven thousand. Theoretically, he could do a lot more, but there are limits to the diligence of even the most obsessed person."

"Actually," said Gurney with the dawning excitement of a scientist who finally sees a pattern in a sea of data, "eleven thousand would be more than enough."

"Enough to do what?" asked Kline.

"Enough to pull off the six fifty-eight trick, for one thing," said

Gurney. "And that little trick, if it was done the way I'm thinking it was done, would also explain the $289.87 request in the first letter to each of the victims."

"Whoa," said Kline, raising his hand. "Slow down. You're going around the corners a little too fast."

Chapter 45

To rest in peace, act now

Gurney thought it through one more time. It was almost too simple, and he wanted to be sure he hadn't overlooked some obvious problem that would blow a hole in his elegant hypothesis. He noted a variety of facial expressions around the table—mixtures of excitement, impatience, and curiosity—as everyone waited for him to speak. He took a long, deep breath.

"I can't say for certain that this is exactly how it was done. However, it's the only credible scenario that's occurred to me in all the time I've been wrestling with those numbers—which goes back to the day Mark Mellery came to my home and showed me the first letter. He was so baffled and frightened by the idea that the letter writer knew him so well he could predict what number he'd think of when asked to think of any number from one to a thousand. I could feel the panic in him, the sense of doom. No doubt it was the same with the other victims. That panic was the whole point of the game that was being played. *How could he know what number I'd think of? How could he know something so intimate, so personal, so private as a thought? What else does he know?* I could see those questions torturing him—literally driving him crazy."

"Frankly, Dave," said Kline with ill-concealed agitation, "they're driving me crazy, too, and the sooner you can answer them, the better."

"Damn right," agreed Rodriguez. "Let's get to the point."

"If I may express a slightly contrary opinion," said Holdenfield anxiously, "I'd like to hear the detective explain this in his own way at his own pace."

"It's embarrassingly simple," said Gurney. "Embarrassing to me, because the longer I stared at the problem, the more impenetrable it seemed to be. And figuring out how he pulled off his trick with the number nineteen didn't cast any light on how the six fifty-eight business worked. The obvious solution never occurred to me—not until Sergeant Wigg told her story."

It was not clear whether the grimace on Blatt's face resulted from an effort to pinpoint the revelatory element or from stomach gas.

Gurney offered Wigg a nod of acknowledgment before going on. "Suppose, as the sergeant has suggested, our obsessed killer devoted two hours a day to writing letters and at the end of a year had completed eleven thousand—which he then mailed out to a list of eleven thousand people."

"What list?" Jack Hardwick's voice had the intrusive rasp of a rusty gate.

"That's a good question—maybe the most important question of all. I'll come back to it in a minute. For the moment let's just assume that the original letter—the same identical letter—was sent out to eleven thousand people, asking them to think of a number between one and a thousand. Probability theory would predict that approximately eleven people would choose each of the one thousand available numbers. In other words, there is a statistical likelihood that eleven of those eleven thousand people, picking a number entirely at random, would pick the number six fifty-eight."

Blatt's grimace grew to comical proportions.

Rodriguez shook his head in disbelief. "Aren't we crossing the line here from hypothesis to fantasy?"

"What fantasy are you referring to?" Gurney sounded more bemused than offended.

"Well, these numbers you're throwing around, they don't have any evidentiary basis. They're all imaginary."

Gurney smiled patiently, although patience was not what he felt. For a moment he was distracted by the awareness of his own dissembling presentation of his emotional reaction. It was a lifelong habit—this reflexive concealment of irritation, frustration, anger, fear, doubt. It served him well in thousands of interrogations—so well he'd come to believe it was a talent, a professional technique, but of course at root it wasn't that at all. It was a way of dealing with life that had been part of him for as long as he could remember.

"So your father never paid attention to you, David. Did that make you feel bad?"

"Bad? No, not bad. No feelings about it at all, really."

And yet, in a dream, one could drown in sadness.

Good Lord, no time for introspection now.

Gurney refocused in time to hear Rebecca Holdenfield say in that no-nonsense Sigourney Weaver voice of hers, "I personally find Detective Gurney's hypothesis far from imaginary. In fact, I find it compelling—and I would ask again that he be allowed to complete his explanation."

She addressed this request to Kline, who turned up his palms as if to say that this was everyone's obvious intention.

"I'm not saying," said Gurney, "that exactly eleven of the eleven thousand people picked the number six fifty-eight—only that eleven is the most likely number. I don't know enough about statistics to quote probability formulas, but maybe someone can help me out with that."

Wigg cleared her throat. "The probability attaching to a range would be far higher than for any specific number within the range. For example, I wouldn't bet the house that a particular number between one and a thousand would be picked by exactly eleven people out of eleven thousand—but if we added a plus-or-minus range of, say, seven in either direction, I might be tempted to bet that the number of people picking it would fall within that range—in this case that six fifty-eight would be picked by at least four people and no more than eighteen people."

Blatt squinted at Gurney. "Are you saying that this guy sent out mailings to eleven thousand people and the same secret number was hidden inside all those little sealed envelopes?"

"That's the general idea."

Holdenfield's eyes widened in amazement as she spoke her thoughts aloud to no one in particular. "And each person, however many there were, who happened to pick six fifty-eight for whatever reason, and then opened that little envelope inside, and found the note saying that the writer knew him well enough to know he'd pick six fifty-eight ... My God, what an impact that would have!"

"Because," added Wigg, "it would never occur to him that he wasn't the only one getting that letter. It would never occur to him that he was just the one out of every thousand who happened to pick that number. The handwriting was the icing on the cake. It made it all seem totally personal."

"Jesus F. Christ," croaked Hardwick, "what you're telling us is that we've got a serial killer using a direct-mail campaign to prospect for victims!"

"That's one way of looking at it," said Gurney.

"That just might be the craziest thing I've ever heard," said Kline, more stunned than disbelieving.

"Nobody writes eleven thousand letters by hand," declared Rodriguez flatly.

"Nobody writes eleven thousand letters by hand," repeated Gurney. "That's exactly the reaction he was banking on. And if it wasn't for Sergeant Wigg's story, I don't think the possibility would ever have occurred to me."

"And if you hadn't described your father's card trick," said Wigg, "I wouldn't have thought of the story."

"You can congratulate each other later," said Kline. "I still have questions. Like why did the killer ask for $289.87, and why did he ask that it be sent to someone else's post-office box?"

"He asked for money for the same reason the sergeant's con man asked for money—to get the right prospects to identify themselves. The con man wanted to know which people on his list were seriously worried about what they might have been photographed doing. Our killer wanted to know which people on his list had picked six fifty-eight and were sufficiently unnerved by the experience to pay money to find out who knew them well enough to predict it. I think the amount was as large as it was to separate the terrified—and Mellery was one of those—from the merely curious."

Kline was leaning so far forward he was barely on his chair. "But why that exact dollars-and-cents amount?"

"That's nagged at me from the beginning, and I'm still not sure, but there's at least one possible reason: to ensure that the victim would send a check instead of cash."

"That's not what the first letter said," pointed out Rodriguez. "It said the money could be sent either by check or by cash."

"I know, and this sounds awfully subtle," said Gurney, "but I think the apparent choice was intended to distract attention from the vital need that it be a check. And the complex amount was intended to discourage payment in cash."

Rodriguez rolled his eyes. "Look, I know *fantasy* isn't a popular word here today, but I don't know what else to call this."

"Why was it vital that the payment be sent as a check?" asked Kline.

"The money itself didn't matter to the killer. Remember, the checks weren't cashed. I believe he had access to them at some point in the delivery process to Gregory Dermott's box, and that's all he wanted."

"All he wanted—what do you mean?"

"What's on a check other than the amount and the account number?"

Kline thought for a moment. "The account holder's name and address?"

"Right," said Gurney. "Name and address."

"But why . . . ?"

"He had to make the victim identify himself. After all, he'd sent out thousands of these mailings. But each prospective victim would be convinced that the letter he'd received was uniquely about him, from someone who knew him very well. What if he just sent back an envelope with the requested cash in it? He'd have no reason to include his name and address—and the killer couldn't ask him specifically to include it, because that would destroy the whole 'I know your intimate secrets' premise. Getting those checks was a subtle way to get the respondents' names and addresses. And maybe, if the surreptitious process of accessing the check information occurred in the post office, the easiest way of disposing of the checks afterward was simply to pass them along in their original envelopes to Dermott's box."

"But the killer would have to steam open and reseal the envelopes," said Kline.

Gurney shrugged. "An alternative would be to get some kind of access after Dermott opened the envelopes himself but before he had a chance to return the checks to their senders. That wouldn't require steaming and resealing, but it does raise other problems and questions—things we need to look into regarding Dermott's living arrangements, individuals with possible access to his home, and so forth."

"Which," rasped Hardwick loudly, "brings us back to my question—which Sherlock Gurney here characterized a little while ago as the most important question of all. Namely, who the hell is on that list of eleven thousand murder candidates?"

Gurney raised his hand in the familiar traffic-cop gesture. "Before we try to answer that, let me remind everyone that eleven thousand is only a guesstimate. It's a feasible number of letters from an executional point of view, and it's a number that statistically supports our six fifty-eight scenario. In other words, it's a number that works. But as Sergeant Wigg pointed out originally, the actual number could be anywhere from five thousand to fifteen thousand. Any quantity within that range would be small enough to be doable and large enough to produce a handful of people randomly choosing six fifty-eight."

"Unless, of course, you're barking up the wrong tree entirely," pointed out Rodriguez, "and all this speculation is just a colossal waste of time."

Kline turned to Holdenfield. "What do you think, Becca? Are we onto something? Or just up another tree?"

"I find aspects of the theory absolutely fascinating, but I'd like to reserve my final opinion until I hear the answer to Sergeant Hardwick's question."

Gurney smiled, this time genuinely. "He rarely asks a question unless he already has a pretty good idea of the answer. Care to share, Jack?"

Hardwick massaged his face with his hands for several seconds— another of the incomprehensible tics that had irritated Gurney so much when they worked together on the Piggert matricide-patricide case. "If you look at the most significant background characteristic all the victims have in common—the characteristic referred to in the threatening poems—you might conclude that their names were part of a list of people with serious drinking problems." He paused. "Question is, what list would that be?"

"Alcoholics Anonymous membership list?" suggested Blatt.

Hardwick shook his head. "No such list. They take that anonymity shit seriously."

"How about a list compiled from public-record data?" said Kline. "Alcohol-related arrests, convictions?"

"A list like that could be put together, but two of the victims wouldn't appear on it. Mellery has no arrest record. The pederast priest does, but the charge was endangering the morals of a minor—nothing about alcohol in the public record, although the Boston detective I spoke to told me the good father later had that charge dismissed in exchange for pleading to a lesser misdemeanor, blaming his behavior on his alcoholism and agreeing to go to long-term rehab."

Kline squinted thoughtfully. "Well, then, could it be a list of the patients at that rehab?"

"It's conceivable," said Hardwick, screwing up his face in a way that said it wasn't.

"Maybe we ought to look into it."

"Sure." Hardwick's almost insulting tone created an awkward silence, broken by Gurney.

"In an effort to see if I could establish a location connection among the victims, I started looking into the rehab issue a while ago. Unfortunately, it was a dead end. Albert Rudden spent twenty-eight days in a Bronx rehab five years ago, and Mellery spent twenty-eight days in a Queens rehab fifteen years ago. Neither rehab offers long-term treatment—meaning the priest must have gone to yet another facility. So even if our killer had a job at one of those places and his job gave him access to thousands of patient records, any list he put together that way would include the name of only one of the victims."

Rodriguez turned in his chair and addressed Gurney directly. "Your theory depends on the existence of a giant list—maybe five thousand names, maybe eleven thousand, I heard Wigg say maybe fifteen thousand—whatever, it seems to keep changing. But there isn't any source for such a list. So now what?"

"Patience, Captain," said Gurney softly. "I wouldn't say there isn't any source—we just haven't figured it out yet. I seem to have more faith in your abilities than you do."

The blood rose in Rodriguez's face. "Faith? In my abilities? What's that supposed to mean?"

"At one time or another, did all the victims go to rehab?" asked Wigg, ignoring the captain's outburst.

"I don't know about Kartch," said Gurney, glad to be drawn back to the subject. "But I wouldn't be surprised."

Hardwick chimed in. "Sotherton PD faxed us his record. Portrait of a real asshole. Assaults, harassment, public drunkenness, drunk and disorderly, menacing, menacing with a firearm, lewd behavior, three DWIs, two trips upstate, not to mention a dozen visits to county jail. The alcohol-related stuff, especially the DWIs, makes it virtually certain he's been pushed into rehab at least once. I can ask Sotherton to look into it."

Rodriguez pushed himself back from the table. "If the victims didn't meet in rehab or even go to the same rehab at different times, what difference does it make that they were in rehab at all? Half the unemployed bums and bullshit artists in the world go to rehab these days. It's a goddamn Medicaid-funded racket, a taxpayer rip-off. What the hell does it mean that all these guys went to rehab? That they were likely to be murdered? Hardly. That they were drunks? So what? We already knew that." Anger, Gurney noted, had become Rodriguez's ongoing emotion, leaping like a brushfire from issue to issue.

Wigg, at whom the tirade was directed, seemed unaffected by its nastiness. "Senior Investigator Gurney once said that he believed all the victims were likely to be connected through some common factor beyond drinking. I was thinking rehab attendance could be that factor, or at least be part of it."

Rodriguez laughed derisively. "Maybe this, maybe that. I'm hearing a lot of maybes but no real connections."

Kline looked frustrated. "Come on, Becca, tell us what you think. How firm is our footing here?"

"That's a difficult question to answer. I wouldn't know where to begin."

"I'll simplify it. Do you buy Gurney's theory of the case—yes or no?"

"Yes, I do. The picture he painted of Mark Mellery's being mentally tortured by the notes he was receiving—I can see that as a plausible part of a certain kind of murder ritual."

"But you look like you're not entirely convinced."

"It's not that, it's just . . . the uniqueness of the approach. Torturing the victim is a common enough part of serial-murder pathology, but I've never seen an instance of its being carried out from such a distance in such a cool, methodical manner. The torture component of such murders generally relies on the direct infliction of physical agony in order to terrorize the victim and give the killer the feeling of ultimate power and control that he craves. In this case, however, the infliction of pain was entirely cerebral."

Rodriguez leaned toward her. "So you're saying it doesn't fit the serial-murder pattern?" He sounded like an attorney attacking a hostile witness.

"No. The pattern is there. I'm saying that he has a uniquely cool and calculated way of executing it. Most serial killers are above average in intelligence. Some, like Ted Bundy, are far above average. This individual may be in a class by himself."

"Too smart for us—is that what you're saying?"

"That's not what I said," replied Holdenfield innocently, "but you're probably right."

"Really? Let me get this on the record," said Rodriguez, his voice as brittle as thin ice. "Your professional opinion is that BCI is incapable of apprehending this maniac?"

"Once again, that's not what I said." Holdenfield smiled. "But once again you're probably right."

Once again Rodriguez's sallow skin reddened with anger, but Kline intervened. "Surely, Becca, you're not implying that there's nothing we can do."

She sighed with the resignation of a teacher saddled with the dullest students in the school. "The facts of the case so far support three conclusions. First, the man you're chasing is playing games with you, and he's very good at it. Second, he is intensely motivated, prepared, focused, and thorough. Third, he knows who's next on his list, and you don't."

Kline looked pained. "But getting back to my question . . ."

"If you're looking for a light at the end of the tunnel, there's one small possibility in your favor. As rigidly organized as he is, there's a chance he may fall apart."

"How? Why? What do you mean, 'fall apart?'"

As Kline asked the question, Gurney felt a tightening in his chest. The raw feeling of anxiety arrived with a cinematically sharp scene in his imagination—the killer's hand gripping the sheet of paper with the eight lines Gurney had so impulsively put in the mail the previous day:

> *I see how all you did was done,*
> *from backwards boots to muffled gun.*
> *The game you started soon will end,*
> *your throat cut by a dead man's friend.*

Beware the snow, beware the sun,
the night, the day, nowhere to run.
With sorrow first his grave I'll tend
and then to hell his killer send.

Methodically, seemingly contemptuously, the hand crumpled the paper into a diminishing ball, and when the ball was improbably small, no larger than a nugget of chewed gum, the hand slowly opened and let it fall to the floor. Gurney tried to force the disturbing image from his mind, but the scenario had not quite run its course. Now the killer's hand held the envelope in which the poem had been mailed—with the address side up, the postmark clearly visible, the Walnut Crossing postmark.

The Walnut Crossing . . . *Oh, God!* A draining chill spread from the pit of Gurney's stomach down through his legs. How could he have overlooked such an obvious problem? *God, calm down. Think.* What could the killer do with that information? Could it lead him to the actual address, to their home, to Madeleine? Gurney felt his eyes widening, his face growing pale. How could he have been so obsessively focused on launching his pathetic little missive? How could he not have anticipated the postmark problem? What danger had he exposed Madeleine to? His mind careened around that last question like a man racing around a burning house. How real was the danger? How imminent? Should he call her, alert her? Alert her to what, exactly? And frighten her half to death? God, what else? What else had he overlooked in his tunnel-vision focus on the adversary, the battle, the puzzle? Who else's safety—who else's life—was he ignoring in his headstrong determination to win the game? The questions were dizzying.

A voice intruded into his near panic. He tried to fasten on to it, use it to regain his balance.

Holdenfield was speaking. " . . . an obsessive-compulsive planner with a pathological need to make reality conform to his plans. The goal that controls him absolutely is to be in absolute control of others."

"Of everyone?" asked Kline.

"His focus is actually very narrow. He feels he must completely dominate through terror and murder the members of his target-victim group, who seem to represent some subset of middle-aged male alcoholics. Other people are irrelevant to him. They're of no interest or importance."

"So where does the 'falling apart' business come in?"

"Well, it so happens that committing murder to create and maintain a sense of omnipotence is a fatally flawed process—no pun intended. As a solution to the craving for control, serial killing is profoundly dysfunctional, the equivalent of pursuing happiness by smoking crack."

"They need more and more of it?"

"More and more to achieve less and less. The emotional cycle becomes increasingly compressed and unmanageable. Things that weren't supposed to happen do happen. I suspect something of that nature occurred this morning, resulting in that police officer's being killed instead of your Mr. Dermott. These unforeseen events create serious emotional tremors in a killer obsessed with control, and these distractions lead to more mistakes. It's like a machine with an unbalanced drive shaft. When it reaches a certain speed, the vibration takes over and tears the machine apart."

"Meaning what, in this specific case?"

"The killer becomes increasingly frantic and unpredictable."

Frantic. Unpredictable. Again the cold dread spread out from the pit of Gurney's stomach, this time up into his chest, his throat.

"Meaning the situation is going to get worse?" asked Kline.

"In a way better, in a way worse. If a murderer who used to lurk in a dark alley and occasionally kill someone with an ice pick suddenly bursts out into Times Square swinging a machete, he's likely to get caught. But in that final mayhem, a lot of people might lose their heads."

"You figure our boy might be entering his machete stage?" Kline looked more excited than revolted.

Gurney felt sick. The macho-bullshit tone that people in law enforcement used to shield themselves from horror didn't work in certain situations. This was one of them.

"Yes." The flat simplicity of Holdenfield's response created a silence in the room. After a while the captain spoke with his predictable antagonism.

"So what are we supposed to do? Issue an APB for a polite thirty-year-old with a vibrating drive shaft and a machete in his hand?"

Hardwick reacted to this with a twisted smile and Blatt with an explosive laugh.

Stimmel said, "Sometimes a grand finale is part of the plan." He got the attention of everyone except Blatt, who kept laughing. When Blatt quieted down, Stimmel continued, "Anybody remember the Duane Merkly case?"

No one did.

"Vietnam vet," said Stimmel. "Had problems with the VA. Problems with authority. Had a nasty Akita guard dog that ate one of his neighbor's ducks. Neighbor called the cops. Duane hated cops. Next month the Akita ate the neighbor's beagle. Neighbor shot the Akita. Conflict escalates, and more shit happens. One day the Vietnam vet takes the neighbor hostage. Says he wants five thousand dollars for the Akita or he's going to kill the guy. Local cops arrive, SWAT team arrives. They take up positions around the perimeter of the property. Thing is, nobody looked into Duane's service record. So nobody knew he was a demolitions specialist. Duane specialized in rigging remote-detonation land mines." Stimmel fell silent, letting his audience imagine the outcome.

"You mean the fucker blew everybody up?" asked Blatt, impressed.

"Not everybody. Six dead, six permanently disabled."

Rodriguez looked frustrated. "What's the point of this?"

"Point is, he'd purchased the components for the mines two years earlier. The grand finale was always the plan."

Rodriguez shook his head. "I don't get the relevance."

Gurney did, and it made him uneasy.

Kline looked at Holdenfield. "What do you think, Becca?"

"Do I think our man has big plans? It's possible. I do know one thing. . . ."

She was interrupted by a perfunctory knock at the door. The door opened, and a uniformed sergeant stepped halfway into the room and addressed Rodriguez.

"Sir? Sorry to interrupt. You've got a call from a Lieutenant Nardo in Connecticut. I told him you were in a meeting. He says it's an emergency, has to talk to you now."

Rodriguez sighed the sigh of a man unfairly burdened. "I'll take it on the one here," he said, tilting his head toward the phone on the low filing cabinet against the wall behind him.

The sergeant retreated. Two minutes later the phone rang.

"Captain Rodriguez here." For another two minutes, he held the phone to his ear in tense concentration. "That's bizarre," he said finally. "In fact, it's so bizarre, Lieutenant, I'd like you to repeat it word for word to our case team here. I'm putting you on speakerphone now. Please go ahead—tell them exactly what you told me."

The voice that came from the phone a moment later was tense and hard. "This is John Nardo, Wycherly PD. Can you hear me?" Rodriguez said yes, and Nardo continued, "As you know, one of our officers was killed on duty this morning at the home of Gregory Dermott. We are presently on site with a crime-scene team. Twenty minutes ago a phone call was received for Mr. Dermott. He was told by the caller, quote, 'You're next in line, and after you it's Gurney's turn.'"

What? Gurney wondered if he could possibly have heard right.

Kline asked Nardo to repeat the phone message, and he did.

"Have you gotten anything yet from the phone company on the source?" asked Hardwick.

"Cell phone within this general area. No GPS data, just the location of the transmitting tower. Obviously, no caller ID."

"Who took the call?" asked Gurney. Surprisingly, the direct threat was having a calming effect on him. Perhaps because anything specific, anything with names attached to it, was more limited and therefore more manageable than an infinite range of possibilities. And perhaps because neither of the names was Madeleine.

"What do you mean, who took the call?" asked Nardo.

"You said a call was received *for* Mr. Dermott, not *by* Mr. Dermott."

"Oh, yes, I see. Well, Dermott happened to be lying down with a migraine when the phone rang. He's been kind of incapacitated since finding the body. One of the techs answered the phone in the kitchen. The caller asked for Dermott, said he was a close friend."

"What name did he give?"

"Odd name. Carbis . . . Cabberdis . . . No, wait a second, here, the tech wrote it down—Charybdis."

"Anything odd about the voice?"

"Funny you should ask. They were just trying to describe it. After Dermott came to the phone, he said he thought it sounded like some foreign accent, but our guy thought it was fake—someone trying to disguise his voice. Or maybe *her* voice—neither one of them was sure about that. Look, guys, sorry, but I have to get back to our situation here. Just wanted to give you the basic facts. We'll be back in touch when we have something new."

After the sound of the call disconnecting, there was a restless silence around the table. Then Hardwick cleared his throat so loudly that Holdenfield flinched.

"So, Davey boy," he growled, "once again you're the center of attention. *'It's Gurney's turn.'* What are you, a magnet for serial murderers? All we got to do is dangle you on a string and wait for them to bite."

Was Madeleine dangling on a string as well? Perhaps not yet. Hopefully not yet. After all, he and Dermott were at the head of the line. Assuming the lunatic was telling the truth. If so, it would give him some time—maybe time to get lucky. Time to make up for his oversights. How could he have been so stupid? So unaware of her safety? Idiot!

Kline looked troubled. "How did you get to be a target?"

"Your guess is as good as mine," said Gurney with a false lightness. His guilt gave him the impression that both Kline and

Rodriguez were eyeing him with unfriendly curiosity. From the beginning he'd had misgivings about writing and mailing that poem, but he'd buried them without defining or articulating them. He was appalled at his ability to ignore danger, including danger to others. What had he felt at the time? Had the risk to Madeleine come anywhere close to his consciousness? Had he had an inkling and dismissed it? Could he have been that callous? *Please, God, no!*

In all this angst, he was sure of at least one thing. Sitting there in that conference room discussing the situation any further was not a tolerable option. If Dermott was next on the killer's list, then that's where Gurney had the best chance of finding the man they were looking for and ending the risk before it crept any closer. And if he himself was next after Dermott, then that was a battle he wanted to fight as far from Walnut Crossing as possible. He slid his chair back from the table and stood.

"If you'll excuse me, there's somewhere I need to be."

At first this generated only blank looks around the table. Then the meaning registered with Kline.

"Jesus!" he cried. "You're not thinking of going to Connecticut?"

"I have an invitation, and I'm accepting it."

"That's crazy. You don't know what you're walking into."

"Actually," said Rodriguez with a dismissive glance in Gurney's direction, "a crime scene crawling with cops is a pretty safe place."

"That would normally be true," said Holdenfield. "Unless . . ." She let the thought dangle, as though she were walking around it to view it from different angles.

"Unless what?" snapped Rodriguez.

"Unless the killer is a cop."

Chapter 46

A simple plan

It seemed almost too easy.

Killing twenty well-trained police officers in twenty seconds should require more complex planning. A deed of that magnitude should be more difficult. After all, it would be the largest such eradication ever achieved—at least in America, at least in modern times.

The fact that no one had done it before, despite its apparent simplicity, both stimulated and troubled him. The idea that finally put his mind to rest was this: For a man of weaker intellect or less formidable powers of concentration, the project might indeed be daunting, but not for him, not with his clarity and focus. Everything was relative. A genius could dance through obstacles that would hopelessly entangle ordinary men.

The chemicals were laughably easy to acquire, quite economical, and 100 percent legal. Even in large quantities, they aroused no suspicion, since they were sold in bulk every day for industrial applications. Even so, he'd prudently purchased each one (there were only two) from a different supplier to avoid any hint of their eventual combination, and he'd acquired the two fifty-gallon pressure tanks from a third supplier.

Now, as he was putting the finishing touches with a soldering iron on a bit of jerry-rigged piping to combine and deliver the lethal mixture to its recipients, he had a thrilling thought—a possible scenario with a climactic image—that so tickled his imagination a gleaming smile burst across his face. He knew that what he was imagining *wasn't likely to happen—the chemistry was too unpredictable—but it could happen. It was at least conceivable.*

On the Chemical Hazards website was a warning he had memorized. The warning was in a red box surrounded by red exclamation points. "This mixture of chlorine and ammonia not only produces a fatally toxic gas but in the proportions indicated is highly unstable and with the catalyst of a spark may explode." The image that delighted him was of the entire Wycherly police department caught in his trap, involuntarily gasping the poison fumes into their lungs just as the catalyzing spark was applied, blowing each of them to pieces from the inside out. As he pictured it, he did something he almost never did. He laughed out loud.

If only his mother could grasp the humor of it, the beauty of it, the glory of it. But perhaps that was asking too much. And, of course, if the policemen were all blown to pieces—little tiny pieces—he wouldn't get to cut their throats. And he very much wanted to cut their throats.

Nothing in this world was perfect. There were always pluses and minuses. One had to make the best of the hand one was dealt. See the glass as half full.

That was reality.

Chapter 47

Welcome to Wycherly

After brushing aside the predictable objections and concerns regarding his intended trip, Gurney went to his car and called the Wycherly police department for the address of Gregory Dermott's home, since all he had up to that point was the P.O. box number on Dermott's letterhead. It took a while to explain to the officer on duty exactly who he was, and even then he had to wait while the young woman called Nardo and got permission to divulge the location. It turned out that she was the only member of the small force not already at the scene. Gurney entered the address in his GPS and headed for the Kingston-Rhinecliff Bridge.

Wycherly was located in north-central Connecticut. The trip took a little over two hours, much of which Gurney spent pondering his gross failure to think of his wife's safety. The lapse so disturbed and depressed him that he became desperate to focus on something else, and he began to examine the main hypothesis developed at the BCI meeting.

The notion that the killer had somehow accessed or compiled a list of several thousand individuals with a history of drinking problems—individuals suffering from the deep-seated fears and guilt arising from an alcoholic past—and then managed to ensnare a handful of them through that simple number trick, and then tormented them with the series of creepy poems, leading up to their ritual murders . . . that entire process, outlandish as it was, now seemed to Gurney entirely credible. He remembered discovering that serial murderers, when they were children, often found pleasure in torturing insects and small animals—for example, by burning them with sunlight concentrated through a magnifying glass. One of his own famous arrests, Cannibal Claus, had blinded a cat exactly that way at the age of five. Burning with a magnifying glass. It seemed disturbingly similar to focusing a victim on his past and intensifying his fears until he was writhing in pain.

Seeing a pattern, fitting the pieces of the puzzle together—it was a process that normally elated him, but that afternoon in the car it didn't feel as good as it usually did. Perhaps it was the lingering perception of his inadequacies, his missteps. The thought was acid in his chest.

He concentrated loosely on the road, the hood of his car, his hands on the wheel. Strange. His own hands—he didn't recognize them. They looked surprisingly old—like his father's hands. The little splotches had grown in number and size. If just a minute earlier he'd been shown photographs of a dozen hands, he wouldn't have been able to identify his own among them.

He wondered why. Perhaps changes, if they occur gradually enough, are not regularly noted by the brain until the discrepancy reaches some critical magnitude. Perhaps it even went further than that.

Would it mean that we always see familiar things to some extent the way they used to be? Are we stuck in the past not out of simple nostalgia or wishful thinking but by a data-processing shortcut in our neural wiring? If what one "saw" was supplied partly from the optic nerves and partly from memory—if what one "perceived" at any given moment was actually a composite of current impressions and stored impressions—it gave new meaning to "living in the past." The past would thus exercise a peculiar tyranny over the present by supplying us with obsolete data in the guise of sensory experience. Might that not relate to the situation of a serial killer driven by a long-ago trauma? How distorted might his vision be?

The theory momentarily excited him. Turning over a new idea, testing its solidity, always made him feel a little more in control, a little more alive, but today those feelings were hard to sustain. His GPS alerted him that it was two-tenths of a mile to the Wycherly exit.

At the end of the exit ramp, he turned right. The area was a hodgepodge of farm fields, tract houses, strip malls, and ghosts of another era's summer pleasures: a dilapidated drive-in movie, a sign for a lake with an Iroquois name.

It brought to mind another lake with another Indian-sounding name—a lake with an encircling trail that he and Madeleine had hiked one weekend when they were searching for their perfect place in the Catskills. He could picture her animated face as they stood atop a modest cliff, holding hands, smiling, looking out over the breeze-crinkled water. The memory came with a stab of guilt.

He hadn't called her yet to let her know what he was doing, where he was going, the likely delay in his homecoming. He still wasn't sure how much he should tell her. Should he even mention the postmark? He decided to call her now, play it by ear. *God help me say the right thing.*

Considering the level of stress he was already feeling, he thought it wise to pull over to make the call. The first place he could find was a scruffy, gravelly parking area in front of a farm stand shuttered for the winter. The word for his home number in the voice-activated dialing system was, efficiently but unimaginatively, *home.*

Madeleine answered on the second ring with that optimistic, welcoming voice phone calls always elicited from her.

"It's me," he said, his own voice reflecting only a fraction of the light in hers.

There was a one-beat pause. "Where are you?"

"That's what I'm calling to tell you. I'm in Connecticut, near a town called Wycherly."

The obvious question would have been, "Why?" But Madeleine didn't ask obvious questions. She waited.

"There's been a development in the case," he said. "Things may be coming to a head."

"I see."

He heard a slow, controlled breath.

"Are you going to tell me anything more than that?" she asked.

He gazed out the car window at the lifeless vegetable stand. More than closed for the season, it looked abandoned. "The man we're after is getting reckless," he said. "There may be an opportunity to stop him."

"The man we're after?" Now her voice was thin ice, fissuring.

He said nothing, jarred by her response.

She went on, openly angry. "Don't you mean the bloody murderer, the serial killer, the man who never misses—who shoots people in their neck arteries and cuts their throats? Isn't that who you're talking about?"

"That's . . . the man we're after, yes."

"There aren't enough cops in Connecticut to handle this?"

"He seems to be focused on me."

"What?"

"He seems to have identified me as someone working on the case, and he may try to do something stupid—which will give us the opportunity we need. It's our chance to take the fight to him rather than just mopping up one murder after another."

"What?" This time the word was less a question than a pained exclamation.

"It's going to be all right," he said unconvincingly. "He's starting to fall apart. He's going to self-destruct. We just have to be there when it happens."

"When it was your job, you had to be there. You don't have to be there now."

"Madeleine, for Chrissake, I'm a cop!" The words exploded from him like an obstructed object blown loose. "Why the hell can't you understand that?"

"No, David," she responded evenly. "You *were* a cop. You're not a cop now. You don't have to be there."

"I'm already here." In the ensuing silence, his temper subsided like a retreating wave. "It's all right. I know what I'm doing. Nothing bad is going to happen."

"David, what is the matter with you? Do you just keep running at the bullets? Running at the bullets? Until one goes through your head? Is that it? Is that the pathetic plan for the rest of our lives together? I just wait, and wait, and wait for you to get killed?" Her voice cracked with such raw emotion on the word *killed* that he found himself speechless.

It was Madeleine who eventually spoke—so softly he could just make out the words. "What is this really about?"

"What's it about?" The question hit him from an odd angle. He felt off balance. "I don't understand the question."

Her intense silence from a hundred miles away seemed to surround him, press in against him.

"What do you mean?" he asked. He could feel his heart rate rising.

He thought he heard her swallow. He sensed, somehow *knew*, she was trying to make a decision. When she did answer him, it was with another question, again spoken so softly he barely heard it.

"Is this about Danny?"

He could feel the pounding of his heart in his neck, his head, his hands.

"What? What would it have to do with Danny?" He didn't want an answer, not now, not when he had so much to do.

"Oh, David," she said. He could picture her, shaking her head sadly, determined to pursue this most difficult of all subjects. Once Madeleine opened a door, she invariably walked through it.

She took a shaky breath and pressed on. "Before Danny was killed, your job was the biggest part of your life. Afterward, it was the only part. The only part. You've done nothing but work for the past fifteen years. Sometimes I feel like you're trying to make up for something, forget something . . . *solve* something." Her strained inflection made the word sound like the symptom of a disease.

He tried to maintain his footing by holding on to the facts at hand. "I'm going to Wycherly to help capture the man who killed Mark Mellery." He heard his voice as if it belonged to someone else—someone old, frightened, rigid—someone trying to sound reasonable.

She ignored what he said, following her own train of thought. "I hoped if we opened the box, looked at his little drawings . . . we could say good-bye to him together. But you don't say good-bye, do you? You never say good-bye to anything."

"I don't know what you're talking about," he protested. But that wasn't true. When they'd been about to move from the city up to Walnut Crossing, Madeleine had spent hours saying good-bye. Not only to neighbors but to the place itself, things they were leaving behind, houseplants. It had gotten under his skin. He'd complained about her sentimentality, said talking to inanimate objects was weird, a waste of time, a distraction, that it was only making their departure more difficult. But it was more than that. Her behavior was touching something in him that he didn't want touched—and now she'd put her finger on it again—the part of him that never wanted to say good-bye, that couldn't face separation.

"You stuff things out of sight," she was saying. "But they're not gone, you haven't really let go of them. You have to look at them to let go of them. You have to look at Danny's life to let go of it. But you obviously don't want to do that. You just want to . . . what, David? What? *Die?*" There was a long silence.

"You want to die," she said. "That's really it, isn't it?"

He experienced the kind of emptiness he imagined existed at the eye of a hurricane—an emotion that felt like a vacuum.

"I have a job to do." It was a banal thing to say, stupid, really. He didn't know why he bothered to say it.

There was a lengthy silence.

"No," she said softly, swallowing again. "You don't have to keep doing this." Then, barely audibly, despairingly, she added, "Or maybe you do. Maybe I was just hoping."

He was at a loss for words, a loss for thoughts.

He sat for a long while, his mouth slightly open, breathing rapid, shallow breaths. At some point—he wasn't sure when—the phone connection was broken. He waited in a kind of vacant chaos for a calming thought, an actionable thought.

What came instead was a sense of absurdity and pathos—the thought that even at the moment when he and Madeleine were emotionally stripped, raw and terrified, they were literally a hundred miles apart, in different states, exposing themselves to empty space, to cell phones.

What also came to mind was what he'd failed to speak about, had failed to reveal to her. He hadn't said a single word about his postmark stupidity, how it might point the killer to where they lived, how the oversight arose from his own obsessive focus on the investigation. With that thought came a sickening echo, the realization that his similar preoccupation with an investigation fifteen years earlier had been a factor in Danny's death—maybe the ultimate cause of it. It was remarkable that Madeleine had connected that death with his current obsession. Remarkable and, he had to admit, unnervingly acute.

He felt he had to call her back, admit his mistake—the peril he'd created—warn her. He dialed their number, waited for the welcoming voice. The phone rang, rang, rang, rang. Then the voice he heard was his own recorded message—a little stiff, almost stern, hardly welcoming—then the beep.

"Madeleine? Madeleine are you there? Please pick up if you're there." He felt a kind of sinking sickness. He couldn't think of anything to say that would make sense in a one-minute message, nothing that wouldn't be likely to cause more damage than it would prevent, nothing that wouldn't create panic and confusion. All he ended up saying was, "I love you. Be careful. I love you." Then there was another beep, and once again the connection was broken.

He sat and stared at the dilapidated vegetable stand, aching and confused. He felt like he could sleep for a month, or forever. Forever would be best. But that made no sense. That was the kind of dangerous thinking that caused weary men in the Arctic to lie down in the snow and freeze to death. He must regain his focus. Keep moving. Push himself forward. Bit by bit, his thoughts began to coalesce around the unfinished task awaiting him. There was work to do in Wycherly. A madman to be apprehended. Lives to be saved. Gregory Dermott's, his own, perhaps even Madeleine's. He started the car and drove on.

The address to which his GPS finally delivered him belonged to an unremarkable suburban Colonial set well back on an oversize lot on a secondary road with little traffic and no sidewalks. A tall, dense arborvitae hedge provided privacy along the left, rear, and right sides of the property. A chest-high boxwood hedge ran across the front, except for the driveway opening. Police cars were everywhere—more than a dozen, Gurney estimated—pulled up at all angles to the hedge, partially obstructing the road. Most bore the Wycherly PD insignia. Three were unmarked, with portable red flashers atop their dashboards. Notably missing were any Connecticut state police vehicles—but perhaps not surprisingly so. Although it might not be the smartest or most effective approach, he could understand a local department's wanting to maintain control when the victim was one of their own. As Gurney nosed into a tight available patch of grass at the edge of the asphalt, an enormous young uniformed cop was pointing to a route around the parked cruisers with one hand and with the other urgently motioning him away from where he was trying to stop. Gurney got out of the car and produced his ID as the mammoth officer approached, tense and tight-lipped. His bulging neck muscles, at war with a collar a size and a half too small, seemed to extend up into his cheeks.

He examined the card in Gurney's wallet for a long minute with increasing incomprehension, finally announcing, "This says New York State."

"I'm here to see Lieutenant Nardo," said Gurney.

The cop gave him a stare as hard as the pecs straining his shirtfront, then shrugged. "Inside."

At the foot of the long driveway on a post the same height as the mailbox was a beige metal sign with black lettering: GD SECURITY SYSTEMS. Gurney ducked under the yellow police tape that seemed to be strung around the entire property. Oddly, it was the coldness of the tape as it brushed against his neck that for the first time that day diverted his attention from his racing thoughts to the weather. It was raw, gray, windless. Patches of snow, previously melted and refrozen, lay in the shadows at the feet of the boxwood and arborvitae plantings. Along the driveway there were patches of black ice filling shallow depressions in the tarred surface.

Affixed to the center of the front door was a more discreet version of the GD Security Systems sign. Next to the door was a small sticker indicating that the house was protected by Axxon Silent Alarms. As he reached the brick steps of the columned entry porch, the door in front of him opened. It was not a welcoming gesture. In fact, the man who opened it stepped out and closed it behind him. He took only peripheral note of Gurney's presence as he spoke with loud irritation into a cell phone. He was a compact, athletically built man in his late forties, with a hard face and sharp, angry eyes. He wore a black windbreaker with the word POLICE in large yellow letters across the back.

"Can you hear me now?" He moved off the porch onto the faded, frost-wilted lawn. "Can you hear me now? . . . Good. I said I need another tech on the scene ASAP. . . . No, that's no good, I mean I need one right now. . . . Now, before it gets dark. The word is spelled n-o-w. What part of that word don't you understand? . . . Good. Thank you. I appreciate that."

He pushed the disconnect button on the phone and shook his head. "Goddamn idiot." He looked at Gurney. "Who the hell are you?"

Gurney did not react to the aggressive tone. He understood where it was coming from. There was always a sense of heightened emotion at the scene of a cop killing—a kind of barely controlled tribal rage. Besides, he recognized the voice of the man who'd sent the officer to Dermott's house—John Nardo.

"I'm Dave Gurney, Lieutenant."

A lot seemed to go through Nardo's mind very quickly, most of it negative. All he said was, "What are you here for?"

Such a simple question. He wasn't sure he knew even a fraction of the answer. He decided to opt for brevity. "He says he wants to kill Dermott and me. Well, Dermott's here. Now I'm here. All the bait the bastard could want. Maybe he'll make his move and we can wrap this up."

"You think so?" Nardo's tone was full of aimless hostility.

"If you'd like," said Gurney, "I can bring you up to date on our piece of the case, and you can tell me what you've discovered here."

"What I discovered here? I discovered that the cop I sent to this house at your request is dead. Gary Sissek. Two months away from retirement. I discovered that his head was nearly severed by a broken whiskey bottle. I discovered a pair of bloody boots next to a freaking lawn chair behind that hedge." He waved a little wildly toward the rear of the house. "Dermott never saw the chair before. His neighbor never saw it before. So where did the freaking thing come from? Did this freaking lunatic bring a lawn chair with him?"

Gurney nodded. "As a matter of fact, the answer is probably yes. It seems to be part of a unique MO. Like the whiskey bottle. Was it by any chance Four Roses?"

Nardo stared at him, blankly at first, as if there were a slight tape delay in the transmission. "Jesus," he said. "You better come inside."

The door led into a wide, bare center hall. No furniture, no rugs, no pictures on the walls, just a fire extinguisher and a couple of smoke alarms. At the end of the hall was the rear door—beyond which, Gurney assumed, was the porch where Gregory Dermott that morning had discovered the cop's body. Indistinct voices outside suggested that the scene-of-crime processing team was still busy in the backyard.

"Where's Dermott?" Gurney asked.

Nardo raised his thumb toward the ceiling. "Bedroom. Gets stress migraines, and the migraines make him nauseous. He's not in what you'd call a good mood. Bad enough before the phone call saying he was next, but then . . . Jesus."

Gurney had questions he wanted to ask, lots of them, but it

seemed better to let Nardo set the pace. He looked around at what he could see of the ground floor of the house. Through a doorway on his right was a large room with white walls and a bare wood floor. Half a dozen computers sat side by side on a long table in the center of the room. Phones, fax machines, printers, scanners, auxiliary hard drives, and other peripherals covered another long table placed against the far wall. Also on the far wall was another fire extinguisher. In lieu of a smoke alarm, there was a built-in sprinkler system. There were only two windows, too small for the space, one in the front and one in the rear, giving it a tunnel-like feeling despite the white paint.

"He runs his computer business from down here and lives upstairs. We'll use the other room," said Nardo, indicating a doorway across the hall. Similarly uninviting and purely functional, the room was half the length of the other and had a window at only one end, making it more like a cave than a tunnel. Nardo flipped a wall switch as they entered, and four recessed lights in the ceiling turned the cave into a bright white box containing file cabinets against one wall, a table with two desktop computers against another wall, a table with a coffeemaker and a microwave against a third wall, and an empty square table with two chairs in the middle of the room. This room had both a sprinkler system and a smoke alarm. It reminded Gurney of a cleaner version of the cheerless break room at his last precinct. Nardo sat in one of the chairs and gestured for Gurney to sit in the other. He massaged his temples for a long minute, as if trying to squeeze the tension out of his head. From the look in his eyes, it wasn't working.

"I don't buy that 'bait' shit," he said, wrinkling his nose as if the word *bait* smelled bad.

Gurney smiled. "It's partly true."

"What's the other part?"

"I'm not sure."

"You come here to be a freaking hero?"

"I don't think so. I have a feeling my being here may help."

"Yeah? What if I don't share that feeling?"

"It's your show, Lieutenant. You want me to go home, I'll go home."

Nardo gave him another long, cynical stare. In the end he appeared to change his mind, at least tentatively. "The Four Roses bottle is part of the MO?"

Gurney nodded.

Nardo took a deep breath. He looked as if his whole body ached. Or as if the whole world ached. "Okay, Detective. Maybe you better tell me everything you haven't told me."

Chapter 48

A house with a history

Gurney talked about the backwards snow prints, the poems, the unnatural voice on the phone, the two unsettling number tricks, the alcoholic backgrounds of the victims, their mental torture, the hostile challenges to the police, the "REDRUM" graffiti on the wall and the "Mr. and Mrs. Scylla" sign-in at The Laurels, the high intelligence and hubris of the killer. He continued to provide details from the three killings he was familiar with until Nardo's attention span looked like it might be reaching its breaking point. Then he concluded with what he considered most important:

"He wants to prove two things. First, that he has the power to control and punish drunks. Second, that the police are impotent fools. His crimes are intentionally constructed like elaborate games, brain teasers. He's brilliant, obsessive, meticulous. So far he hasn't left behind a single inadvertent fingerprint, hair, speck of saliva, clothing fiber, or unplanned footprint. He hasn't made any mistakes that we've discovered. The fact is, we know very little about him, his methods, or his motives that he hasn't chosen to reveal to us. With one possible exception."

Nardo raised a weary but curious eyebrow.

"A certain Dr. Holdenfield, who wrote the state-of-the-art study of serial murder, believes he's reached a critical stage in the process and is about to launch some sort of climactic event."

Nardo's jaw muscles rippled. He spoke with fierce restraint.

"Which would make my slaughtered friend on the back porch a warm-up act?"

It wasn't the kind of question one could, or should, answer. The two men sat in silence until a slight sound, perhaps the sound of an irregular breath, drew their attention simultaneously to the doorway. Incongruously for such a surreptitious arrival, it was the NFL-size hulk who'd earlier been guarding the driveway. He looked like he was having a tooth drilled.

Nardo could see what was coming. "What, Tommy?"

"They've located Gary's wife."

"Oh, Christ. Okay. Where is she?"

"On her way home from the town garage. She drives the Head Start school bus."

"Right. Right. Oh, fuck. I should go myself, but I can't leave here now. Where the fuck is the chief? Anybody find him yet?"

"He's in Cancún."

"I know he's in freaking Cancún. I mean, why the fuck doesn't he check his messages?" Nardo took a long breath and closed his eyes. "Hacker and Picardo—they were probably closest to the family. Isn't Picardo the wife's cousin or something? Send Hacker and Picardo. Christ. But tell Hacker to come see me first."

The gigantic young cop went as quietly as he'd come.

Nardo took another long breath. He began speaking as though he'd been kicked in the head and hoped that speaking would help him clear his mind. "So you're telling me they were all alcoholics. Well, Gary Sissek wasn't an alcoholic, so what does that mean?"

"He was a cop. Maybe that was enough. Or maybe he got in the way of a planned attack on Dermott. Or maybe there's some other connection."

"What other connection?"

"I don't know."

The back door slammed, sharp footsteps approached, and a wiry man in plainclothes appeared at the door. "You wanted to see me?"

"Sorry to do this to you, but I need you and Picardo to—"

"I know."

"Right. Well. Keep the information simple. Simple as you can. 'Fatally stabbed while protecting the intended victim of an attack. Died a hero.' Something like that. Jesus fucking Christ! What I mean is, no awful details, no pool of blood. You understand what I'm trying to say? The details can come later if they have to. But for now . . ."

"I understand, sir."

"Right. Look, I'm sorry I can't do it myself. I really can't leave. Tell her I'll come by the house tonight."

"Yes, sir." The man paused at the doorway until it was clear that Nardo had nothing more to say, then marched back the way he came and closed the rear door behind him, this time more quietly.

Again Nardo forced his attention back to his conversation with Gurney. "Am I missing something, or is your understanding of this case pretty much theoretical? I mean, correct me if I'm wrong, but I didn't hear anything about a list of suspects—in fact, no concrete leads to pursue at all, is that right?"

"More or less."

"And that shitload of physical evidence—envelopes, notepaper, red ink, boots, broken bottles, footprints, taped phone calls, cell-tower transmission records, returned checks, even messages written in skin oil from this freaking lunatic's fingertips—none of that led anywhere?"

"That's one way of looking at it."

Nardo shook his head in a manner that was getting to be a habit. "Bottom line, you don't know who you're looking for or how to find him."

Gurney smiled. "So maybe that's why I'm here."

"Why is that?"

"Because I have no idea where else to go."

It was a simple admission of a simple fact. The intellectual satisfaction of figuring out the tactical details of the killer's MO was little more than a distraction from the lack of progress on the central issue so plainly articulated by Nardo. Gurney had to face the fact that despite his eureka insights into the peripheral mysteries of the case, he was almost as far from identifying and capturing his man as he'd been on the morning Mark Mellery brought him those first baffling notes and asked for his help.

There was a small shift in Nardo's expression, a relaxation of its sharp edge.

"We've never had a murder in Wycherly," he said. "Not a real one, anyway. Couple of manslaughter plead-outs, couple of vehicular homicides, one questionable hunting accident. Never had a killing here that didn't involve at least one completely intoxicated asshole. At least not in the past twenty-four years."

"That how long you've been on the job?"

"Yep. Only guy in the department longer than me is . . . was . . . Gary. He was just shy of twenty-five. His wife wanted him out at twenty, but he figured if he stayed another five . . . Damn!" Nardo wiped his eyes. "We don't lose many guys in the line of duty," he said, as though his tears needed a rational explanation.

Gurney was tempted to say he knew what it was like to lose a colleague. He'd lost two in one bust gone bad. Instead he just nodded in sympathy.

After a minute or so, Nardo cleared his throat. "You have any interest in talking to Dermott?"

"Matter of fact, yes. I just don't want to get in your way."

"You won't," said Nardo roughly—making up, Gurney supposed, for his moment of weakness. Then he added in a more normal tone, "You've spoken to this guy on the phone, right?"

"Right."

"So he knows who you are."

"Right."

"So you don't need me in the room. Just fill me in when you're through."

"Whatever you say, Lieutenant."

"Door on the right at the top of the stairs. Good luck."

As he ascended the plain oak staircase, Gurney wondered if the second floor would be any more revealing of the occupant's personality than the first, which had no more warmth or flair than the computer equipment it housed. The landing at the top of the stairs echoed the redundant security motif established downstairs: a fire extinguisher on the wall, a smoke alarm and sprinklers in the ceiling. Gurney was getting the impression that Gregory Dermott was definitely a belt-and-suspenders guy. He knocked at the door Nardo had indicated.

"Yes?" The response was pained, hoarse, impatient.

"Special Investigator Gurney, Mr. Dermott. May I see you for a minute?"

There was a pause. "Gurney?"

"Dave Gurney. We've spoken on the phone."

"Come in."

Gurney opened the door into a room darkened by partly closed blinds. It was furnished with a bed, a nightstand, a bureau, an armchair, and a tablelike desk against the wall with a folding chair in front of it. All the wood was dark. The style was contemporary, superficially upscale. The bedspread and carpet were gray, tan, essentially colorless. The room's occupant sat in the armchair facing the door. He sat tilted a little to one side, as though he'd found an odd position that mitigated his discomfort. To the extent that the underlying personality was visible, it struck Gurney as the techie type one might expect in the computer business. In the low light, his age was less definable. Thirtysomething would be a reasonable guess.

After studying Gurney's features as if trying to discern in them the answer to a question, he asked in a low voice, "Did they tell you?"

"Tell me what?"

"About the phone call . . . from the crazy murderer."

"I heard about that. Who answered the phone?"

"Answered it? I assume one of the police officers. One came to get me."

"The caller asked for you by name?"

"I guess. . . . I don't know. . . . I mean, he must have. The officer said the call was for me."

"Was there anything familiar about the caller's voice?"

"It wasn't normal."

"How do you mean that?"

"Crazy. Up and down, high like a woman's voice, then low. Crazy accents. Like it was some kind of creepy joke, but serious, too." He pressed his fingertips against his temples. "He said that I was next, then you." He seemed more exasperated than frightened.

"Were there any background sounds?"

"Any what?"

"Did you hear anything other than the caller's voice—music, traffic, other voices?"

"No. Nothing."

Gurney nodded, looking around the room. "Do you mind if I sit down?"

"What? No, go ahead." Dermott gestured broadly to the room as though it were full of chairs.

Gurney sat on the edge of the bed. He had a strong feeling that Gregory Dermott held the key to the case. Now, if only he could think of the right question to ask. The right subject to raise. On the other hand, sometimes the right thing to say was nothing. Create a silence, an empty space, and see how the other guy would choose to fill it. He sat for a long while staring down at the carpet. It was an approach that took patience. It also took good judgment to know when any more empty silence would just be a waste of time. He was approaching that point when Dermott spoke.

"Why me?" The tone was edgy, annoyed—a complaint, not a question—and Gurney chose not to respond.

After a few seconds, Dermott went on, "I think it might have something to do with this house." He paused. "Let me ask you something, Detective. Do you personally know anyone in the Wycherly police department?"

"No." He was tempted to ask the reason for the question but assumed he'd soon enough discover it.

"No one at all, present or past?"

"No one." Seeing something in Dermott's eyes that seemed to

demand further assurance, he added, "Before I saw the check-mailing instructions in the letter to Mark Mellery, I didn't even know Wycherly existed."

"And no one ever told you about anything happening in this house?"

"Happening?"

"In this house. A long time ago."

"No," said Gurney, intrigued.

Dermott's discomfort seemed to exceed the effects of a headache.

"What was it that happened?"

"It's all secondhand information," said Dermott, "but right after I bought this place, one of the neighbors told me that twenty-some-odd years ago there was a horrible fight here—apparently a husband and wife, and the wife was stabbed."

"And you see some connection . . . ?"

"It may be a coincidence, but . . ."

"Yes?"

"I'd pretty much forgotten about it. Until today. This morning when I found—" His lips stretched in a kind of nauseous spasm.

"Take your time," said Gurney.

Dermott placed both his hands to his temples. "Do you have a gun?"

"I own one."

"I mean with you."

"No. I haven't carried a gun since I left the NYPD. If you're worried about security, there are more than a dozen armed cops within a hundred yards of this house," said Gurney.

He didn't look particularly reassured.

"You were saying you remembered something."

Dermott nodded. "I'd forgotten all about it, but it came back to me when I saw . . . all that blood."

"What came back to you?"

"The woman who was stabbed in this house—she was stabbed in the throat."

Chapter 49

Kill them all

Dermott's recollection that the neighbor (now deceased) had placed the event "twenty-some-odd years ago" meant that the number could easily be less than twenty-five—and that, in turn, would mean that both John Nardo and Gary Sissek would have been on the force at the time of the attack. Although the picture was far from clear, Gurney could feel another piece of the puzzle starting to rotate into position. He had more questions for Dermott, but they could wait until he got some answers from the lieutenant.

He left Dermott sitting stiffly in his chair by the drawn blinds, looking stressed and uncomfortable. As he started down the staircase, a female officer in scene-of-crime coveralls and latex gloves in the hallway below was asking Nardo what to do next with the areas outside the house that had been examined for trace evidence.

"Keep it taped and off-limits, in case we have to go over it again. Transport the chair, bottle, anything else you've got to the station. Set up the back end of the file room as a dedicated area."

"What about all the junk on the table?"

"Shove it in Colbert's office for now."

"He's not going to like it."

"I don't give a flying— Look, just take care of it!"

"Yes, sir."

"Before you leave, tell Big Tommy to stay in front of the house, tell Pat to stay by the phone. I want everyone else out knocking on doors. I want to know if anyone in the neighborhood saw or heard anything out of the ordinary the past couple of days, especially late last night or early this morning—strangers, cars parked where they aren't normally parked, anyone hanging around, anyone in a hurry, anything at all."

"How large a radius you want them to cover?"

Nardo looked at his watch. "Whatever they can cover in the next six hours. Then we'll decide where to go from there. Anything of interest turns up, I want to be informed immediately."

As she went off on her mission, Nardo turned to Gurney, who was standing at the foot of the stairs. "Find out anything useful?"

"I'm not sure," said Gurney in a low voice, motioning Nardo to follow him back into the room they'd been sitting in earlier. "Maybe you can help me figure it out."

Gurney sat in the chair facing the doorway. Nardo stood behind the chair on the opposite side of the square table. His expression was a combination of curiosity and something Gurney couldn't decipher.

"Are you aware that someone was once stabbed in this house?"

"What the hell are you talking about?"

"Shortly after Dermott bought the place, he was told by a neighbor that a woman who'd lived here years ago had been attacked by her husband."

"How many years ago?"

Gurney was sure he saw a flicker of recognition in Nardo's eyes.

"Maybe twenty, maybe twenty-five. Somewhere in there."

It seemed to be the answer Nardo expected. He sighed and shook his head. "I hadn't thought about that for a long time. Yeah, there was a domestic assault—about twenty-four years ago. Not too long after I joined the force. What about it?"

"Do you remember any of the details?"

"Before we go down memory lane, you mind addressing the relevance issue?"

"The woman who was attacked was stabbed in the throat."

"Is that supposed to mean something?" There was a twitch at the corner of Nardo's mouth.

"Two people have been attacked in this house. Of all the ways that someone could be attacked, it strikes me as a notable coincidence that both of those people were stabbed in the throat."

"You're making these things sound the same by the way you say it, but they got zip in common. What the hell does a police officer murdered on a protection assignment today have to do with a domestic disturbance twenty-four freaking years ago?"

Gurney shrugged. "If I knew more about the 'disturbance,' maybe I could tell you."

"Fine. Okay. I'll tell you what I can tell you, but it's not much." Nardo paused, staring down at the table, or more likely into the past. "I wasn't on duty that night."

An obvious disclaimer, thought Gurney. *Why does the story demand a disclaimer?*

"So this is pretty much secondhand," Nardo went on. "As in most domestics, the husband was drunk out of his mind, got into an altercation with his wife, apparently picked up a bottle, whacked her with it, I guess it broke, she got cut, that's about it."

Gurney knew damn well that wasn't *it.* The only question was how to jar the rest of the story loose. One of the unwritten rules of the job was to say as little as possible, and Nardo was carefully obeying the rule. Feeling that there was no time for a subtle approach, Gurney decided to plunge head-on into the barrier.

"Lieutenant, that's a crock of shit!" he said, looking away with disgust.

"Crock of shit?" Nardo's voice was pitched menacingly just above a whisper.

"I'm sure what you told me is true. The problem is what's missing."

"Maybe what's missing is none of your freaking business." Nardo was still sounding tough, but some of the confidence had gone out of the belligerence.

"Look, I'm not just some nosy asshole from another jurisdiction. Gregory Dermott got a phone call this morning threatening my life. *My* life. If there's any possible way what's going on here could be connected to your so-called domestic disturbance, I goddamn well have a right to know about it."

Nardo cleared his throat and gazed up at the ceiling as if the right words—or an emergency exit—might suddenly appear there.

Gurney added in a softer tone, "You could start by telling me the names of the people involved."

Nardo gave a little nod, pulled out the chair he'd been standing behind, and sat down. "Jimmy and Felicity Spinks." He sounded resigned to an unpleasant truth.

"You say the names like you knew them pretty well."

"Yeah. Well. Anyway . . ." Somewhere in the house, a phone rang once. Nardo seemed not to hear it. "Anyway, Jimmy used to drink a bit. More than a bit, I guess. Came home drunk one night, got into a fight with Felicity. Like I said, he ended up cutting her pretty bad with a broken bottle. She lost a lot of blood. I didn't see it, I was off that night, but the guys who were on the call talked about the blood for a week." Nardo was staring at the table again.

"She survived?"

"What? Yeah, yeah, she survived, but just barely. Brain damage."

"What happened to her?"

"Happened? I think she was put in some kind of nursing home."

"What about the husband?"

Nardo hesitated. Gurney couldn't tell whether he was having a hard time remembering or just didn't want to talk about it. "Claimed self-defense," he said with evident distaste. "Ended up getting a plea deal. Sentence reduced to time served. Lost his job. Left town. Social services took their kid. End of story."

Gurney's antenna, sensitized by a thousand interrogations, told him there was still something missing. He waited, observing Nardo's discomfort. In the background he could hear an intermittent voice—probably the voice of whoever had answered the phone—but couldn't make out the words.

"There's something I don't understand," he said. "What's the big deal about that story, that you didn't just tell me the whole thing to begin with?"

Nardo looked squarely at Gurney. "Jimmy Spinks was a cop."

The frisson that swept through Gurney's body brought with it half a dozen urgent questions, but before he could ask any, a square-jawed woman with a sandy crew cut appeared suddenly at the doorway. She wore jeans and a dark polo shirt. A Glock in a quick-draw holster was strapped under her left arm.

"Sir, we just got a call you need to know about." An unspoken *immediately* flashed in her eyes.

Looking relieved at the distraction, he gave the newcomer his full attention and waited for her to go on. Instead she glanced uncertainly toward Gurney.

"He's with us," said Nardo without pleasure. "Go ahead."

She gave Gurney a second glance, no friendlier than the first, then advanced to the table and laid a miniature digital phone recorder down in front of Nardo. It was about the size of an iPod.

"It's all on there, sir."

He hesitated for a moment, squinting at the device, then pushed a button. The playback began immediately. The quality was excellent.

Gurney recognized the first voice as that of the woman standing in front of him.

"*GD Security Systems.*" Apparently she'd been instructed to answer Dermott's phone as though she were an employee.

The second voice was bizarre—and thoroughly familiar to Gurney from the call he'd listened in on at Mark Mellery's request. It seemed so long ago. Four deaths had intervened between that call and this one—deaths that had shaken his sense of time. Mark in Peony, Albert Rudden in the Bronx, Richard Kartch in Sotherton (*Richard Kartch*—why did that name always bring with it an uneasy feeling, a feeling of discrepancy?), and Officer Gary Sissek in Wycherly.

There was no mistaking that weirdly shifting pitch and accent.

"*If I could hear God, what would He tell me?*" the voice asked with the menacing lilt of a horror-movie villain.

"*Excuse me?*" The female cop on the recording sounded as taken aback as any real receptionist might have been.

The voice repeated, more insistently, *"If I could hear God, what would He tell me?"*

"I'm sorry, could you repeat that? I think we may have a bad connection. Are you using a cell phone?"

Speaking quickly to Nardo, she interjected some live commentary. "I was just trying to prolong the call, like you said, to keep him talking as long as possible."

Nardo nodded. The recording went on.

"If I could hear God, what would He tell me?"

"I don't really understand that, sir. Could you explain what you mean?"

The voice, suddenly booming, announced, *"God would tell me to kill them all!"*

"Sir? I'm pretty confused here. Did you want me to write this message down and pass it along to someone?"

There was a sharp laugh, like cellophane crumpling.

"It's Judgment Day, no more to say. / Dermott be nimble, Gurney be quick. / The cleanser is coming. Tick-tock-tick."

Chapter 50

Re-search

he first to speak was Nardo. "That was the whole call?"

"Yes, sir."

He leaned back in his chair and massaged his temples. "No word yet from Chief Meyers?"

"We keep leaving messages at his hotel desk, sir, and on his cell phone. No word yet."

"I assume the caller's number was blocked?"

"Yes, sir."

"'Kill them all,' huh?"

"Yes, sir, those were his words. Do you want to hear the recording again?"

Nardo shook his head. "Who do you think he's referring to?"

"Sir?"

"'Kill them all.' All who?"

The female cop seemed to be at a loss. Nardo looked at Gurney.

"Just a guess, Lieutenant, but I'd say it's either all the remaining people on his hit list—assuming there are any—or all of us here in the house."

"And what about 'the cleanser is coming,'" said Nardo. "Why 'the cleanser'?"

Gurney shrugged. "I have no idea. Maybe he just likes the word—fits his pathological notion of what he's doing."

Nardo's features wrinkled in an involuntary expression of distaste.

Turning to the female cop, he addressed her for the first time by name. "Pat, I want you outside the house with Big Tommy. Take diagonal corners opposite each other, so together you'll have every door and window under surveillance. Also, get the word around—I want every officer prepared to converge on this house within one minute of hearing a shot or any kind of disturbance at all. Questions?"

"Are we expecting an armed attack, sir?" She sounded hopeful.

"I wouldn't say 'expecting,' but it's sure as hell possible."

"You really think that crazy bastard is still in the area?" There was acetylene fire in her eyes.

"It's possible. Let Big Tommy know about the perp's latest call. Stay super alert."

She nodded and was gone.

Nardo turned grimly to Gurney. "What do you think? Think I ought to call in the cavalry, tell the state cops we got an emergency situation? Or was that phone call a bunch of bullshit?"

"Considering the body count so far, it would be risky to assume it was bullshit."

"I'm not assuming a freaking thing," said Nardo, tight-lipped.

The tension in the exchange led to a silence.

It was broken by a hoarse voice calling from upstairs.

"Lieutenant Nardo? Gurney?"

Nardo grimaced as if something were turning sour in his stomach. "Maybe Dermott's got another recollection he wants to share." He sank deeper into his chair.

"I'll look into it," said Gurney.

He stepped from the room into the hallway. Dermott was standing at his bedroom door at the top of the staircase. He looked impatient, angry, exhausted.

"Could I speak to you . . . please?" The "please" was not said pleasantly.

Dermott looked too shaky to negotiate the staircase, so Gurney went up. As he did, the thought came to him that this wasn't really a home, just a place of business with sleeping quarters appended to it. In the city neighborhood where he was raised, it was a common arrangement—shopkeepers living above their shops, like the wretched deli man whose hatred of life seemed to increase with each new customer, or the mob-connected undertaker with his fat wife and four fat children. Just thinking about it made him queasy.

At the bedroom door, he shoved the feeling aside and tried to decipher the portrait of unease on Dermott's face.

The man glanced around Gurney and down the stairs. "Is Lieutenant Nardo gone?"

"He's downstairs. What can I do for you?"

"I heard cars driving away," said Dermott accusingly.

"They're not going far."

Dermott nodded in an unsatisfied way. He obviously had something on his mind but seemed in no rush to get to the point. Gurney took the opportunity to pursue a few questions of his own.

"Mr. Dermott, what do you do for a living?"

"What?" He sounded both baffled and annoyed.

"Exactly what sort of work do you do?"

"My work? Security. I believe we had this conversation before."

"In a general way," said Gurney, smiling. "Perhaps you could give me some details."

Dermott's expressive sigh suggested that he viewed the request as an irritating waste of his time. "Look," he said, "I need to sit down." He returned to his armchair, settling into it gingerly. "What kind of details?"

"The name of your company is GD Security Systems. What sort of 'security' do these 'systems' provide, and for whom?"

After another loud sigh, he said, "I help companies protect confidential information."

"And this help comes in what form?"

"Database-protection applications, firewalls, limited-access protocols, ID-verification systems—those categories would cover most projects we handle."

"We?"

"I beg your pardon?"

"You referred to projects 'we' handle."

"That's not meant *literally*," said Dermott dismissively. "It's just a corporate expression."

"Makes GD Security Systems seem a bit bigger than it is?"

"That's not the intention, I assure you. My clients love the fact that I do the work myself."

Gurney nodded as though he were impressed. "I can see how that would be a plus. Who are these clients?"

"Clients for whom confidentiality is a major issue."

Gurney smiled innocently at Dermott's curt tone. "I'm not asking you to reveal any secrets. I'm just wondering what sort of businesses they're in."

"Businesses whose client databases entail sensitive privacy issues."

"Such as?"

"Personal information."

"What sort of personal information?"

Dermott looked like he was evaluating the contractual risks he might be incurring by going any further. "The sort of information collected by insurance companies, financial-service companies, HMOs."

"Medical data?"

"A great deal of it, yes."

"Treatment data?"

"To the extent that it is captured in the basic medical coding system. What's the point of this?"

"Suppose you were a hacker who wanted to access a very large medical database—how would you go about it?"

"That's not an answerable question."

"Why is that?"

Dermott closed his eyes in a way that conveyed frustration. "Too many variables."

"Like what?"

"Like what?" Dermott repeated the question as though it were an embodiment of pure stupidity. After a moment he went on with his eyes still closed. "The hacker's goal, the level of expertise, his familiarity with the data format, the database structure itself, the access protocol, the redundancy of the firewall system, and about a dozen other factors that I doubt you have the technical background to understand."

"I'm sure you're right about that," said Gurney mildly. "But let's say, just for example, that a skilled hacker was trying to compile a list of people who'd been treated for a particular illness . . ."

Dermott raised his hands in exasperation, but Gurney pressed on. "How difficult would that be?"

"Again, that's not answerable. Some databases are so porous they might as well be posted on the Internet. Others could defeat the most sophisticated code-breaking computers in the world. It all depends on the talent of the system designer."

Gurney caught a note of pride in that last statement and decided to fertilize it. "I'd be willing to bet my pension there aren't many people better at it than you are."

Dermott smiled. "I've built my career on outwitting the sharpest hackers on the planet. No data-protection protocol of mine has ever been breached."

The boast raised a new possibility. Might the man's ability to stymie the killer's penetration of certain databases have something to do with the killer's decision to involve him in the case via his post-office box? The idea was certainly worth considering, even though it created more questions than answers.

"I wish the local police could claim the same degree of competence."

The comment brought Gurney back from his speculation. "What do you mean?"

"What do I mean?" Dermott seemed to be thinking long and hard about the answer. "A murderer is stalking me, and I have no confidence in the ability of the police to protect me. There is a madman loose in this neighborhood, a madman who intends to kill me, then kill you, and you respond to this by asking me hypothetical questions about hypothetical hackers accessing hypothetical databases? I have no idea what you're trying to do, but if you're trying to settle my nerves by distracting me, I assure you it's not helping. Why don't you concentrate on the real danger? The problem is not some academic software issue. The problem is a lunatic creeping up on us with a bloody knife in his hand. And this morning's tragedy is proof positive that the police are worse than useless!" The angry tone of this speech had by the end spun out of control. It brought Nardo up the stairs and into the bedroom. He looked first at Dermott, then at Gurney, then back at Dermott.

"The hell's going on?"

Dermott turned away and stared at the wall.

"Mr. Dermott doesn't feel adequately protected," said Gurney.

"Adequately prot—" Nardo burst out angrily, then stopped and began again in a more reasonable way. "Sir, the chances of any unauthorized person getting into this house—much less 'a lunatic with a bloody knife' if I heard you right—are less than zero."

Dermott continued staring at the wall.

"Let me put it this way," Nardo continued. "If the son of a bitch has the balls to show up here, he's dead. He tries to get in, I'll eat the son of a bitch for dinner."

"I don't want to be left alone in this house. Not for a minute."

"You're not hearing me," growled Nardo. "You're not alone. There are cops all over the neighborhood. Cops all around the house. Nobody's getting in."

Dermott turned toward Nardo and said challengingly, "Suppose he already got in."

"The hell are you talking about?"

"What if he's already in the house?"

"How the hell could he be in the house?"

"This morning—when I went outside to look for Officer Sissek— suppose when I was walking around the yard . . . he came in through the unlocked door. He could have, couldn't he?"

Nardo stared at him incredulously. "And gone where?"

"How would I know?"

"What do you think, he's hiding under your freaking bed?"

"That's quite a question, Lieutenant. But the fact is, you don't know the answer, do you? Because you didn't really check the house thoroughly, did you? So he *could* be under the bed, couldn't he?"

"Jesus Christ!" cried Nardo. "Enough of this shit!"

He took two long strides to the footboard, grabbed the bottom of it, and with a fierce grunt heaved the end of the bed into the air and held it at shoulder height.

"Okay now?" he snarled. "You see anyone under there?"

He let the bed down with a thud and a bounce.

Dermott glared at him. "What I want, Lieutenant, is competence, not childish drama. Is a careful search of the premises too much to ask?"

Nardo eyed Dermott coldly. "You tell me—where could someone hide in this house?"

"Where? I don't know. Basement? Attic? Closets? How should I know?"

"Just to set the record straight, sir, the first officers on the scene did go through the house. If he was here, they would have found him. Okay?"

"They went through the house?"

"Yes, sir, while you were being interviewed in the kitchen."

"Including the attic and basement?"

"Correct."

"Including the utility closet?"

"They checked all the closets."

"They couldn't have checked the utility closet!" cried Dermott defiantly. "It's padlocked, and I have the key, and nobody asked me for it."

"Which means," countered Nardo, "if it's still padlocked, nobody could have gotten into it to begin with. Which means it would have been a waste of time to check it."

"No—what it means is that you're a damn liar for claiming that the whole house had been searched!"

Nardo's reaction surprised Gurney, who was bracing himself for an explosion. Instead the lieutenant said softly, "Give me the key, sir. I'll take a look right now."

"So," Dermott concluded, lawyerlike, "you admit that it was overlooked—that the house was not searched the way it should have been!"

Gurney wondered if this nasty tenacity was the product of Dermott's migraine, or a bilious streak in his temperament, or the simple conversion of fear into aggression.

Nardo seemed unnaturally calm. "The key, sir?"

Dermott muttered something—something offensive, by the look on his face—and pushed himself up out of his chair. He took a key ring out of his nightstand drawer, extricated a key smaller than the rest, and tossed it on the bed. Nardo picked it up with no visible reaction and left the room without another word. His footsteps receded slowly down the stairs. Dermott dropped the remaining keys back in the drawer, started to close it, and stopped.

"Shit!" he hissed.

He picked up the keys again and began working a second one off the stiff little ring that held them. Once he'd removed it, he started for the door. After taking no more than a step, he tripped on the bedside throw rug and stumbled against the doorjamb, banging his head. A strangled cry of rage and pain emerged from his clenched teeth.

"You all right, sir?" asked Gurney, stepping toward him.

"Fine! Perfect!" The words were sputtered out furiously.

"Can I help you?"

Dermott seemed to be trying to calm down. "Here," he said. "Take this key and give it to him. There are two locks. With all the ridiculous confusion . . ."

Gurney took the key. "You're okay?"

Dermott waved his hand disgustedly. "If they came to me to begin with like they should have . . ." His voice trailed off.

Gurney gave the wretched-looking man a final assessing glance and went downstairs.

As in most suburban houses, the stairs to the basement descended behind and beneath the stairs to the second floor. There was a door leading to them, which Nardo had left open. Gurney could see a light on below.

"Lieutenant?"

"Yeah?"

The source of the voice seemed to be located some distance from the foot of the rough wooden stairs, so Gurney went down with the key. The odor—a musty combination of concrete, metal pipes, wood, and dust—kicked up a vivid memory of the apartment-house basement of his childhood—the double-locked storeroom where tenants stored unused bicycles, baby carriages, boxes of junk; the dim light cast by a few cobwebby bulbs; the shadows that never failed to give him a hair-raising chill.

Nardo was standing at a gray steel door at the opposite end of an unfinished concrete room with exposed joists, dampness-stained walls, a water heater, two oil tanks, a furnace, two smoke alarms, two fire extinguishers, and a sprinkler system.

"The key only fits the padlock," he said. "There's also a dead bolt. What's with this redundant security mania? And where the hell's the other key?"

Gurney handed it to him. "Says he forgot. Blames it on you."

Nardo took it with a disgusted grunt and stuck it directly into the lock. "Rotten little fucker," he said, pushing the door open. "I can't believe I'm actually checking— What the hell . . . ?"

Nardo, followed by Gurney, walked tentatively through the doorway into the room beyond, which was considerably larger than a utility closet.

At first, nothing they saw made sense.

Chapter 51

Show-and-tell

Gurney's immediate reaction was that they'd entered the wrong door. But that didn't make any sense, either. Apart from the door at the top of the stairs, it was the only door in the basement. But this was no mere storage space.

They were standing in the corner of a large, softly lighted, traditionally furnished, richly carpeted bedroom. In front of them was a queen-size bed with a flowery quilt and a ruffled skirt extending around the base. Several overstuffed pillows with matching ruffles were propped up against the headboard. At the foot of the bed was a cedar hope chest. On it sat a big stuffed bird made of some sort of patchwork quilting. An odd feature in the wall to Gurney's left attracted his attention—a window that seemed at first glance to provide a view of an open field, but the view, he quickly realized, was a poster-size color transparency illuminated from the rear, presumably intended to relieve the claustrophobic atmosphere. He simultaneously became aware of the low hum of some sort of air-circulation system.

"I don't get it," said Nardo.

Gurney was about to agree when he noticed a small table a little farther along the same wall as the fake window. On the table was a low-wattage lamp in whose circle of amber light stood three simple black frames of the sort used to display diplomas. He moved closer for a clearer view. In each frame was a photocopy of a personal check. The checks were all made out to X. Arybdis. They were all in the amount of $289.87. From left to right, they were from Mark Mellery, Albert Rudden, and R. Kartch. These were the checks Gregory Dermott had reported receiving, the originals of which he'd returned uncashed to their senders. But why had he made copies before returning them? And, more troubling, why the hell had he framed them? Gurney picked them up one at a time, as if a closer inspection might provide answers.

Then, suddenly, while he was peering at the signature on the third check—R. Kartch—the uncomfortable feeling he'd had about that name resurfaced. Except this time not just the feeling came to him, but the reason for it.

"Damn!" he muttered at his earlier blindness to the now obvious discrepancy.

Simultaneously, an abrupt little sound came from Nardo. Gurney looked at him, then followed the direction of his startled gaze to the opposite corner of the wide room. There—barely visible in the shadows, beyond the reach of the feeble light cast by the table lamp on the framed checks, partly concealed by the wings of a Queen Anne armchair and camouflaged by a nightgown of the same dusty-rose hue as the upholstery, a frail woman sat with her head bent forward on her chest.

Nardo unclipped a flashlight from his belt and aimed its beam at her.

Gurney guessed that her age might be anywhere from fifty to seventy. The skin was deathly pale. The blond hair, done up in a profusion of curls, had to be a wig. Blinking, she raised her head so gradually it hardly seemed to be moving, turning it toward the light with a curiously heliotropic grace.

Nardo looked at Gurney, then back at the woman in the chair.

"I have to pee," she said. Her voice was high, raspy, imperious. The haughty upward tilt of her chin revealed an ugly scar on her neck.

"Who the hell is this?" whispered Nardo, as though Gurney ought to know.

In fact, Gurney was sure he knew exactly who it was. He also knew that bringing the key down to Nardo in the basement had been a terrible mistake.

He turned quickly toward the open doorway. But Gregory Dermott was already standing in it, with a quart bottle of Four Roses whiskey in one hand and a .38 Special revolver in the other. There was no trace of the angry, volatile man with a migraine. The eyes, no longer screwed up into an imitation of pain and accusation, had reverted to what, Gurney assumed, was their normal state—the right keen and determined, the left dark and unfeeling as lead.

Nardo also turned. "Wha . . . ?" he began, then let the question die in his throat. He stood very still, eyeing Dermott's face and gun alternately.

Dermott took a full step into the room, adroitly reached back with his foot, and hooked his toe around the edge of the door, slamming it shut behind him. There was a heavy metallic click as the lock snapped into place. A small, unsettling smile lengthened the thin line of his mouth.

"Alone at last," he said, mocking the tone of a man looking forward to a pleasant chat. "So much to do," he added. "So little time." He apparently found this amusing. The cold smile widened for a moment like a stretching worm, then contracted. "I want you to know in advance how much I appreciate your participation in my little project. Your cooperation will make everything so much better. First, a minor detail. Lieutenant, may I ask you to lie facedown on the floor?" It wasn't really a question.

Gurney could read in Nardo's eyes a kind of rapid calculation, but he couldn't tell what options the man was considering. Or even if he had any idea what was really going on.

To the degree that he could read anything in Dermott's eyes, it looked like the patience of a cat watching a mouse with nowhere to run.

"Sir," said Nardo, affecting a kind of pained concern, "it would be a real good idea to put the gun down."

Dermott shook his head. "Not as good as you think."

Nardo looked baffled. "Just put it down, sir."

"That's an option. But there's a complication. Nothing in life is simple, is it?"

"Complication?" Nardo was speaking to Dermott as though he were an otherwise harmless citizen temporarily off his medication.

"I plan to put down the gun after I shoot you. If you want me to put it down right away, then I'll have to shoot you right away. I don't want to do that, and I'm sure you don't want that, either. You see the problem?"

As Dermott spoke, he raised the revolver to a point at which it was aimed at Nardo's throat. Whether it was the steadiness of his hand or the calm mockery in Dermott's voice, something in his manner convinced Nardo he needed to try a different strategy.

"You fire that gun," he said, "what do you think happens next?"

Dermott shrugged, the thin line of his mouth widening again. "You die."

Nardo nodded in tentative agreement, as though a student had given him an obvious but incomplete answer. "And? What then?"

"What difference does it make?" Dermott shrugged again, gazing down the barrel at Nardo's neck.

The lieutenant seemed to be making quite an effort at maintaining control, over either his fury or his fear.

"Not much to me, but a lot to you. You pull that trigger, in less than a minute you'll have a couple dozen cops up your ass. They'll fucking rip you to pieces."

Dermott seemed amused. "How much do you know about crows, Lieutenant?"

Nardo squinted at the non sequitur.

"Crows are incredibly stupid," said Dermott. "When you shoot one, another one comes. When you shoot that one, another comes, and then another, and another. You keep shooting them, and they keep coming."

It was something Gurney had heard before—that crows would not let one of their own die alone. If a crow was dying, others would come and stand next to him, so he wouldn't be alone. When he'd first heard that story, from his grandmother when he was ten or eleven years old, he had to leave the room because he knew he was going to cry. He went into the bathroom, and his heart ached.

"I saw a picture once of a crow shoot on a farm in Nebraska," said Dermott with a mixture of amazement and contempt. "A farmer with a shotgun was standing next to a pile of dead crows that came up to his shoulder." He paused, as if to allow Nardo time to appreciate the suicidal absurdity of crows and the relevance of their fate to the current situation.

Nardo shook his head. "You really think you can sit in here and shoot one cop after another as they come through the door without getting your head blown off? It's not going to happen that way."

"Of course it isn't. Didn't anyone ever tell you a literal mind is a small mind? I like the crow story, Lieutenant, but there are more efficient ways to exterminate vermin than shooting them one at a time. Gassing, for example. Gassing is very efficient, if you have the right sort of delivery system. Perhaps you've noticed that every room in this house is equipped with sprinklers. Every one except this one." He paused again, his livelier eye sparkling with self-congratulation. "So if I shoot you and all the crows come flying in, I open two little valves on two little pipes, and twenty seconds later . . ." His smile became cherubic. "Do you have any idea what concentrated chlorine gas does to a human lung? And how rapidly it does it?"

Gurney watched Nardo struggling to assess this frighteningly contained man and his gassing threat. For an unnerving moment, he thought the cop's pride and rage were about to propel him into a fatal leap forward, but instead Nardo took a few quiet breaths, which seemed to let some of the tension out of the spring, and spoke in a voice that sounded earnest and anxious.

"Chlorine compounds can be tricky. I worked with them in an antiterrorism unit. One guy accidentally produced some nitrogen trichloride as a by-product of another experiment. Didn't even realize it. Blew his thumb off. Might not be as easy as you think to run your chemicals through a sprinkler system. I'm not sure you could do that."

"Don't waste your time trying to trick me, Lieutenant. You sound like you're trying a technique from the police manual. What does it say—'Express skepticism regarding the criminal's plan, question his credibility, provoke him into providing additional details'? If you want to know more, there's no need to trick me, just ask me. I have no secrets. What I do have, just so you know, are two fifty-gallon high-pressure tanks, filled with chlorine and ammonia, driven by an industrial compressor, linked directly to the main sprinkler pipe that feeds the system throughout the house. There are two valves concealed in this room that will join the combined one hundred gallons, releasing an enormous amount of gas in a highly concentrated form. As for the unlikely peripheral formation of nitrogen trichloride and the resultant explosion, I would regard that as a delightful plus, but I will be content with the simple asphyxiation of the Wycherly PD. It would be great fun to see you all blasted to pieces, but one must be content. The best must not be made the enemy of the good."

"Mr. Dermott, what on earth is this all about?"

Dermott wrinkled his brow in a parody of someone who might be considering the question seriously.

"I received a note in the mail this morning. *'Beware the snow, beware the sun, / the night, the day, nowhere to run.'*" He quoted the words from Gurney's poem with sarcastic histrionics, shooting him an inquisitive glance as he did so. "Empty threats, but I must thank whoever sent it. It reminded me how short life can be, that I should never put off till tomorrow what I can do today."

"I don't really get what you mean," said Nardo, still in his earnest mode.

"Just do what I say, and you'll end up understanding perfectly."

"Fine, no problem. I just don't want anyone to get hurt unnecessarily."

"No, of course not." The stretchy, wormlike smile came and went. "Nobody wants that. In fact, to avoid unnecessary hurt, I really do need you to lie down on the floor right now."

They had come full circle. The question was, what now? Gurney was watching Nardo's face for readable signs. How much had the man put together? Had it dawned on him yet who the woman in the chair might be, or the smiley psychopath with the whiskey bottle and the gun?

At least he must have finally realized, if nothing else, that Dermott was the murderer of Officer Sissek. That would account for the hatred he couldn't quite conceal in his eyes. Suddenly the tension was back in the spring. Nardo looked wild with adrenaline, with a primitive, consequences-be-damned emotion far more powerful than reason. Dermott saw it, too, but far from cowing him, it seemed to elate him, to energize him. His hand tightened just a little on the handle of the revolver, and for the first time the slithery smile revealed a lively glimmer of teeth.

Less than a second before a .38 slug would surely have ended Nardo's life, and less than two seconds before a second slug would have ended his own, Gurney broke the circuit with a furious, guttural shout.

"Do what the man said! Get down on the fucking floor! Get down on the fucking floor NOW!"

The effect was stunning. The antagonists were frozen in place, the insidious momentum of the confrontation shattered by Gurney's raw outburst.

The fact that no one was dead persuaded him that he was on the right track, but he wasn't sure exactly what that track was. To the extent that he could read Nardo, the man looked betrayed. Beneath his more opaque exterior, Dermott seemed disconcerted but was striving, Gurney suspected, not to let the interruption undermine his control.

"Very wise advice from your friend," Dermott said to Nardo. "I'd follow it at once if I were you. Detective Gurney has such a good mind. Such an interesting man. A famous man. You can learn so much about a person from a simple Internet search. You'd be amazed at what sort of information pops up with a name and a zip code. So little privacy anymore." Dermott's sly tone sent a wave of nausea through Gurney's chest. He tried to remind himself that Dermott's specialty was persuading people that he knew more about them than he really did. But the idea that his own failure to think ahead regarding the postmark problem could in any way have put Madeleine in jeopardy was intrusive and nearly unbearable.

Nardo reluctantly lowered himself to the floor, eventually lying on his stomach in the position of a man about to do a push-up. Dermott directed him to clasp his hands behind his head, "if it's not too much to ask." For a terrible moment, Gurney thought it might be the setup for an immediate execution. Instead, after gazing down with satisfaction at the prone lieutenant, Dermott carefully put the whiskey bottle he'd been carrying on the cedar hope chest next to the big stuffed bird—or, as Gurney now realized, the big stuffed *goose*. With a sickening chill, he recalled a detail from the lab reports. *Goose down.* Then Dermott reached down to Nardo's right ankle, pulled a small automatic pistol out of a holster strapped there, and placed it in his own pocket. Again the humorless grin waxed and waned.

"Knowing where all the firearms are located," he explained with a creepy earnestness, "is the key to avoiding tragedy. So many guns. So many guns in the wrong hands. Of course, an argument is often made that guns don't kill people, people kill people. And you have to admit that there's some truth in that. People do kill people. But who would know that better than men in your profession?"

Gurney added to the short list of things he knew to be true the fact that these archly delivered speeches to Dermott's captive audience—the polite posing, the menacing gentility, the same elements that characterized his notes to his victims—had one vital purpose: to fuel his own fantasy of omnipotence.

Proving Gurney right, Dermott turned to him and like an obsequious usher whispered, "Would you mind sitting over there against that wall?" He indicated a ladder-back chair on the left side of the bed next to the lamp table with the framed checks. Gurney went to the chair and sat without hesitation.

Dermott looked back down at Nardo, his icy gaze at odds with his encouraging tone. "We'll have you up and around in no time at all. We just need to get one more participant in place. I appreciate your patience."

On the side of Nardo's face visible to Gurney, the jaw muscle tightened and a red flush rose from the neck into the cheek.

Dermott moved quickly across the room to the far corner and, leaning over the side of the wing chair, whispered something to the seated woman.

"I have to pee," she said, raising her head.

"She really doesn't, you know," said Dermott looking back toward Gurney and Nardo. "It's an irritation created by the catheter. She's had a catheter for years and years. A discomfort on the one hand, but a real convenience, too. The Lord giveth, and the Lord taketh away. Heads and tails. Can't have one without the other. Wasn't that a song?" He stopped as though trying to place something, hummed a familiar tune with a perky lilt, then, still holding the gun in his right hand, helped the old woman up from the chair with his left. "Come along, dear, it's beddy-bye time."

As he led her in small, halting steps across the room to the bed and assisted her into a semireclining position against the upright pillows, he kept repeating in a little boy's voice, "Beddy-bye, beddy-bye, beddy-bye, beddy-bye."

Pointing the gun at a rough midpoint between Nardo on the floor and Gurney in the chair, he looked unhurriedly around the room, but not *at* anything in particular. It was hard to tell whether he was seeing what was there or overlaying on it another scene from another time or place. Then he looked at the woman on the bed in the same way and said with a kind of fey Peter Pan conviction, "Everything's going to be perfect. Everything's going to be the way it always should have been." He began humming very softly a few disconnected notes. As he went on, Gurney recognized the tune of a nursery rhyme, "Here We Go Round the Mulberry Bush." Perhaps it was the uncomfortable reaction he'd always had to the antilogic of nursery rhymes; perhaps it was this one's dizzying imagery; perhaps it was the colossal inappropriateness of the music to the moment; but whatever it was, hearing that melody in that room made him want to puke.

Then Dermott added words, but not the right words. He sang

like a child, "Here we get into the bed again, the bed again, the bed again. Here we get into the bed again, so early in the morning."

"I have to pee," the woman said.

Dermott continued singing his weird ditty as though it were a lullaby. Gurney wondered how distracted the man actually was— sufficiently to permit a leaping tackle across the bed? He thought not. Would a more vulnerable moment come later? If Dermott's chlorine-gas story was an action plan, not just a scary fantasy, how much time did they have left? He guessed not much.

The house above was deadly still. There was no indication that any of the other Wycherly cops had yet discovered their lieutenant's absence or, if they had, realized its significance. There were no raised voices, no scuttling feet, no hint of any outside activity at all—which meant that saving Nardo's life and his own would probably depend on what Gurney himself could come up with in the next five or ten minutes to derail the psychopath who was fluffing up the pillows on the bed.

Dermott stopped singing. Then he stepped sideways along the edge of the bed to a point at which he could aim his revolver with equal ease at either Nardo or Gurney. He began moving it back and forth like a baton, rhythmically, aiming it at one and then the other and back again. Gurney got the idea, perhaps from the movement of the man's lips, that he was waving the gun in time to *eeny meeny miney mo, catch a tiger by the toe.* The possibility that this silent recitation might in a few seconds be punctuated with a bullet in one of their heads seemed overwhelmingly real—real enough to jar Gurney right then into taking a wild verbal swing.

In the softest, most casual voice he could muster he asked, "Does she ever wear the ruby slippers?"

Dermott's lips stopped moving, and his facial expression reverted to a deep, dangerous emptiness. His gun lost its rhythm. The direction of its muzzle settled slowly on Gurney like a roulette wheel winding down to a losing number.

It wasn't the first time he'd been at the wrong end of a gun barrel, but never in all the forty-seven years of his life had he felt closer to death. There was a draining sensation in his skin, as though the blood were retreating to some safer place. Then, bizarrely, he felt calm. It made him think of the accounts he'd read of men overboard in an icy sea, of the hallucinatory tranquillity they felt before losing consciousness. He gazed across the bed at Dermott, into those emotionally asymmetric eyes—one corpselike from a long-ago battlefield, the other alive with hatred. In that second, more purposeful eye, he sensed a rapid calculation under way. Perhaps Gurney's reference to the pilfered slippers from The Laurels had served its purpose—raising questions that needed resolution. Perhaps Dermott was wondering how much he knew and how such knowledge might affect the consummation of his endgame.

If so, Dermott resolved these matters to his satisfaction with disheartening speed. He grinned, showing for the second time a glimpse of small, pearly teeth.

"Did you get my messages?" he asked playfully.

The peace that had enveloped Gurney was fading. He knew that answering the question the wrong way would create a major problem. So would not answering it. He hoped that Dermott was referring to the only two things resembling "messages" that had been found at The Laurels.

"You mean your little quote from *The Shining*?"

"That's *one*," said Dermott.

"Obviously, signing in as Mr. and Mrs. Scylla." Gurney sounded bored.

"That's *two*. But the third was the best, don't you think?"

"I thought the third was stupid," said Gurney, desperately stalling, racing back through his recollections of the eccentric little inn and its half owner, Bruce Wellstone.

His comment produced a quick flash of anger in Dermott, followed by a kind of caginess. "I wonder if you really know what I'm talking about, Detective."

Gurney suppressed his urge to protest. He'd discovered that often the best bluff was silence. And it was easier to think when you weren't talking.

The only peculiar thing he could remember Wellstone saying was something about birds, or bird-watching, and that something about it didn't make sense at that time of year. *What the hell kind of birds were they? And what was it about the number? Something about the number of birds . . .*

Dermott was getting restless. It was time for another wild swing.

"The birds," said Gurney slyly. At least he hoped he sounded sly and not inane. Something in Dermott's eyes told him the wild swing may have connected. But how? And what now? What was it about the birds that mattered? What was the *message*? The wrong time of year for what? *Rose-breasted grosbeaks!* That's what they were! But so what? What did rose-breasted grosbeaks have to do with any-thing?

He decided to push the bluff and see where it led. "Rose-breasted grosbeaks," he said with an enigmatic wink.

Dermott tried to hide a flicker of surprise under a patronizing smile. Gurney wished to God he knew what it was all about, wished he knew what he was pretending to know. What the hell was the number Wellstone had mentioned? He had no idea what to say next, how to parry a direct question should it come. None came.

"I was right about you," said Dermott smugly. "From our first phone call, I knew you were smarter than most members of your tribe of baboons."

He paused, nodding to himself with apparent pleasure.

"That's good," he said. "An intelligent ape. You'll be able to appreciate what you're about to see. As a matter of fact, I think I'll follow your advice. After all, this is a very special night—a perfect night for magic slippers." As he was speaking, he was backing up toward a chest of drawers against the wall on the far side of the room. Without taking his eyes off Gurney, he opened the top drawer of the chest and removed, with conspicuous care, a pair of shoes. The style reminded Gurney of the open-toe, medium-heel dress shoes his mother used to wear to church—except that these shoes were made of ruby-colored glass, glass that glistened like translu-cent blood in the subdued light.

Dermott nudged the drawer shut with his elbow and returned to the bed with the shoes in one hand and the gun in the other, still leveled at Gurney.

"I appreciate your input, Detective. If you hadn't mentioned the slippers, I wouldn't have thought of them. Most men in your position wouldn't be so helpful." The unsubtle ridicule in the comment was meant to convey, Gurney assumed, the message that Dermott was so completely in control that he could easily turn to his own advantage anything anyone else might say or do. He leaned over the bed and removed the old woman's worn corduroy bedroom slippers and replaced them with the glowing red ones. Her feet were small, and the shoes slipped on smoothly.

"Is Dickie Duck coming to bed?" the old woman asked, like a child reciting her favorite part of a fairy tale.

"He'll kill the snake and cut off its head. / Then Dickie Duck will come to bed," he replied in a singsong voice.

"Where's my little Dickie been?"

"Killing the cock to save the hen."

"Why does Dickie do what Dickie does?"

"For blood that's as red / as a painted rose. / So every man knows / he reaps what he sows."

Dermott looked at the old woman expectantly, as though the ritual exchange was not finished. He leaned toward her, prompting her in a loud whisper, "What will Dickie do tonight?"

"What will Dickie do tonight?" she asked in the same whisper.

"He'll call the crows till the crows are all dead. / Then Dickie Duck will come to bed."

She moved her fingertips dreamily over her Goldilocks wig, as though she imagined she were arranging it in some ethereal style. The smile on her face reminded Gurney of a junkie's rush.

Dermott was watching her, too. His gaze was revoltingly unfilial, the tip of his tongue moving back and forth between his lips like a small, slithering parasite. Then he blinked and looked around the room.

"I think we're ready to begin," he said brightly. He got up on the bed and crawled over the old woman's legs to the opposite side—taking the goose from the hope chest as he did so. He settled himself against the pillows beside her and placed the goose in his lap. "Almost ready now." The cheeriness of this assurance would have been appropriate for someone placing a candle on a birthday cake. What he was doing, however, was inserting his revolver, finger still on the trigger, into a deep pocket cut into the back of the goose.

Jesus bloody Christ, thought Gurney. *Is that the way he shot Mark Mellery? Is that how the residue of down stuffing ended up in the neck wound and in the blood on the ground? Is that possible—that at the moment of his death Mellery was staring at a fucking goose?* The picture was so grotesque he had to choke back a crazed urge to laugh. Or was it a spasm of terror? Whatever the emotion was, it was sudden and powerful. He'd faced his share of lunatics—sadists, sex murderers of every persuasion, sociopaths with ice picks, even cannibals—but never before had he been forced to devise a solution to such a complex nightmare while just a finger twitch away from a bullet in the brain.

"Lieutenant Nardo, please stand. It's time for your entrance." Dermott's tone was ominous, theatrical, ironic.

In a whisper so low that Gurney wasn't sure at first whether he was hearing it or imagining it, the old woman began muttering, "Dickie-Dickie-Dickie Duck. Dickie-Dickie-Dickie Duck. Dickie-Dickie-Dickie Duck." It was more like a clock ticking than a human voice.

Gurney watched as Nardo unclasped his hands, stretching and clenching his fingers. He rose from his position on the floor at the foot of the bed with the resilient spring of a man in very good condition. His hard glance shifted from the odd couple on the bed to Gurney and back again. If anything in that scene surprised him, his stony face didn't show it. The only obvious thing, from the way he eyed the goose and Dermott's arm behind it, was that he'd figured out where the gun was.

In response, Dermott began stroking the back of the goose with his free hand. "One last question, Lieutenant, regarding your intentions before we begin. Do you plan to do as I say?"

"Sure."

"I'll take that answer at face value. I'm going to give you a series of directions. You must follow them precisely. Is that clear?"

"Yeah."

"If I were a less trusting man, I might question your seriousness. I do hope you appreciate the situation. Let me put all my cards on the table to prevent any lingering misunderstanding. I've decided to kill you. That issue is no longer open for discussion. The only question that remains is *when* I will kill you. That piece of the equation is up to you. Do you follow me so far?"

"You kill me. But I decide when." Nardo spoke with a kind of bored contempt that seemed to amuse Dermott.

"That's right, Lieutenant. You decide when. But only up to a point, of course—because, ultimately, everything will come to an appropriate end. Until then you can remain alive by saying what I tell you to say and doing what I tell you to do. Still following me?"

"Yeah."

"Please remember that at any point you have the option of dying instantly through the simple expedient of not following my instructions. Compliance will add precious moments to your life. Resistance will subtract them. What could be simpler?"

Nardo stared at him unblinkingly.

Gurney slid his feet a few inches back toward the legs of his chair to put himself in the best possible position to propel himself at the bed, expecting the emotional dynamic between the two men to explode within seconds.

Dermott stopped stroking the goose. "Please put your feet back where they were," he said without taking his eyes off Nardo. Gurney did as he was told, with a new respect for Dermott's peripheral vision. "If you move again, I'll kill you both without saying another word. Now, Lieutenant," Dermott continued placidly, "listen carefully to your assignment. You are an actor in a play. Your name is Jim. The play is about Jim and his wife and her son. The play is short and simple, but it has a powerful ending."

"I have to pee," said the woman in a pixilated voice, her finger-tips again drifting back over her blond curls.

"It's all right, dear," he answered without looking at her. "Everything will be all right. Everything will be the way it always should have been." Dermott adjusted the position of the goose slightly in his lap, refining, Gurney supposed, the aim of the revolver inside it at Nardo. "All set?"

If Nardo's steady gaze were poison, Dermott would have been dead three times over. Instead there was only a flicker around his mouth, which might have been a smile or a twitch or a touch of excitement.

"I'll take your silence for a yes this time. But a friendly word of warning. Any further ambiguity in your responses will result in the immediate termination of the play and your life. Do you under-stand me?"

"Yeah."

"Good. The curtain rises. The play begins. The time of year is late autumn. The time of day is late evening, already dark. It's rather bleak, some snow on the ground outside, some ice. In fact, the night is very much like tonight. It's your day off. You've spent the day in a local bar, drinking all day, with your drunken friends. That's the way you spend all your days off. You arrive home as the play begins. You stagger into your wife's bedroom. Your face is red and angry. Your eyes are dull and stupid. You have a bottle of whiskey in your hand." Dermott pointed to the Four Roses on the hope chest. "You can use that bottle there. Pick it up now."

Nardo stepped forward and picked it up. Dermott nodded approvingly. "You instinctively evaluate it as a potential weapon. That's very good, very appropriate. You have a natural sympathy with the mind-set of your character. Now, with that bottle in your hand, you stand, swaying from side to side, at the foot of your wife's bed. You glare with a stupid rage at her and her little boy and his little stuffed goose in the bed. You bare your teeth like a stupid rabid dog." Dermott paused and studied Nardo's face. "Let me see you bare your teeth."

Nardo's lips tightened and parted. Gurney could see that there was nothing artificial about the rage in that expression.

"That's right!" enthused Dermott. "Perfect! You have a real talent for this. Now you stand there with bloodshot eyes, with spittle on your lips, and you shout at your wife in the bed, 'What the fuck is he doing in here?' You point at me. My mother says, 'Calm down, Jim, he's been showing me and Dickie Duck his little storybook.' You say, 'I don't see any fucking book.' My mother tells you, 'Look, it's right there on the bedside table.' But you have a filthy mind, and it shows in your filthy face. Your filthy thoughts are oozing like the oily sweat through your stinking skin. My mother tells you that you're drunk and you should go to sleep in the other room. But you start taking your clothes off. I scream at you to get out. But you take off all your clothes, and you stand there naked, leering at us. You make me feel like I'm going to vomit. My mother screams at you, screams at you not to be so disgusting, to get out of the room. You say, 'Who the fuck are you calling disgusting, you slut bitch?' Then you smash the whiskey bottle on the footboard, and you jump up on the bed like a naked ape with the broken bottle in your hand. The nauseating stink of whiskey is all over the room. Your body stinks. You call my mother a slut. You—"

"What's her name?" interrupted Nardo.

Dermott blinked twice. "It doesn't matter."

"Sure it does."

"I said it doesn't matter."

"Why not?"

Dermott seemed taken aback by the question, if only a little. "It doesn't matter what her name is because you never use her name. You call her things, ugly things, but you never use her name. You never show her any respect. Maybe it's so long since you've used her name you don't even know what it is anymore."

"But you know her name, don't you?"

"Of course I do. She's my mother. Of course I know my mother's name."

"So what is it?"

"It doesn't matter to you. You don't care."

"Still, I'd like to know what it is."

"I don't want her name in your filthy brain."

"If I'm going to pretend to be her husband, I have to know her name."

"You have to know what I want you to know."

"I can't do this if I don't know who that woman is. I don't care what you say—it makes absolutely no goddamn sense for me not to know my own wife's name."

It wasn't clear to Gurney where Nardo was going with this.

Had he finally realized that he was being directed to reenact the drunken assault by Jimmy Spinks on Felicity Spinks that had occurred twenty-four years ago in this same house? Had it dawned on him that this Gregory Dermott who a year earlier had purchased this house might very well be Jimmy and Felicity's child—the eight-year-old Spinks boy whom social services had taken into their care in the aftermath of that family disaster? Had it occurred to him that the old woman in the bed with the scar on her throat was almost certainly Felicity Spinks—reclaimed by her grown son from whatever long-term nursing facility the trauma had consigned her to?

Was Nardo hoping to change the homicidal dynamic of the little "play" in progress by revealing what it was all about? Was he trying to create a psychological distraction, in the hope of finding some way out? Or was he just fumbling around in the dark—trying to delay as long as he could, however he could, whatever Dermott had in mind?

Of course, there was another possibility. What Nardo was doing, and how Dermott was reacting to it, might not make any rational sense at all. It could be the sort of ridiculously trivial sidetrack issue over which small boys beat each other with plastic shovels in sandboxes and angry men beat each other to death in bar fights. With a sinking heart, Gurney suspected that this last guess was as good as any.

"Whether you think it makes sense is of no importance," said

Dermott, again adjusting by a quarter inch the angle of the goose, his gaze fixed on Nardo's throat. "Nothing you think is of any importance. It's time for you to take your clothes off."

"First tell me her name."

"It's time for you to take your clothes off and smash the bottle and jump up on the bed like a naked ape. Like a stupid, drooling, hideous monster."

"What's her name?"

"It's time."

Gurney saw a slight movement in the muscle in Dermott's forearm—meaning that his finger was tightening on the trigger.

"Just tell me her name."

Any doubt Gurney had about what was happening was now gone. Nardo had drawn his line in the sand, and all his manhood—indeed his life—was invested in making his adversary answer his question. Dermott, likewise, was invested 100 percent in maintaining control. Gurney wondered whether Nardo had any idea how important this matter of control was to the man he was trying to face down. According to Rebecca Holdenfield—in fact, according to everyone who knew anything about serial killers—control was the goal worth any price, any risk. Absolute control—with the feeling of omniscience and omnipotence it engendered—was the ultimate euphoria. To threaten that goal head-on without a gun in your hand was suicidal.

It seemed that blindness to that fact had put Nardo once again an inch from death, and this time Gurney couldn't save him by shouting him into submission. That tactic wouldn't work a second time.

Murder was moving now like a racing storm cloud into Dermott's eyes. Gurney had never felt so helpless. He couldn't think of any way to stop that finger on the trigger.

It was then he heard the voice, clean and cool as pure silver. It was, without a doubt, Madeleine's voice, saying something she'd said to him years ago on an occasion when he felt stymied by a seemingly hopeless case.

"There's only one way out of a dead end."

Of course, he thought. How absurdly obvious. *Just walk in the opposite direction.*

Stopping a man who has an overwhelming need to be in total control—who has an overwhelming need to kill to achieve that control—required that you do exactly the opposite of what all your instincts told you. And with Madeleine's sentence clear as spring-water in his mind, he saw what he needed to do. It was outrageous, patently irresponsible, and legally indefensible if it didn't work. But he knew it would.

"Now! Now, Gregory!" he hissed. "Shoot him!"

There was a shared moment of incomprehension as both men seemed to struggle to absorb what they had just heard, as they might struggle to understand a thunderclap on a cloudless day. Dermott's deadly focus on Nardo wavered, and the direction of the gun-in-the-goose moved a little toward Gurney in the chair against the wall.

Dermott's mouth stretched sideways in his morbid imitation of a grin. "I beg your pardon?" In the affected nonchalance, Gurney sensed a tremor of unease.

"You heard me, Gregory," he said. "I told you to shoot him."

"You . . . *told* . . . me?"

Gurney sighed with elaborate impatience. "You're wasting my time."

"Wasting . . . ? What the hell do you think you're doing?" The gun-in-the-goose moved farther in Gurney's direction. The nonchalance was gone.

Nardo's eyes were widening. It was hard for Gurney to gauge the mix of emotions behind the amazement. As though it were Nardo who'd demanded to know what was going on, Gurney turned toward him and said, as offhandedly as he could manage, "Gregory likes to kill people who remind him of his father." There was a stifled sound from Dermott's throat, like the beginning of a word or cry that got stuck there. Gurney remained determinedly focused on Nardo and went on in the same bland tone. "Problem is, he needs a little nudge from time to time. Gets bogged down in the process. And, unfortunately, he makes mistakes. He's not as smart as he thinks. Oh, my goodness!" He paused and smiled speculatively at Dermott, whose jaw muscles were now visible. "That has possibilities, doesn't it? *Little Gregory Spinks—not as smart as he thinks.* How about it, Gregory? Do you think that could be a new poem?" He almost winked at the rattled murderer but decided that might be a step too far.

Dermott stared at him with hatred, confusion, and something else. What Gurney hoped it was was a swirl of questions that a control freak would be compelled to pursue before killing the only man capable of answering them. Dermott's next word, with its strained intonation, gave him hope.

"Mistakes?"

Gurney nodded ruefully. "Quite a few, I'm afraid."

"You're a liar, Detective. I don't make mistakes."

"No? What do you call them, then, if you don't call them mistakes? Little Dickie Duck's fuckups?"

Even as he said it, he wondered whether he had now taken that fatal step. If so, depending on where the bullet struck him, he might never know. In any event, there was no safe retreat route left. A wave of the tiniest vibrations unsettled the corners of Dermott's mouth. Reclining incongruously on that bed, he seemed to be gazing at Gurney from a perch in hell.

Gurney actually knew of only one mistake Dermott had made—a mistake involving the Kartch check, which had finally gotten through to him only a quarter of an hour earlier when he'd looked at the framed copy of that check on the lamp table. But suppose he were to claim that he'd recognized the mistake and its significance from the beginning. What effect would that have on the man who was so desperate to believe he was in complete control?

Again Madeleine's maxim came to mind, but in reverse. *If you can't back up, then full speed ahead.* He turned toward Nardo, as if the serial killer in the room could safely be ignored.

"One of his silliest fuckups was when he gave me the names of the men who'd sent checks to him. One of the names was Richard Kartch. The thing is, Kartch sent the check in a plain envelope with no cover note. The only identification was the name printed on the check itself. The name on the check was R. Kartch, and that's also the way it was signed. The *R* could have stood for Robert, Ralph, Randolph, Rupert, or a dozen other names. But Gregory knew it stood for Richard—yet at the same time he claimed no other familiarity or contact with the sender than the name and address on the check itself—which I saw in the mail at Kartch's house in Sotherton. So I knew right away from the discrepancy that he was lying. And the reason was obvious."

This was too much for Nardo. "You knew? Then why the hell didn't you tell us so we could pick him up?"

"Because I knew what he was doing and why he was doing it, and I had no interest in stopping him."

Nardo looked like he'd stepped into an alternate universe where the flies were swatting the people.

A sharp clicking noise drew Gurney's attention back to the bed. The old woman was tapping her red glass shoes together like Dorothy leaving Oz on her way home to Kansas. The gun-in-the-goose on Dermott's lap was now pointed directly at Gurney. Dermott was making an effort—at least Gurney hoped it required an effort—to appear unfazed by the Kartch revelation. He articulated his words with a peculiar precision.

"Whatever game you're playing, Detective, I'm the one who's going to end it."

Gurney, with all the undercover acting experience he could bring to the moment, tried to speak with the confidence of a man who had a concealed Uzi zeroed in on his enemy's chest. "Before you make a threat," he said softly, "be sure you understand the situation."

"Situation? I fire, you die. I fire again, he dies. The baboons come through the door, they die. That's the situation."

Gurney closed his eyes and leaned his head back against the wall, uttering a deep sigh. "Do you have any idea . . . any idea at all . . . ?" he began, then shook his head wearily. "No. No, of course you don't. How could you?"

"Any idea of what, Detective?" Dermott used the title with exaggerated sarcasm.

Gurney laughed. It was an unhinged sort of laugh, meant to raise new questions in Dermott's mind, but actually energized by a rising tide of emotional chaos in himself.

"Guess how many men I've killed," he whispered, glaring at Dermott with a wild intensity—praying that the man wouldn't recognize the time-consuming purpose of his desperate ad-libbing, praying that the Wycherly cops would soon take note that Nardo was missing. Why the hell hadn't they noticed already? Or had they? The glass shoes continued to click.

"Stupid cops kill people all the time," said Dermott. "I couldn't care less."

"I don't mean just any men. I mean men like Jimmy Spinks. Guess how many men like him I've killed."

Dermott blinked. "What the hell are you talking about?"

"I'm talking about killing drunks. Ridding the world of alcoholic animals, exterminating the scum of the earth."

Once again there was an almost imperceptible vibration around Dermott's mouth. He had the man's attention, no doubt about that. Now what? What else but ride the wave. There was no other transportation in sight. He composed his words as he spoke them.

"Late one night in the Port Authority bus terminal, when I was a rookie cop, I was told to roust some derelicts from the rear entryway. One wouldn't leave. I could smell the stink of the whiskey from ten feet off. I told him again to get out of the building, but instead of going out the door, he started coming toward me. He pulled a kitchen knife out of his pocket—a little knife with a serrated blade like you'd use to slice an orange. He brandished the knife in a threatening manner and ignored my order to drop it. Two witnesses who saw the confrontation from the escalator swore that I shot him in self-defense." He paused and smiled. "But that's not true. If I'd wanted to, I could have subdued him without even breathing hard. Instead I shot him in the face and blew his brains out the back of his head. You know why I did that, Gregory?"

"Dickie-Dickie-Dickie Duck," said the old woman in a rhythm quicker than the clicking of her shoes. Dermott's mouth opened a fraction of an inch, but he said nothing.

"I did it because he looked like my father," said Gurney with an angrily rising voice, "looked like my father looked the night he smashed a teapot on my mother's head—a fucking stupid teapot with a fucking stupid clown face on it."

"Your father wasn't much of a father," said Dermott coldly. "But then again, Detective, neither were you."

The leering accusation removed any doubt in Gurney's mind about the extent of Dermott's knowledge. At that moment he seriously considered the option of absorbing a bullet to get his hands on Dermott's throat.

The leer intensified. Perhaps Dermott sensed Gurney's discomfort. "A good father should protect his four-year-old son, not let him get run over, not let the driver get away."

"You piece of shit," muttered Gurney.

Dermott giggled, seemingly crazed with delight. "Vulgar, vulgar, vulgar—and I thought you were a fellow poet. I hoped we could keep trading verses. I had a little ditty all ready for our next exchange. Tell me what you think of it. 'A hit-and-run without a trace, / the star detective fell on his face. / What did the little boy's mother say / when you came home alone that day?'"

An eerie animal sound rose from Gurney's chest, a strangled eruption of rage. Dermott was transfixed.

Nardo had apparently been waiting for the moment of maximum distraction. His muscular right arm accelerated up and around in a mighty circular overhand motion, hurling the unopened Four Roses bottle with tremendous force at Dermott's head. As Dermott sensed the movement and began to swivel the gun-in-the-goose toward Nardo, Gurney launched himself in a headlong diving leap at the bed, landing chest-first on the goose, just as the thick glass base of the full whiskey bottle smashed squarely into Dermott's temple. The revolver discharged beneath Gurney, filling the air around him with an atomized explosion of down stuffing. The bullet passed under Gurney in the direction of the wall where he'd been sitting, shattering the table lamp that had provided the room's sole illumination. In the darkness he could hear Nardo breathing hard through clenched teeth. The old woman started to make a faint wailing sound, a sound with a quavering pitch, a sound like a half-remembered lullaby. Then there was the sound of a terrific impact, and the heavy metal door of the room flew open, swung around, and hit the wall—followed immediately by the huge hurtling figure of a man and a smaller figure behind him.

"Freeze!" shouted the giant.

Chapter 52

Death before dawn

The cavalry had finally arrived—a little late, but that was a good thing. Considering Dermott's history of precise marksmanship and his eagerness to pile up the crows, it was possible that not only the cavalry but Nardo and Gurney would have ended up with bullets in their throats. And then, when the gunshots brought the whole department swarming into the house and Dermott opened the valve, sending the pressurized chlorine and ammonia through the sprinkler system . . .

As it was, the only major casualty other than the lamp and the doorframe was Dermott himself. The bottle, propelled by all of Nardo's combative rage, had struck him with sufficient force to produce what looked like a possible coma. In a related minor injury, a curved shard of glass had splintered from the bottle on impact, embedding itself in Gurney's head at the hairline.

"We heard a shot. What the fuck's going on here?" snarled the hulking man, peering around the mostly dark room.

"Everything's under control, Tommy," said Nardo, his jagged voice suggesting he wasn't yet part of the everything. In the dim light coming in from the other part of the basement, Gurney recognized the smaller officer who'd rushed in on Big Tommy's heels as the crew-cut Pat with the acetylene-blue eyes. Holding a heavy nine-millimeter pistol at the ready and keeping a close watch on the ugly scene in the bed, she edged around to the far corner of the room and switched on the lamp that stood next to the wing chair where the old woman had been sitting.

"You mind if I get up?" said Gurney, who was still lying across the goose on Dermott's lap.

Big Tommy glanced at Nardo.

"Sure," said Nardo, his teeth still partly clenched. "Let him get up."

As he rose carefully from the bed, blood began flowing freely down his face—the sight of which was probably what restrained Nardo from immediately assaulting the man who had minutes earlier encouraged a demented serial killer to shoot him.

"Jesus," said Big Tommy, staring at the blood.

An overload of adrenaline had kept Gurney unaware of the wound. He touched his face and found it surprisingly wet; then he examined his hand and found it surprisingly red.

Acetylene Pat looked at Gurney's face without emotion. "You want an ambulance here?" she said to Nardo.

"Yeah. Sure. Make the call," he said without conviction.

"For them, too?" she asked with a quick nod toward the odd couple in the bed. The red glass shoes caught her eye. She squinted as if trying to banish an optical illusion.

After a long pause, he muttered a disgusted, "Yeah."

"You want the cars called in?" she asked, frowning at the shoes that seemed to be disconcertingly real after all.

"What?" he said after another pause. He was staring at the remains of the smashed lamp and the bullet hole in the drywall behind it.

"We've got cars on patrol and guys out there on door-to-door inquiries. You want them called in?"

The decision seemed harder for him than it should have been. Finally he said, "Yeah, call them in."

"Right," she said, and strode out of the room.

Big Tommy was observing with evident distaste the damage to Dermott's temple. The Four Roses bottle had come to rest upside down on the pillow between Dermott and the old woman, whose curly blond wig had shifted in a way that made the top of her head look like it had been unscrewed a quarter of a turn.

As Gurney gazed at the bottle's floral label, the answer came to him that had eluded him earlier. He remembered what Bruce Wellstone had said. He said that Dermott (aka Mr. Scylla) had claimed he'd seen *four rose-breasted grosbeaks* and that he had made a particular point of the number *four*. The "translation" of *four rose-breasted grosbeaks* struck Gurney almost as quickly as the words. *Four Roses!* Like signing the register "Mr. and Mrs. Scylla," the message was just another little dance step advertising his cleverness— Gregory Dermott showing how easily he could toy with the dumb evil cops. *Catch me if you can.*

A minute later Pat returned, grimly efficient. "Ambulance on the way. Cars recalled. Door-to-doors canceled." She regarded the bed coldly. The old woman was making sporadic sounds somewhere between keening and humming. Dermott was morbidly still and pale. "You sure he's alive?" she asked without evident concern.

"I have no idea," said Nardo. "Maybe you ought to check."

She pursed her lips as she walked over and probed for a neck pulse.

"Uh-huh, he's alive. What's the matter with her?"

"That's Jimmy Spinks's wife. You ever hear about Jimmy Spinks?"

She shook her head. "Who's Jimmy Spinks?"

He considered this for a while. "Forget it."

She shrugged—as if forgetting things like that were a normal part of the job.

Nardo took a few slow, deep breaths. "I need you and Tommy upstairs to keep the place secured. Now that we know this is the little fucker who killed everyone, the forensics team will have to come back and run the house through a sieve."

She and Tommy exchanged uneasy looks but left the room with no argument. As Tommy passed Gurney, he said as casually as if he were commenting on a speck of dandruff, "You got a piece of glass sticking out of your head."

Nardo waited until their footsteps had climbed the stairs and the basement door at the top of the stairs was closed before speaking.

"Back away from the bed." His voice was a bit jerky.

Gurney knew he was really being told to back away from the weapons—Dermott's revolver in the now-blasted stuffing of the goose and Nardo's ankle pistol in Dermott's pocket and the formidable whiskey bottle on the pillow—but he complied without objection.

"Okay," said Nardo, struggling, it seemed, to control himself. "I'm giving you a chance to explain."

"You mind if I sit down?"

"I don't care if you stand on your fucking head. Talk! Now!"

Gurney sat in the chair by the splintered lamp. "He was about to shoot you. You were two seconds away from a bullet in the throat, or the head, or the heart. There was only one way to stop him."

"You didn't tell him to stop. You told him to shoot me." Nardo's fists were clenched so tightly that Gurney could see the white spots on the knuckles.

"But he didn't, did he?"

"But you told him to."

"Because it was the only way to stop him."

"The only way to stop . . . Are you out of your fucking mind?" Nardo was glaring like a killer dog waiting to be loosed.

"The fact is, you're alive."

"You're saying I'm alive because you told him to kill me? What kind of lunatic shit is that?"

"Serial murder is about control. Total control. For crazy Gregory that meant controlling not only the present and the future but also the past. The scene he wanted you to act out was the tragedy that occurred in this house twenty-four years ago—with one crucial difference. Back then little Gregory wasn't able to stop his father from cutting his mother's throat. She never really recovered, and neither did he. The grown-up Gregory wanted to rewind the tape and start it over so he could change it. He wanted you to do everything his father did up to the point of raising the bottle. Then he was going to kill you—to get rid of the horrible drunk, to save his mother. That's what all the other murders were about—attempts to control and kill Jimmy Spinks by controlling and killing other drunks."

"Gary Sissek wasn't a drunk."

"Maybe not. But Gary Sissek was on the force when Jimmy Spinks was, and I bet Gregory recognized him as a friend of his father. Maybe even a casual drinking buddy. And the fact that you were also on the force back then probably in Gregory's mind made you a perfect stand-in—the perfect way for him to reach back and change history."

"But you told him to shoot me!" Nardo's tone was still argumentative, but, to Gurney's relief, the conviction behind it was weakening.

"I told him to shoot you because the only way to stop a control-freak killer like that when your only weapon is words is to say something that makes him doubt he's really in control. Part of the control fantasy is that he's making all the decisions—that he's the all-powerful one, and no one has power over him. The biggest curveball you can throw at a mind like that is the possibility that he's doing exactly what you want him to do. Oppose him directly and he'll kill you. Beg for your life and he'll kill you. But tell him you want him to do exactly what he's about to do and it blows the circuit."

Nardo looked like he was trying hard to find a flaw in the story. "You sounded very . . . authentic. There was hatred in your voice, like you really wanted me dead."

"If I hadn't been convincing, we wouldn't be having this conversation."

Nardo switched gears. "What about the shooting in Port Authority?"

"What about it?"

"You shot some bum because he reminded you of your drunk father?"

Gurney smiled.

"What's funny?"

"Two things. First: I never worked anywhere near Port Authority. Second: In twenty-five years on the job, I never fired my gun, not even once."

"So that was all bullshit?"

"My father drank too much. It was . . . a difficult thing. Even when he was there, he wasn't there. But shooting a stranger wouldn't have helped much."

"So what was the point of talking all that shit?"

"The point? The point is what happened."

"The hell does that mean?"

"Christ, Lieutenant, I was just trying to hold Dermott's attention long enough to give you a chance to do something with that two-pound bottle in your hand."

Nardo stared at him a little blankly, as though all this information wasn't quite fitting into the available spaces in his brain.

"That stuff about the kid being hit by the car . . . that was all bullshit, too?"

"No. That was true. His name was Danny." Gurney's voice became hoarse.

"They never got the driver?"

Gurney shook his head.

"No leads?"

"One witness said that the car that hit my boy, a red BMW, had been parked in front of a bar down the street all afternoon and that the guy who came out of the bar and got into it was obviously drunk."

Nardo thought about this for a while. "Nobody in the bar could ID him?"

"Claimed they never saw him before."

"How long ago this happen?"

"Fourteen years and eight months."

They were quiet for some minutes; then Gurney resumed speaking in a low, hesitant voice. "I was taking him to the playground in the park. There was a pigeon walking in front of him on the side-

walk, and Danny was following it. I was only half there. My mind was on a murder case. The pigeon walked off the sidewalk into the street, and Danny followed it. By the time I saw what was happening, it was too late. It was over."

"You have other kids?"

Gurney hesitated. "Not with Danny's mother."

Then he closed his eyes, and neither man said anything for a long time. Nardo eventually broke the silence.

"So there's no doubt Dermott's the guy who killed your friend?"

"No doubt," said Gurney. He was struck by the exhaustion in both of their voices.

"And the others, too?"

"Looks that way."

"Why now?"

"Hmm?"

"Why wait so long?"

"Opportunity. Inspiration. Serendipity. My guess is that he found himself designing a security system for a big medical-insurance database. It may have dawned on him that he could write a program to extract all the names of men who'd been treated for alcoholism. That would be the starting point. I suspect he became obsessed with the possibilities, eventually came up with his ingenious scheme for trolling through the list to find men scared and vulnerable enough to send him those checks. Men he could torture with his vicious little poems. Somewhere along the line, he got his mother out of the nursing home where the state had put her after the attack left her incapacitated."

"Where was he all those years before he showed up here?"

"As a kid, either in a state facility or in foster care. Could've been a nasty path. Got involved with computer software at some point, I assume through games, got good at it. Very good—eventually got a degree from MIT."

"And sometime along the way he changed his name?"

"Probably when he turned eighteen. I bet he couldn't stand

having his father's name. Come to think of it, I wouldn't be surprised if Dermott was his mother's maiden name."

Nardo's lip curled. "Would've been nice if you'd thought to run him through the state's name-change database at the start of this freaking mess."

"Realistically, there was no reason to do that. And even if we did, the fact that Dermott's childhood name was Spinks wouldn't have meant a damn thing to anyone involved in the Mellery case."

Nardo looked like he was trying to store all this away for reflection when his head was clearer. "Why did the crazy son of a bitch come back to Wycherly at all?"

"Because it was the scene of the attack on his mother twenty-four years ago? Maybe because the weird notion of rewriting the past was taking hold of him? Maybe he heard the old house was for sale and couldn't resist it? Maybe it offered an opportunity for getting even not only with drunks but with the Wycherly police department? Unless he chooses to tell us the whole story, we'll never know for sure. I don't think Felicity is likely to be much help."

"Not much," agreed Nardo, but he had something else on his mind. He looked troubled.

"What is it?" asked Gurney.

"What? Nothing. Nothing, really. Just wondering . . . how much it really bothered you that someone was killing drunks."

He didn't know what to say. The proper answer might have something to do with not sitting in judgment on the worthiness of the victim. The cynical answer might be that he cared more about the challenge of the game than the moral equation, more about the game than the people. Either way, he had no appetite for discussing the issue with Nardo. But he felt he ought to say something.

"If what you're asking me is whether I was enjoying the pleasures of vicarious vengeance on the drunk driver who killed my son, the answer is no."

"You sure about that?"

"I'm sure."

Nardo eyed him skeptically, then shrugged. Gurney's reply

didn't seem to convince him, but neither did he seem inclined to pursue the matter.

The explosive lieutenant had apparently been defused. The rest of the evening was occupied with the triage process of sorting through the immediate priorities and routine details of concluding a major murder investigation.

Gurney was taken to Wycherly General Hospital along with Felicity Spinks (née Dermott) and Gregory Dermott (né Spinks). While Dermott's incoherent mother, with her ruby glass slippers still on her feet, was examined by a blandly upbeat PA, Dermott was rushed off, still unconscious, to radiology.

Meanwhile the gash in Gurney's head was being cleaned, stitched, and bandaged by a nurse whose manner seemed unusually intimate—an impression fostered in part by the breathiness of her voice and by how close to him she stood as she worked gently on his wound. It was an impression of immediate availability that he found incongruously exciting under the circumstances. Although that was clearly a perilous path, not to mention insane, not to mention pathetic, he did decide to take advantage of her friendliness in another way. He gave her his cell number and asked her to call him directly if there was any significant change in Dermott's condition. He didn't want to be out of the loop, and he didn't trust Nardo to keep him in it. She agreed with a smile—after which he was driven by a taciturn young Wycherly cop back to Dermott's house.

En route he called Sheridan Kline's emergency night line and got a recording. He left a compact message covering the essential points. Then he called home, got his own recording, and left a message for Madeleine, referring to the same events—minus the bullet, the bottle, the blood, and the stitches. He wondered if she was out somewhere or actually standing there, listening to him leaving the message, unwilling to speak to him. Lacking her uncanny insight into such matters, he had no feeling for the right answer.

By the time they arrived back at Dermott's house, over an hour had passed and the street was full of Wycherly, county, and state police vehicles. Big Tommy and square-jawed Pat were standing sentry on the porch. Gurney was directed into the small room off the center hallway where he'd had his introductory conversation with Nardo. Nardo was there again, sitting at the same table. Two crime-scene specialists in white coveralls, booties, and latex gloves were just leaving the room on their way to the basement stairs.

Nardo pushed a yellow pad and a cheap pen across the table toward Gurney. If there was any dangerous emotion left in the man, it was well hidden under a thick layer of bureaucratic rigmarole.

"Have a seat. We need a statement. Start at your point of arrival at this site this afternoon, with the reason for your presence. Include all relevant actions by you and direct observations by you of the actions of others. Include a timeline, indicating at which points it is based on specific information and at which points it is estimated. You may conclude the statement at the time you were escorted to the hospital, unless during your treatment at the hospital additional relevant information came to light. Any questions?"

Gurney spent the next forty-five minutes following these directions, with Nardo mostly out of the room, filling four lined pages with small, precise handwriting. There was a copying machine on the table against the far wall of the room, and Gurney used it to make two copies of the signed and dated statement for himself before submitting the original to Nardo.

All the man said was, "We'll be in touch." His voice was professionally neutral. He didn't offer a handshake.

Chapter 53

Ending, beginning

By the time Gurney had crossed the Tappan Zee Bridge and begun the long Route 17 leg of his journey, the snow was falling more heavily, effectively shrinking the visible world. Every few minutes he'd open his side window for a blast of cold air to keep his mind in the moment.

A few miles from Goshen, he nearly drove off the road. It was his tires vibrating loudly against the ribbed surface of the shoulder that kept him from heading over an embankment.

He tried to think of nothing but the car, the steering wheel, and the road, but it was impossible. He began instead to imagine the potential media coverage to come, beginning with a press conference at which Sheridan Kline would surely congratulate himself for the role of his investigatory staff in making America safer by ending the bloody career of a devilish criminal. The media, in general, got on Gurney's nerves. Their moronic coverage of crime was a crime in itself. They made a game of it. Of course, in his own way, so did he. He generally viewed a homicide as a puzzle to be solved, a murderer as an opponent to be outmaneuvered. He studied the facts, figured the angles, tripped the snare, and delivered his quarry into the maw of the justice machine. Then on to the next death from unnatural causes that demanded a clever mind to sort out. But sometimes he saw things in quite a different way—when he was overcome by the weariness of the chase, when darkness made all the puzzle pieces look alike or not like puzzle pieces at all, when his harried brain wandered from its geometric grid and followed more primitive paths, giving him glimpses of the true horror of the subject matter in which he'd chosen to immerse himself.

On the one hand, there was the logic of the law, the science of criminology, the processes of adjudication. On the other, there was Jason Strunk, Peter Possum Piggert, Gregory Dermott, pain, murderous rage, death. And between these two worlds there was the sharp, unsettling question—what had one to do with the other?

He opened the side window again and let the hard-blown snow sting the side of his face.

Profound and pointless questions, inner dialogues leading nowhere, were as familiar in his inner landscape as estimating the chances of a Red Sox win might be in another man's. It was a bad habit, this sort of thinking, and it brought him nothing good. On the occasions when he'd insist on exposing it to Madeleine, it would be met with boredom or impatience.

"What's really on your mind?" she'd sometimes ask, putting down her knitting and looking him in the eye.

"What do you mean?" he'd ask in reply, dishonestly, knowing exactly what she meant.

"You can't possibly care about that nonsense. Figure out what's actually bothering you."

Figure out what's actually bothering you.

Easier said than done.

What *was* bothering him? The vast inadequacies of reason in the face of feral passions? The fact that the justice system is a cage that can no more keep the devil contained than a weather vane can stop the wind? All he knew was that something was there, in the back of his mind, chewing at his other thoughts and feelings like a rat.

When he tried to identify the most corrosive problem amid the day's chaos, he found himself lost in a sea of unmoored images.

When he tried to clear his mind—to relax and think of nothing—two images would not disappear.

One was the cruel delight in Dermott's eyes when he recited his hideous rhyme about Danny's death. The other was the echo of the accusatory fury with which he himself had slandered his own father in the fictional account of the attack on his mother. That was no mere acting. Rising up from somewhere beneath it, saturating it, was a terrible anger. Did its authenticity mean he actually hated his father? Was the rage that exploded in the telling of that ugly tale the suppressed rage of abandonment—the fierce resentment of a child toward a father who did nothing but work and sleep and drink, a father who was forever receding into the distance, forever unreachable? Gurney was startled at how much, and how little, he had in common with Dermott.

Or was it the reverse—a smoke screen covering the guilt he felt for abandoning that chilly, insular man in his old age, for having as little to do with him as possible?

Or was it a displaced self-hatred arising out of his own double failure as a father—his fatal lack of attention toward one son and his active avoidance of the other?

Madeleine would probably say that the answer could be any of the above, all of the above, or none of the above; but whatever it was wasn't important. What was important was to do what one believed in one's heart to be the right thing to do, right here and now. And lest he find that concept daunting, she might suggest that he begin by returning Kyle's phone call. Not that she was particularly fond of Kyle—in fact, she didn't seem to like him at all, found his Porsche silly, his wife pretentious—but for Madeleine personal chemistry was always secondary to doing the right thing. Gurney marveled at how a person so spontaneous could also lead such a principled life. It was what made her who she was. It was what made her a beacon in the murkiness of his own existence.

The right thing, right now.

Inspired, he pulled over at the broad, scruffy entrance area of an old farm and took out his wallet to get Kyle's number. (He'd never bothered to enter Kyle's name in his phone's voice-recognition system, an omission that gave his conscience a twinge.) Calling him at

3:00 A.M.—midnight in Seattle—seemed a little crazy, but the alternative was worse: He would put it off, and put it off again, and then rationalize not calling at all.

"Dad?"

"Did I wake you?"

"Actually, no. I was up. Are you all right?"

"I'm fine. I, uh . . . I just wanted to talk to you, return your call. I wasn't being very good about that, seemed like you'd been trying to reach me for a long time."

"You sure you're all right?"

"I know it's an odd time to call, but don't worry, I'm fine."

"Good."

"I did have a difficult day, but it turned out okay. The reason I didn't return your calls sooner . . . I've been in the middle of a complicated mess. But that's no excuse. Was there anything you needed?"

"What kind of mess?"

"What? Oh—usual kind, homicide investigation."

"I thought you were retired."

"I was. I mean, I am. But I got involved because I knew one of the victims. Long story. Next time I see you, I'll tell you all about it."

"Wow. You did it again!"

"Did what?"

"You caught another mass murderer, right?"

"How'd you know that?"

"*Victims.* You said *victims,* plural. How many were there?"

"Five that we know of, plans for twenty more."

"And you got him. Damn! Mass murderers don't have a chance against you. You're like Batman."

Gurney laughed. He hadn't done much of that lately. And he couldn't remember the last time he'd done so in a conversation with Kyle. Come to think of it, this was an unusual conversation in other ways as well—considering that they'd been talking for at least two minutes without Kyle's mentioning something he'd just bought or was about to buy.

"In this case Batman had a lot of help," said Gurney. "But that's not why I called. I wanted to return your calls, find out what was happening with you. Anything new?"

"Not much," said Kyle drily. "I lost my job. Kate and I broke up. I may change careers, go to law school. What do you think?"

After a second of shocked silence, Gurney laughed even louder. "Jesus Christ!" he said. "What the hell happened?"

"The financial industry collapsed—as you may have heard—along with my job and my marriage and my two condos and my three cars. Funny, though, how quickly you can adjust to unimaginable catastrophe. Anyway, what I'm really wondering about now is whether I should go to law school. That's what I wanted to ask you. You think I have the right kind of mind for that?"

Gurney suggested that Kyle come up from the city that weekend, and they could talk about the whole situation in as much detail as he wanted for as long as he wanted. Kyle agreed—even seemed happy about it. When the call ended, Gurney sat for a good ten minutes, amazed.

There were other calls he had to make. In the morning he'd call Mark Mellery's widow and tell her that it was finally over—that Gregory Dermott Spinks was in custody and that the evidence of his guilt was clear, concrete, and overwhelming. She'd probably already have gotten a personal call from Sheridan Kline and maybe from Rodriguez as well. But he'd call her anyway because of his relationship with Mark.

Then there was Sonya Reynolds. According to their arrangement, he owed her at least one more of his special mug-shot portraits. It seemed so unimportant now, such a trivial waste of time. Still, he'd call her and at least talk about it and would end up doing whatever he'd originally agreed to do. But nothing else. Sonya's attention was pleasing, ego-gratifying, maybe even a little thrilling, but it came with too high a price, too great a danger to things that mattered more.

The 160-mile trip from Wycherly to Walnut Crossing took five hours instead of three because of the snow. By the time Gurney turned off the county highway onto the lane that meandered up the mountain to his farmhouse, he'd fallen into a kind of autopilot numbness. The window, open a crack for the last hour, had kept enough of a chill on his face and oxygen in his lungs to make driving possible. As he reached the gently sloping pasture that separated the big barn from the house, he noted that the snowflakes that had earlier been racing horizontally across the roads were now floating straight down. He drove slowly up through the pasture, turning eastward at the house before stopping, so that the warmth of the sun, later in the day when the storm had passed, could keep the windshield free of ice. He sat back, almost unable to move.

He was so deeply exhausted that when his phone rang, it took him several seconds to recognize the sound.

"Yes?" His greeting could have been mistaken for a wheeze.

"Is David there?" The female voice sounded familiar.

"This is David."

"Oh, you sounded . . . odd. This is Laura. From the hospital. You wanted me to call . . . if anything happened," she added with enough of a pause to suggest a hope that his desire for the call might have deeper roots than the reason he'd given.

"That's right. Thank you for remembering."

"My pleasure."

"Did something happen?"

"Mr. Dermott passed away."

"Excuse me? Could you say that again?"

"Gregory Dermott, the man you wanted to know about—he died ten minutes ago."

"Cause of death?"

"Nothing official yet, but the MRI they did on admission showed a skull fracture with a massive hemorrhage."

"Right. I guess it's not a surprise, with that kind of damage." It seemed to him that he was feeling something, but the feeling was far away and had no label.

"No, not with that kind of damage."

The feeling was faint but disturbing, like a small cry in a loud wind.

"No. Well, thank you, Laura. It was good of you to call."

"Sure. Is there anything else I can do for you?"

"I don't think so," he said.

"You better get some sleep."

"Yeah. Good night. And thanks again."

First he switched off the phone, then he switched off the headlights of the car and sank back against the seat, too drained to move. In the sudden absence of the headlights, everything around him was impenetrably dark.

Slowly, as his eyes adjusted, the absolute blackness of the sky and the woods shifted to a deep gray and the snow-covered pasture to a softer gray. Out where he imagined he could just discern the eastern ridge, where the sun would rise in another hour, there seemed to be a faint aura. The snow had stopped falling. The house beside the car was massive, cold, and still.

He tried to see what had happened in the simplest terms. The child in the bedroom with his lonely mother and demented drunk of a father . . . the screams and the blood and the helplessness . . . the terrible lifelong physical and mental damage . . . the homicidal delusions of revenge and redemption. So the little Spinks boy grew into the Dermott madman who murdered at least five men and was on the verge of murdering twenty more. Gregory Spinks whose father had cut his mother's throat. Gregory Dermott who had his skull fatally smashed in the house where it all began.

Gurney gazed out at the barely visible outline of the hills, knowing there was a second story to consider, a story he needed to understand better—the story of his own life, the father who'd ignored him, the grown son he in turn had ignored, the obsessive career that had brought him so much praise and so little peace, the little boy who'd died when he wasn't looking, and Madeleine who seemed to understand it all. Madeleine, the light he'd almost lost. The light he'd endangered.

He was too tired now to move even a finger, too far toward sleep to feel a thing, and into his mind came a merciful emptiness. For a while—he wasn't sure how long—it was as though he didn't exist, as though everything in him had been reduced to a dimensionless point of consciousness, a pinprick of awareness and nothing more.

He came to suddenly, opening his eyes just as the burning rim of the sun began to glare through the bare trees atop the ridge. He watched the radiant fingernail of light slowly swell into a great white arc. Then he became aware of another presence.

Madeleine, in her bright orange parka—the same one she'd worn the day he'd followed her to the overlook—was standing by the side window of the car looking at him. He wondered how long she'd been there. Tiny ice crystals glimmered on the fleecy edge of her hood. He lowered the window.

At first she said nothing, but in her face he saw—saw, sensed, felt, he didn't know by what route her emotion reached him—an amalgam of acceptance and love. Acceptance, love, and a deep relief that once again he'd come home alive.

She asked with a touching matter-of-factness whether he'd like some breakfast.

With the vitality of a leaping flame, her orange parka captured the rising sun. He got out of the car and put his arms around her, holding her as though she were life itself.

Acknowledgments

My thanks to my superb editor, Rick Horgan, who was a constant source of good ideas, whose inspired and inspiring guidance made everything so much better, who came up with the perfect title, and who had the courage in today's difficult publishing environment to take a chance on the first novel of an unpublished writer; to Lucy Carson and Paul Cirone for their advocacy, enthusiasm, and efficiency; to Bernard Whalen for his advice and encouragement early on; to Josh Kendall for a thoughtful critique and a wonderful suggestion; and finally to Molly Friedrich, simply the best and brightest agent in the world.

About the Author

After a successful career in the advertising industry, John Verdon retired with his wife, Naomi, to the rural mountains of upstate New York—an ironically tranquil environment for creating the Dave Gurney series of thrillers.

Read on for an excerpt from
international bestselling author John Verdon's
latest Dave Gurney novel,

Peter Pan Must Die

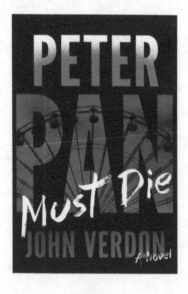

CROWN

Available wherever books are sold

Long Before the
Killing Began

*T*here was a time when he dreamt of being the head of a great nation. A nuclear power.

As the president, he would have his finger on the nuclear trigger. With a twitch of that finger he could launch nuclear missiles. He could obliterate huge cities. He could put an end to the human stink. He could wipe the rotten slate clean.

With maturity, however, had come a more practical perspective, a more realistic sense of what was possible. He knew that the nuclear trigger would never be within his reach.

But other triggers were available. One day at time, one trigger-pull at a time, much could be accomplished.

As he thought about it—and through his teenage years he'd thought about little else—a plan for his future slowly took shape. He came to know what his specialty would be—his art, his expertise, his field of excellence. And that was no small thing, since previously he had known almost nothing about himself, had no sense of who or what he was.

He had so few memories of anything before he was twelve.

Only the nightmare.

The nightmare that came again and again.

The circus. His mother, smaller than the other women. The terrible laughter. The music of the merry-go-round. The deep, constant growling of the animals.

The clown.

The huge clown who gave him money and hurt him.

The wheezing clown whose breath smelled like vomit.

And the words. So clear in the nightmare that their edges were as jagged as ice smashed against stone. "This is our secret. If you tell anyone, I'll feed your tongue to the tiger."

Chapter 1

The Shadow of Death

In the rural Catskill Mountains of upstate New York, August was an unstable month, lurching back and forth between the bright glories of July and the gray squalls of the long winter to come.

It was a month that could erode one's sense of time and place. It seemed to feed Dave Gurney's confusion over where he was in his life—a confusion that had begun with his retirement from the NYPD three years earlier, after twenty-five years on the job, and had intensified when he and Madeleine had moved out to the country from the city where they'd both been born, raised, educated, and employed.

At that moment, a cloudy late afternoon in the first week of August, with low thunder grumbling in the distance, they were climbing Barrow Hill, following the remnant of a dirt road that linked three small bluestone quarries, long abandoned and full of wild raspberry brambles. He was trudging along behind Madeleine as she headed for the low boulder where they normally stopped to rest, doing his best to take her frequent advice: *Look around you. You're in a beautiful place. Just relax and absorb it.*

"Is that a tarn?" she asked.

Gurney blinked. "What?"

"That." She inclined her head toward the deep, still pool that filled the broad hollow left years ago by the removal of the bluestone. Roughly round, it stretched from where they sat by the trail to a row of water-loving willow trees on the far side—a glassy expanse perhaps two hundred feet across that mirrored the weeping branches of the trees so precisely, the effect resembled trick photography.

"A *tarn?*"

"I was reading a wonderful book about hiking in the Scottish Highlands," she said earnestly, "and the writer was forever coming upon 'tarns.' I got the impression that it was some kind of rocky pond."

"Hmm."

His nonresponse led to a long silence, broken finally by Madeleine. "See down there? That's where I was thinking we should build the chicken coop, right by the asparagus patch."

Gurney had been staring bleakly at the reflection of the willows. Now he followed her line of sight down a gentle slope through an opening in the woods formed by an abandoned logging road.

One reason that the boulder by the old quarry had become their habitual stopping place was that it was the only point on the trail from which their property was visible—the old farmhouse, the garden beds, the overgrown apple trees, the pond, the recently rebuilt barn, the surrounding hillside pastures (long untended and full this time of year with milkweed and black-eyed Susans), the part of the pasture by the house that they mowed and called a lawn, the swath up through the low pasture that they mowed and called a driveway. Madeleine, perched now on the boulder, always seemed pleased at this uniquely framed view of it all.

Gurney didn't feel the same. Madeleine had discovered the spot herself shortly after they'd moved in, and from the first time she had shown it to him all he could think of was that it was the ideal location for a sniper to target someone entering or leaving their house. (He had the good sense not to mention this to her. She did work three days a week in the local psychiatric clinic, and he didn't want her thinking he was in need of treatment for paranoia.)

The need to build a chicken coop, its projected size and appearance, and the site where it should be built had become daily topics of conversation—obviously exciting to her, mildly irritating to him. They had acquired four chickens in late May at Madeleine's urging and had been housing them in the barn—but the idea of moving them up to new quarters by the house had taken hold.

"We could build a nice little coop with an enclosed run between the asparagus patch and the apple tree," she said brightly, "so on hot days they'd have shade."

"Right." The word came out more wearily than he'd intended.

The conversation might have deteriorated from there had Madeleine's attention not been diverted. She tilted her head.

"What is it?" asked Gurney.

"Listen."

He waited—not an unusual experience. His hearing was normal, but Madeleine's was extraordinary. A few seconds later, as the breeze rustling the foliage subsided, he heard something in the distance, somewhere down the hill, perhaps on the town road that dead-ended into the low end of their pasture "driveway." As it grew louder, he recognized the distinctive growl of an oversized, undermuffled V8.

He knew someone who drove an old muscle car that sounded exactly like that—a partially restored red 1970 Pontiac GTO—someone for whom that brash exhaust note was the perfect introduction.

Jack Hardwick.

He felt his jaw tightening at the prospect of a visit from the detective with whom he had such a bizarre history of near-death experiences, professional successes, and personality clashes. Not that he hadn't been anticipating the visit. In fact, he'd known it was coming from the moment he'd heard about the man's forced departure from the State Police Bureau of Criminal Investigation. And he realized that the tension he felt now had a lot to do with what had happened prior to that departure. A serious debt had been incurred, and some kind of payment would have to be made.

A formation of low dark clouds was moving quickly over the far ridge as though retreating from the violent sound of the red car—now visible from where Gurney was sitting—as it made its way up the mowed pasture swath to the farmhouse. He was briefly tempted to stay on the hill until Hardwick left, but he knew that would accomplish nothing—only extend the period of discomfort before the inevitable meeting. With a small grunt of determination he got up from his place on the boulder.

"Were you expecting him?" asked Madeleine.

Gurney glanced down the slope. The GTO came to a stop by his own dusty Outback in the little makeshift parking area by the side of the house. The big Pontiac engine roared louder for a couple of seconds as it was revved prior to being shut down.

"I was expecting him in a general way," said Gurney, "not necessarily today."

"Do you want to see him?"

"I'd say he wants to see me, and I'd like to get it over with."

Madeleine nodded and stood up, pushing her short brown hair back from her forehead.

As they turned to start down the trail, the mirror surface of the quarry pool shivered under a sudden breeze, dissolving the inverted image of the willows and the sky into thousands of unrecognizable splinters of green and gray.

If Gurney were the kind of man who believed in omens, he might have seen the shattered image as a sign of the destruction to come.

Also by John Verdon

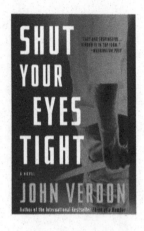

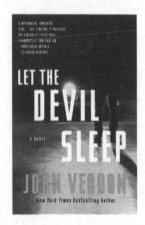

B\D\W\Y

AVAILABLE WHEREVER BOOKS ARE SOLD